Changeling
Moon

Changeling Moon

Dani Harper

BRAVA

KENSINGTON PUBLISHING CORP.

www.kensingtonbooks.com

BRAVA BOOKS are published by

Kensington Publishing Corp.
119 West 40th Street
New York, NY 10018

All Kensington titles, imprints, and distributed lines are available at special quantity discounts for bulk purchases for sales promotion, premiums, fund-raising, educational, or institutional use.

Special book excerpts or customized printings can also be created to fit specific needs. For details, write or phone the office of the Kensington Special Sales Manager: Kensington Publishing Corp., 119 West 40th Street, New York, NY 10018, Attn: Special Sales Department. Phone: 1-800-221-2647.

Brava and the B logo Reg. U.S. Pat. & TM Off.

ISBN-13: 978-0-7582-6514-2
ISBN-10: 0-7582-6514-X

First Kensington Trade Paperback Printing: June 2011

10 9 8 7 6 5 4 3 2   1

Printed in the United States of America

Writing is a solitary art and yet no writer can work her craft alone. This story is for my husband, Ron Silvester, who believed in me from the beginning, who shares the dream and cheers me on.

There aren't enough words to thank you for your unwavering encouragement, patience, enthusiasm, and acceptance—not to mention the humor, hugs, coffee and chocolate. Your love inspires me every day.

ACKNOWLEDGMENTS

Thank you to Stephany Evans, my wonderful agent, and to Alicia Condon, my terrific editor, for taking a chance on me. I feel so fortunate to be able to work with you both. Thanks to everyone at FinePrint and Kensington who helped to make *Changeling Moon* the best it could be.

Afterward we will be as one animal of the forest and be so close that neither one can tell that one of us is one and not the other. Can you not feel my heart be your heart?

—ERNEST HEMINGWAY

Prologue

The wolf wanted out.

Heavy clouds obscured the moon and washed the night with icy rain. The cold, damp air brought a myriad of intriguing scents. The man slunk along the sidewalk, his limbs tingling as his body instinctively drew energy from the earth.

The wolf wanted out *now*.

Full of hunger and rage, the wolf writhed under the man's skin in anticipation as he turned into a familiar alley behind the town hall. It was dark there, overgrown with trees and bushes, flanked with leaning fences, sagging garages, and numberless garbage cans. There was a spot where no light reached, a perfect spot to—

The wolf snarled its impatience and the man cursed back. He was *trying* to hurry, dammit, but his body refused to cooperate. To human eyes, he was just an old drunk, sixty going on eighty. In reality, he was far older than even those like him could guess. When his wolf wanted out, he could no longer keep it leashed for long. And truth be told, he didn't want to. Because once he took on his lupine form, all his aches and pains would disappear, and he'd be strong and powerful again.

The wolf within whispered: *Tonight we will hunt. And become even stronger.*

Chapter One

Freezing rain sliced out of the black sky, turning the wet pavement to glass. Zoey stared out at the freakish weather and groaned aloud. With less than two days left in the month of April, the skies had been clear and bright all afternoon. Trees were budding early and spring had seemed like a sure bet. Now *this*. Local residents said if you didn't like the weather this far north, just wait fifteen minutes. She gave it five, only to watch the rain turn to sleet.

Perhaps she should have asked more questions before taking the job as editor of the *Dunvegan Herald Weekly*. She was getting the peace and quiet she'd wanted, all right, but so far the weather simply sucked. Winter had been in full swing when she'd arrived at the end of October. Wasn't it ever going to end?

Sighing, she buttoned her thin jacket up to her chin and hoisted the camera bag over her shoulder in preparation for the long, cold walk to her truck. All she wanted before bed was a hot shower, her soft flannel pajamas with the little cartoon sheep on them, the TV tuned to *Late Night*, and a cheese and mushroom omelet. Hell, maybe just the omelet. She hadn't eaten since noon, unless the three faded M&Ms she'd found at the bottom of her bag counted as food.

As usual, the council meeting for the Village of Dunvegan had gone on much too long. Who'd have thought that such a small community could have so much business to discuss? It was well past ten when the mayor, the councilors, and the remnants of a long-winded delegation filed out. Zoey had lingered only a few moments to scribble down a couple more notes for her article but it was long enough to make her the last person out of the building.

The heavy glass door automatically locked behind her, the metallic sound echoing ominously. Had she taken longer than she thought? There wasn't a goddamn soul left on the street. Even the hockey arena next door was deserted, although a senior men's play-off game earlier had made parking difficult to find. Now, her truck—a sturdy, old red Bronco that handled the snow much better than her poor little SUV had—was the only vehicle in sight.

The freezing rain made the three-block trek to the truck seem even longer. Not only did the cold wind drive stinging pellets of ice into her face, but her usual business-like stride had to be shortened to tiny careful steps. Her knee-high leather boots were strictly a fashion accessory—her bedroom slippers would have given her more traction on the ice. If she slipped and broke her ankle out here, would anyone even find her before morning?

The truck glittered strangely as she approached and her heart sank. Thick sheets of ice coated every surface, sealing the doors. Nearly frozen herself, she pounded on the lock with the side of her fist until the ice broke away and she could get her key in. "Come on, dammit, come on!"

Of course, the key refused to turn, while the cold both numbed and hurt her gloveless fingers. She tried the passenger door lock without success, then walked gingerly around to the rear cargo door. No luck there either. She'd have to call a tow—

Except that her cell phone was on the front seat of her truck.

Certain that things couldn't get any worse, she tested each door again. Maybe one of the locks would loosen if she kept trying. If not, she'd probably have to walk all the way home, and wasn't that a cheery prospect?

Suddenly a furtive movement teased at her peripheral vision. Zoey straightened slowly and studied her surroundings. There wasn't much to see. The streetlights were very far apart, just glowing pools of pale gold that punctuated the darkness rather than alleviating it. Few downtown businesses bothered to leave lights on overnight. The whispery hiss of the freezing rain was all she could hear.

A normal person would simply chalk it up to imagination, but she'd been forced to toss *normal* out the window at an early age. Her mother, aunts, and grandmother were all powerful psychics—and the gene had been passed down to Zoey. Or at least a watered-down version of it. The talent was reliable enough when it worked, but it seemed to come and go as it pleased. *Like right now.* Zoey tried hard to focus yet sensed absolutely nothing. It was her own fault perhaps for trying to rid herself of the inconvenient ability.

No extrasensory power was needed, however, to see something large and black glide silently from one shadow to another near the building she'd just left. *What the hell was that?* There was nowhere to go for help. The only two bars in town would still be open, but they were several blocks away, as was the detachment headquarters for the Royal Canadian Mounted Police. There was a rundown trailer park a block and a half from the far side of the arena, but

Zoey knew there were no streetlights anywhere along that route.

A dog? Maybe it's just a big dog, she thought. *A really big dog or a runaway cow. After all, this was a rural community. And a northern rural community at that, so maybe it's just a local moose, ha, ha. . . .* She struggled to keep her fear at bay and redoubled her efforts on the door locks, all the while straining to listen over the sound of her own harsh breathing.

The rear door lock was just beginning to show promise when a low, rumbling growl caused her to drop her keys. She spun to see a monstrous shape emerge from the shadows, stiff-legged and head lowered. *A wolf?* It was bigger than any damn wolf had a right to be. *Jesus.* Some primal instinct warned her not to run and not to scream, that the animal would be on her instantly if she did so.

She backed away slowly, trying not to slip, trying to put the truck between herself and the creature. Its eyes glowed green like something out of a horror flick, but this was no movie. Snarling black lips pulled back to expose gleaming ivory teeth. The grizzled gray fur around its neck was bristling. Zoey was minutely aware that the hair on the back of her own neck was standing on end. Her breath came in short shuddering gasps as she blindly felt for the truck behind her with her hands, sliding her feet carefully without lifting them from the pavement.

She made it around the corner of the Bronco. As soon as she was out of the wolf's line of sight, she turned and half skated, half ran for the front of the truck as fast as the glassy pavement would allow. *Don't fall, don't fall!* It was a litany in her brain as she scrambled up the slippery front bumper onto the icy hood. With no hope of outrunning the creature and no safe place in sight, the roof of the truck seemed like her best bet—if she could make it. *Don't fall, don't fall!* Flailing for a handhold, she seized an ice-crusted windshield wiper, only to have the metal frame snap off in her hand. She screamed as she slid back a few inches.

The wolf sprang at once. It scrabbled and clawed, unable to find a purchase on the ice-coated metal. Foam from its snapping jaws sprayed over her as the beast roared its frustration. Finally it slipped back to the ground and began to pace around the truck.

Zoey managed to shimmy up the hood until she was able to put her back against the windshield, and pulled her knees up to her chin. She risked a glance at the roof behind her—she had to get higher. Before she could move, however, the wolf attacked again, scrambling its way up the front bumper. Vicious jaws slashed at her. Without thought, Zoey kicked out at the wolf, knocking one leg out from under it. It slid backward but not before it clamped its teeth on her calf. The enormous weight of the creature dragged at her and she felt herself starting to slide. . . .

One hand still clutched the broken windshield wiper and she used it, whipping the creature's face and muzzle with the frozen blade until she landed a slice across one ungodly glowing eye. The rage-filled snarl became a strangled yelp; the wolf released her leg and slipped from the hood. This time Zoey didn't look, just turned and launched herself upward for the roof rack. She came down hard, adrenaline keeping her from feeling the impact of the bruising metal rails. She was conscious only of the desperate need to claw and grasp and cling and pull until she was safely on the very top of the vehicle.

Except she *wasn't* safe. Not by a long shot. *Crap.* She could plainly see that she wasn't high enough. *Crap, crap,*

crap. The enraged wolf leapt upward in spite of the fact that its feet could find little traction on the ice-coated pavement. What it couldn't gain in momentum, the wolf made up for in effort, hurling itself repeatedly against the Bronco. Its snapping jaws came so close that Zoey could see the bleeding welts across its face, see that one of its hellish eyes was now clouded and half-closed. She slashed at it again, catching its tender nose so it howled in frustration and pain as it dropped to the ground. Snarling, it paced back and forth like a caged lion, watching her. Waiting.

The wind picked up and the freezing rain intensified. Huddled on her knees in the exact center of the icy roof, Zoey's adrenaline began to ebb. She was cold and exhausted, and parts of her were numb. But she wasn't helpless; she wouldn't allow herself to think that way. The thin windshield wiper was badly bent with pieces of it missing, but she'd damn well punch the wolf in the nose with her bare fist if she had to. If she still could. . . .

The wolf sprang again.

Dr. Connor Macleod cursed himself for the hundredth time for not bringing another veterinarian into his practice. His family and friends, and particularly his receptionist, had been on his case about it for the past two years. He'd always handled everything himself, but it was time to face facts—his practice had grown too large.

The second calving season of the year was in full swing, and Connor had been out on farm calls since five o'clock that morning. He wouldn't have minded except he'd gotten only an hour of sleep after performing an emergency cesarean on a heifer. That case had been touch and go for most of the night. He'd had a few choice words for the farmer who had bred the young animal to a bull of a much larger breed, creating a huge calf that couldn't possibly be born on its own. The man had been defensive and angry, but Connor didn't care. He had every patience with animals and none at all for those who deliberately misused them.

Right now he had no patience left for anything, and the unseasonal weather didn't improve his mood. He needed coffee. And food. And sleep, but that was less likely than the other two. Fortunately he wasn't human and as long as he ate enough, his body could deal with a serious sleep deficit—at least for a while.

As the lights of Dunvegan came into view, uneasiness twisted his gut. The ice storm had been far more intense here. The road was glassed over and treacherous, yet his feelings had nothing to do with the driving conditions. He switched off the radio and pulled to the side of the road for a few moments, needing to think, to focus and unravel the sudden surge of energies he sensed.

Suddenly the darkness brightened as everything around him—the dashboard, his hands on the steering wheel, the road signs—began to glow with a silvery light. It was a phenomenon that only he could see, a precursor to *farsight*. . . .

He yelled out. He couldn't help it. A hideous premonition spawned a violent and bloody image in his mind. A woman was in terrible danger, and what was threatening her was no more human than he was.

In the blink of an eye the image was gone and the otherworldly light yielded to the natural darkness. Connor pulled back onto the deserted highway and sped toward the village, heedless of the glaring ice. The truck had studded tires and four-wheel drive, both necessary in harsh northern winters and unpredictable northern springs, and Connor was a skilled driver. Nevertheless, his pickup stayed on the road largely because he *willed* it to. As he drove into town, the vehicle fishtailed repeatedly but recovered each time. Then he turned onto a side street.

Close. He knew he was close, he could feel it. Suddenly, as he swung the truck hard onto Hemstock Avenue—he saw a huge wolf leap at a parked truck. He leaned on the horn and stepped on the accelerator as the snarling creature fell back into the road. One of its eyes flashed green in the bright headlights, as it turned to look at the oncoming truck—

—then vanished without a trace. But not before Connor recognized it: a Changeling.

Like himself.

He slowed his pickup and pulled up behind a red Bronco that had seen better days. He scanned the ice-covered windows, expecting the woman to be inside—until a faint movement drew his eyes upward. His mouth fell open. *She was on the goddamn roof.* Slippery as it was, it was only a matter of moments before the wolf would have reached her, killed her. Or worse.

She was soaked and pale, her long hair plastered to her head and caked with ice. Her amber eyes overwhelmed her white face, but they weren't tearful and frightened. Instead, her direct gaze took him by surprise. A creature out of legend had just attacked her, yet instead of falling apart, she was taking Connor's measure. He was suddenly reminded of a falcon he had treated last year. The small predator had showed a fierce courage out of all proportion to its size.

And it nearly took my thumb off, he reminded himself. *Best to step carefully here, Macleod.* "I don't know what you said to that wolf to get him so riled up," he ventured. "Do you always insult the local wildlife?" The deliberate absurdity of the question surprised a small grin from her.

"I just can't help myself," she said, a little thickly. "You shoulda heard what I said to the grizzly and the moose that were here." Her lips and face were obviously numb, making it difficult to shape the words.

"Let me help you down from there. I'm betting you could use some coffee."

"A hot tub full of it."

He held out his hand to her as she shifted to swing her legs around. The cold had made her movements awkward, almost wooden. She paused and glared at Connor. "Don't you dare be an ax murderer."

"I won't. I'm not." He dared to smile a little—but only a little. Damn, but her expression reminded him of that falcon. Beautiful and downright ferocious. If she was ever truly pissed off, he'd bet she could nail someone to the nearest wall with only a look. "I'll remove that from my résumé, pronto. In fact, let me take off *serial killer* and *stalker* while I'm at it."

Her face relaxed into that grin as she took his outstretched hand. He immediately grasped her other hand as well, willing his body heat into her frozen fingers. He was about to lift her down when the tang of fresh blood snapped his senses into high alert.

"Hold on a minute." Connor began inspecting her right leg. The lower pant leg was shredded, the tall leather boot beneath it full of holes. Blood welled from the punctures, dripping to the ice-covered sidewalk below, where it quickly congealed. His own blood chilled. It was all he could do to compose his face, keep his tone light.

"I think we might need a little first-aid here. Are you okay for a minute while I do a fast field dressing?"

She nodded and he fumbled in his coat pocket, producing a bright roll of elastic bandage which he set in her lap. As he did so, something clattered to the pavement.

"Sorry." He picked up a windshield wiper, or what was left of it. She held her hand out, but it was a long moment before Connor recovered from his astonishment enough to give it to her. Scent told him there was blood on the thin strip of metal, and it wasn't human. His exquisite night vision showed him bits of fur stuck to it as well. Wolf fur.

Christ.

Grown men, strong men, often surrendered to terror against creatures like her attacker. Yet this woman had battled for her life with the most meager of weapons and had actually held the beast at bay. Connor handed back the wiper as solemnly as a warrior might award a sword.

She took it and shrugged. "The damn thing had hold of me. I had to make it let go."

"Good job," he managed. What an understatement. She had no idea what she'd done, what she'd saved herself from. An ordinary wolf could exert enough bite force to crack the heavy thighbones of moose and bison. But the creature that had attacked her could have taken her leg off. Easily.

Still, what *had* happened was bad enough. He turned his attention back to the wound. "This might hurt a bit." She hissed in a breath but said nothing as he unzipped the boot and eased it off.

Pushing back the shredded pant leg, he sucked in his own breath as he surveyed the damage. There were the deep prints of a monstrous wolf's teeth on both sides of her shapely calf. The front incisors had only dented the skin but the fanglike canines had driven through both leather and soft skin like nails. And following them were the savage stabs of the pointed molars. A wolf's molars weren't meant for chewing and grinding like a human's. Instead, they were *carnassials*, designed to shear flesh. The boot's leather had protected her to a degree. But had the wolf had a better grip; if it had jerked its head to one side or the other. . . .

Connor shook off the grisly thoughts as he tore strips from the hem of her jeans. Deftly, he folded them into pads and placed them against the worst of the wounds, wrapping her leg with the bandage so the thick cloth pads put some pressure on the torn flesh. "This should slow the bleeding," he explained.

She surveyed his work, clearly puzzled. "Orange isn't really my color . . ."

He laughed a little. "These bandages only come in fluorescents for some warped reason. You ought to see this orange stuff on a black cat. It's like some bad Halloween joke."

"A cat? Why would you—"

"—wrap up a cat? Because I'm the local vet. I wrap up cows and horses too. Had to put a cast on a lizard last week."

"I thought you were a paramedic or something."

"Sorry. The EMTs had a previous engagement." He placed his hands gently around her waist and then lifted her down to the icy sidewalk. He was about to release her when her knees suddenly buckled and he found himself supporting her.

"Am I drunk?" she asked as she struggled to get her feet under her, her hands hanging onto his coat. She looked surprised, almost bewildered. "I don't remember drinking anything. I was going to make an omelet, not a margarita . . . I'm so sorry."

"No need to be sorry. You're not at your best right now." Her sudden confusion worried him. "Come on, we're going to sit in my truck for a while and warm up."

"But I don't know you." She tried to push away from him, might even have succeeded if he'd been less determined—and human. But her legs were unsteady and so he kept his hands firmly on her waist. "I can't get in a truck with a stranger!" she protested.

Uh-huh. "Okay, I'm Connor Macleod, and I'm the guy who's presently holding you up." He studied her face with growing concern. "As I mentioned, I'm the vet around here and I just finished delivering a calf out at Peterson's. I was going to stop at the corner store for some hot coffee before I went home and then I saw you out here playing with wolves. So now I'm not a stranger." He turned a mock suspicious eye on her. "Say, I don't know you either. Maybe I should ask who *you* are before I let you in my vehicle."

"Zoey Tyler," she murmured, then frowned. "I shouldn't tell you that. Have I been drinking?" Her words were definitely slurring now, her eyelids fluttering down. "I just need to get into my Bronco and I'll be fine."

Connor shook his head. "Good survival instincts, but a little misplaced right now. You can sue me later, Zoey Tyler." She mumbled a brief objection as he scooped her up and carried her to his truck.

The vehicle had been left running and the heat was thick and heavenly. Connor was seldom bothered by cold but pins and needles heralded the return of feeling to his fingers and toes. How much longer had Zoey been outside in the freezing rain? He regretted his decision to dress her wounds—he should have gotten her out of the weather first. Her eyes had opened for only a moment when he put her in the truck and hadn't opened since. She was shaking now, her teeth chattering. Carefully he worked at getting the soggy jacket off her as her head lolled forward, water dripping from the curtain of her long, thick hair.

Connor reached behind the seat for a big plaid blanket. He wrapped it around Zoey like a shawl, taking care to cover her head to prevent further heat loss from her body. She was barely conscious. Exhaustion probably. Delayed shock likely. Even hypothermia was a strong possibility. There was no hospital in the village and he couldn't take her to the medical clinic. He'd heard the dispatcher over his radio talking about a nasty accident earlier with three cars involved. Both of Dunvegan's doctors had accompanied the injured to the city. Well, it wouldn't be the first time he'd filled in for the human medical professionals in an emergency. Although this was a bit different from splinting a broken arm or stitching up a gashed thumb.

Shoving back the driver's seat, Connor tilted the steering wheel out of the way, then sat with his back against the door. He opened his coat and pulled Zoey inside it, onto his lap. It took some maneuvering—and some cussing—in such tight quarters but he finally managed to get her feet to rest on the dashboard above the glove box. Elevating them would keep blood in her internal organs, standard treatment for anyone suffering from shock. It would help her wounded leg to stop bleeding too.

Now if he could only get her warm. . . .

Chapter Two

In the middle of a dark and stormy night, Connor Macleod was sitting in his truck with a strange woman in his arms. Why didn't it feel odd? Instead, it seemed like the most natural thing in the world, and that in itself was just plain weird.

Resting his chin lightly on her head, he had to admit that she fit very nicely. Zoey was shorter than he was—so was almost everyone he had ever met—but she was taller than most women. And not tiny and fragile by any means. She felt solid, strong. Come to think of it, she had fought the wolf and would probably try to kick *his* butt too if she woke up and caught him cuddling her like this. Connor couldn't help smiling a little at the thought of her fierce amber eyes.

So what did he really know about her? Of course he'd recognized her name at once. As the new editor of the *Dunvegan Herald Weekly*, she'd been behind some major changes at the eighty-three-year-old newspaper. The name banner across the top had been replaced with a new full-color graphic. And her first front-page photo was not of the members of the local service club presenting a check to charity. Instead, it was an exciting action shot from the annual dogsled races. Zoey Tyler had captured two teams running neck and neck, snow flying, and almost every paw off the ground. The dogs looked airborne, ethereal. Connor had clipped it and put it on the bulletin board at the clinic, marveling at the talent of the photographer. He kept meaning to order a print that he could frame for his office.

And the updates to the *Weekly* went far beyond appearance. When residents pulled the paper from their mailboxes, the front page displayed actual news instead of instructions on how to make yet another version of Saskatoon berry jam. And that first editorial—well, he'd wondered what the hell was going on when he saw a large group of people standing around talking at the post office. He hadn't seen a natural gathering that big since Murray Clements jumped off the Peace River Bridge with a homemade parachute. Then someone had handed him a newspaper. . . .

He had to credit Zoey Tyler—she really knew how to get people involved. No sensationalism, no tabloid tricks, just good solid research and the ability to shine a light on an issue. Some of her editorials had gotten results too, like the construction of new crosswalks on Fourth Street. But would Zoey's talent create a problem for the Pack? She'd just been viciously attacked by a wolf in the middle of town. What would she write about *that*?

Deep in thought, he ran his hand down Zoey's back—and jerked to attention. The woman in his arms was now perfectly still, her shaking subsided, but he knew that wasn't a good sign, not so soon. He tipped her head back so he could see her face. It seemed whiter than ever and her lips were pale and bluish. He placed the back of his hand against her cheek. A human would feel cool to him anyway—his ambient body temperature ran between 103 and 104 degrees—but he knew instantly that she was much colder than she should be. If her core temperature had fallen. . . .

The heater was already on full blast. Connor often complained that the temperature control had two settings, *North Pole* and *Hell*. He'd been too warm within the first few moments of entering the vehicle and now he was cooking. Beads of sweat trickled down his forehead and stung his tired eyes and yet the oppressive heat was having no effect on Zoey.

"Hey there, wake up for me. Wake up now!" Connor massaged her back through the blanket, ran his hands over her arms, stroked her head, patted her cheeks. "Zoey!" Finally he slapped her face lightly, but she remained unresponsive, her breathing so faint he could barely hear it. Connor reached under the blanket for her wrist. The weak and thready pulse, coupled with his own preternatural senses, confirmed his worst suspicions. *Shit.*

There was no lack of recorded incidents in which accident survivors appeared completely unhurt, had even walked around and tended to others, yet nonetheless died from untreated shock. Hypothermia could be fatal as well, even to Changelings like himself. A human being was far more fragile.

"Come on, little falcon, I'm fighting for you, but you have to help me. Just a little bit, honey." Connor sat her up, framed her face in his large hands. He usually held his psychic abilities in reserve, declining to use them on humans out of courtesy. But politeness be damned, he *had* to make a connection with this woman before it was too late. "Look at me, Zoey. Listen to me. Come back." His voice was coaxing at first but rapidly hardened to commanding. He willed her to respond, his mind reaching for hers as he had never done with a human. Still he felt her floating away from him. Good Christ, he was going to lose her.

No. The word stood out in his mind as something within him stirred and came to the forefront. Telepathy was every Changeling's birthright and Connor's abilities were formidable. But his greatest power came from his wolfen form. He couldn't Change now, couldn't become the wolf. Yet the wolf had come to *him*, unexpectedly lending its strength. Connor didn't stop to wonder at this strange occurrence. He focused everything he had on Zoey. "Come back right now!"

He could feel her mentally resist him, even slap at him. See her with his mind's eye, adrift in a gray haze. She was tired and cold, and wanted to rest in the soft, warm depths into which she had spiraled. She had no way of knowing she might not wake up.

"Come back!" he commanded her. Confused, angry, but finally unable to resist him, he sensed her swimming slowly up through layers of awareness, a great gray sea. *Come on, Zoey, just a little closer, you can do it. Come back. . . .* Finally she neared the surface where he could reach her with his energy, wrap it around her like a lifeline and anchor her to him, keep her from again drifting downward.

Connor sensed the change in her at once. He cradled her close against his chest and sought her wrist again. The pulse was stronger, there was no imagining it. He closed his eyes and brought her wrist to his lips, then held her hand to his cheek. He could hear her breathing, steady and deep. He breathed easier too. The wolf within him, apparently satisfied with Zoey's condition, receded, but not very far. Connor could feel it just beneath the surface of his human

self, watchful and alert. Christ, was it *guarding* her? Connor
had lived a long time, yet his wolf had never emerged unbidden, never behaved like this.

This night could not get any stranger—

And then it did. A sudden rapid blur of images flashed
across Connor's mind. He saw creatures of all kinds—deer,
bear, puma, fox, elk, eagle, even a falcon. All glowing with
the strange silvery light of *farsight* . . . and in their midst
stood Zoey Tyler.

The vision lasted mere seconds, then vanished. *What the
hell was that?* Connor was sweating and this time it had
nothing to do with the heat in the truck. His *farsight* was
usually literal, not symbolic—after all, it had told him that a
human woman was in trouble and then led him directly to
her. Why would he see a parade of unrelated animals surrounding Zoey?

Had to be a brain fart of some kind. *Had to be.* Obviously
he was a lot more tired than he realized.

Strands of Zoey's hair dried in the heat and curled out
from under the blanket. Connor seized a stray lock and
wound it around his finger. The darkness couldn't hide the
color of her hair from his acute vision and he found himself marveling at the hue. Not red, not gold, but a deep
blend of both, like an autumn apple. *Russet.* It suited his
fierce little falcon.

His?

He shook his head to clear it. He was just oversensitive
to this woman after the strong psychic connection he had
made, right? That had to account for the powerful sense of
familiarity. He really didn't know her, not yet. Now that
she was a little more stable, he needed to get her home and
look after those bite wounds properly.

And apply silver nitrate to them as soon as possible. . . .

Carefully Connor lifted Zoey away from him, easing her over to the passenger seat once more. As he did so, the blanket fell from her head, pulling her russet hair back from her face. Much of her color had returned and now he saw a riot of golden freckles that marched across her nose and over her cheekbones in such numbers that they met in places. He was instantly captivated, and his fingers found themselves wandering over her face in a kind of caress—

Suddenly she jerked awake. Zoey's gaze snapped and smoldered as she turned to regard Connor, fury in every cell of her body. Slowly he pulled his hand away, his eyes never leaving hers, fully aware he had overstepped a major boundary. And glad that she didn't know she'd just spent a considerable amount of time in his lap—at least, he sure as hell *hoped* she didn't know.

Zoey's eyes didn't waver, although she shoved a hand roughly through her long hair and brought it forward to curtain the left side of her face. The defensive gesture bothered him deeply and he quelled an impulse to brush the beautiful hair back over her shoulder, touch her face again, soothe her frown. Kiss every one of those freckles. . . .

"What did you think you were doing?" Her voice was low, almost shaking with anger. Both hands were now fisted in her lap; her body shifted just enough to let her use them.

Connor eased back behind the steering wheel. "Some of your color's come back, so I happened to be checking your skin temperature. And I admit it, I was admiring your freckles."

She blushed furiously then, which only charmed him further. "Do you always look with your hands?" she demanded.

"Well, yes, I guess I do." He nodded, considering.

"Checking out cows and cats and dogs and whatnot every day—I never really thought about it, but I guess I use my hands as much as my eyes." And he did. Although there was no point mentioning he had the ability to sense what the animal was feeling by touching it. Or that he had used some of the same ability to forge a psychic link with Zoey.

"I see." She looked away from him and rubbed her hands over her face. "Geez, I feel awful. My leg hurts and it's *boiling* in here."

"I'll bet you feel worse than awful. But the fact that you've noticed it's hotter than the seventh ring of hell in here is encouraging," said Connor. Gratefully he turned the heat down and opened his window a little to let in some fresh air. "I'm glad you're awake. I was getting worried." *There's an understatement. You scared the bejeezus out of me.* "Now that you're warmed up and not so shocky, I'll take you home. You've got a real nasty bite, and we need to look after that leg properly."

"*Shocky*? Is that a word?"

"You *are* an editor, aren't you? Ask any EMT—it's probably classed as slang, but they use the word all the time."

She objected most of the way to her apartment building, insisting that she could drive herself if he would only *take her to her truck*. It was obvious that she didn't feel well enough to do more than complain, but still, Connor was relieved to hear it. Human or animal, if the patient was putting up a fuss, they were going to be fine. *With a little help*, he reminded himself as he patted the pocket of his coat where he always kept a small bottle of silver nitrate.

Zoey's protests fell on deaf ears. Not only did this man not take her to her Bronco, but he insisted on carrying her up to her apartment, wrapped in a blanket like somebody's invalid granny. She lived on the top floor of what was jok-ingly referred to as "Dunvegan's Skyscraper," a four-story complex that was just slightly taller than the lone office building. The guy wasn't even winded when he got to her door and set her on her feet. He must work out, she de-cided. With shoulders like that, he probably bench-pressed cows or something. And he was so warm. . . .

Get a grip, girl. It's dark, you're tired, and no one's ugly after midnight. Zoey shook her head, hoping to clear it, as he produced her keys from somewhere and opened the door. The man—damn, she'd forgotten his name—had told her repeatedly that she hadn't been drinking, but her body felt like she'd spent the entire evening guzzling shooters in a bar. Acted like it too. She stumbled as she crossed the threshold, but then, missing one high-heeled boot probably had something to do with that. The man seized her arm and steered her carefully into the living room and onto the couch.

"I can work on this leg a lot better if you lie down," he said as he knelt beside her and started to take the blanket off.

Suddenly, Zoey jerked and just as quickly gritted her teeth to suppress a groan. She wasn't fast enough to fool this guy, though.

"What's wrong?" he demanded.

"Nothing, I'm fine."

He frowned, his pale eyes darkening into a stormy sea. "Like hell. You've gone even whiter than you were. Spill it or I'm taking more than the blanket off. Did you get bitten somewhere else?"

"No." Pain was sawing at her now, and she just didn't have the strength to argue. "My ribs are just sore. I think it's from climbing the roof rack. It's nothing."

"I'll tell you if it's nothing. I don't want you to puncture a lung when you roll over in your sleep because we didn't check for broken ribs."

Zoey blinked and wondered if she had passed out for a moment. She was sitting on the edge of the couch with her shirt open and large, warm hands were gently skimming her battered rib cage. A *stranger's* hands, she reminded herself but her instincts refused to agree. Instead she felt curiously safe. She frowned and grasped the edges of her shirt to yank them together. Considered decking the guy, just on principle. Instead, she did absolutely nothing. The man's touch was feather light. Soothing. Wherever his fingers trailed, the pain seemed to ease. She could breathe easier, and was surprised to realize how difficult breathing had been up to now.

"You've got some bruising, but no breaks." Deftly he buttoned her shirt and eased her back onto the couch so he could turn his attention to her leg. "Take it easy tomorrow, okay? You're hurting now, but the second day is usually a lot worse. Do you have some ibuprofen around, something for pain?"

She nodded. "Hell, yeah. I get migraines so I've practically got my own pharmacy on hand."

"You're shivering again." He searched the bedroom, came back with an armful of quilts, and tucked them carefully around her. Zoey protested a little at having to lie down but she was far too tired and in too much pain to resist. The last thing she saw was the tall man pulling a roll of gauze from his pocket.

The pickup bounced over unseen potholes as Connor drove into the abandoned farmyard. Rows of broken-down granaries and sheds floated in a sea of yellowed grass made golden in the early morning light. The two barns were leaning, their roofs losing shingles like dying dragons shedding scales. The house alone was still square, its cracked windows curtained with patched and dirty blankets. All the buildings were a uniform weathered gray with not a speck of paint among them. Not a sign of ice or even rain. Last night's freakish weather hadn't reached this far. Or perhaps even nature avoided this place.

The tall vet walked to the door and rapped it sharply, his senses alert, his gaze flicking over the windswept grass as if he expected something to leap from it.

"Go to hell, Macleod." The voice from within the house was low and gravelly. Human hearing would have missed it but Connor could pick it up easily.

"We need to talk, Bernie. I'm betting you need some patching up, too."

"I don't need nuttin' from you. Get off my property."

"Yeah, yeah, yeah. After we've talked—" Connor rattled the doorknob. "You know damn well I'm not leaving, so open up."

There was a long, long silence. Connor was patient by nature but the attack on Zoey had brought out something else. He had been every bit a healer as he cared for her, held her, warmed her, tended her wounds. But once he'd left her apartment, a cold, hard anger had taken hold. His mind was made up, his resolve certain.

He was about to kick in the door when suddenly it flew open. Frowning, he stooped to fit under the low doorframe and disappeared into the dark interior.

Chapter Three

The snapping jaws were so close that droplets of spittle struck her face...

Zoey flailed awake and tumbled from the couch, yelping as her battered ribs made contact with the floor. Disjointed memories of the past night crowded into her awareness as she fought clear of the pile of quilts and struggled to sit up.

"A wolf! Holy crap, a *wolf*, a goddamn wolf right in the middle of town!" Her system was hollering for coffee, aspirin, and food, but she had other priorities. The first was to phone the RCMP, the local Fish and Wildlife office, Dunvegan's mayor and whoever was in charge of animal control in this area. The creature was still out there somewhere and Zoey wasn't going to let anyone else be attacked if she could help it. People needed to be warned, and once she'd talked to the authorities, she'd write up one helluva front-page story.

"The paper comes out on Monday, but is that soon enough? Maybe I should put up posters or . . . ow!" She paused in the middle of getting to her feet, eased herself to the couch instead, and inspected her right leg. It was wrapped neatly from ankle to knee in white gauze, but there was a sharp-edged ache in many places beneath the smooth, even bandage. The veterinarian had probably done a good job but she should have her leg checked out by one of the clinic doctors or—

The vet. *Omigod.* Her face heated as she remembered all too clearly being carried up the stairs to her apartment like Scarlett fricking O'Hara. Although Scarlett hadn't complained so much about it. *Please, please, please don't let any of the neighbors have seen us.* But the stranger had done more than carry her and treat the bite. He had saved her life. Embarrassing or not, she knew she'd needed the rescue. She could have been killed. She could have *died* last night if it wasn't for that man showing up when he did.

She sat down on the couch and hugged herself until the shaking subsided. Suddenly making all those phone calls could wait. She was alive, and she just wanted to savor that for a while.

Connor was almost sorry for the exquisite night vision he possessed. Had he been human, the darkened house would have softened the effect of what he was seeing. The old man's face was bruised and swollen, flayed open diagonally in several places. One eye was puffed shut, a jagged cut across the purple lid still leaking blood, staining the white beard stubble on his cheek.

The damage was daunting from a medical point of view. The healer in him winced inwardly at the sight, yet his usual sympathy was far outweighed by his growing respect for Zoey—and his determination to keep her safe. *You did a good job of defending yourself, little falcon. The vicious old bastard deserved everything he got and more.*

"I see you went out on the town last night, Bernie," Connor said calmly as he opened his kit. His working hands were steady and sure, like his voice, never betraying the waves of rage that flooded his gut. "I thought we had agreed that you were going to stay here, lock yourself in the cellar or at least come to me when the urge became too strong." The man hissed as antiseptic bubbled over the fearful cuts. "You've been losing control for a while now, Bernie. You've always been a selfish bastard, a nasty drunk, even a thief. The Pack has looked the other way, let you live however you chose. But now you're a killer."

"Piss off. I don't need a lecture from a goddamn dog doctor." The man tried to shove Connor away and get up, but Connor only moved in closer. One large hand pressed down hard on Bernie's plaid-shirted shoulder.

"This is no lecture, Bernie. This can't go on. You killed a dozen animals in Ralph Wharton's herd last month. You didn't need to eat; you just killed for the pure pleasure of it. Last night you tried to kill a human being, a woman."

Bernie went still. "I don't remember that," he rasped slowly, a look like fear creeping into his good eye. "I wouldn't do that. I've never done that! That's not true, you son-of-a-bitch, Macleod. You're trying to trick me."

Connor shook his head, his hand unmoving, the pressure unwavering. "No tricks, Bernie. You're too dangerous to be allowed to Change anymore and you know it. I let you talk me out of it last time, but not today. I saw you in the road. I knew it was you. And the woman you attacked defended herself, cut your face. Marked you."

He held a tight rein on his emotions, kept his voice calm but he knew Bernie would see the rage plainly in his eyes if he looked. Something primal was frighteningly close to the surface, and Connor was sweating with the effort of holding it back. *Please, dear God, let him accept this. If I have to fight with him, I just may kill him. And I'll want to.*

"You know what has to happen, Bernie. Jessie leads the Pack and she's ordered it." And even if she hadn't ordered it, Connor knew he would still be here, still be doing this. Because of Zoey.

The older man opened his mouth as if to protest, but no sound came out. Moments passed. Suddenly Bernie turned his ruined face to the wall and remained motionless as Connor rolled the frayed shirtsleeve up, swabbing the inside of the arm over a vein. The vet drew a large syringe from the kit, then reached in his pocket for the same bottle of silver nitrate he'd used on Zoey's wounded leg.

The young RCMP officer flipped his notepad closed, put his hat back on, and left. Zoey knew he hadn't believed her about the wolf even though she'd unwrapped her bitten calf for the sake of evidence. He'd been sympathetic and hadn't treated her like an idiot—the deputy mayor had already done that over the phone—but it was still very clear that the cop thought it was a dog attack.

She threw her slipper across the room, which only irritated her aching ribs. "I may be from the city but I know damn well that was no dog!" In February she had photographed a major dogsled race on the frozen river. Every breed of sled dog was present, and even some dogs that were genuinely half wolf. She'd watched in horror as two teams suddenly sprang on each other between races, and vividly remembered the blood-chilling sound of twenty large dogs roaring and snapping at each other while their owners waded into the melee to haul them apart. Still, nothing looked remotely like the beast that had attacked her, nothing was that big, that bent on killing.

Zoey sat back and surveyed the large teeth marks on her calf, thankful that she wasn't squeamish. It was a bad bite, but it looked clean and there wasn't a lot of swelling. There were butterfly closures on several of the punctures and they seemed to be doing their job—there was only a little blood on the gauze she'd removed. Still, she didn't kid herself. There was no denying that if the wolf had been able to get any traction on the slippery ice, if she hadn't hit the beast just right on its sensitive nose and muzzle, she might well have lost a sizeable chunk of her leg. *At the very least.* She'd seen the horrible results of two separate dog attacks in Vancouver. One of the victims, an elderly woman, had died. The other, a strong young man, had been maimed for life.

She shivered and turned her attention to the dilemma at hand. How could she warn people if she couldn't get the authorities to believe there was a wolf? The village officials thought she'd been bitten by a large dog, which was an unpleasant but relatively more acceptable problem. Maybe she should work with that.

"Okay, okay, the point is that people need to be on the lookout for *something*," she said aloud, testing the idea. "So what if they're looking for a big ferocious dog instead of a wolf? Does it really matter?" It was a tough call. *Tell the truth and be labeled a loony.* Then the story would be dismissed. No one would bother looking for a creature of any kind, no one would be on alert. *Tell a half-truth and maybe people would at least be careful.* Maybe no one else would get hurt.

Zoey sighed and tried to rewrap the gauze on her leg, feeling clumsy as she did so. She felt clumsy about the story too. She could just see the headline now: *Giant dog bites editor. Details on page 11.*

Of course she wouldn't title it like that, but frankly, she didn't know if she could make it sound much better. She might not mention who the victim was either, although she knew darn well it wouldn't stay a secret in such a small town. But she *could* place the article somewhere on the front page where it would be seen and people might be on their guard for a while. Might be a little more alert, might watch their children a little more closely.

But damn it all, it had been a *wolf*, a genuine call-of-the-wild wolf that had attacked her, and not being able to say so was frustrating beyond all words.

Thankfully, it had been a quiet day at the clinic. No calvings, no emergencies, no urgent calls. Connor had left Bernie, dragged himself through the morning's scheduled surgeries, then gone home at noon. To bed. The strain of many days without adequate rest and the intense emotions of the past twenty-four hours combined to send him into a dreamless sleep almost before his head hit the pillow.

It was well past midnight when he finally awakened. He lay on his back looking up at the bright moon through the tall windows that stretched almost floor to ceiling on the west wall of the master bedroom. His headache was gone but his heart hurt. There was little anger left in him now, only a deep aching sadness and questions that had no answers. Why hadn't Bernie asked for help? The old Changeling had no love for the Pack, but the Pack was bound by its own laws to assist him, work with him. Younger, stronger Changelings could have been assigned to watch over him when he was in wolfen form and keep him out of trouble. Keep him from hurting anyone. If all else failed, every Pack maintained a *haven*, an iron-barred place of safety in which an out-of-control wolf could be confined until his senses returned.

At least Bernie would have still been able to Change.

Applied to the wound within twelve hours of being bitten, silver nitrate would prevent a human from becoming a Changeling. Applied at least once more, the colorless liquid not only stopped the genetic shift in its tracks, it reversed it. Silver nitrate had just as dramatic of an effect on someone who had been born a Changeling, and only a single ample dose was required. Once injected into Bernie's veins, it would have quickly spread to every cell. By now, his inner wolf would be permanently suppressed, forever a prisoner in its human form.

What would it do to the old Changeling to look up at the moon, knowing he could never answer its call again? How would he stand it?

Connor got up and went to the balcony door, clad in only plaid pajama bottoms. The air was cold on his exposed skin as he stepped outside, but it blunted the painful emotions a bit. He stood for a long time, scenting the air, then walked to the cedar steps that led from the balcony to the ground. *Come.* He called out the wolf within and trotted briskly downward, first on two feet, then on four. Paused in the yard and shook himself all over. His silvery pelt was marked with a blanket of black over his shoulders—a rare saddleback wolf. Soundless, he bounded away into the night.

Behind him, the only evidence of the Change was a faint whiff of ozone in the air, a crackle of static electricity, and a handful of tiny blue sparks that fell to the ground and winked out at the foot of the stairs.

The wolf was nature's perfect running machine. With long loping strides that ate up the miles, Connor raced for hours until flecks of foam began to fly from his lolling tongue. He finally slowed near the top of a hill, his flanks heaving, mouth wide and lungs burning for air. He slaked his thirst at a tiny spring, then padded to the crest. The moon was high now and brilliant in the clear starry sky, almost blinding to look at directly. Instead he looked out across the river valley and lay down with his head on his paws.

In the small hours of the morning, Bernie was awakened by the howling of a wolf. He lifted his ravaged face, his swollen eye crusted with a mixture of dried blood and tears. Humans usually couldn't tell the direction such a sound was coming from, but the old man knew at once that the wolf must be up on Elk Point, said to be a sacred place. The animal sang as if its heart was broken, the mournful refrain taken up by the wolves in the surrounding hills.

Bernie swore softly. He knew the sorrow-filled song was for him, knew it was Connor who sang it. The tears began again.

Chapter Four

Zoey headed down the hall to the front door, determined that her next editorial would be in favor of legalizing the murder of people who knocked at ungodly hours. True, she was usually awake at those hours but still . . . *The building had better be on fire.*

She flung open the door, expecting anyone but Connor Macleod. At least, she assumed that's who was nearly filling her doorframe. She didn't remember him being quite that tall, or so wide of shoulder. Didn't recall the dark, glossy hair that fell forward into his face and tumbled over the collar of his denim jacket. Or the strong angles of his jaw line, now accented with dark beard stubble. But those pale gray eyes . . . Those she remembered very well.

"Hello, ma'am. I'm conducting a survey to see how many people will answer the door this early in the morning. I'll just put you down as a *yes*."

"It's six A.M. on a Saturday." She stared up at him warily for a long moment. "What are you doing here?"

"I'm a desperate man. The Finer Diner doesn't open 'til six-thirty and I might die if I don't find coffee soon."

Her mouth curved but she kept a hand on the door. Yesterday she'd been too nervous to phone him and here he was today in the flesh. Damn sexy flesh too. Did she really want him to come inside? "So I'd be saving your life if I let you in?"

"God, yes."

What could it hurt? "Well, I couldn't possibly refuse an emergency like that. I'd be violating some sort of Good Samaritan law." She waved him inside and led the way to the kitchen.

He squeezed into a chair behind her little bistro table, then his eyes widened and he gave a low, appreciative whistle. "That's a hell of a setup you've got here. I may never go to the Finer Diner again."

"I take my coffee seriously." She did too. The kitchen was small but one half of the counter space was devoted to espresso and latte machines in addition to a regular coffeemaker, two different grinders, and an assortment of glass canisters containing dark beans. Huge bright coffee mugs marched along a shelf, while colorful paintings of steaming cups were hung on the wall. "But you can't discount the Finer Diner entirely. The food is incredible there." She knew it for a fact. She'd made a habit of eating there frequently and was already on a first name basis with Bill and Jessie Watson, the couple that ran the place.

"True, Bill's an artist when it comes to food. He'd rather cook than breathe."

"You know them? Oh wait, I guess you've been here a lot longer than I have." She kept forgetting that people in a small town knew each other. In Vancouver, she'd lived in an apartment building for years without knowing the names of the people who lived on the same floor.

"Well, it's true that we've been friends for a long time. But it was inevitable—where else could a single hardworking vet go to eat around here with the kind of hours I keep?"

She didn't miss the fact that he was telling her outright he was available, and the news sent a pleasant tingle through her. "So does this hardworking vet prefer his coffee plain or would he like a mocha grande with double espresso?"

Connor hesitated for a moment and she realized that he looked tired. Very tired. "I'll tell you what," she decided. "I'll get some strong coffee going because it'll brew fast. After you've had a cup, I'll make you that mocha."

"Thanks. That sounds great."

Long practice had the coffee brewing within moments. Zoey found the biggest mug she had and placed it in front of him, scooping her pile of papers off the table before she sat down. The table looked a lot smaller than usual with a good-looking man looming over it. Suddenly she remembered her appearance and ran her hands hurriedly through her hair. God, here she was entertaining in her bathrobe! Worse, beneath it were turquoise flannel pajamas with little green frogs on them. She tugged the collar of the bathrobe higher in a useless bid to hide them—the pant legs were plainly visible below the robe. So were the furry slippers. . . .

"It's pretty."

"What?"

"Your hair. It's nice. The color, the waves."

"Thanks." Maybe the pajamas were okay after all. "So were you out delivering a calf?"

"Probably."

"You don't know?"

He scrubbed a hand over his face and grinned. "This morning I wouldn't swear to anything without checking with the dispatcher first. I'm pretty much running on automatic pilot."

"I've done that myself a few times. Sounds like veterinary practice can be a lot like the newspaper business."

"Not here, surely."

"No, thank God. It's a lot quieter here."

"Is that why you came to Dunvegan? For the quiet?"

Not exactly, Zoey thought, but if she told him about that little ability she'd inherited, the one she was trying to leave behind, he'd surely think she was weird. She didn't want to take a chance on chasing him off, not yet. He looked just too good in her kitchen. . . . So she gave him the same standard answer she'd given her former boss and co-workers, her new publisher, everyone in fact. "Big city journalism is not your career, it's your life. I wanted a slower pace and a chance to write more human interest stories, instead of just pieces about murders and robberies."

"Instead, you got wolves."

"Beats the heck out of human wolves," she countered. The coffeemaker beeped and Zoey took off the pot, poured Connor's cup.

"Thanks." He brought it to his face and inhaled deeply. "Smells like heaven." Sipped. "Tastes like it too. I'm saved!"

"The miracle of freshly ground beans." She poured herself a cup as well.

"Really? I didn't see you grinding any." His eyes were full of humor as they looked at her over his coffee mug.

She paused with the pot in her hand and sighed. "Okay, I'll come clean. I was already awake, been up for over an hour. I'm one of those annoying morning people and I get my best writing done around five. Go ahead"—she waved a hand at him—"recoil in horror."

He laughed. "My mother always said there was something magic about mornings. Must be true, since I'm sitting with a pretty woman and drinking good coffee. But I'll confess too. I saw your lights on when I was driving by and knew you were up. And what I really came here for is to make sure you're okay."

"I *am* okay, thanks to you. As much as I love wrestling wolves, I admit I was getting a little tired when you came along the other night."

"Did you get that bite checked at the clinic?"

"I called a couple of times yesterday, but neither of the doctors was in. By the time I called again, the clinic was closed."

He frowned. "The message machine has an emergency number. The doctors aren't that hard to reach."

"Well, it didn't feel like an emergency. I checked my leg—it looked clean and it wasn't bleeding. I washed it and doused it with peroxide just in case." That had stung like crazy at first but at least the peroxide hadn't foamed up around the punctures, as it would have if they'd been dirty or infected. "So I thought it could wait until today." She smiled but for some reason he was still frowning. Excuses suddenly came tumbling out of her mouth as if she was in grade school facing a glowering teacher. "I've been pretty busy. In case you didn't notice, I have a newspaper to run and deadlines to make. I had to assign someone to take photos of the damage from the ice storm—there was a fallen tree blocking Main Street. And there were other calls to make, stories to be written. I just lost track of the time and well, *forgot*." Crap. That sounded completely lame even to her. And why was she trying to explain herself to this man?

"Pretty tough to forget that a wolf used your leg for a chew toy."

"Well, of course I didn't forget *that*. My leg feels like it was caught in a bear trap, okay?" She couldn't keep the defensive tone out of her voice, and that pissed her off. She glared at him, wondering how the hell this man had managed to knock her off-balance so easily with less than three sentences.

There was a pause. Then his mouth twitched so slightly that she wasn't sure she'd seen it. "I see I've left my manners in the truck. Can I have a do-over if I apologize and promise to stop grilling you?" He held out his cup and grinned. "I really don't want to risk losing out on more of your great coffee."

She rolled her eyes but topped off his cup, her anger deflating like a balloon. "I'm sorry too. I'm just stressed, I guess. I can put a lot of things to the side—like making repeated calls to doctors' offices—when I have other priorities, and my main priority has been to try to convince people that there's a dangerous animal out there. I've been on the phone a lot."

"Yeah? Who did you call?"

"The usual. The cops and the mayor's office and the Fish and Wildlife guys for starters. Most wouldn't even listen. Well, the RCMP listened enough to send an officer over. He was nice about it but it was obvious he thought it was a dog attack. Said they'll definitely keep their eyes open. If an animal is found and its owner is determined, they'll lay charges. He's going to refer my case to the local bylaw official, but I don't know what good that will do. I'd already called *him* myself."

"You told all those people and no one believed you?"

"Hey—city girl, media type, new in town—what do *you* think?"

"No credibility at all, eh?"

"Not a shred. So I figure I'll write up the story as if it

was a big nasty dog, say it was acting strangely—no exaggeration there—and maybe people will think it could be rabid, maybe they'll be a little bit worried." She stopped and thought then. "What am I saying, *I* should be the one that's worried. What if it did have rabies?" Her hand went to her head. *Stupid, stupid, stupid.* She should have crawled to the damn clinic if she had to and gotten herself checked out.

"I doubt that you have to worry. There's very little incidence of rabies in this part of the country. I haven't seen a case in ten years."

"Really? That's a huge relief. Well, I can still write the story so at least people will be on the lookout for a weird dog, and maybe no one else will get bitten."

"Sounds like a plan. Are you sure you're going to be okay with that, with letting people think it was a dog? You know what it was."

"I know what it was." She looked at him sharply then. "Hey, so do you!" Why hadn't she thought of it before? "I don't have any proof that the wolf was a wolf but maybe you could back me up. The village officials would listen to you. Or maybe you could give me a couple of quotes I can use in my article." She couldn't keep the hopeful note out of her voice. A hope that faded as Connor shook his head slowly.

"It's true that it was a wolf, but the truth can be misused. The local farmers and ranchers are likely to get gun-happy and wipe out every wolf they can find. Wolves aren't a protected species here," he explained. "I'm not happy that one attacked you but it's out of character for wolves in general. It may have been sick, or too old to hunt regular game."

Like some lions that become man-eaters in Africa, she thought with a shiver. "I guess humans are very easy prey."

"Unless they have windshield wipers."

She snorted at that. Still, she couldn't help agreeing with what he'd said. "Look, I don't want to start a wolf extermination either. I just want people to be safe, and a dog attack story will probably do the job. But it bothers me that no one will be looking for this animal. Old or sick or just plain crazy, it should be stopped."

"That much I can promise you."

"But the authorities—"

"Are not the only people capable of tracking down a rogue wolf," he finished. "Trust me, my family and friends are on it as we speak. The wolf will be dealt with." Connor placed his hand over hers.

She hoped her hand wasn't shaking. It was completely swallowed by his. She could feel the heat of it, and the rough palm that was the signature of a working man. It was sexy as hell and she caught herself wondering what that hand would feel like sliding slowly under the bathrobe, stroking her bare skin. . . . Her cheeks heated suddenly and she pulled her hand away.

"I promised you a double-shot mocha," she said as she got up and began pulling out canisters. She risked a quick glance at his face as she worked. There was humor in his eyes, as if he was laughing at her for pulling her hand away. Thank God he didn't know what she had been thinking. Yesterday she'd felt nervous at the thought of seeing him again. And here she was in her pajamas and bathrobe, making him coffee in her own kitchen while thinking bedroom thoughts. And hoping like crazy she wasn't blushing.

"You know, there's another reason why the town officials didn't take you seriously."

"What would that be?"

"They don't want the stories about werewolves to start up again."

"Excuse me?"

"Werewolves. Two years ago the paper carried a number of stories about werewolves attacking area residents."

She stopped dead and stared at him, the carafe forgotten in her hand. "You've got to be kidding."

"Nope. Wish I was. Of course, there were only three people interviewed, all of them regulars at the same bar, mind you. Didn't stop some of the bigger city papers from picking up the story. We even had a television crew visit the sites of the alleged attacks. Dunvegan ended up on the national news and for a while it was impossible to go to the post office without running into reporters. It was all very X-Files."

Zoey shook her head slowly. She was in the news business—how had she not heard about the story before she came here? Had she been so intent on avoiding the paranormal that she had missed it? Of course, she would have been focused on "real" news, automatically filtering out anything that reeked of tabloid tales. "No one ever mentioned a word of it at the newspaper. I had no idea—wait, wait just a minute." She held up a finger as several puzzle pieces clicked into place.

"Oh. My. God. I'll bet that's why the publisher asked me during the job interview if I'd ever reported a UFO story or interviewed a dead celebrity! I thought he just had a bizarre sense of humor." She laughed as she said it, but she'd been terrified during the interview, fearful that Ted Biegel had heard rumors, had somehow discovered the truth behind her reputation for breaking stories or worse, had discovered her real last name. What a relief to know that the man's odd questions hadn't had a thing to do with her, her psychic ability, or her unusual family.

Connor chuckled. "I imagine old Ted feared a repeat of history. He was on vacation when the werewolf stories came out. When he came back, the editor responsible not only resigned but left town."

"I imagine that's *resigned* as in *fired*."

"That's what everyone figured."

"I'm really glad you told me this before I wrote about the attack." She wanted nothing to do with any supernatural stories. No werewolves, no woo-woo, *nothing* that might direct any attention her way. Sure, she'd changed her name years ago, but one whiff of the paranormal around her and another reporter would have little trouble uncovering who she really was. "I could have destroyed my credibility as a journalist without even knowing it. No wonder the deputy mayor was so rude."

She'd have to shelve all the research she'd done on wolves, along with the draft of her article. Maybe she could rework it and sell it to a magazine—in another part of the country. And the "dog attack" story for the newspaper? She would have to choose her words carefully so as not to remind local residents—or her publisher—about those werewolf tales. Or anything else of that nature. . . . Zoey put a pair of frothy cups on the table and tried to lighten things up. "God, can you imagine the headlines if a bigger paper picked up the story? *Werewolf Attacks Editor, Town Under Siege by Wolfman.* That would be great for my career—not!"

Connor awarded two thumbs up to the mocha, then asked, "So, can I drive you over to the clinic now and get that wound looked at?"

She shook her head. "Thanks, but I haven't even checked to see if they're open on a Saturday. I really should have done it yesterday."

He smiled and pulled out a cell phone, waggled it in his hand, then went out onto her balcony. A few moments later, he returned and pocketed the phone. "Lowen says to bring you in. He'll open the place in twenty minutes."

"I—what? Who's Lowen?"

"Lowen Miller, husband of Bev Miller. They're the doctors here. And my friends."

"That's a wonderful offer but—"

"It's not an offer, it's an order from Lowen. He's threatening to come down here if you don't show up. Says a bite like that is nothing to fool around with, and I happen to agree with him."

Zoey stared for a long moment, slightly stunned. The amiable and charming Connor Macleod had just neatly transformed into a brick wall. The expression on his face was still pleasant yet something in his eyes had hardened. Her lips were forming a protest—hopefully something more mature than *you're not the boss of me*—when a familiar tingly sensation settled over her. And expanded. Her gift, usually so tiny, flared brightly as she looked at the man standing in her kitchen, giving her a sudden clarity of perception.

He wasn't threatening her, she could feel that. There was only good intent. But no mistake, Connor Macleod was fully prepared to do whatever was necessary to get her to the clinic. If she argued, she would not win. If she refused, he would probably carry her. That rankled more than a little but then she shook herself mentally, letting the gift show her more. *He was afraid for her*—

The gift winked out abruptly and she wondered how

long she'd been staring at Connor. "You're right," she said simply. And he was. She'd been an *idiot* for not getting her leg looked at—what had she been thinking? It was just like that time she had gotten so involved with covering an ongoing murder trial that she'd neglected to eat for a day and a half. And had fainted on the courthouse steps like a ninny. Mortified, she'd made a promise to take better care of herself. It was just that she got so darn focused, so intent. . . .

She thanked him and went to get dressed.

Chapter Five

After the trip to the clinic, Connor drove Zoey back to her apartment to pick up her camera and her truck. He'd hoped to talk her into having breakfast with him, but she insisted she had to go to work. He knew full well that the newspaper office wasn't open on Saturday, but maybe she just wanted to get some writing done. Or maybe she just needed to assert herself.

He'd been prepared for a hell of an argument over going to the doctor, and then over whether or not he could drive her there. She did *not* like being told what to do. He felt her bristle at his words, saw her plant her feet, fist her hands at her sides, resist with every part of her being. She'd glared at him eye-to-eye when suddenly the ferocity slipped away, replaced by something akin to his own *farsight*. The power of it had radiated from her like the electrical energy that heralded the Change from human to wolf. It had lasted only a few seconds, but it was long enough to change her mind. Long enough to make him wonder.

Now he slipped into the back door of the clinic, headed up the stairs to the living quarters where he knew his friends were waiting. He could smell Earl Grey steeping, Bev's favorite. She was a pediatrician while Lowen was actually the area's coroner as well as a surgeon. Rather than retire, the couple had chosen to leave the big city and their lucrative practices to set up a clinic in a small town that needed them. With the nearest hospital two hours away and doctors in short supply in northern Canada, little Dunvegan was extremely lucky to have them. Connor felt lucky himself to count them as friends. Particularly because they knew what he was.

He was barely through the door when Bev handed him a mug of fragrant tea and pointed to the living room. Lowen wandered in a few moments later and tossed Connor a small empty bottle before ensconcing himself in his favorite recliner.

"You oughta keep that one, wolf-boy."

"This?" Connor looked at the bottle.

"No, that long-legged gal you brought in. She's a smart one. I like her editorials. So this silver nitrate you palmed me is supposed to stop her from becoming what you are?"

"Yes." Legends and folk tales claimed that anyone bitten by a Changeling would become one. They were absolutely right. The secret was in the saliva. A single bite, even a very small one, sent saliva into the bloodstream. The saliva activated an otherwise innocuous gene already present in all humans. Only silver nitrate could stop the process, and only if used in time. Treatment had to be started within twelve hours or all the silver in the world wouldn't help. "Injection is more effective because you only need to do it once, but it's pretty tough to explain to a human patient what the shot is for. Especially when we're talking about a hundred or so cc's."

"That's a damn big shot," snorted Lowen. "So that's why you decided to go with a topical application?"

"Exactly. More applications but easier to pass off. Two's usually enough as long as it's started within twelve hours of the bite, but there was a full moon behind the clouds the night Zoey was bitten. A Changeling's bite tends to be more virulent then, so I'm playing it safe by giving her three applications."

"The whole thing sounds like a damn B-movie." Lowen shook his head. "Well, I followed your instructions to the letter, doused every puncture with it. Acted like I was flushing the wounds. The stuff looks just like distilled water."

"Colloidal silver is touted for its antibiotic properties." Bev came and sat on the couch next to Connor. "People often take it internally."

"Yeah, well, people take a lot of questionable things internally," grunted Lowen. "Too much of that silver nitrate stuff and you turn into a giant Smurf. Skin's blue, permanently. I once had a case where—"

"So has Zoey had the three applications now?" Bev cut her husband off with such practiced ease that Connor had to hide a smile. It was likely a talent she'd developed in self-defense, since Lowen could reminisce for hours once he got started.

"I gave her one the night of the attack. Lowen gave her the second one this morning. Ideally they should be a day or two apart, so I've got to find a way to get her another one Monday or Tuesday."

"Ha. That won't be hard." The old doctor slurped the last of his tea and banged the cup down on a side table. "I suggested she let *you* check her leg and change the dressings."

Connor was surprised. "Why would you tell her that? I'm a vet."

"And the most talented healer I've ever come across. The medical profession lost out when you decided to patch up cows instead of people."

"Thanks but still, it's one thing to pinch hit in an emergency and—"

"But there's no emergency," replied Lowen. "Exactly. She's due back in a week so I can officially look at the wound to make sure there's still no infection, but until then she's on her own. And that's where you come in. I told her I want the dressings changed frequently, the wounds washed and treated with antibiotic cream. So you'll have plenty of opportunities to apply the silver nitrate and ask her out."

Connor laughed then. "You're devious, Lowen."

"So my poker opponents tell me. Now reassure me of one thing."

"What?"

"That there's no chance of rabies from this bite. I know it's rare in this part of the country, but it's still standard procedure to ship a bite victim off to the city for shots when we can't locate the animal and test it."

"Changelings don't carry rabies."

"And you know for certain it wasn't a real wolf?" asked Bev.

"Better. I know who the wolf was." Connor's gray eyes darkened. "And I also know he won't be a wolf again. Ever."

Lowen's eyebrow went up. "Sounds personal."

God, yes, it was personal. "He would have killed her, Lowen." No sooner had he formed the words than his inner wolf began snarling and snapping. With enormous effort, Connor leashed it firmly, startled at the strength of it, puzzled by its purpose. The wolf clearly intended to protect Zoey Tyler. No matter what.

* * *

Zoey spent most of the day at the office, then took photos at a service club meeting where scholarships were
being awarded to some bright and promising high school
seniors. After supper she returned to the office to download the photos and write up an article.

The *Dunvegan Herald Weekly* office was silent except for
clocks ticking and the dripping of the staff room faucet.
She liked having the place to herself. How on earth had
she ever gotten anything done in the middle of a big busy
newsroom? It was so much easier to work when it was
quiet. Easier, until she played her phone messages and
found one from Connor. It was nothing much, just a simple request that she call him, but his deep melodious voice
did strange things to her insides. God, he even *sounded* hot.
Did he do that on purpose?

It ruined her concentration for writing. She'd barely get
a sentence down before she began thinking of Connor. His
eyes for instance, and how they were almost silver at times.
With such a color they should have seemed cold, even icy,
and yet they were anything but. There was warmth and
ready humor in them. Until—

Zoey contemplated the glimpse she'd gotten of another
side of Connor Macleod. The one who'd stood in her
kitchen ready to do whatever was necessary to get her to
the clinic. His eyes had been different then, darker. The
warmth was gone, replaced with a decided coolness. Yet
there was no chill directed toward her. Of that she was certain. It was more like the coolness of metal armor, the determined chill of a sword, as he readied for battle. As he
stood to protect her, even from herself.

She shivered at the sheer sexiness of it, of him. Ran her
hands through her hair and rubbed them lightly over her
face, feeling the heat that had flared in her cheeks. *Heat.* In

his truck, she had awakened to the sensation of Connor stroking her cheek. In her kitchen, he'd placed that big hand over hers. She could still feel the unusual heat that had radiated from his skin on both occasions. Not the parched heat of a fever but more like the banked coals of a campfire, something that beckoned her to relax, to stretch out and simply bask in the pleasure of it.

Sitting behind her desk as she had sat at her bistro table, her hand resting palm down on the smooth surface, she smiled. The table had been so tiny, she could have reached out and touched Connor easily. Could have indulged the urge she'd felt to brush the glossy dark hair from his face, indulged that wish to slide her palm over the stubble on his jaw. She imagined stirring her mocha slowly, lazily, and skimming the chocolate froth onto the spoon. Licking it off with quick little flicks of her tongue while he watched her with silvery eyes. . . .

Omigod. She put a hand on her chest where her heart was pounding and took several deep breaths. If she was going to make a habit of fantasizing about Connor at work, she'd have to start keeping a vibrator in her desk! Zoey looked up at the clock, then at her laptop screen. She had a whopping six and a half sentences to show for an hour's work. Crap. *Crap, crap, crap.* Desperate to get her mind off a certain tall, sexy veterinarian, she seized her camera bag. Maybe the fresh evening air would cool her down. Maybe a short walk would ease the stiffness that had set into her aching leg and work off some of her unexpected, uh, *tension.* Oh hell. Maybe she'd be really lucky and find another wolf to beat up. . . .

There were no wolves wandering the streets but Zoey enjoyed the fresh spring air. Temperatures had risen to normal and the only evidence left of the freak ice storm was a

scattering of twigs and branches on the ground, some saw-
dust where the fallen tree at the top of Main Street had
been removed, and a few puddles. She walked slowly, favor-
ing her injured calf. Lowen Miller had ordered her to stay
off it, but she'd been in a chair all day—surely it wouldn't
hurt anything to stretch a bit?

The sun was low in the sky when Zoey reached the little park by the fire hall. It was too early in the year for
flowers. There didn't seem to be anything worth photographing and she was ready to turn back when Lucinda
Perkins's minivan turned the corner. Mabel Rainier was
riding shotgun. The pale green vehicle was festooned with
homemade signs identifying it as the DNP–Dunvegan
Neighborhood Patrol.

It took only a wave from Zoey for the van to pull over.
Lucinda and Mabel were from the local senior's lodge,
where in recent months a small group had formed the
DNP in response to a rash of vandalism. The seniors
worked hard to repair or replace the many flower boxes,
both in the park and along the downtown streets, and were
determined to protect them. So far, the patrol idea seemed
to be working.

The women willingly posed by a newly built planter, excited that they were going to be in the newspaper. Zoey
couldn't help being charmed—it wasn't an attitude she'd
encountered much as a journalist in the city. People just
seemed to be more cynical there, either unimpressed by attention from the media or demanding it as their due. She
diligently took down information and quotes for what
would be a nice little story for Page Three.

"I'm so glad we have an editor who takes an interest in
community events," said Lucinda.

Zoey smiled. "Isn't that what an editor does?"

"Well," said Mabel. "You'd think so, but nothing's quite the same as it used to be. Everyone's been looking for the sensational ever since those werewolf stories started up all over again a couple years ago."

Again? Zoey lowered her steno pad. "I heard a little about what happened then. Have there been stories before?" Connor hadn't mentioned any earlier episodes.

Lucinda patted her arm as if to soothe her confusion. "Well, it's one of those things, dear. Every area has its local legends, stories you tell around campfires on a dark night."

"Except here, instead of ghosts, it's werewolves," supplied Mabel. "Usually it dies down in a little while and people forget all about it. Then those men—"

"Those *drunks* you mean," sniffed Lucinda.

"Those drunks," amended Mabel with a chuckle. "They said they saw the wolf right in the middle of town, and this time the story just didn't go away."

Lucinda nodded. "It was the TV that did it. Some news station really put Dunvegan on the map this time and I imagine we'll stay on it. Now we get all sorts of visitors coming here, asking questions about wolves. Why, there's been an investigator here for a week now, interviewing everyone he can find."

"Really? He hasn't come by the newspaper office yet," said Zoey. Strange—it was the first thing she would have done as a reporter in a new town.

"Oh that's likely because Ted Biegel would string him up on sight. Ted's part of the Chamber of Commerce," said Mabel. "The whole werewolf thing really steams them up. They don't want to be like that little town on the border that put in the UFO landing pad."

Zoey's eyes widened. "They did *what?*"

"Some say it was foolish, but I think it was sharp as

tacks," said Lucinda, sitting on a park bench and tugging Zoey down beside her. "Some folks claimed to be seeing UFOs in the area. The Chamber there noticed that it brought a lot of business to their little town, so they built a big round concrete pad. Put up colored lights and signs to invite UFOs. They get all kinds of tourists now who want to get their picture taken standing on it. Local stores sell a lot of souvenirs. And you can bet when somebody claims to see a flying saucer, it makes their local newspaper."

"Not like here. Ted wouldn't publish a story like that at gunpoint," declared Mabel, folding her arms. "That one poor editor who wrote about the werewolves while Ted was on vacation? Fired on the spot. A shame, really."

"So Dunvegan has its very own urban legend?" pressed Zoey.

"It's an *old* legend," corrected Mabel. "Dates all the way back to before Dunvegan existed." She lowered her voice to a conspiratorial whisper. "The museum on Third Avenue used to have an old diary on display, and cross my heart, it's got an entry about a man becoming a wolf."

The other woman gasped. "Don't let Kathleen Summers hear you telling people that! She'll have a conniption if anyone comes asking about it. That diary's been under lock and key in the archives ever since that page got photographed and put in the paper."

"She doesn't want people to know?" asked Zoey, trying not to smile at the wealth of information Lucinda had just blurted.

Lucinda shook her head. "Kathleen just doesn't want to lose her job. She likes running the museum. You seem to be good at your job too, and if you want to keep it, you ought to know that the town's of two minds. Half would like to cover up the wolf stories, and the other half knows better. I don't mind sharing the stories, but I don't want to see Kathleen in trouble."

"So what do the stories say exactly? I promise I won't bother your friend."

Zoey saw them exchange glances. Some unspoken agreement seemed to be reached and Mabel was the first to speak. "We've got some coffee in the van. It's too cool out here for such a long story."

Zoey's brain felt like a hamster in a wheel as she walked slowly back to the office where she'd parked her truck. Lucinda and Mabel had been eager to tell her everything they knew about the local werewolf legends—which was considerable—stopping only when Mabel remembered it was movie night at the lodge. They'd left Zoey with plenty to think about, and a new understanding of Dunvegan. It made even more sense now why none of the village officials wanted to hear about her wolf encounter. No doubt about it, she'd have to write the story up as a dog attack if she wanted to stay here. Her goal was still to warn people, and she had cautioned the ladies before they'd left to be watchful for big aggressive dogs. They'd clucked over her bandaged leg, given her plenty of advice—then looked at her strangely. Surely they didn't suspect that she wasn't telling them the truth? She felt a twinge of guilt but Mabel had been right; if Zoey wanted to keep her job, she had to step carefully.

Maybe Connor was stepping carefully too, only telling her about the most recent episode of the ongoing werewolf tale. He certainly hadn't mentioned that his own family was linked to the legend! According to her new friends, rumors had surrounded the Macleods since the family first homesteaded in the area over a century ago. Was that the real reason he didn't want her to write about the wolf? Maybe he had a vested interest in preventing the werewolf legends from surfacing again.

And maybe she had more in common with Connor Macleod than she had thought. After all, she knew only too well what it was like to have your family considered *different*. Or strange. And to be tarred with the same brush.

Chapter Six

Zoey's thoughts were interrupted as she found it increasingly difficult to walk. The bite wound had begun throbbing and burning horribly. Had she overdone it, used her leg too much, too soon? *Dear God, please don't let it be infected.*

Suddenly a grizzled old drunk in a torn plaid shirt rounded the corner, almost colliding with her. "Just the gal I'm looking for!" he bellowed into her face, stinging her eyes with the reek of alcohol on his breath. His face was a mass of nasty cuts and scabs, interspersed with several days' growth of scraggly white beard. Zoey dodged him as he made a grab for her.

"I got somethin' for your little newspaper," he yelled and made another unsuccessful swipe. He was neither quick enough nor coordinated enough to catch her. Instead he fell sprawling to the sidewalk. Zoey hurried away as fast as her injured leg would let her, gritting her teeth against the pain, leaning one hand on the storefronts as she made her way down the street. The man got up and staggered after her, shouting, swearing, and raving about a story he had to tell her, something he wanted to show her.

"For Pete's sake," she muttered. She wasn't scared, just annoyed. The old coot obviously recognized her—one of the drawbacks to working for the media—and even if she managed to put some distance between them and get off his radar now, it was likely he'd show up in her office sometime in the future. *There's one or two in every community. . . .*

"Where the hell's the Neighborhood Patrol when I need them?" Although she'd almost be embarrassed to call for help. The man was far too drunk to catch her, and even if he did, she imagined she would have little trouble defending herself. He already looked like he'd been on the losing end of a fight. Meanwhile, the slow-motion chase would no doubt make great YouTube material—*the gimpy victim fleeing the staggering boozehound.* Or perhaps a *zombie footrace,* a little humor for a low-budget horror movie.

Finally making it to her Bronco, she risked a look back. The drunk was still following her, but was better than half a block away now. She pulled the door open and grabbed her phone off the seat just as he launched into a fresh tirade, his gravelly voice echoing down the deserted street.

"That damn vet thinks he can tell me *what to do,*" he confided loudly to his reflection in the dark store windows. "Macleod thinks he's so goddamn perfect, but he's just like me. Just like me." He suddenly fell to his knees, his hands over his face, groaning and sobbing loudly. "It wasn't s'posed to work like that. It wasn't s'posed to *be* like that. It should have been you, ya fucking bastard! Damn you, Connor Macleod!"

Zoey had the cell phone to her ear, but froze at the mention of the vet's name.

The drunk staggered to his feet, his rage returned. He shook both fists at the empty street. "You hear me, Macleod? But you're not so smart. You wait, Macleod. I

called him, told him. Hear me? I told him fucking everything and he knows what you are!" His tirade was suddenly
redirected as a patrol car swung lazily around the corner as
if on cue and stopped in front of him. "It's about time you
showed up!" he hollered.

"Looks like you got an early start tonight, Bernie." A
young officer got out and opened the back door for him,
stood patiently as the old man staggered over, still complaining loudly. "How's that face feeling today? Maybe we
could get Doc Miller to come by the station and check it
out for you."

The man stiffened and straightened. Zoey gasped as he
swung a hand around and pointed directly at her. "That
newspaper bitch wouldn't listen to me. I got something to
show her, and she wouldn't listen. You ought to do your
damn job and arrest *her*!" He clambered clumsily into the
back of the patrol car, continuing his rants.

The officer closed the door with obvious relief and
walked over to Zoey. "Are you all right? Has he been bothering you?"

"I'm fine. He just yelled at me." Up close, this guy
looked even younger than the one who had questioned
her about the animal attack.

"He does a lot of that. He'll be doing it all night too, I
imagine. You can press charges, you know. You don't have
to put up with harassment."

She laughed. "I'm in the newspaper business. Getting
yelled at is sometimes part of the job. No harm done. But
can you tell me who he is?"

"Are you going to write about this? Because technically,
I'm not supposed to give out that information."

"What kind of story would it make? *Editor shouted at by*

drunk. Yeah, that'll sell a lot of papers. I just like to know the names of the people who are upset with me. Helps me to avoid them."

The young officer grinned. "Bernard Gervais. He's in a fantasy world most of the time, so I wouldn't worry about anything he says." He touched his hat and returned to the cruiser and its irate passenger.

Gervais. Lucinda and Mabel had talked about a Gervais. Is that a French name? Zoey could still hear the man in the backseat raving at full volume, even though all the car windows were closed. Saw the officer shaking his head as he drove away. "Glad I'm not you," she murmured and climbed into her truck. She sat for several long minutes, grateful beyond words to be off her feet and especially off her injured leg. What could the drunken old geezer possibly have against Connor Macleod? Was the guy a farmer, had Connor treated his livestock? Maybe he was upset about the bill. . . .

She heaved an irritated sigh as she found herself wanting to defend the tall veterinarian. All that walking, all that work, and here she was thinking about Connor all over again. Exasperated, she looked over at her office window and resolutely climbed out of the truck. Maybe it was time to check out those newspaper articles that Lucinda and Mabel had mentioned. Her psychic gift was silent but her reporter's intuition was tingling, and she would bet money that the old drunk was involved in the wild story.

The werewolf stories were surprisingly easy to find. Just over two years had passed since Barry Gordon, Bernard Gervais, and Jeb Luken had called the police and then the newspaper, claiming that a werewolf had chased them.

The men had left the Jersey Pub after last call and were

winding their way on foot to Luken's house. "A great and enormous gray wolf came out of the shadows. It had green glowing eyes and was snarling like a pit bull," Luken told the reporter. "Straight out of hell it was and no mistake it was going to attack us."

Zoey sat down abruptly amid the piles of newspapers. *Green glowing eyes.* The wolf that attacked her also had strange eyes, demonic, as if lit from within. She still saw them in her dreams. Still heard that horrible throaty snarling. . . .

Cut that out, dammit! With an effort she shoved the memories away and focused on the article. Luken and Gordon had scrambled into a Dumpster, holding down the metal lid with all the strength they could muster. They didn't know where Gervais had gone, didn't hear anything but growling as the monstrous creature had sniffed around the Dumpster. "The wolf jumped right on top of it, bold as brass," Luken was quoted as saying. "We could hear him walking back and forth, pawing and scratching at the lid. Damn, I don't mind saying I was some scared. Scared shitless, both of us."

Gervais claimed he had hidden inside the covered bed of a parked pickup. "I got separated from my buddies when the wolf showed up. It was every man for himself. I just dove for cover like everyone else." A photo of the trio confirmed what Zoey already knew, thanks to the officer. Bernard Gervais was the drunk who had pursued her down Main Street.

The *Dunvegan Herald Weekly* had published the report on one of the inside pages and below the crease, no doubt hoping to bury the story. It hadn't worked. A veritable flood of letters followed in subsequent issues, some of them complaining about the press the men were getting for such a wild tale, but others claiming to have seen similar creatures.

Zoey scanned the letters. Enormous wolves in every color had been sighted at various times in the area, but never in town. Some people had sighted very large wolves running as a pack near Elk Point. All of the stories could be chalked up to ordinary sightings of ordinary wolves. After all, her own research had shown that wolves could reach 175 pounds or more. With so much wilderness to roam in and an abundance of game, it stood to reason that this part of northern Canada simply produced big wolves.

Reason didn't have an answer for the diary entry however. Just as Mabel and Lucinda had said, a page had been photographed and printed. The caption said the journal had belonged to one Jack Harrison, a schoolteacher who had homesteaded in the Spirit River area and established a ranch there. Zoey squinted to read the ornate scrawl.

February 28, 1904.

Got a big black wolf in my trapp today, biggest I ever saw. Had a white star on its chest and white on its nose and tail like a dog. Thought it were a bear at first until it puts its ears up and looked at me. Rifle jammed up and then there was no wolf in the trapp, just a young man. Snow was deep but he had no coate or boots. Asked him where my wolf was because I wanted that pelt, but he shook his head. Then he opened the trapp with his bare hands. Knew he must be one of the wolf people my dad told me about because two good men aren't strong enough to open that trapp without the key. He pulled his leg out and it was bleeding bad but then it stopped right quick. I tried to unjam the rifle in case he might want to kill me but he just walked away and headed west to Macleod's land.

"Omigod," breathed Zoey. Connor's family was actually

named. And guilt by association undoubtedly followed. Sure enough, a small letter made it to print in the very next issue of the newspaper, pointing to the Macleods as the cause of all the trouble.

It's about time someone called a spade a spade, and revealed the creatures who think to live among us undetected. Families like the Macleods have blurred the line between man and beast for decades, intermingling with humans and converting them to their kind. They look like us on the outside but underneath they're all teeth and claws, just waiting for a chance to use them.

The bizarre letter was signed by Roderick Harrison. Good grief, was he a descendant of the man who wrote the diary? *It's almost like a feud,* thought Zoey. Harrisons and Macleods instead of Hatfields and McCoys. She empathized with Connor. No wonder he hadn't wanted the werewolf stories to resurface. Just look at the craziness he'd have to deal with—something Zoey could certainly relate to.

She shook her head, trying to get back to business. Harrison's letter should never have been published—any newspaper that printed such a personal attack was opening itself up to a lawsuit. Maybe it wasn't so surprising that Ted had fired the editor responsible. Most of the publications Zoey had worked for would have done the same simply as damage control.

Subsequent editorials were allegedly devoted to quelling the "mass hysteria" yet special feature articles appeared on the myths and legends surrounding *werewolves.* So-called experts flew in from all over, and *The Herald* dutifully interviewed most of them. Even the one who insisted the U.S. government was conducting the top secret testing of a breed of superwolves in the Canadian north, *and* the one who claimed that aliens were masquerading on this planet as wildlife. Zoey rolled her eyes and wondered how the reporter had managed to keep a straight face.

To her surprise, the story died out abruptly only eight issues later—not a very long run for such a sensational event. Zoey scanned all the issues up to the present, but no further mention of wolves, *were* or otherwise, was ever made. Undoubtedly, her hot-tempered publisher had killed the story the moment he returned to the office. She had little trouble picturing Ted Biegel's wrath descending on the parties responsible. She smiled as she remembered Mabel Rainier's words. Zoey only had to check the issue following the last werewolf update to see a change in the editor's name!

No wonder the village officials had been rude. She supposed she might even have to do some sort of damage control herself, to make certain she didn't become affiliated with the werewolf stories in any way. But it rankled. She had never hesitated to take a stand with a story, no matter how unpopular it might be. As a professor had once told her, the concept of journalistic impartiality was a myth the public made up. No reporter could write without taking sides at least a little.

But this was different. There was no lone citizen taking on city hall, no one's rights to be defended, no issues to be brought to light and championed. Just a bite from an animal she couldn't prove was a wolf and reports of werewolves from the local drunks. No doubt Larry, Moe, and Curly would have more credibility than that trio. And as a stranger in town, her own credibility wouldn't be much better.

It was long past midnight when Zoey finally drove home. She was going to feel like dirt in the morning, but thank heavens it would be a Sunday. She shook her head as she limped up the stairs to her apartment. *Werewolves*, for God's sake. She'd stayed up all night researching were-wolves. Who'd have thought? She hadn't read anything to make her believe in the creatures, but the description given by Jeb Luken and some of the letter-writers matched what she herself had seen only a few days before. A wolf, a *real* wolf, obviously roamed this area. And it wasn't afraid of people. The fact that it had wandered right into town made it every bit as dangerous as a garbage-eating bear. She had the proof of that on her very own leg.

Yet when the trio had reported it two years ago, the RCMP and the Fish and Wildlife officers hadn't appeared overly concerned. The newspaper had quoted them re-peatedly as saying the animal was a dog. Maybe a wild or feral dog, but a *dog*. Nothing more. Which was pretty much the reaction Zoey had gotten when she'd called those de-partments after the attack.

Was it so damn far-fetched that there could be a real wolf? Wolves were certainly native to northern Canada and known to live in the Dunvegan area. They weren't en-dangered here as a species, were plentiful in fact, and ranchers and farmers routinely shot them. However, pre-vailing theories claimed that wolves never attacked peo-ple—although there was an incident a few years ago with campers in Tofino, and more recently, a hiker killed in Saskatchewan. There was that poor teacher up in Alaska too. . . . Still, it all made for poor statistics. *Three* recorded attacks in over a century? Obviously Connor was right; the wolf was sick or old and not acting normally. But it wouldn't be sick for two years . . . it would either have died or re-covered. If it recovered, could attacking humans be a bad habit now? She'd have to ask Connor about that.

Connor again. Her mind had come full circle and she was once more thinking about the tall, dark-haired vet. So much for trying to distract herself. Zoey was far too tired to fight it and instead just let her imagination roam. She fell asleep clutching her pillow and pretending she was snuggled up with him, moaning a little as she dreamed of those big workingman's hands stroking her naked skin.

Chapter Seven

"Thank God this day is over," breathed Connor, flipping the clinic's window sign to *Closed*. To borrow words from a patient's young owner, it had been "a totally rotten, no-good, very bad day." To make it worse, it was probably his own damn fault. He'd insisted that he could handle things just fine while Birkie Peterson was on vacation, that he didn't need any temporary help.

What the hell had he been thinking?

His white-haired receptionist and friend had mentored at least three or four veterinarians before him, and her efficiency bordered on the supernatural. More than that, she was well known for her unflappable nature. If a fire-breathing dragon came through the doors of the North Star Animal Hospital, Connor had no doubt that Birkie would simply take its name and direct it to a chair, probably hand it a cup of coffee and a magazine.

The fire-breathing dragon would have looked good today, he thought as he poured the scorched dregs from the coffeemaker into a Styrofoam cup. Other than the fact that he was still vertical, the day had had few redeeming qualities. He'd semen-tested six young bulls that had been brought in last minute by 83-year-old Ivan Chirikov, then dehorned the lot. Ivan had no phone, seldom came to town, and didn't believe in appointments. He was also mostly deaf. It was simply easier to perform whatever un-scheduled procedures he was asking for rather than try to argue. At least it would be six months or so before the old farmer returned with another batch of unplanned patients.

Next was emergency surgery on a cat hit by a car. It was noon before Connor could get back to his regular appoint-ments, which included a few patients he'd rather not have seen. Ever.

One was an old dog that was scheduled for euthanasia. The big Chesapeake was blind, arthritic, and had soiled the carpet one too many times, including that very morning. Connor's Changeling senses could easily read the animal's confusion. She didn't understand why her owners had left her there alone. She did know that they were cross with her. It was instinctive for a canine to keep its den clean, a source of shame to the dog when it failed. Connor ran his hands over the chocolate fur, now dulled to mud-brown with age. *It's not your fault, old girl.* He had soothed the ani-mal's mind and comforted it as he injected the lethal sub-stance. It was over almost instantly, but unexpectedly he had spent the next few minutes in the bathroom splashing his face with cold, cold water. Euthanasia was part and par-cel of veterinary practice, but this time it reminded him far too much of what he had been forced to do to Bernie. Oh sure, Bernie was still alive. But only part of him.

A cesarean case came in right before closing time. The calf was already dead and had been for a while, the cow nearly so because of the extreme toxicity. It had been a god-awful mess. Connor had done his very best, used every tal-ent and skill he had at his disposal, but the unfortunate cow likely wouldn't survive the night.

A goddamn perfect ending to a goddamn perfect day. He

sipped the terrible coffee, half wished it was something much stronger. Like his father's favorite whiskey for instance. Connor sighed and wondered how Birkie was doing in Scotland. She'd been his mother's best friend since forever, and had gone with his sister, Kenzie, to visit his parents. He would've liked to have joined them, but that would have meant closing down the clinic completely.

Of course, things would be different if he'd listened to his friends and family and advertised for a partner. Most of the time he resisted the idea. After all, he'd handled the workload on his own just fine for years. Lately, however, he had to admit that his practice had grown much bigger than one vet—even if he was a Changeling—could handle. The North Star Animal Hospital served a large chunk of the Peace River country, and the traveling alone was taking up a helluva lot of his time.

Birkie, bless her, had done her best. She'd brought in a steady stream of Animal Health Technicians who needed a few months of practical work experience in order to complete their diploma. The extra hands were invaluable, and thank God he had three techs on hand right now, but there was a limit to what they could do. He needed to bite the bullet and advertise for another partner.

And he ought to ask Zoey Tyler out.

Connor picked up a newspaper from a waiting room chair. Zoey hadn't returned his calls yet, but maybe she was just busy. Or maybe she wasn't interested. He recalled her face when he had covered her hand with his. She had been flustered, and he hadn't needed Changeling senses to discern the jump in her pulse even as she pulled her hand away. There was interest there all right. Attraction. Maybe he could build on that.

God knew there was attraction on his side. And a curious familiarity. He felt as though he knew Zoey, had known her for a long time. *That* he might attribute to the strong psychic link he had been forced to make the night of the attack. But the attraction—well, that was apparent from the time he'd first spotted her soaking wet and defiant on the roof of her truck. Might as well admit it, he thought. Those amber eyes had him just this side of mesmerized. Her freckles did too. And as for the rest of her, well . . . as tired as he was at night, he still couldn't help thinking about those long legs, and imagining them wrapped around him.

Of course, there were things to consider. She was human. She was also a journalist, and from her writings he could see she had no love for sensationalism. Instead, she paid close attention to detail and delivered solid facts. She'd laughed when he told her about the werewolf stories— how would she react if she knew they were true, that Changelings existed? And that it was a Changeling, not a wolf, that had chewed on her?

How would she handle it if she knew that she was in real danger of becoming one?

Zoey's leg needed a final treatment in order to prevent that possibility. And, thanks to Lowen, Connor had a perfectly good excuse for seeing her again. He patted his jacket pocket where the bottle of silver nitrate was nestled. He'd refilled it this morning in the clinic pharmacy, then loaded his other pockets with gauze and such so he'd be ready to rewrap the wound tomorrow. And maybe he'd work on asking her out then too.

Switching his coffee cup to the other hand, he snatched up a doughnut—an apple fritter, courtesy of a client—and a half dozen boxes of number 4 sutures, juggling them all as

CHANGELING MOON   71

he headed down the clinic hallway, scanning the *Dunvegan Herald Weekly*.

Police are advising residents to be particularly watchful, after an animal attacked and bit a local woman Thursday night. The incident occurred after 11 P.M. when the woman was approached by a large canine similar to one of the sled-dog types raised in this area . . .

Zoey had skillfully managed to present a credible and balanced story without ever using the word *wolf*. She'd gone back to the police, the mayor's office, Fish and Game, and even the dogcatcher, and secured quotes from every last one of them. Somehow she'd managed to overcome their first impression of her as a hysterical woman literally crying wolf. The article spoke of the possibility of coyotes within town limits or dogs gone feral, with references to previous occurrences of both. But no mention was made of wolves.

Damn good job. Damn good *professional* job, thought Connor. He tucked the paper under his arm and stuck the doughnut in his mouth so he could open the door to his office. All his carefully balanced cargo fell to the floor, however, when he spotted the enormous black wolf inside.

"Christ, Culley!" Connor slammed the door behind him as the creature turned strange blue-gold eyes in his direction. "What the hell are you doing here?" Although the building was empty, instinct had him switching to mind-speech so he couldn't be overheard. *I mean it, Culley, have you gone completely crazy? What if someone sees you?*

The black wolf was sprawled on the battered couch that Connor used for napping when surgeries kept him late. The bone-crushing jaws opened wide as the creature yawned hugely, exposing long, sharp teeth. *Dog.*

Oh sure, right, like you could pass for a dog! Get the hell out of here before you scare my patients. The cows in the livestock wing were unlikely to react to the scent of a Changeling, but still. . . .

Dog. The wolf shook itself. Relaxed its body language, dampened its appearance of alertness. Half-closed its eyes. Slowly, one erect tulip-shaped ear flopped down, then the other. The massive head dropped, the powerful shoulders slouched. Coupled with a toothy grin and lolling tongue, the large creature suddenly looked friendly, almost comical. *Dog.*

It'll never work. Connor wasn't about to admit that the small changes were incredibly effective, particularly when combined with Culley's natural coloration. His long black muzzle had a snippet of solid white right down the middle of it that circled his nose, and there were white hairs in his eyebrows. There was a very *un*-wolflike star on his chest and the tip of his tail was pure white too. *What are you doing here, anyway? Don't you have some electronic gadgets to fix somewhere?*

Can't a guy visit his big brother? Haven't seen you in weeks. Bill and Jessie sent me to haul your ass to their house for dinner tonight or—

A sudden knock at the door made Connor jump. His heart jumped, too, when Zoey Tyler poked her beautiful head inside.

"I was just in the neighborhood—" She glanced down. "Gee, I was going to ask if you'd read the paper yet. Sure hope that's not your opinion of my article."

Connor followed her gaze to the lumpy fritter soaking up spilled coffee like a sea sponge. The packages of sutures had fallen clear of the puddle, but the newspaper had been ground zero. "No, no, I was just clumsy. I—uh—was just about to get some paper towels from the lunchroom." He put a hand on the doorknob, hoping to guide her back into the hall before she looked up and spotted the wolf but it was already too late. Her eyes grew wide as she stared at the massive black creature.

"Oh. My. God."

To Connor's astonishment, Zoey opened the door further and stepped inside. She had a hand on his arm but her expression was one of wonder, not fear. "That is the biggest, most humongous dog I have ever seen in my entire life. Is that one of those Belgian Shepherds I've been hearing about? Somebody must have crossed it with a Pyrenees to make it so big."

Connor latched onto that idea a little desperately. "He's definitely an unusual mix."

"He must have some malamute or husky in him too. Just look at those gorgeous eyes. Can I touch him? Is he friendly?"

Any hope he had of getting Zoey out of his office was dashed as the big black animal jumped off the couch, seemingly as awkward and clumsy as any puppy. It rushed over, wagging its tail so madly that its entire rear section was in motion. "It's okay, he's safe," Connor reassured Zoey. Mentally, he wasn't so calm. *If you scare her away, Culley, I'll personally kick your hairy butt all over creation, do you hear me?*

The creature whined ever so slightly, looked almost hurt. *Good dog.*

My ass. But you damn well better act like one now.

Zoey was far from terrified. She laughed as she buried her hands in the thick ruff around the creature's neck and scratched behind its floppy ears. It chuffed and whined, rubbing its massive head against her for more attention. It looked around her and up at Connor with a smug expression and winked a hazel eye at him. *Dog.*

How would you like to be neutered?

The animal curled its lips back in answer, showing its fangs. Then Connor heard his brother's laughter in his mind as the black "dog" shook itself and suddenly stood on its hind legs. It towered over Zoey, resting its paws lightly on her shoulders—and licked her face thoroughly.

"Hey!" Connor inserted himself between them and shoved the creature off balance, forcing it to return to all fours. *Mine!* Instinctively he broadcast the primal word with a psychic punch behind it. The wolf skittered backward a few inches as if struck. Planted its feet and stared up at Connor, speculation in those blue-gold eyes. Then it ambled off to sprawl on the couch.

"It wasn't hurting me," said Zoey from behind him.

"Well, yeah but—but he can't be allowed to jump up on people like that. Nothing worse than bad manners in a big dog, and it can be downright dangerous for old people and children, you know." He shot a glare at the creature. It chuffed out a breath at him and looked away, clearly insulted. Connor threw an arm around Zoey's shoulders and gently steered her out of the office, closing the door firmly behind them.

"You're sweating. Are you okay?"

"Just warm," he lied. He felt very far from *okay*. The wolf within him was awake. Wide, wide, awake and he didn't understand why. Nor did he have the faintest idea why he'd reacted so primitively to his brother licking Zoey's face. For one fleeting instant he'd very nearly Changed. Another second and he would have been at Culley's throat.

He grabbed a bottle of water out of the lunchroom

fridge and guzzled most of it down before he remembered he had a guest. "I'm sorry. Would you like anything?" He opened the fridge door again to show off the contents, but she shook her head.

"I can't stay—I'm due at the Rotary Club in twenty, gotta write up something on their guest speaker. Really, I just came by to see if I could talk to your receptionist. I'm doing a story on local wildflowers and someone told me she knows a lot about plants."

Knows a lot was an understatement. "She's certainly the right source for that. Birkie gathers plants for medicinal uses, grows her own herbs. I know she'd be happy to help you, but she's in Scotland right now."

"Wow. I've always wanted to visit Scotland. And Ireland too—my parents are from there. I hear the British Isles are beautiful."

"They are. My folks moved to Scotland a few years ago." He didn't mention that he'd been born there, had spent his entire childhood there, until a rogue Changeling had killed a human, and the hunts began. The entire sept of Clan Macleod had been forced to flee, and his parents had brought him and his siblings to the Peace River country of northern Canada. The hills and coulees of Dunvegan bore a striking resemblance to the land they'd left behind. . . .

"I guess you don't get to see your folks much then."

"Not as much as I'd like. It's pretty hard to get away from the practice." Another reason for bringing in a partner. "My sister, Kenzie, went along with Birkie this time."

"I know what it's like to be busy. You must wish you were with them."

"Not at this moment." It was true. He was enjoying the scenery right where he was. Connor could feel that his wolf was close to the surface but it was merely watchful.

Observing. Maybe it was enjoying Zoey's freckles too. Her fine features were awash in fragments of gold. The delightful speckling continued unabated down her throat, over her collarbones and down—

He yanked his eyes up before he started peering down her blouse but couldn't help wondering if her breasts were covered in golden freckles too. He fervently hoped so, and a slow, lazy grin pulled at the corners of his mouth, which he suppressed quickly with a cough into his hand. And more water. He drained the bottle and tossed it into the blue bin for recyclables. Remembered to grab a roll of paper towels from a cupboard and tucked it under his arm. "You know, before my newspaper met an untimely end, I caught your article on the *canine* attack." He made quotation marks in the air around the word *canine*. "Nice work."

"You think people will take it seriously? Enough to be on their guard? Because it's really been bothering me. I don't want anybody to get hurt because I made the decision *not* to call a spade a spade."

"Or a wolf a wolf. Yeah, I think you struck just the right tone with the story."

She looked relieved and smiled at him, that little smile he'd first noticed when he'd been holding her close in his truck . . . and he really, *really* wanted to hold her close again. Now. Right now.

Instead he forced himself to walk her to the front doors of the clinic and watch her cross the parking lot to her old red truck. He hadn't had the chance to observe her from behind before. Even her injured leg couldn't disguise her distinctive walk. The way she moved set off all kinds of intriguing thoughts . . . like just where did those freckles end?

"She's pretty, bro."

Connor spun at Culley's voice behind him. "You! What the hell did you think you were doing?"

His younger brother was an inch shorter than he, a little leaner, yet the shape of his face was similar to Connor's, the bone structure and set of his jaw too. It was obvious they were Macleods, but there the resemblance ended. Culley was the family prankster, with a ready grin and hazel eyes that seemed constantly amused by the world. *Full of the devil*, as their mother was fond of saying.

"Just yanking your chain a little, bro. Wasn't anyone in the clinic but us at the time." Culley surveyed Connor and let out a low whistle. "But let's talk about *you*. You look like shit. And you're damn testy today too."

"Thanks a bunch. I was doing just fine until you showed up. Speaking of appearances, I'm almost used to you showing up without shoes, but where the hell are your pants?"

Culley looked down. He had a shirt on, and it was even buttoned for once. But instead of his usual jeans, he wore *Homer Simpson* flannel pajama bottoms—with holes in both knees. There was a big hole in the toe of one mismatched sock as well. "Huh. Guess I was in a hurry."

"You're always in a hurry. Get some clothes from my office before somebody sees you and thinks you're strange."

Connor shook his head as his younger brother disappeared. Anything present within the aura of a Changeling's body as it shifted into wolfen form was automatically taken along for the ride. That meant clothing certainly, but also objects such as wallets, jewelry, even tools and cell phones. All were somehow suspended in a separate dimension until human form was resumed. Culley's twin, Devlin, had made it his mission in life to discover the how and why of this, constantly experimenting with the phenomenon. He also studied recent scientific discoveries in quantum physics which had led to the development of something called *String Theory*. Connor didn't quite understand the principle—although Devlin expounded on it at every opportunity—only that this new theory maintained there were far more dimensions than the three that humans were aware of.

Culley, on the other hand, couldn't care less about the physics of Changeling abilities. He lived for the pure joy of the Change, the freedom of his wolfen self, the oneness with the earth. He was quick to Change at any opportunity—and often a little too quick, Changing before making certain it was completely safe. He also seldom made sure he was fully clothed before he shifted. It was a constant source of amusement to the Pack to see how Culley would turn up next, but every one of them had also warned him—someday he'd have to return to human form unexpectedly, and there would be a lot of explaining to do.

He's going to show up naked on Main Street one of these days. Connor headed back to his office. Once there, he found the soggy mess had already been cleaned up, and his sutures were stacked neatly on his desk. Relieved, he tossed the paper towels he'd been carrying onto the couch beyond and sank into his chair. He watched Culley digging through the dresser over by the en suite sans pajama bottoms. The scar on his right leg was still visible although more than a century had passed. . . .

"Geez, Connor, half the clothes in this dresser should be burned. Where the hell do you shop?"

"The farm supply store mostly."

"It shows. Where is your sense of style? Even your patients have more fashion sense."

"My style is just fine, thanks. And I want those back when you're done with them."

Culley rolled his eyes as he yanked on a pair of nondescript jeans and buttoned them. "Just how much sleep have you been getting lately, bro?"

"Why are you still here? And why are you asking so many questions?"

"Hey, I'm on a mission. I've got orders to invite you to supper and not to take *no* for an answer. Bill and Jessie are worried about you. We all are."

Connor swiveled the chair to face his brother. "About me? Why?"

"Duh! Your practice has grown way too large for one person." Culley switched to mindspeech and added: *Even for a Changeling.*

"God, you sound just like Birkie." Connor rubbed a hand over his eyes, then gratefully drained the fresh cup of coffee he found on his desk. "I'll get to it."

"At the rate you're *getting* to it, your former assistant, Morgan, will be able to apply for the job. And she has three years of veterinary college left."

"So I'm a slow mover."

"Well now, there's an understatement. Why the hell didn't you ask that long-legged editor to go out with you?"

Annoyance resurfaced. "Maybe I would have if I hadn't been distracted by a goddamn wolf in my office!" Or, more likely, his own wolf within. He still felt shaken by its near-emergence.

"And there's that temper again." Culley folded his arms and tsked. "Completely out of character for you, bro. And so was that little display of force when I licked your gal's pretty face. I'll bet it pissed you off that I kissed her first. Almost Changed, didn't you?"

"Okay, okay, yeah." It was pointless to deny it. Most of them could mask their thoughts at will—a natural defense among telepaths—but any Changeling could tell when another was about to become a wolf. It took energy, lots of it, and it was instinctively drawn from the earth itself, gathered from the very air. The static charge that built around a Changeling vibrated in the air like an approaching thunderstorm. "I guess I'm a lot more tired than I thought."

"You were seconds away from tearing my head off my shoulders with your teeth! You think it was just a matter of not enough sleep?"

"Isn't that what you were complaining about, that I'm working too hard?"

His brother shook his head and checked his watch. "I give up. You'll have to figure it out for yourself. For now, just get in the truck."

"I've got a herd vaccination in an hour at—"

"—at Hal Bremner's place, I know. Devlin and I already did it. Now let's move out."

"You didn't have to do that," protested Connor, but his brother was already halfway down the hall. He might have known his brother wasn't out of earshot though.

The hell I didn't. Jessie will have both our butts in a sling if you're not at that dinner table pronto. Connor had no problem imagining that. Jessie was leader of the Pack for good reason, and it had nothing to do with her phenomenal cooking skills.

But her cooking skills were ample reason to heed her summons.

He chuckled and hurried down the hall after his brother.

Chapter Eight

The waning moon was veiled with a dark wisp of cloud as the old man shuffled slowly through the overgrown yard. Bernie needed to be outside where he could breathe the scents on the wind. The open expanse of sky was vivid with stars, as wild streamers of cloud tumbled and twisted past them. A coyote yipped in the distant forest and was forcefully answered by a pair of wolves. *Our land. Ours.*

Depression threatened to crush him, exacerbated by the tall bottle of Black Velvet he'd been nursing most of the day. Bernie hadn't been able to Change, not since Macleod had injected him with the only poison that could affect him: silver. It wasn't supposed to have happened, he had taken steps to make sure it didn't happen. There shouldn't have been anything but water in the bottle. *Shoulda done it myself, shoulda taken care of it myself.*

What if there had been a tiny amount of actual nitrate left in the small bottle before Macleod filled it? The syringe had been huge, taking in the entire contents of the bottle and delivering them into Bernie's veins. At full-strength, it would have been a massive dose. But what if it didn't really take that much to do the job? What if just a drop or two of silver nitrate mixed with water was enough?

Bernard Gervais had run wild and free for several human

lifetimes. He was strong and powerful, answering to no one, not even to Jessie, the Pack Leader. Hell, he was a lot older than all of them. He should be leading the Pack, not that smart-mouthed woman. She couldn't tell him what to do and neither could that young pup, Connor. *Damn them both, damn all of them!*

He knew it was futile after his first few attempts at Changing, but he couldn't seem to stop trying. He sank down in the tall grass, exhausted. By day he drank heavily, raging at Connor, hating him. By night he grieved and hated his life, hated himself and what he'd become. Human. Stupid, weak, sniveling *human.*

Bernie stretched out full length on the ground, seeking some shred of comfort from the earth. He was cold, something he had seldom been before. *It can't be gone, it can't be over.* Surely his gift could not have left him completely after so many, many years. It was all the more frustrating now that he'd found an incredible source of energy, a human with a powerful bloodline, blood that could make him all but invincible. And now the Macleods would have it all to themselves, would once again have the power that should be his.

Drawing a shuddering breath, he closed his eyes and willed once more—and for the first time he felt an answering shift in his body. He could hardly believe it, sitting up in his excitement, inhaling in short sharp gasps. He willed again, and again he could feel a response. It wasn't his imagination. A low gurgling laugh emerged from his lips, a frightening blend of growl and hysteria. *You're going to pay, Macleod. And so is that red-haired bitch. She's going to pay for what she did to my face. Right after she gives me what I want.*

A wicked smile drew his lips back unnaturally, exposing both upper and lower teeth, causing most of the cuts on his face to crack and bleed again. The blood oozed black in the moonlight. A few moments later, the smile was replaced by the grinning jaws of a wolf.

God, the bed felt like heaven. Connor was glad he'd gone to Bill and Jessie's home. The company was good, of course. His brothers, Culley and Devlin, always kept the conversation lively. He'd lost track of how many helpings of the venison stew and fresh bread he'd had, but it was the first time in a long time he felt like he'd gotten enough to eat. The Change burned up a hell of a lot of calories. So did working like a man possessed. Culley and Birkie, Jessie and Bill, all of them had been right: He needed to take action on hiring another vet.

First thing in the morning, he murmured. *Tomorrow.*

Banners of moonlight moored windows to floor, the silvery streamers making the shadows of his room darker, deeper. Connor's eyes closed blissfully. His breathing slowed, his large frame sprawled and relaxed. He had just achieved the nirvana state of full sleep when the phone on the night table rang.

Miles away, Zoey thrashed in the grip of a nightmare. She was running through the darkened streets of Dunvegan, pursued by the grizzled gray wolf. Every now and then she'd risk a glance behind her and see the glowing eyes, the snarling, snapping jaws. She climbed fences, ran through buildings, even drove her car for a while, but still the monstrous creature followed her. It was like the lupine version of *The Terminator.* She could neither hide from it nor outrun it, and it was coming closer and closer. Gurgling snarls filled her ears, and she could feel its hot breath on the backs of her legs. Any second it was going to bite her, take her down like a deer and kill her. . . . She wanted to scream but no sound would come out.

Suddenly another wolf, larger, darker, appeared on the sidewalk directly in front of her. Zoey dove off to one side to avoid it and fell onto the grass. She expected to feel her pursuer's teeth, expected the newcomer to attack her as well. Instead, the gray wolf launched itself at the bigger wolf's throat and a furious battle ensued. She wanted to run, wanted to get away while the animals fought, but she found herself unable to move. She was frozen, paralyzed. Helpless.

And when the gray wolf lay in a bloodied heap on the ground, she could only wait for the victor to look in her direction, wait for its strange gray eyes to fasten on her. Wait for it to spring with bared and bloody teeth. . . .

Her own scream awakened her. Zoey practically leapt out of her bed, turning on every light she could find, and rubbing her hands up and down her arms to stave off the chill effects of the nightmare. "Voices," she said. "I need voices." She bundled herself in an afghan on the couch and reached for the remote, hoping a little television would anchor her in some sort of reality.

A few minutes later she was rolling her eyes. She should have known that television in the wee hours of morning was the wrong place to turn to for reality. After flipping through a variety of scary movies, including one about werewolves no less, she turned off the set and threw the remote onto another chair in disgust. It was going to be a long, long night. . . .

She nearly jumped out of her skin when the phone rang beside her. At this time of night the only reason to call a small-town newspaper editor was *fire*. Any other disasters would wait until morning. Alert and all business, she grabbed the receiver but didn't get a chance to say a word.

"Thank God you're there! Look, I'm sorry to ask, but I really need your hands."

"Connor?"

"Yeah, it's me. You're not squeamish, are you?"

"No—hey, are you okay?"

"I'm at the clinic, about to be up to my ass in puppies. I swear I'll buy you the most exotic coffee on the planet— hell, I'll buy you a whole coffee *plantation*, if you'll just come help."

"I don't have any experience, but I'll come."

"You have two hands, that's all I need."

"I—" The phone went dead and she stared at the receiver for a long moment, then hurried to her room to get dressed. She wasn't certain how much help she could be, but hanging out with a hot veterinarian sure beat sitting up all night afraid to go to sleep.

The clinic doors were open. Only the night-lights were on in the reception area, and Zoey was grateful she'd been there earlier. At least she had some idea where things were. She passed the examination rooms, the lab, the lunchroom, heading down the hallway to where bright light spilled out of a doorway. She looked inside and caught only a fleeting glimpse of Connor before he grabbed her by the shoulders and kissed her forehead loudly.

"Thanks for coming. I got this emergency call an hour ago." He took her hand and led her to a stainless steel table where a large reddish-gold dog lay panting heavily. Her shaved belly was the size and color of a prize-winning pumpkin. "This is Millie. She's got enough puppies in there for a football team but the poor gal's not making any progress. I'm going to do a C-section but I have to have someone to watch her vitals and to take the puppies as I hand them off." He looked at Zoey then, measuring her. "You sure you're up to this? Because once we get started, it's going to go fast. There's no time to get sick or faint."

"Hey, city reporter here. I've covered the crime beat," she protested. "You just tell me what to do."

He grinned and patted her shoulder. "Okay, tough gal, here we go."

It did go fast. One moment Connor was showing her how to check the dog's pulse, and the next, he was making the first incision. Somewhere between those tasks, he'd managed to start an IV, feed a tube down Millie's windpipe, start the anesthetic and reposition the now-sleeping dog on the table, all the while giving Zoey instructions on what to do with the puppies when they arrived. She held a towel in her hands, nervous but ready, checking the dog's pulse frequently. Millie's heart was strong and steady. Like Connor, she thought. She watched him work, admiring the efficiency and artistry that went into the surgery.

Suddenly he handed her something that looked like a slimy gray jelly bean—if jelly beans were the size of Idaho potatoes. It squirmed a little in her towel and she realized with a start that it was a puppy, totally encased in an amniotic sac. *Omigod*. She peeled the sac away to reveal the wet blond puppy underneath and rubbed it vigorously with the towel. It began squeaking and she watched, fascinated, as it blindly waved its little blunt nose around. It sounded almost indignant. A rush of warmth shot through her and she had to blink hard to clear her eyes of unexpected moisture. She looked up to find Connor grinning at her.

"Congratulations. You've just witnessed the start of a brand-new life."

"Is it like this for you too?"

"Every single time. It never gets old. It does get rushed though. Put that one under the heat lamp. His brothers and sisters are ready to come out and play."

He wasn't kidding. Zoey would no sooner get a puppy rubbed down than Connor was handing her another. And another. At one point she was rubbing two at a time. "Holy cow, how many are there?"

"At least a dozen. Retrievers usually have big litters, but Millie's outdone herself. Check her pulse for me, will you?"

Zoey hurried to do so, but the mother dog was fine. The next puppy wasn't, however. It looked different from its siblings, smaller and unmoving. "Connor, I can't get this one to breathe."

"Use the bulb syringe, suction the fluid out of its mouth."

She did her best but felt clumsy with the unfamiliar tool. The pup lay limp.

"Shake it very gently, upside down. The lungs may need to drain a little."

That was harder. She was fearful of hurting it, but as the pup continued to be unresponsive, she jiggled it harder. Nothing. "Connor!"

"Don't panic yet. The bottle on the table is a respiratory stimulant. Put a drop on its tongue and then keep rubbing it with the towel. Keep its head down."

She had tears in her eyes as she opened the tiny mouth. Everything was so delicate, so perfect. She applied the drop and resumed rubbing. "C'mon, c'mon, breathe! You can do it, little guy, c'mon."

"I've got another puppy that can't wait. You're going to have to juggle them."

Flustered, she tucked the limp pup under her sweatshirt to keep it warm, took the new pup, and was relieved when it squeaked almost immediately. She was just placing it in the box under the heat lamp with its siblings when a faint movement next to her skin caught her attention. She reached in and found the troubled pup squirming feebly. "Oh, look at you! What a wonderful fellow you are!" She crooned to the puppy as she rubbed it with the towel. Tears ran down her face when it finally made a faint squeak.

"Way to go, Dr. Tyler."

"He's the one that did it, he kept trying."

"So did you. And here's two more for you."

In the end there were fifteen puppies nestled in a squirming mass under the heat lamp. Connor finished suturing the mother as he adjusted the gas, explaining that he had to wean Millie off the anesthetic. "She's going to wake up pretty soon and we'll see if we can talk her into nursing these pups a little. The first milk produced has all sorts of antibodies and such that the pups are going to need. But after that, we're going to bottle feed them for a meal or two while she rests and recovers. Bring along a couple of the pups."

Zoey gathered up the two biggest puppies and followed as Connor carried Millie into his office and placed her on an enormous sheepskin pillow on the floor. It was surrounded by wide planks nailed together to form a box of sorts and positioned in front of the couch. Connor took the dog's pulse, pushed open first one eyelid, then the other and looked in her eyes. The dog pulled her head back and shook it. "She's waking up just fine. Put the pups with her and let's go get the rest."

Zoey nestled them close to the mother, and was amazed at how they immediately flailed about in search of a nipple. One fastened on right away. "How do they know what to do?"

"Instinct. All the instructions are hardwired into them, so they don't have to know anything. They just do."

It took several trips, but finally, the pups were arranged two deep along the mother's belly. Connor turned the lights off except for a small lamp. Zoey thought they were leaving but instead, he stretched out on the old couch. "I have to keep an eye on Millie for a while. She's an experienced mom but she might be disoriented," he explained and extended his arm in invitation. "Why don't you scootch right in here and have a nap? You worked hard tonight."

She hesitated for a second, then realized she was far too tired to drive home. Besides, the idea of cuddling up to the tall vet was a temptation she really didn't want to resist.

The battered couch was surprisingly comfortable. It was long and wide, and although Connor filled the length of it, when he turned sideways there was just the right amount of room for her to spoon in front of him. He wrapped a powerful arm around her waist and pulled her snugly against him. God, it felt good. Heat seemed to flow from him, working its way into her tired body as if she had a campfire at her back. She watched as Millie lifted her head and began nosing her puppies, tentatively at first then licking them enthusiastically. "Look, she's discovering her new family."

Connor's voice rumbled pleasantly in her ear. "This is

the best part, after it's all over and you can just enjoy watching them bond."

"You're really good at what you do. And you like it a lot, don't you?"

"Can't imagine doing anything else. But you were great tonight yourself."

"I don't know about that."

"I do. You helped a helluva lot. I might have lost a couple of those pups, trying to do it all myself. Or I could have been a little too slow and lost Millie. So, thanks."

"Thanks for asking me."

He planted a kiss on her cheek, hugged her tight. "Go to sleep now."

She did. She had fully intended to continue watching the puppies but instead fell headlong into dreamless slumber, secure in Connor's arms.

Zoey awakened to the sound of squeaking puppies. She opened her eyes to find Connor kneeling by the box, bottle-feeding one of the pups. Millie didn't appear to mind or perhaps she was just preoccupied. The mother dog seemed to be nosing the squirming mass of hungry pups into some sort of order.

"Morning," she managed.

He looked up from his task and smiled. "Sorry if I woke you. I tried not to make noise, but this crew was ready to riot. There's fresh coffee and cinnamon buns in the lunchroom if you want."

"Holy cow, you baked?"

"Nope, Dell Mackie brought them by. I offered to marry her again but she turned me down as usual."

"I see. You must be heartbroken," she ventured.

"Devastated. She's eighty-nine, but nobody makes cinnamon buns like she does."

Zoey laughed and tried to sit up, but discovered she was buried in quilts. She struggled out from under them, sat up, and ran her hands through her hair. "God, I must look a sight."

"A sight for sore eyes, and one I'd like to see more of."

"But I don't know how to make cinnamon buns."

"Every relationship has its challenges."

She chuckled as she knelt by the box. "Where's the littlest guy, the one I had trouble with last night?"

"Left hand side, bottom row, with the rest of Millie's little black sheep." Connor nodded in the general direction, his attention taken up with feeding a second pup in his hands.

"Her what?"

"Look closer at the pups. Notice anything unusual?"

Their fuzzy puppy coats were dry now and Zoey thought the variety of colors made quite a picture. Eight were reddish gold like their mother. Three were blond. They were plump, their rounded features similar. She frowned as she realized the remaining four were different. Even though their newborn features were blunt and undeveloped, it was obvious that their shape, their build, was nothing like the others. Leaner. Shorter coat. And the color—three were chestnut with white markings, white feet. The smallest pup, the one that had been tucked in Zoey's shirt, was a mix of white and brindle. "Why are they so different?"

"Different father I imagine. The owners will be furious. Millie's a purebred with a ritzy pedigree and this will call the breeding into question."

Zoey stared at him. "Different fathers? In one batch?"

"It happens with dogs and cats. The owners had Millie bred to a champion stud. But it looks like another dog got to her afterward while she was still in estrus. My money's on old Bruce Granger's boxer." Connor shook his head. "Millie's owners will want the whole litter put down."

"*What?*"

"A lot of folks breed dogs as a business. For some, it's only a business. If the pups have no future in the show ring, if they can't command top price, then they're disposed of."

Disposed. Zoey was horrified. She'd helped them take their first breaths. For a fleeting and foolish moment she thought about adopting them all, then realized the impossibility of it. "Why can't they just find homes for them?"

"Most breeders would do that. They keep their potential champions and they sell their pet quality animals. But these folks are more hard-headed than most. They think it devalues their stock to put pets on the market." He snorted at that. "As if the average family was able to buy one of their five-thousand-dollar bluebloods."

"I'm keeping this one." Zoey reached into the box and picked up the small brindle and white pup and held it to her cheek. "I don't care what the owners say or what they want for it, I'm keeping him. He's *not* disposable."

Connor looked stricken. "God, I didn't mean—I should have thought before I spoke. You don't have to worry about these puppies, Zoey. I'm not going to let anything happen to them."

"Honest?"

"Cross my heart."

"But the owners—"

"Knowing the owners as I do, I think it's best that they

never know about these four little door prizes. Millie had *eleven* pups. Capiche?"

"My lips are sealed. But I still want this puppy." And she did. Zoey had never had a dog of her own. She definitely didn't want one like the massive black pony that had been in Connor's office, but she had to admit she liked the enthusiastic affection.

"He'll be ready for you to take home in about six weeks. If I can't find a surrogate mom for these four, I'll get someone to hand-raise them for me."

It wouldn't be the first time he'd done this, Zoey realized. "Do you try to save everything?"

He laughed a little. "My hired man, Jim Neely, asks me that every time I bring home another orphan. He complains that I'm turning the farm into a petting zoo, but then he always finds a place for the animal. More than a few have been rehabilitated thanks to him. My sibs help too."

"So a love for animals runs in the family?"

"I guess you could say that. Maybe it's more a respect for nature. But don't put me on too high of a pedestal. This is a veterinary practice, and I have to put down animals as well. I get my share of cases where there's no other option. Luckily this isn't one of them."

The puppy in her arms squeaked and nuzzled blindly. "I think he's hungry."

"Then it's his turn." Connor held out the bottle to her.

"I don't know how to do this!"

"Sure you do. Hold him like this"—he rearranged her arms a little—"and introduce him to the bottle."

She didn't have to do anything more. The little creature attacked the rubber nipple with a will and began drinking greedily. She shifted a little, trying to get comfortable, and found herself leaning against Connor. It felt just right.

Chapter Nine

Connor checked his watch. Zoey had insisted on going home, but not before inviting him to stop by for coffee later.

Now wasn't exactly *later*—in fact, she'd barely been gone an hour—but the silver nitrate had to be applied a final time. Today. He'd already spent time making arrangements for the four puppies, and he didn't dare risk getting caught up in his work and forgetting, or being distracted by the emergencies that were common to his practice. Connor was determined to make certain that Zoey didn't become the very thing that had attacked her. He thought for a moment of her russet hair. She'd no doubt make a beautiful wolf, but she wouldn't enjoy it if it was forced on her.

Geoff Lassiter's wife, Melly, had been well prepared for the Change. She was accustomed to her husband shifting from human to wolf, had no fear of it and was willing to join him. Okay, if the truth be told, she was *itching* to join him—Melly had pestered Geoff daily about it. Geoff, however, had coached her for a long time before he would grant her the single bite—just a tiny nip that barely broke the skin—that would alter her life forever. At the next full moon, Connor had watched over the pair of them in the forest, stood guard as Geoff held Melly tenderly, encouraged her, talked her through it. It was like a birth of sorts, and there had been joy when Melly at last stood on four feet, clad in rich black fur. Geoff Changed then and the pair ran and played like cubs. When Melly finally shifted back, she had been flushed and laughing, happy and filled with the deep peace that came of the very earth itself.

There was no such peace for those who made that initial transition unaided. The very first Change was hard even on those born to it, painful yet bearable if relaxed into, embraced. Humans who found themselves Changing into something they didn't even believe existed could die from sheer terror and shock, or be driven into insanity. The pain was often magnified beyond human endurance as they fought their own bodies. Death frequently followed.

Connor had seen that happen only last year.

He and Bill had been enjoying a four-footed run under the full moon when they'd heard distant screams in the river valley. There, they'd discovered a young human teenager alone in the woods, screaming in fear and pain as his body shifted and Changed, for the first time—and he'd had no idea what was happening to him. Connor and Bill had been unable to help the boy, although Connor had brought all of his psychic power to bear. There was no reaching him in this condition, no convincing him that they could help. The boy had died moments after the Change was complete.

Folklore claimed that werewolves magically shifted back to their human form after death. It wasn't so. Whatever you were when you died, you stayed that way. The body, even a Changeling body, had no life force, no energy to call on to do otherwise. Connor had found it particularly sad, however, that the boy had remained in death the very thing that had terrified him in the last hours of his life. Sadder still that his family would never know what had happened to him. Bill and Connor had buried the small gray wolf near Elk Point, a sacred spot, and planted wild rose bushes over the site.

Jessie had convened the Pack, but it was a formality only. None of them would have bitten the boy. None would have risked Changing an unknowing human even to save their own lives.

That left Bernie as the natural suspect. A lone wolf by his own choice, the old man acknowledged no leader and no law. Plus he was well-known for being both vicious and self-centered. But there was no proof, no scent left in the area after nearly a month of heavy rain. The boy could have been bitten anytime after the previous full moon. Now, after the attack on Zoey, it seemed even more likely that Bernie had been the culprit. He wouldn't have cared what the boy suffered.

Bernie wouldn't care if Zoey suffered either.

And so he would do everything in his power to prevent it, Connor thought as he parked his car outside Zoey's apartment building. He reached into his coat pocket and held the small clear, glass bottle of silver nitrate like a talisman as he climbed the stairs to Zoey's apartment, trying to shake off the melancholy that had enveloped him. He knocked. A window at the end of the hallway let the early morning sun flood in, but it suddenly seemed to pale when Zoey opened the door.

Her russet hair spilled over her shoulders in tousled waves, her amber eyes seemed a little tired but were as arresting as ever. She was in her bathrobe again, and the dark blue plush only enhanced her fairness. He didn't see any flannel pajamas this time, however, and Connor's mouth dried without warning. A mere flip of his finger would undo the tie—would it also unveil her soft skin and its unique coloration? Frame the lush curves of her body in the color of the night sky. . . .

She smiled up at him. "I didn't think you'd need coffee so soon. I just got out of the shower."

Suddenly he remembered to breathe, and then his brain kicked in. "I wanted to check on that leg of yours before I get started on another day. Lowen mentioned you might need the dressings changed." Connor managed a smile and rubbed at the stubble on his jaw, wishing he had thought to shave. Wishing, too, that he could stop thinking about that damn little tie on her robe. "Hope I don't look too scary."

"You do but I'm very brave." She led the way to the living room. He was surprised to find the television on at such an early hour. As if she'd read his mind, Zoey waved a hand at the TV screen. "You're just in time to join me for cartoons. Everyone thinks a reporter should watch the news first thing, but trust me, cartoons are the only way to start the day. Oh, and you have to eat sugar-frosted cereal while you watch or you don't get the full experience."

Connor accepted a bowl of Cocoa Crunchies with a chuckle. As a Changeling, he could scent the chemical signatures of food coloring and preservatives, but mentally shrugged it off. *Calories are calories and God knows I could use more of them these days.*

Zoey settled onto the couch beside him. They lounged companionably, feet on the coffee table, talking while the cartoons provided a carefree backdrop.

Connor decided to venture a question. "You mentioned last night that you hadn't been sleeping well. I was wondering if there was a reason?"

"Just some dreams," she said, flipping channels with the remote. "Why?"

"Well, it's not every day a person gets attacked by a wolf. I was just wondering if you were having nightmares, anxiety attacks, anything out of the ordinary."

She settled on a channel and picked up her own bowl of cereal. "You mean something like post-traumatic stress. I confess to having had a few nightmares about wolves. It isn't fun but it's to be expected, you know? But last night's dream was different. Another wolf showed up, not the same one that bit me. This wolf was bigger and it was silver with black markings. Kind of pretty really."

"Black markings?" His throat constricted suddenly.

"Sort of like a black blanket over his back. I've seen lots of photos of wolves, but nothing like it. Of course things tend to be a little weird in dreams. Probably comes of eating too late at night."

"I hope you weren't eating these things." Connor's head was already ringing a little from the quantity of sugar. Or maybe it was because Zoey had seen a saddleback wolf in her dream. He knew better than to believe in coincidence, but what could it mean?

"Nope, pizza."

"What?"

"You were hoping I didn't eat Cocoa Crunchies before bed. It was cold pizza. It was so damn real . . . but of course it wasn't."

"The pizza wasn't real?" He teased her, a little anxious to steer the subject away from dreams and wolves.

"No, I meant the *dream*," she laughed. "Look, don't mess with my head this morning, okay? I'm tired and easily confused."

"I doubt that you get confused very often. You're pretty smart."

"Ha. You haven't seen me try to balance my checkbook."

"So you're better with words than with numbers. So what? My mother used to say that everyone's good at something. I'm a much better vet, thank God, than I am a farmer."

"My publisher mentioned that you now own a farm that his cousin used to have."

"Well, he's half right. I own the farm and I live there. Other than that, I don't do any farming to speak of."

"Because you're so busy?"

He snorted at that. "More because Jim begged me not to. I seem to have a condition known as *black thumb*."

"Your hired man said that? But I hear you're fantastic with animals. How can a healer not do well with plants too?"

"My family asks the very same question, but not so nicely. So I stick with being a vet. Speaking of which, how about putting your foot up on the coffee table and letting me take a look at those dressings?"

To his surprise, she obliged at once. "I was just thinking about calling the doctor this morning—the bite looks worse today." Her robe fell back to her hip on one side, exposing a long and shapely leg, beautifully freckled with gold. The bandaged calf didn't spoil the view a bit, and all Connor could think was that he'd asked for it. He swallowed hard and set to work, trying to keep his eyes on the task at hand. Once he'd unwrapped the gauze, however, he had no trouble focusing. He let out a long low whistle at the color of her calf. The tiny white butterfly bandages that held the deeper punctures closed nearly glowed in sheer contrast.

Zoey leaned forward, resting her hand on his shoulder. "See what I mean? It didn't look this bad yesterday. Is it okay? It's not infected is it?"

"No, no, it's all right. This is just the bruising that's finally come to the surface. It's a little swollen but the wounds are clean." He examined it carefully. There didn't seem to be a square inch of skin between her knee and her toes that wasn't somewhere between pale lavender-blue and the bright color of grapes.

"It can't be all right! For God's sake, it's purple all over."

"And you're likely to see a whole rainbow of colors as time goes on. I admit, it's pretty spectacular, but it's not surprising. A wolf can have a bite pressure of 1,500 or more pounds per square inch, a lot more than even a very large dog. There's more trauma to the skin and muscle than just the bite wounds." *But not as much as there could have been.* Connor repressed a shudder as he carefully sponged the silver nitrate over each and every puncture.

"What is that, distilled water?"

"Antibacterial." Close enough. It would act as one, even though that wasn't the real reason he was using it.

"I wonder if the cops would believe me if they saw this now," she mused.

"Probably not. They're not exactly trained to know the difference between a dog attack and a wolf attack. You can't blame them for thinking it was a dog that chewed on you." He pulled a fresh roll of gauze from his pocket and began to wrap her calf. "I'm amazed you're walking on this, you know. It looks pretty painful."

"It's not too bad. It's achy and the skin feels a little tight. It gets painful if I'm walking on it too much, and I know I've overdone it more than once."

"Maybe you should take it easy for a couple of days, stay

off it as much as you can. Elevate your leg and put some ice on it to get the swelling down."

"That's exactly what the doctor said."

"You should listen to him. Lowen's one of the best." He finished the dressing and she flexed her toes experimentally.

"So are you, apparently. It feels pretty good, doc."

Connor just shook his head. Wolves had 42 teeth. So did Changelings, and Bernie had applied more than half of his teeth to Zoey's calf. She was far tougher than she looked. Most people would have been unable to walk with such an injury. And most people wouldn't have her resilient spirit either—

"So do you have to work at the clinic today?" she asked.

"Hmm? Not till later, thank God. My brothers conspired with my assistants to cancel everything for the morning. Can't do that very often though—the practice has grown a lot over the last few years. I need to start looking for another vet."

"My cousin's a vet. Just graduated a couple years ago."

"If he's not attached to a practice, have him send me a résumé." Connor looked around, studying the surroundings for the first time. "So you don't have any pets?"

"Not at present, although I seem to have decided on a certain puppy I met last night," she laughed. "Actually, I've wanted a pet for a long time but it's been hard to make the decision. My new pet is going to have such a tough act to follow. I had this big orange tomcat named Fester when I was growing up—well, technically, he had been my mom's cat until I came along. After that, though, he was all mine. I didn't have any brothers or sisters, and there weren't any kids my age in our neighborhood, so I grew up playing with Fester. He was such a good sport. I dressed him up and took him for rides in my doll buggy and my bike carrier. I remember playing doctor and bandaging him up with toilet paper. I must have used the entire roll because he looked like a mummy when I was done, with only his eyes peeking out. And he just sat there and waited until I decided he was *all better* and took it off him. He was so patient that way. Fester slept on my bed every night, and I used to read stories to him—I swear he liked it."

"I'll bet you miss him."

"Every day. I'd just graduated high school and was getting ready for college in the fall—I was so worried about having to leave him behind. Then I got up one morning, and he was on my bed next to me just like always. But he didn't wake up."

"That must have been really hard."

"Yeah, it was. I cried for days. But he was twenty years old—what could I expect? And actually, I'm glad it happened before I left, that I was there."

"You must have taken really good care of him. Twenty is a ripe old age for a cat. I've met only one that's lived longer. His name is Poodle."

"His name is what?"

"No kidding, it's *Poodle*." Connor told her about the ancient Siamese cat and his equally ancient owner, Mrs. Enid Malkinson. "They even look alike—they both have these watery blue eyes that are just a little bit crossed."

"Oh come on, you're making that up!"

He put his hand over his heart. "I swear it's true. I'll introduce you. I think they've lived so long because there's a kind of symbiotic relationship between the two of them. Poodle seems to thrive on finding trouble. And Enid seems to thrive on every little drama in her cat's life. Not that she wants anything to happen to him," he explained. "Far from it. But she has no family to talk about, so every little adventure Poodle has provides exciting news that she can share. Trust me, nearly everyone in town, whether they're interested or not, is well informed about that cat's current health."

"I'm surprised I haven't heard about him. Maybe I should pay a visit to Mrs. Malkinson and see if I can do a story about Poodle."

"Really? She'd be thrilled, but a cat's not exactly front-page news. How would you make a story out of it?"

"The first rule of journalism is that everything's a story. And besides, people love to read about animals. You said the cat was older than Fester was, right?"

"Yeah, Enid claims he's thirty and I don't think that's too far off. I'll see if Birkie can find some old records at the clinic that would give us a better estimate."

"Well, that's worth an article right there, don't you think? You're right, it's not front-page news but an unusually long-lived cat could make a nice little feature story. I can look up what the world record is, add that in for interest. And you could give me a couple of quotes about the care of geriatric pets or something. It would be great."

Connor looked at Zoey's animated face. "I know someone else who's great," he murmured as he leaned into her and gently brushed her smiling mouth with his lips. Asking, just asking.

She answered. Her lips were tentative for only a moment, then her hands reached up to tangle in his hair. She met him kiss for kiss, gentle and sweet, demanding and bold. It was a heady mixture and Connor rapidly discovered that a simple taste wasn't going to be enough. He leaned further, instinctively using his weight to gently urge her into a reclining position. She resisted for a moment as if considering, then drew him down with her onto the plush couch.

Connor trailed his fingers along her throat, following them with soft openmouthed kisses. Nuzzled along her sensitive collarbone as he pushed the robe from her right shoulder. A jolt of electricity shot through him as he realized she had nothing on under the robe. Nothing but more of those glorious golden freckles. His body hardened instantly and he nearly groaned aloud.

Instead, he brushed his lips over the smooth skin, relishing the taste, the scent of her. Breathed her in, pulled her essence into his lungs and held it there near his heart. Kissed his way back to the little hollow at the base of her throat. Slid the material from her left shoulder, nuzzled and kissed the newly exposed skin. The tie that held her robe together slipped, spilling her soft rounded breast into Connor's hand. He palmed the delicate weight of it, brushing his thumb lightly over the nipple as he again sought her full lips. God, he wanted her, wanted all of her, here and now—

Without warning, the wolf within him surged forward. Connor reacted at once, pulling back from Zoey so fast that he ended up on the floor. He sat there, stunned and breathing hard. *What the hell?*

"Are you okay?" Zoey asked, looking flustered. Her beautiful breast and shoulders disappeared as she pulled her robe around her, but it was probably safer that way. She had no way of knowing that he was hanging onto his control by his fingernails, that he was fighting the Change.

"I'm sorry. I—well, I didn't mean to get so carried away."

"Geez, Connor, we're not in high school."

She sounded disappointed and those amber eyes had

gone fierce, but he couldn't think of a damn thing to say. *Sorry, I was turning into a werewolf.* "I—uh, I didn't want you to get the wrong idea." Where did that come from? Good God, could he sound any lamer? Meanwhile, the wolf within had retreated, but not far. Not nearly far enough.

"The wrong idea?"

Yup, *lame.* He got to his feet slowly, knowing that any sudden movement might cause his control to slip. "Look, I'm fairly sure that's not what I meant. But since I'm really tired and not making sense even to myself, I'd better go."

Zoey studied him for a long moment. "Okay. You do look pretty wasted."

"I feel wasted." He did too. Fighting off the Change was physically hard, and only a Changeling in his prime could manage it. Thank God he wasn't Bernie's age. . . .

There were a dozen different things Connor wanted to do. Finish what they had started together, for one. Kiss Zoey good-bye, for two. Three, ask if he could see her again. He dared do none of them. Instead, he forced himself to walk out the door, get in his truck, and drive away.

Within him, the wolf growled until the sound threatened to spill from his human lips. It wasn't until Connor turned into the laneway of his farm that the wolf finally gave up and receded into sulking silence.

Chapter Ten

"Ms. Tyler, I'm Tad Helfren, Paranormal Investigations. I understand you've got werewolves around here."

Startled, Zoey looked up from behind her desk at the short, heavyset man who was extending his hand to her. Her senses jolted as if electrified and she declined the invitation. "We've got *what*?"

"Werewolves, you heard me. Come on, it was in your newspaper just a couple years back. I've got all the clippings. I've just come back from Wisconsin, following up on some fresh evidence of the Bray Road Beast. Lycanthropy. Shapeshifters. Skinwalkers. Changelings. A werewolf by any other name. . . . I'm sure you know what I'm talking about. In fact, you're in the media business, you've probably run across my work."

"Your work?" she repeated dumbly. Had she just stepped into the Twilight Zone? It had to be a joke, but something in the man's face warned her just how serious he was. "I'm sorry, what publication are you with?"

"*OtherWorld News*." Helfren tossed several copies onto her desk. It was no tabloid. She couldn't help noticing each paper was full broadsheet size, as professional looking as the *Globe* and *Mail* and several sections thick. "Maybe you've seen our website? Hard copy circulation is nearly three million in the States alone, online subscriptions number eleven million worldwide. So you can see, this isn't a newsletter spit out of a photocopier, Ms. Tyler. We are the world leader in paranormal information."

"You're a reporter."

His eyes flashed at that. "I'm no reporter, lady. I'm a professional investigator."

Reporter, she thought.

"So, tell me, what's the wolf activity in this area like right now?"

Dear Lord, there had to be some way to get this guy out of her office. Zoey wished she had a button on the floor like the ones in banks, some signal that tied in to the RCMP office down the road. Better yet, she wished she had a pager to Ted Biegel. Her publisher would delight in showing this werewolf fan to the door—or through it— but a glance at the clock showed that Ted was still in a meeting over at the Elks Club. *Damn.*

"I've been told we have a few," Zoey said, trying to sound casual. "They're native to the Peace River region, just like most of the Canadian north. Really, we have far more coyotes than any other predator, and plenty of black bears. An occasional cougar. I suggest you read my story in the second section of this week's paper for details." Right after the attack, she'd written a carefully researched story on wolves. She hadn't dared publish it at the time, but came up with a way to use it later by planning a series of articles about local wildlife. *All* the local wildlife. This week's article had been a general introduction to the series. Next week would feature black bears, since the sports reporter had come up with a lucky photo of a pair of bear cubs on someone's back porch. She'd planned to publish the feature on wolves after that, but with this strange character in her

office, a story on chipmunks seemed much more appealing.

"So do you like wolves, Ms. Tyler?"

"Actually I prefer housecats."

"But these werewolf stories—"

Enough was enough. "Look, I wasn't the editor at the
time, Mr. Helfren. I just moved here, so you know about
as much as I do, probably more. I really can't help you."
She stood, signaling an end to the meeting. "I suggest
you contact the local Fish and Wildlife officers. You'll find
their office in the government building across from the
library."

"Been there. Interviewed them both. That's why I'm
here talking to *you*." He sat down then, made himself comfortable in the armchair facing her desk. His broad face
didn't reveal so much as a hint of smugness as he looked up
at her expectantly. He appeared relaxed, even friendly, but
Zoey's intuition told her plainly it was a mask. She had a
chilling impression of thick muscle veiled beneath his loose
jacket, of dangerous intent in his mind. She remained
standing, believing that showing the slightest fear or weak-
ness would be a serious mistake.

"Ms. Tyler, the officers say you claimed to have been attacked by a wolf only a few days ago," he continued. "And
that apparently you were bitten."

She tried to keep her face passive as anger warred with
surprise. Fish and Wildlife employees were supposed to follow the same strict privacy policies as the RCMP—but she
had no doubt that Helfren was adept at prying information
out of people. Part hardcore detective and part aggressive
trial lawyer, she decided—and all shark. To refuse to talk to
him at all would likely piss him off. Could she satisfy him
with some basic information, show him there was no story

here? She measured her words carefully. "It's no secret that I was bitten by a dog. You can read all about that in the paper. It was a very large dog, probably a malamute or other large sled dog. We have a number of mushers in the region who raise them, who run sleds for tourists and compete in races. We had a race right here only a few months ago."

"You told the officers that it was a wolf, that it had glowing eyes."

She was *so* going to have words with them. "It was the middle of the night and I was terrified. I've never seen a wolf in my entire life, not even in a zoo. *Of course* the animal looked like a wolf to me. Later, when I'd recovered, I realized it was a dog. Just a big, nasty dog, and I hope they catch the wretched thing before it bites someone else."

"Real wolves don't attack humans, Ms. Tyler. A person of your education has surely heard that."

"Of course, and so you see, it wasn't a wolf."

He continued as if she hadn't spoken. "Werewolves *do* attack people, Ms. Tyler. And there are rarely survivors. But even if you get away, no one escapes completely. Do you understand what I'm saying to you?"

"*You* need to understand that I have an appointment in ten minutes, Mr. Helfren." She didn't, but she would damn well create one to go to. "Please leave now."

"Once bitten by a werewolf, the victim becomes one at the next full moon. You have approximately twenty days left of your human existence."

I'm so outta here. Zoey moved swiftly around her desk then, intending to walk out. The reporter was faster, leaping up from the chair to block the door and grabbing her arm. She repressed a gasp and refused to struggle, knowing that he wanted her to be afraid, he would enjoy her fear—

and she refused to give it to him. Instead, she focused all of her anger into a hot glare. Her voice was firm—and she tried to make it loud enough to alert the other people in the office. Hoped like crazy that there *were* other people in the office. Her stomach sank as she realized it was Friday. Not just Friday, but *noon* on Friday. There might as well be tumbleweeds rolling through the *Dunvegan Herald Weekly*. *Shit!* "Let go of me. I will not hesitate to press charges."

He ignored her. "You could be a rich woman, a very rich woman. Do you know what my publishers would pay you to show them what you are?"

"Let go, *now!*" Was she going to be reduced to screaming in order to get some help? And how on earth was she supposed to scream when she wasn't afraid? Her fear had transmogrified into white-hot anger. He was squeezing her arm with iron fingers but she refused to flinch. The anger welled up thick and hot within her, a reservoir of volatile energy. Zoey tried to shift her footing without alerting the man, attempting to get into a position to defend herself.

The reporter seemed to sense her intent, because he turned abruptly and pressed closer to her, throwing her off balance against the desk, his face close to hers. His smile was cold, slick, and smug with pleasure. "You call me after the full moon and we'll talk terms. I'm authorized to make a substantial offer. We could even write a book together, Ms. Tyler. Tour the talk shows. No more small-town newspapers—"

Zoey's free hand closed over an ancient office stapler, a relic from the fifties that weighed a couple of pounds. She swung it with all of her strength into the back of Helfren's skull. And was shocked when he neither went down nor let go of her arm. Instead he snarled a curse in her face as he knocked the weapon from her hand. And drew his fist back to retaliate.

The blow didn't connect. With his back to the door, Helfren never saw the huge tattooed arm reach for him, only felt the shock of a beefy hand seizing his collar. The distraction let Zoey pull herself free. She watched, dumbstruck, as Bill Watson hauled the reporter out into the reception area and shook him like a crash test dummy before letting his feet touch the ground. "You think you're a tough guy, do you? Think you can waltz in here and lay hands on a friend of mine just like that?" Helfren tried to throw a punch but the big man was amazingly fast. In a blur of motion, Bill let go of the reporter's collar with one hand and decked him with the other, sending him flying back against the service counter.

Helfren was no lightweight, but Bill was nearly as tall as Connor, twice as wide—and very, very angry. He seized the front of the man's jacket with both hands and gave him another hard shake. "You ever come in here again, ever come *near* this woman again, and I'll have your guts for garters. Are we clear on that?"

Helfren's mouth was bleeding and so was the gash on the back of his head where Zoey's stapler had connected. The moment Bill released him, the reporter staggered for a moment, then abruptly shoved his way out the door. Flecks of blood spattered the counter, the floor. Bill simply collected himself, tugged the hem of his T-shirt down, and ambled over to Zoey. "Are you all right then? Did that rotter hurt you?"

"I'm fine now, thanks." The red-haired giant was grinning at her and she tried to muster a smile in return.

Bill picked up the countertop phone and punched in

numbers. It was an old-style phone with a large receiver—her publisher hated to spend money on new equipment—but it still looked ridiculously small in his hand. "Fitz? You'll want to get down to the newspaper. Someone was trying to rough up the lady editor. Yeah, *was*. I gave him a little lesson in manners before he left." Bill laughed at something and hung up the phone. "Sergeant Fitzpatrick'll be here right quick. He wanted to know if the guy left under his own power or if I threw him through the window."

"Hey, I was just getting ready to toss him through the window myself when you interrupted."

"Thatta girl." He said it like a proud parent. "But you got some licks in—he was bleedin' afore I smacked him. Say, are you certain you're okay?"

"Yeah, but I'm going to sit down." She made it to the receptionist's chair but sitting turned out to be a lot more like *collapsing* as her knees gave way. "Geez—he didn't even hit me and I feel wobbly."

"Adrenaline, lovey. Tends to leave abrupt-like as soon as you don't need it no more. Learned that the hard way, I did, my first time wrestling in Europe. Fell flat on my face after I got out of the ring in Brussels. What about your wing?"

"My—you mean my arm?" She lifted the arm that Helfren had been gripping. There were red marks above the elbow where his fingers had been and the skin was tight. Swollen probably. She moved it experimentally. "A little sore, but it works okay. What a rotten jerk!"

"I got better words than that for the bloody bastard, but you don't need to hear 'em. Say, where is everybody? I thought you had folks working in this office."

"Friday afternoon," Zoey explained. "The publisher's

having lunch at his Elks meeting. Both reporters have the day off because they have a lot of events to cover this weekend. The composers have finished all the ads for Monday's paper, so they're gone too." She glanced at the clock. "Our receptionist is still on lunch, and after that she has to go to the post office and the bank. The office is usually closed while Lindsey's gone but Helfren must have come in just before she left. Otherwise she would have locked the door behind her."

An RCMP officer with sergeant's stripes pushed through the door. "Hey Bill," he said, but his eyes were on Zoey. "Are you all right, Ms. Tyler?"

She was a lot more *all right* now. The officer wasn't as tall as Bill or Connor, but he looked like he could take on either—or both. The uniform enhanced his muscular frame. There were streaks of gray in the sergeant's black hair but they only set off his rugged features. In another life he must have been a cowboy, she decided. Or a Marine. What was it about Dunvegan that attracted so many good-looking men? Of course, none of them, not even Fitzpatrick, stirred her as Connor did. She nearly sighed as she realized she missed him. She was still disappointed and downright annoyed after he'd all but run out of her apartment Tuesday morning. He hadn't called either—but she missed him.

"Ms. Tyler?"

She blinked and shook herself mentally. "I'm fine. Really. Although, I seem to be having a rough week between w—*wild dogs* and crazy people." She'd almost said *wolf*. She took a deep breath and began again, relating the events calmly, answering questions from both men but avoiding any mention of wolves, *were-* or otherwise.

Fitzpatrick made rapid notes, then surveyed her arm. "I'd advise you to go see Lowen Miller right away about that. It probably just needs some ice but you'll want the injury on record for court purposes."

"Right. I'll do that." Zoey cussed inwardly. Helfren would and should be charged as soon as the police found him, but she would have to appear in court and testify. She covered Dunvegan's local court proceedings twice a month and knew the drill. It would probably take up most of a day just waiting in the courtroom for her turn. Geez, what a pain in the—

"Did he leave anything behind, Ms. Tyler?"

"Um, yeah, he left some papers and a business card on my desk." She pointed to her office and Fitz disappeared inside for a few moments.

When he emerged, he was holding a copy of *OtherWorld News* and looking grimmer than he had a few moments earlier. "Ms. Tyler, I'm not sure I've got all the details about what Helfren wanted from you." He looked at her expectantly.

"I told you that I was bitten by an animal the other night and that somehow he found out about it." She met his green eyes, and wondered anew why Dunvegan seemed to be home to so many hot men. *Tall*, hot men. Was there something in the water? She sighed and relented. "Helfren thinks I was bitten by a werewolf, or at least, he's convinced he can make a story out of it for his readership. He talked about writing a book, about doing talk shows and how his publishers would pay me a lot if I turn into a werewolf too. And he got ugly when I didn't fall at his feet and say *make me a star*."

Bill made a noise that sounded surprisingly like a growl. Fitzpatrick looked troubled, and she couldn't decide if he was upset at Helfren or bothered by the mention of were-wolves. "Look," she said, standing up. "I could use a break here. I don't want this werewolf crap to get started all over again, and I'm sure you don't either. And for purely personal reasons, I don't want to be known as that hysterical editor who believes in Nessie and the Sasquatch."

Fitzpatrick's mouth twitched ever so slightly and he closed his notebook. "Okay, I hear you. I don't have to write the werewolf part down in the report. But do I know everything now?"

"As much as I do."

"All right then. Don't forget to see the doc. I'll be in touch." He put on his hat and left, taking the newspaper with him.

"Is there another one of those?" Bill asked.

"Helfren's rag? Sure, there must be four or five on my desk. If you want one, take it. I sure don't need the souvenir. You know, what I *really* need is some advice on how I might have broken his hold on me."

He looked at her appraisingly, head to one side. "You don't scare easy, eh? You got some real spirit, girl. No wonder our Connor's smitten."

What? She didn't know how to respond to that, and could only nod as Bill warned her to be careful in case Helfren hung around, promised her a few street fighting lessons, then walked away with a copy of *OtherWorld News* tucked under a massive bicep. When he reached the door, he turned and called back to her. "Almost forgot! I came to invite you over. Jessie's firing up the grill tonight at about seven for all our mates. First barbecue of the season, you know. Gotta bring summer in proper. The house is smack behind the store, so you can't miss." He shot her a knowing grin. "Your vet'll be there too."

She forced a smile, thanked him, and waited until he'd gone. Locked the office door behind him, counted to ten, then twenty. And exploded. "My vet, my *ass!*" She hadn't heard a word, not one word, from Connor since his hasty exit Tuesday morning. Sure, her reasonable side said he was busy, but after he'd gotten her all hot and bothered and, and, *aroused . . .* wonderfully aroused . . . well, couldn't he at least call or something? And how about an explanation for his abrupt departure? It wasn't lack of sleep that had him putting moves on her and then suddenly tearing himself away like he expected a damn alien to pop out of her.

All the tension of the past hour was channeled into Zoey's rant. And when the tension was gone, she was left facing what she really wanted. To be held and comforted. By Connor.

She sighed and considered calling him, but what would she say? *Hi, I need a hug because this strange guy wants me to turn into a werewolf.* Zoey shook her head—

—and nearly jumped out of her skin when the village siren went off. Decades ago, it had been an air raid siren to warn against bombers that never came. Now it signaled to the volunteer fire brigade that there was a blaze somewhere. Grateful for the diversion, she grabbed her camera bag and headed for her truck.

Chapter Eleven

Zoey dumped her bag onto the bistro table in her kitchen. Didn't even bother to check the fridge—*as if* there would be anything interesting in it anyway—and headed straight for the couch. She was tired, dirty from head to toe, and smelled like smoke after spending the afternoon watching the Dunvegan Volunteer Fire Department battle a tractor fire that had spread to a farmyard and several outbuildings. She'd gotten some good photos and some useful story material but all she wanted right now was to get off her feet. That, and close her stinging eyes for a while before the migraine that was brewing on the right side of her head could erupt. . . .

The dream ambushed her at once. The gray grizzled wolf burst through the balcony doors in a shower of glass. She leapt from the couch, hoping to make the hallway door but the creature cornered her effortlessly in the kitchen, glaring at her with those damn glowing eyes and snapping at her with foam-flecked jaws. Zoey held one of her metal bistro chairs in front of her, with thoughts of clubbing the monster with it, but it was too close. If she lifted the chair to swing it, she'd leave herself vulnerable just long enough for those wicked teeth to reach her. Instead, all she could do was hold the wolf away from her as he lunged. The chair began to grow heavy, almost too heavy to hold up, as the wolf bit at the metal legs. It was so close she could see the scars crisscrossing its face. "Help, I need help in here!" she yelled but couldn't seem to make a sound above a whisper.

Suddenly an unearthly howl filled the room. It was long and loud, and seemed to vibrate right through her to resonate in her bones. Another wolf appeared behind her attacker. Zoey recognized the great silvery beast by the blanket of black over its shoulders and feared it was here to join in the kill. But to her surprise, the grizzled wolf roared and spun, twisting its body as it did so to lunge at the other's throat. The savage growls and choking snarls were deafening as the creatures battled. There was no squeezing past the fight, so Zoey aimed for the quickest way out of the kitchen and climbed onto the table. She had one leg out of the window, feeling for a toehold so she could climb over to the neighbor's balcony when blood suddenly sprayed the wall beside her, splattering her face and arm. She snapped her attention to the now silent apartment where her attacker lay lifeless just a few feet away. The great silver and black wolf lifted its bloodied muzzle and stared at her with pale gray eyes. The eyes darkened to the color of storm as the massive creature took a step toward her. *Omigod, omigod.* She pulled back without thinking and lost her balance, her fingers sliding from the window frame. She was falling, falling—

Zoey awakened on the floor beside the couch with a scream caught in her throat. She choked and sputtered her way to the bathroom to get a drink. Only then could she draw a full breath, leaning on her elbows over the sink. *Omigod. That was a frickin' whopper.*

She spent an extra long time in the shower, trying to

rinse off the residue of the nightmare as much as the smoke and dirt. She really didn't want to go to the barbecue. The dream had left her off-balance—*weirded out*, as the sports reporter was fond of saying. But staying in the apartment wasn't all that appealing at the moment either. Besides, she'd feel guilty if she disappointed Bill and Jessie, especially after Bill had personally come to the office to issue the invitation, and then had ejected that insane reporter for her. Still, as much as she probably needed people around her, some semblance of normalcy after the disturbing dream, she wasn't sure she was up to seeing them.

She stood in front of her closet, studying her choices and shook her head. "It's not the damn barbecue, Zoey Tyler. It's Connor you don't want to see." Okay, she *wanted* to see him but wasn't *ready* to see him. Not until she could sort out her emotions, think clearly. She was still miffed that he'd left so abruptly—but one of the volunteers battling the blaze had shed some light on Connor's life. He'd told her about his pair of champion roping horses, which had broken into a grain shed a few days ago, gorging on barley until they foundered themselves. "They were near gone when I found 'em, almost went for my gun instead of the phone. But Macleod's got a way of pulling critters back from death's door and he didn't disappoint. Stayed the rest of the day and all that night, nursing them along until he was certain they would make it. Damn miracle worker, that guy."

Did that kind of thing happen often? Small wonder the vet was exhausted. He really hadn't looked well when he left. She supposed she could cut him a break for not making a more—what could she call it? *Socially adept exit?* Smooth transition between kissing and leaving? She picked out a turquoise blouse that she knew set off the auburn tones of her hair. "But he could damn well call, couldn't he?"

It shouldn't matter. If she never saw the man again, it really shouldn't matter. After all, it wasn't like they had a relationship or anything. Technically, all they had between them was a little kissing. . . .

Kissing. Who had come up with that word? What a lame term for something so incredible. What the man had done was more along the lines of making love with his lips. Just thinking about it made the heat rise to her cheeks. And speaking of heat . . . What was it with his body temperature? Being near him was like reclining in front of a bright fireplace; a deep and languid relaxation always stole over her. And she had certainly responded to him. No matter that she told herself she didn't want or need a relationship right now, that she was busy, that it wasn't convenient, that she was certain there were reasons, very good reasons if she could just think of them, for not getting involved with Connor Macleod. Her response to him exposed all of those sensible thoughts as the flimsy excuses they were. Because the connection went deeper than a mere physical response, although that alone had been so strong she could still feel it. It was as if some part of her actually recognized Connor, knew him. Psychic gift or heart's intuition, it had been just as clear when he was drinking coffee at her kitchen table as when she was in his arms.

Maybe she was dragging her feet about the barbecue because if she saw Connor there, she'd know why he hadn't been calling. If he avoided her, if he was too casual, maybe distant, then she'd know that he wasn't interested in her. That he'd pulled away from her and left because he didn't want to be too involved.

"That would suck," she said aloud as she put on a pair of

turquoise earrings. But knowing where she stood was better than wondering, and she'd never been one to back away from something she feared. Okay, there was that one time at the advanced ski hill when she'd thought better of going down, but wasn't that just common sense? She'd simply decided her skills weren't yet equal to the steep run and took the lift back to another slope. *So it was the bunny hill. . . .*

She'd definitely decline any further engagements with wolves too. The effects of this afternoon's dream were starting to fade a little but she still had to repress a shudder. And something about it was puzzling her. She could account for the grizzled wolf—after all, it was the one that had attacked her in real life. She expected to see it in her dreams. But what was the meaning of this new wolf, the black and silver one? She'd never seen anything like its distinctive saddleback markings. Did they mean something? And why was this strange wolf popping up as regularly as the real one?

The new wolf had pale gray eyes. Zoey had expected green or brown or something, well, more *animal-like*. But then, huskies had strange eyes, blue or even clear white for instance, so maybe gray eyes were not all that unusual. Still, she had a niggling impression she was missing something, something she ought to know or—

"Good grief. I don't need to sit around here all night and think about wolves," Zoey chided herself, and gathered up her keys and her purse. Bill's barbecue suddenly seemed very appealing. There would be people. Lots of people. Good food, of course, but more importantly, lots and lots of people. Conversation. Laughter. And no wolves.

Although it was just behind Main Street, the Watson home boasted a surprisingly large backyard surrounded by

a tall hedge of blossoming lilacs. Zoey could see the roof of
The Finer Diner rising beyond the flowered bushes. An
enthusiastic yellow Lab met her at the gate.

"Hi," she laughed and fondled the dog's ears. The dog
led the way through the crowd, wagging its tail. Zoey
smiled and waved at a number of people she knew until
the dog halted in front of the enormous stainless steel barbecue. Smoke and steam billowed up from the open lid as
if from a blacksmith's forge and she could barely see the
petite black woman turning steaks behind it. The dog
barked, as if announcing Zoey, and the woman looked up
at once.

"You made it, girl!" Jessie hurried around to hug her
tightly.

"Thanks for inviting—" Zoey flinched as her upper arm
protested the pressure. Jessie was small but powerful.

Her friend released her at once with a frown. "That rotter *did* hurt you. Bill told me about what happened today.
Lemme see that arm." There was no time to object. Jessie
simply seized her loose sleeve and rolled it up as smoothly
as if it were a window shade. She grimaced at the purple
imprints of large fingers on the inside of Zoey's arm just
above the elbow, the skin around the prints darkening ominously as well.

"The dirty bugger," declared Jessie. "It hasn't been a day
and just look at the color of these marks already. Have you
iced this wing yet?" She called her husband to take over
grilling duties and ushered Zoey into the house.

Within a few moments, there was a bag of frozen peas
curved around Zoey's injured arm and an icy glass of
mango slush in her other hand. "I have to admit that feels a
whole lot better," said Zoey. She drew on the straw

thoughtfully, savoring both the fruit and the shot of vodka that enhanced it. "In fact, this is probably the best I've felt all day. Thanks."

"No problem. I've had lots of practice. Bill and I both wrestled for a number of years, and we took turns patching each other up. Well, mostly I patched up Bill," Jessie laughed. "He gets so reckless, so crazy when he's in the ring. Me, I never got hurt too bad—I preferred strategy to the straightforward approach. That's why I can still take him down."

Zoey stared at her. "*You* can take Bill? But he's so *huge!*" she blurted and covered her mouth in embarrassment.

"You think size matters? Haven't you ever heard of Yoda, girl? Brains and agility will beat brawn and muscle every time. And let's not forget the Force," grinned Jessie as she held out some white pills and a glass of water to Zoey. "This'll help with the pain and swelling. Mind you, that's your one and only drink if you take them."

"Gotcha. Did you meet while on the wrestling circuit?" asked Zoey as she peered at the pills. Acetaminophen. She considered the glass in her hand, looked again at the pills, then shook her head. She didn't drink much as a rule but tonight she wouldn't mind a couple more mango slushes or maybe a good dark beer in tribute to her Irish heritage. She was certain she'd seen someone holding a Guinness earlier. . . .

"Not on the usual circuit, that's for sure. Bill was from London. My family was from Louisiana, so we were more than an ocean apart. But we had both signed on with an international group that was doing a three-month stint of tag-team matches in Europe. By the time the tour was up, Bill and I were married." Jessie chuckled. "My mother had conniptions at first, but once she met Bill and saw us together, she had to admit it was meant to be. She's doted on him ever since."

"And you too, I see."

"And me too. Like I told you, *meant to be*. We're still hot for each other after all these years. And speaking of hot—I've been slaving over that barbecue too long." Jessie shrugged out of her overshirt, leaving just a bright coral cami and Zoey noticed a large colored tattoo covering her friend's shoulder and upper arm: A leaping wolf, silvery against the deep mahogany of her skin.

"Oh my—that's gorgeous!" breathed Zoey and meant it, even if wolves weren't her favorite animals at the moment. The tat was a work of art, intricately detailed. There was even expression in the lupine face. She was about to ask why Jessie had chosen a wolf when suddenly the screen door flew open behind her and Connor was there. Holding her arm gently in his strong hands, examining the bruises with a feather touch. Swearing softly under his breath, his eyes storm-dark with anger. Bill was right at his elbow.

"I told you he's a rotten bugger," said the red-haired man. "I shook him around a bit but Zoey got her licks in. Nearly split his thick skull for him, she did. Still, I wish I'd thumped him a bit more now."

Connor's voice was low and hard. "I'd like to thump him myself." He straightened slowly and searched Zoey's face, cupping her elbow carefully in his hand.

"Sorry to disappoint you both, but I've got first thumping rights, the minute I complete my black belt in Karate or Kung Fu or something." She removed her arm from Connor's big hand, ignoring the tiny thrill that zipped through her at the thought of what that hand could do. . . .

"And I'm okay, thanks. My arm's not broken, not even sprained. It'll work just fine for swearing in to testify against that rat bastard." There was a long pause and she felt another tingle, one that wasn't caused by being in close proximity to a tall broad-shouldered man. She didn't need her psychic talent to tell her that Connor was angry—that was plain from his expression. The devil help Helfren if they met face to face anytime soon. But there was something else, something niggling at her senses. She tried to open herself to it—

And found herself nearly nose to nose with a massive wolf, the same silver and black creature from her nightmares, its pale gray eyes fastened intently on hers. Zoey yelped and jumped backward, bashing her hip against the rim of the countertop. The pain served to interrupt the vision and the wolf disappeared abruptly. There were only Connor's eyes, wide with concern.

"Zoey, talk to me. Are you all right? What happened to you?"

"What happened to me? What the hell happened to *you?*" She gripped the counter with one hand and held the other to her throbbing hip. Another day, another bruise, she thought ruefully. Connor stepped closer but she held up a hand—the one that had been on her hip. She didn't dare let go of the counter with the other just yet. "Please don't crowd me for a few minutes, okay? I mean it, just back off and let me breathe." *Let me breathe and try to figure all this out.* This was no doubt what she got for actually trying to use her unwanted psychic ability. She was seeing things, and damn *scary* things at that. Was she more tired than she'd thought? She picked up the nearly empty glass of mango slush and gave it an experimental sniff.

Jessie moved in and put a gentle arm around her. "Hon,

you've had a long and difficult day. I shouldn't have given you that drink without something to eat first. Why, knowing you, I'll just bet you haven't had a thing since breakfast."

Zoey latched onto the idea with relief. "Yeah, that Helfren guy really messed up my lunch hour." And if she hadn't eaten, then maybe her blood sugar was down. Really, really down. Didn't people sometimes hallucinate when that happened? She'd fainted from low blood sugar once before, but maybe seeing things was possible as well. And she *was* tired. . . . That nagging voice within told her she was grasping for straws, but she decided to ignore it.

"What say we find you the most comfortable chair in the yard, and you can just relax and put those hardworking editor's feet up while I get Bill to bring you a steak? I've got my best cajun chicken on the grill too."

"Works for me." Zoey allowed her friend to lead her outside. "Jessie, you just won't believe what I thought I saw—"

Connor watched from the porch as Jessie settled Zoey into a sprawling Adirondack chair. The two women were laughing now but he wasn't cheered. He wanted to kick something. Better yet, he wanted to chase something around and bite it. Preferably Helfren. He would definitely go looking for him in the very near future. . . .

Jessie walked by the grill, still smiling, and spoke to her husband. But as she turned and made her way back to the porch, her expression was all business. Connor followed the Pack leader into the kitchen.

"There was power here just now," she stated. "A helluva lot of it."

"It's Zoey—she has a gift of some kind. It feels like *far-*

sight to me, but it's different. Is that what happened to her? She saw something, didn't she?"

"She saw your wolf."

What? "That's not possible."

"There is only one saddleback wolf, animal or Change-ling, in this part of the country. One black and silver wolf with pale eyes. And she saw it in your face just now."

"Good God, I didn't feel anything, not a thing. My wolf was close to the surface but it was under control. Not like when—" he trailed off. "I meant to talk to you, Jess, about what happened the other day when I was with her. Something really weird is going on."

She snorted at that. "We're Changelings. *Something really weird* is always going on. We'll talk about it after the party, Connor. For now, go get yourself a drink."

Chapter Twelve

Zoey finished the last bite of her chicken and put the plate on the little table beside her, settling back into her chair with a happy sigh. This was *so* what she needed. Great food, a little relaxation, good company. Normally she would have made the rounds, made sure she met everyone, but her leg was bothering her and she was more tired than she'd initially thought. To her delight, most of the party guests wandered over to her and said hello or introduced themselves. For someone who was new in town, she couldn't have felt more welcomed. Geoff and Melly Lassiter had invited her to their goat farm. Holt LaLonde had offered to fly her over the Peace River valley in his Cessna. Martin Beauchamp and René Ghostkeeper had brought over samples from the dessert table, most of which they'd baked themselves. Zoey grinned as she pulled a small notepad from her purse and scribbled a couple of story tips she'd received from Jeannie Rousseau, the bookstore owner. Her grin faded when Connor appeared out of nowhere and sat in the chair next to her.

"So," he said, looking over at the patio where some couples were dancing under bright lanterns. He was pointedly *not* looking at her. "I was wanting to tell you that I'm sorry for having left so abruptly the other day, but I haven't figured out how."

She considered his words carefully. "You were tired," she offered at last.

"No excuse."

"Okay, then you could have picked up the phone."

"I certainly should have. Birkie was right."

"I thought she was in Scotland. She told you to call me?"

"No, no. She's been warning me for quite a while that I've been too wrapped up in my work and need to make time for a life."

That was something she could relate to. "Seems to be the challenge of the twenty-first century. Most of us have to learn how to do that. She sounds very wise."

"There's an understatement. I should pay more attention to what she says, a lot more and a lot sooner." He scrubbed a hand over his face and looked at her then. "You know, I came here tonight hoping to get you alone long enough to apologize, then Bill told me what that Helfren character did and I just saw red. Then, in the kitchen, *you* saw something. . . ." He let it hang.

"Jessie told you?"

"I twisted her arm."

Zoey snorted. "Jessie? Try again."

"Okay, maybe I acted pathetic until she felt sorry for me and told me what I wanted to know."

She wasn't sure she could picture that either. "And what do you know?"

"That you thought you saw a wolf when you looked at me."

"That's hardly your fault, Connor. Jessie was right, I was

tired and my blood sugar had sunk to my shoes. I haven't been sleeping well, so it's not all that surprising that I started seeing things. Pretty disturbing, mind you, but not surprising." She had decided to ignore the fact that the vision had come through her psychic gift, since surely the gift was influenced by her own physical and emotional condition, and therefore suspect. She sighed and shared the conclusion she'd come to. "I hope this doesn't sound dramatic—I'm wondering if I might have a mild case of post-traumatic stress after all."

He nodded. "Makes perfect sense. The wolf attack was a very intense and terrifying experience, and it's going to take some time to fade. But I sure don't like the thought of you being frightened by *me*."

"It wasn't really you. And besides, I'll have you know I *wasn't* scared, I was just startled."

"Startled?" There was a pause. "Is that your story?" His expression lightened considerably.

"And I'm sticking to it," she said. She slid her hand over his on the armrest. Heat radiated from his skin and she caught her breath as her mind painted pictures of other places she'd like to be touching.

"So things are okay between us?" he asked. There was no mistaking the hopeful note in his voice.

"Only if you dance with me." She grinned at him. "Cruel I know, but it's a strict policy of mine. Can't accept an apology that doesn't come with a dance. Sorry."

"What about your leg?"

"I'm light on my feet, and besides, I was hoping for a *slow* dance."

His hand seized hers at once, and she was pulled from the chair and into his powerful arms in the blink of an eye. The heat, the scent of him, surrounded her, filled her

senses, as they began to move together. Her sore leg coop-
erated to the point that she could almost forget it.

"Hey, the dance floor's way over there." Zoey said with a
weak laugh. Every hormone she had was in overdrive at
the proximity of Connor's powerful body. She half-
expected spontaneous combustion to claim her clothing as
her body brushed against his. And didn't *that* just paint a
picture in her mind?

"We'll get there. Eventually." He guided her subtly but
unerringly through the crowd. She was amazed at how
smoothly he moved in spite of his size, and for a moment
she had a vivid impression of a powerful predator stalking
silently in the shadows—

"Zoey?"

"What?" The impression disappeared like a soap bubble,
and she shook her head a little to clear it. "Mind's wandering, I guess. Sorry."

He laughed then, and she could feel the rumble of it in
his chest. Something deep and low within her clenched
delightfully at the vibration, and she gripped his broad
shoulder hard. Her bruised arm protested a little but she
was too busy watching Connor's eyes go from gray to silver
as he lowered his head. Her arms traveled up of their own
volition to circle his neck.

Within two seconds she realized it wasn't going to be
like the last time. There was no trading here, no gentle testing, no give and take. And she was *so* not in control. Connor's mouth was hot and soft yet relentless all at the same
time. Wrapped tightly in his powerful arms, held against his
well-muscled frame, her body was not her own. Not hers
at all. She was already pressed against him from chin to toe
but it wasn't enough, not nearly enough. She wanted to
wrap herself in that luscious glowing heat that radiated

from him. Something between a whimper and a moan escaped her throat as his large, strong hands massaged her back and shoulders, leaving that delicious warmth behind. His heated hands moved lower to knead her bottom. She wound her fingers in his long dark hair. Her breasts felt strangely tight, almost tingly, and she wanted his mouth on them. Needed it.

A burst of distant laughter snapped her to her senses and Zoey pushed away from Connor. She didn't get far—she was pretty much caged in those arms. But frantic glances around her revealed nothing but shadow. She could hear the party somewhere off to her right but she couldn't see much.

"Where the hell are we?"

"Side of the house. Behind the garden shed to be exact."

"I thought we were headed to the dance floor."

"We are," he said as he nuzzled her neck. "This is the scenic route."

She breathed him in, felt her insides melting. He pulled back for a moment and as she looked up into his face, all she could think was *damn fine scenery*. "Well, then"—she grinned—"sign me up for the full tour."

Moments later Zoey's blouse was open and she was thanking the lingerie gods for front-hooking bras. Connor's large hands were hot, one at the small of her back pressing her to him and the other engulfing her breast. He was trailing kisses along her collarbone, working his way lower and lower with his lips and tongue. She could hardly breathe for the anticipation. A low moan escaped her as he closed his questing lips around a nipple.

Oh yes. Yes-yes-yes. Her hands worked through Connor's wavy hair, twisting and tangling, as he worked her tender nipple with his tongue, nibbled it delicately with his teeth.

Drew her breast strongly into his mouth, again and again, until answering pulls from deep within her core had Zoey gasping for breath. He flicked open her jeans then and slid them slowly down her hips, with his mouth still working her breast. A hot burst of moisture dampened her thong just before it went south and she wondered why the cool evening air didn't flash into steam as soon as it brushed her skin. Then Connor's mouth was on hers again. A picture blossomed in her mind, showed her plainly how the subtle thrust of his tongue was symbolic of another, more complete, possession.

And she wanted it. *Needed it.* Needed everything. Needed *him.* She parted her legs for his hand, rocked her pelvis forward to meet his questing fingers. Moaned deep in her throat as one slid inside her. She gripped his shoulders and rode first one finger, then two. She was soaking wet, desperately hot to the point of aching—and nearly cheered when he crooked his fingers *just so*, dragging his fingertips across her most sensitive spot as she moved. She could feel the approaching storm now, bearing down on her like thunderheads on a hot summer night. *Oh geez, oh Connor, oh*— He sealed his lips over hers and she screamed into his mouth, as the violent orgasm flashed through her like sheet lightning.

Tad Helfren was fuming by the time he found Bernard Gervais. The old drunk was in a corner booth of the Jersey Pub with half a dozen empty draft glasses in front of him.

The investigator was in a rotten mood. The huge lump on the back of his head ached like a bitch, and his lip stung as he took a sip of his imported German beer. "Where the hell have you been? I'm paying you for your help, not to drink yourself into a stupor."

"If I wanted a stupor, I'd have started a hell of a lot earlier." Bernie's speech was intelligible, his eyes reasonably clear. "What d'ya want, Helfren?"

"There were a bunch of cattle killed tonight, just west of town. I picked it up on the scanner and the police are saying it was an animal attack. Fish and Wildlife are going out first thing in the morning." Helfren leaned over the table, his voice dropping. "I know they're going to find wolf prints. It's werewolves, isn't it?"

Bernie's scarred face stretched uncomfortably with a slow deliberate smile. "Yeah, must be. Natural killers, those things. The vet's not home tonight either."

"You still think Macleod's the one? I've had his office under surveillance for three stinking weeks but so far I haven't got a thing on him. And that little gift you suggested we leave in his office hasn't been touched yet."

"He's the one. And the newspaper bitch is out tonight too. I'm betting the two of them went after the cattle just for fun."

"But it isn't the full moon yet—would she turn so soon?"

"He's her sire, he can make it happen whenever he likes. You can bet he's initiating her to the kill. Just like he made her cut my face."

Helfren refrained from mentioning that Little Miss Editor had nearly cracked his own skull and Macleod had been nowhere in sight. Gingerly, he fingered the fresh stitches in the midst of the swelling. "But she *will* turn when the moon's full? 'Cause, dammit, I want those photos. You called *me*, remember? Got me to come all the way up here to the middle of nowhere, claiming there would be proof that werewolves exist."

"You said you'd pay for it." Gervais finished his glass.

"When I get proof, you'll get your money. That's the agreement."

"You'd best be prepared to make a down payment then. You still have that equipment set up where I told you? It's turned on?"

"For all the good it's doing," Helfren snorted.

"Make sure you check it in the morning." The old man got to his feet.

"Where the hell do you think *you're* going?"

Gervais chuckled low in his throat, but it wasn't a pleasant sound. "Just going to stir the pot a little. And the next time you see me, you better have your fucking checkbook."

As Zoey's senses returned she found herself draped against Connor like a wet beach towel, and his talented mouth was doing wonderful things to her neck. Her body was weightless, boneless, breathless, a hollowed-out shell blasted clean by the sheer force of release. She was strangely ravenous in spite of the meal she'd had, but that could wait. There were other hungers to be satisfied, she thought and smiled as her fingers worked the buttons of Connor's shirt. She spread the material aside, running her hands over his chest, exploring the dusting of dark hair that accentuated the powerful muscles. God, the man was built, and she couldn't help grinning as she leaned forward to circle her tongue around a nipple. A sudden craving to cover that chest with soft, openmouthed kisses surfaced but was deflected as Connor's big hands drew her close, pressing her skin firmly against his. She'd just experienced the best orgasm of her life, yet the heat of his body seemed to incite a whole new level of languor in her. She just wanted to bask in it, melt into it, become one with it. . . .

Zoey was just starting to fiddle with the zipper of his obviously straining jeans when he stiffened and seized her hands. "What? What is it?" Her hands were still captive but he wasn't paying attention to her, wasn't even looking at her. Instead every fiber of him seemed to be alert. Watching. Listening. She glanced around him frantically. "Is someone coming?" Holy crap, that was all she needed—to be caught with her pants down *literally* in a very small town. Ha, and she'd been worried about werewolf rumors. The post office gossips would have a field day with—

Connor released her so abruptly that she lost her balance and had to grab the side of the house for support. "Hey!" She yanked her clothes together. "What the hell's the matter with you?"

She buttoned frantically as she watched him take a couple of steps forward, all his attention focused outward. Certainly not on her. Zoey listened hard yet heard nothing but the party carrying on in the yard beyond. Saw nothing either, since there were no lights on this side of the house. Her psychic gift also failed to make an appearance but she wasn't surprised by that. After, all, it hadn't warned her of the wolf attack either. When she didn't want the gift, it crowded in on her senses. When she could really use it, it couldn't be found. She wondered crossly what was the point of having a psychic talent if it was going to be so damn unreliable. Wondered with even more annoyance what was the point of trying to be close to Connor—then sudden agony seared through her injured leg like hot metal through butter.

In every novel she'd read, things went black at times like these. Instead the world had gone white. Brilliant, blinding white. She hovered in the heart of the sun for long moments, until the pain released her as abruptly as it had seized her.

Zoey didn't feel herself hit the ground. She was much too busy gasping in great lungfuls of air. She was vaguely aware of Connor kneeling beside her, holding her by the shoulders, his face near hers. A hard shake jarred her senses, made her eyes fly open and her temper flare. "Quit that! I'm okay, goddammit. Let go."

"I thought you were passing out."

"Sorry, I'm not the fainting type. Go find a princess." She sat and rested her arms on her knees, content to just practice breathing for a while. A sudden burst of laughter from the party reached her ears and she looked up to find that Connor was gone. "Hey, I didn't mean now!"

She'd heard of men who ignored their partner's need for foreplay in favor of their own satisfaction, but she'd never heard of a man totally satisfying, then abandoning, his partner. It made no sense. It was too much like what had happened—or rather, *not happened*, in her apartment. At least she had had an orgasm this time, but even though it was definitely the best one she'd ever had, she was still pissed off. What was Connor Macleod's problem? He wasn't shy by any stretch of the imagination. Nor was he hesitant about touching her—and boy, oh boy, did he know *how* to touch her. Impotence wasn't a factor either. He'd had a hell of an impressive erection that made her core clench just thinking about it.

"So why the goddamn disappearing act?" she muttered crossly, rubbing her throbbing leg as she struggled to think. If Connor wasn't interested in her, then why seek her out to apologize in the first place? Or why be so angry at the bruise on her arm from that asshole reporter? For that matter, why would he be upset that she'd briefly imagined a wolf's face when she looked at him? If he really wasn't into her, that should have been the perfect excuse to back away. *Just leave the crazy lady alone.* . . .

No, he'd had ample opportunity to walk away and he hadn't. Zoey didn't need any psychic gifts to tell her that Connor cared, that he had feelings for her. She was sure of it and sure of what she'd seen in his face when she'd suggested the dance, sure of what she'd felt in his touch. She didn't know what Connor's problem was, but she was *so* going to hunt him down and find out!

Her leg still hurt like hell—and just what was *that* all about?—but she managed to limp around the house to the backyard. She leaned on a planting bench and scanned the crowd for Connor under the glowing strings of patio lanterns that crisscrossed the yard. Instead she caught sight of an enormous canine shape as it made an impossible leap over the wall of lilacs. Terror jammed her heart into her throat and she couldn't have shouted a warning if there'd been time. Tumult erupted as the creature landed inside the yard and ran through the party. Someone screamed. People turned to look, some tripped trying to get out of the way and others were knocked down as the huge wolf raced around the yard with snarling, snapping jaws. Jessie's normally placid dog exploded with primal rage and lunged for the intruder, but the wolf was far too fast.

She knew, *knew*, it was coming for her but running had suddenly become impossible. The pain in her leg was now overriding everything, even adrenaline. Slowly she sank to the ground, fighting to stay conscious above the agony, fighting even to draw a breath, yet her fingers walked along the grass and closed over a fallen garden trowel just as the wolf reached the end of the far walkway. It wheeled and headed straight toward her.

Her vision faltered, grayed as she struggled to kneel on her good leg, holding the trowel in front of her with both hands. Then the sudden clarity of the doomed kicked in and she could see everything in vivid detail. The hellish green light in the creature's eyes, the grizzled and scarred muzzle, the gleam on its long pointed teeth—

Just as she expected the wolf to leap and sink those terrible teeth into her, something knocked her flat. For a moment she couldn't see, then realized something dark and massive was blocking her view. Her eyes gradually made out a pattern, a familiar pattern, black on silver. . . . She couldn't even scream as the realization hit her. The saddleback wolf from her dreams was standing over her.

With nerveless fingers she felt for the trowel, even though she knew she'd be dead before she could raise it, but the new wolf didn't even glance at her. All its attention was on its gray opponent, and its black lips peeled back from long white teeth. Zoey's own teeth began to chatter as a deep warning growl resonated from the creature and vibrated into her very bones. Without warning it sprang forward with a horrific roar. The gray wolf wheeled and ran.

The crowd dove out of the way of the pursued and the pursuer. Zoey saw the wolves clear the back gate and disappear into the darkness as strong hands slipped beneath her and lifted her from the grass.

Chapter Thirteen

The wolf had never taken over before, not once in his very long life. Connor had been aware that his lupine side was stirring from the moment he'd uncovered those gorgeous freckled breasts. . . . And when Zoey had screamed out her pleasure in his arms, all he'd wanted was to bury himself in the welcome oasis of her body. Instead, he'd ended up in a losing battle with his own wolf.

The same thing had happened at her apartment. Just when things got hot and heavy, his Changeling nature had emerged unbidden and unwanted. Only this time he couldn't stop it. He'd been forced to leave her, knowing she was in pain, knowing something was very wrong. Forced to slip away to the front of the house and Change behind the profusion of evergreens just off the porch.

But once in wolfen form, his awareness had shifted away from human in a heartbeat, expanded suddenly to include many things at once. He had scented a wolf; sensed a Changeling; identified Bernie. And discerned the old wolf's terrible intent. A raw and primal fury had erupted within Connor then, blinding him. He was beyond all thought, all reason, as he raced around the house to where dozens of humans mingled with Changelings in two-legged form. It didn't matter to him who saw him; it couldn't matter who saw him. All that mattered was that he protect Zoey.

And that he kill Bernie.

He could see the rogue wolf still far ahead, a fleeting pale shape that appeared to fly through the dark streets of Dunvegan. Since when had the old drunk developed such speed? The wolf was weaving a twisted path in and out of side streets and alleys. Connor was running flat out, fueled by anger and adrenaline, yet Bernie maintained his unprecedented lead.

Connor was so intent on his prey that he didn't see the juggernaut that hit him broadside, knocking him breathless in a tangle of limbs and teeth and claws. He rolled and scrambled to a crouch, sides heaving but fangs bared to attack—*Culley?*

Glad you recognize me. The black wolf replied, using the mental speech that most Changelings employed in wolfen form. The words were focused tightly so that only Connor would hear and not their quarry.

What the hell were you doing? You could have been . . . Connor suddenly felt sick. Dear God, what if he'd leapt for Culley's throat without knowing it was him?

I figured an intervention was in order after you showed your wolf to the entire party. Jesus, Connor, what the hell were you thinking?

I don't know. And he didn't. The need to protect Zoey had simply overridden everything. His inner wolf had only a single purpose—to kill Bernie.

Jessie wants Bernie brought to the stone circle at Elk Point, in one piece and still breathing. Are you up for it?

The Pack would gather there to pass judgment on the

crazy old Changeling. And then Jessie would no doubt have some choice words for Connor. He took a long, deep breath, then another as his head cleared. *Let's go get him.*

The trail was easy to pick up, as distinct as if it had been drawn in neon against the dark ground. Sure of their direction, the two wolves ran shoulder to shoulder.

How the hell did Bernie manage to Change in the first place? Culley's voice was loud in Connor's head. *I thought you took care of that.*

I did, dammit. I gave him the injection myself, and I gave him more than enough silver to do the job. The brothers ran flat out, their pace beyond what real wolves could manage, and still Bernie's fleeing form remained far ahead of them.

Clouds obscured the half moon, cloaking everything below in deep shadow. Changeling eyesight could penetrate the gloom easily but human eyes were not designed for it. Judgment of distance, size, shape, speed—all were skewed by the darkness. If anyone happened to catch a fleeting glimpse of two wolves racing by, they were likely to be mistaken for large dogs. Still, Connor would feel much better if they got away from human habitation.

He's heading for the golf course. There was relief in Culley's voice. The Dunvegan Golf Course was small and thick with trees, and bordered the northern edge of the village. On the other side of Fairway Six was deep forest. Together the brothers leapt the high fence that separated the sixth hole from the last row of houses. Then their bellies were again low to the ground as they raced to follow Bernie across manicured grass, around water hazards and sand traps, and finally through brush and trees. It was dark but their natural night vision served them well. Connor could see Bernie ahead of them and knew they were finally closing on the old rogue.

Suddenly a brilliant light flashed. More flashes followed, blinding them. The pair broke stride, confused, and Culley stumbled. *I can't see!*

This way! Nose to my flank.

Culley pressed his muzzle to his brother's hip and followed blindly as Connor veered from the trails at once. Branches slapped at their faces as they crashed through thick underbrush, then followed an overgrown creek bed for more than a mile as Connor led his younger brother to safety. He didn't dare stop until they were under the Gamble Street Bridge. *You okay?*

Still got purple and green spots in front of my eyes, but I'm okay. What the hell happened back there?

Cameras. I spotted a gleam off a trip wire just as Bernie hit it so I was looking down when the flashes started going off. Got a few spots in front of my eyes too.

The clear water splashed and churned over the stones, making a sound like laughter. Culley waded into the tiny creek and began drinking in earnest. Connor was about to follow suit when a familiar sensation settled over him and his fur stood on end.

Bernie led us right into a trap. The cameras were for us.

Culley lifted his head and studied his brother. *You sure about that?*

I can see it. Connor's eyesight wasn't a hundred percent yet but his *farsight* was fully engaged. Silvery images played across his mind like a disjointed movie. A short stocky man pulling equipment from a van. Walking the deer trails that crisscrossed the golf course. Wiring cameras into trees, flashes and floodlights into bushes. Connor saw state-of-the-art equipment, maybe military, in some of the tree stands. Cameras for still shots and video, cameras with night vision, motion sensors, infrared. How many silently recording sentinels had they run past, unaware, before they hit the older, light-dependent equipment? *Bernie's working with somebody else.*

Somebody like, what, a human? Who?

I've never seen him before, but I'm betting it's that reporter.

The one who threatened Zoey? Shit. We'd better Change and go take those cameras out.

Can't. Connor was certain of it. *We can't risk our human selves being recorded as well. Someone's keeping close tabs on that equipment, and they'll be able to make the connection between us and the wolves.*

The black wolf snapped his great jaws on empty air and began loping along the bank. Connor followed. They had to get back and tell Jessie the terrible news.

Bernie had outed the Pack.

Lowen Miller finished wrapping Zoey's leg from ankle to knee with practiced hands. The roll of gauze ended neatly just below her knee and was deftly tucked in. She was just wondering how many hundreds or perhaps thousands of times he'd performed the task, when suddenly he was pointing a finger at her.

"What?"

"Didn't I say to stay off that leg for a few days until those wounds had a chance to close properly?" he asked gruffly, and didn't wait for an answer. "Those are damn deep puncture wounds and they need to heal from the inside out."

Not much bedside manner, she thought. Her publisher had said that Lowen doubled as the local coroner. Maybe he was better at dealing with dead people than live ones. "I guess I can stay in the office, get someone else to cover things for a couple days."

"Not good enough. You need to stay *home* with that leg elevated and iced."

She bristled at his tone but her retort was averted by the hasty intervention of the doctor's wife. With long-practiced ease, Bev neatly inserted herself in front of Lowen. Zoey caught a glimpse of her hand reaching behind and patting his arm. He grunted and moved off like a grizzly in reluctant retreat.

The older woman smiled at her. "My husband's just worried about you. If you walk around on that leg, dear, those wounds are never going to close. You need to give them a chance."

"I guess I can ask for a few days—"

Lowen's voice sounded from the doorway. "I'll tell Ted you're to have all the time you need. He's cheap but he's not an idiot. And make sure you take every last capsule of those antibiotics I gave you!"

"Thanks, honey!" Bev replied cheerfully but firmly. He waved a hand and left. She watched to make sure he was really gone, and then turned back to Zoey. "He's right about the antibiotics, and I'll have George over at Dunvegan Drugstore deliver a second course of them. I don't prescribe them much these days, but we can't take any chances on infection setting into that bite."

"Thank you very much. Thank your husband for me too. I'm sure you came here for fun, not to patch me up."

"I've patched up quite a few people tonight with scratches and bruises. One wrenched ankle. A skinned knee. People had quite a scare. But if you want to feel sorry for someone, pity Sergeant Fitzpatrick. He was just a guest until this happened. Now he has a few dozen complaints to file. I imagine the paperwork will be considerable." She smiled again and left.

Zoey didn't feel too sorry for the sergeant. After all, hadn't she told the RCMP there was a wolf on the loose? It was their own fault for not believing her.

Dear God, what if the wolf had bitten someone else?

Thoughts of vindication began to pop like soap bubbles. Maybe she should have reported the wolf in the newspaper after all and damn the consequences. Had she changed the outcome by calling the animal a dog? What if she *herself* had endangered people?

She was deep in thought when a familiar form sat on the couch beside her. Without hesitation she grabbed his arm and laid her face against his shoulder with more relief than she wanted to feel. "I don't know whether to hit you or kiss you!"

"I'll take the kiss, if it's all the same to you."

It wasn't Connor.

Zoey sat bolt upright and stared at the man beside her. "Omigosh, I'm sorry."

"Hey, I'm used to it. It comes with being a Macleod. I'm Devlin by the way. Saw you with my older brother."

"Zoey." She fervently hoped he hadn't seen his big brother dance her off into the shadows. . . . Quickly she put that thought aside before her face turned red, and focused instead on the family resemblance. Devlin's eyes were green-gold, maybe hazel, but the lines of his face and the set of his shoulders said *Macleod* as plainly as if the name had been stamped on his forehead.

"You'd be the newspaper lady," he said.

"Editor," she corrected, and decided to act like it by asking questions. "Did you see the wolves?"

"Everyone saw something, although plenty of folks weren't sure what they were seeing since it happened so fast. Some people saw two animals, some only saw one.

Several thought it was a big gray dog, or a coyote," Devlin explained.

"A *coyote!*" she sniffed. "How could anyone mistake that huge beast for a coyote?"

"People generally see what they expect to see. And coyotes are expected. After all, they come into town pretty regularly. They like to check out the garbage or pet food left on back porches. One of Jake Griswold's malamutes is also spotted from time to time. They're holy terrors when they get loose." He winced. "The whole string of them ran through Enid Malkinson's flower club picnic one day like a Viking horde. God, what a mess. Half the village was up in arms. You should look it up in your newspaper. I think Ted Biegel even wrote an editorial about it."

"I'll be sure to check that out. But you haven't answered my question. Did *you* see two wolves tonight?"

Devlin sighed. "I did, but I'd rather not be quoted on that. You know about the rumors, and I'd rather not get involved."

"The werewolf rumors?"

"That'd be them."

"Off the record then. You saw two animals, and you knew they were wolves."

"Persistent, aren't you? But off the record, yes and yes. Fletcher knew it too, of course. Upset the old dog quite a bit."

Fletcher was still upset by the sounds of it. Bill had rushed through the house earlier, carrying the big dog bodily. Only a powerful wrestler could have managed it. The normally placid Fletcher had been thrashing and twisting in his arms, snapping and snarling like an animal possessed. Zoey could still hear frantic barking from the basement but it was greatly muffled. "Poor dog."

"That's what Bill said when he brought him a second steak," laughed Devlin. "I'm sure the *poor dog* will have a very good time getting over his trauma. Speaking of trauma, what about you?"

"Me?"

"You're a hell of a brave woman. One wolf bite already and two wolves prepared to fight to the death over you. Yet you didn't even scream."

"There wasn't time," she said simply, then thought about what he'd said. "Wait a minute, you think the wolves were fighting over me? Why would they do that?"

Suddenly Devlin looked distinctly uncomfortable. "Well, it just looked that way. I mean, you were on the ground with an injured leg and all, so it was very *Wild Kingdom*. Sort of like lions fighting over a lame gazelle, don't you think?"

Prey. Zoey suppressed a shiver. "Why me? Why not the steaks, why not the entire buffet? Why not Fletcher, or even Jessie for that matter? She's a lot smaller than me."

He coughed into his hand unexpectedly as if stifling a laugh, then cleared his throat. "Well, that's what wild wolves do. They single out the wounded and the weak from a herd very quickly. Every instinct they have is wired for that purpose."

"Great. What you're saying is that I'm wolf bait." Zoey slumped back on the couch and surveyed her freshly bandaged calf resting on the coffee table. Wondered idly if it was going to be difficult to repair the side seam on the leg of her blue jeans, which Lowen had neatly snipped from ankle to knee. Without warning, her psychic senses flickered into life. She searched Devlin's face and was surprised to learn that despite his pleasant expression, he was extremely angry. Not at her. At the wolves—wait, that wasn't quite right. Only at the *gray* wolf. Fear or surprise she could understand, but why would someone be *angry* toward a wolf? More than angry—*furious*. A chill zipped through her, and she shivered as she rubbed her upper arms. "Do you know where Connor is?"

Devlin draped his jacket around her before she could think to protest. "He went after the wolf, of course."

"He *what*?"

"Just to investigate, mind you," Devlin added hastily. "And Culley went with him—that's my twin brother by the way. They should be back in a couple hours or so."

So much for confronting Connor about ditching her. Zoey looked at her watch. It was already late. "I'd better go home . . ." she began but Devlin held up a hand.

"I'm relieving the bartender in a few minutes, so maybe you'd let me make you a drink first. I'll bet you could use one. Or several." He waggled his brows. "I make a wicked Long Island Iced Tea and a decadent Chocolate Martini, or if you want something more suited to the journalistic field, a Jack Sour."

What the hell. Zoey made a rare decision. "Maybe a friendly bartender is exactly what I need right about now. It's been a very long, very strange day."

Jessie was quiet as Connor delivered the news. She stood with folded arms, the picture of stillness, until he was done. She raised her head then and Connor could feel the punch of raw energy, see the flash of barely suppressed fury in her golden eyes. Her inner wolf was close to the surface, causing Connor's own to be watchful.

"Something's very wrong," she said at last. "But we can't deal with Bernie now. There are still human guests to attend to. The Pack will meet at Elk Point tomorrow night at dusk." She shook her head, and seemed to shake off her anger as well, although Connor had no doubt it had simply gone deep. The Pack would meet, as she said. And then it would go hunting. . . .

He turned to leave but Jessie put a hand on his arm.

"*Two* wolves crashed my party, mister."

"I'm sorry about that, Jess," he said.

"Bad enough that people saw one wolf, without a second one adding to the chaos."

"I know."

She scrutinized him. "You're not the impulsive type, Connor. It wasn't a conscious choice on your part, was it?"

"Hell *no*." It was embarrassing to admit he'd lost control. "The wolf took over."

"That tells me Bernie wasn't just being an asshole. He must have intended to do harm, for your wolf to react like that."

He snorted. "No one else's wolves popped out."

"No, they didn't. Just yours." She looked thoughtful and added, "I'll bet Zoey was the target the whole time then. Bernie must have intended to finish the job he started."

Immediately Connor's inner wolf snarled at the thought. He struggled to hold his alter ego in check as the hair on the back of his neck bristled. "Dammit, Jessie, don't say things like that."

Jessie tightened her grip on his arm and the creature within him quieted somewhat. As Pack leader, Jessie naturally possessed a great deal of power, but it was impossible not to be more than a little amazed when she exerted it. After all, she barely came up to Connor's chest. She amazed him further with her words. "Your inner wolf knows more than you do, or you wouldn't be so surprised by its actions. Zoey Tyler is your mate."

Chapter Fourteen

Connor should have been shocked. At least he figured he *ought* to be a helluva lot more than mildly surprised. Instead, he felt as if a dozen puzzle pieces had suddenly clicked neatly into place. "That's why she saw my wolf tonight, isn't it? And why my wolf is so on edge?"

"Nothing can be hidden from a mate. And our wolves often recognize a mate long before we do. It's happened more than once in our own Pack. Look at Geoff Lassiter."

He nodded. Geoff had known that Melly Chalmers was his mate ever since they were in high school together. He'd had to wait years, however, for her to come to the same conclusion.

"I've known Zoey for just over a week." It felt longer though. And it felt *right*. But from a human standpoint, it was far too soon to tell her so. He'd have to be patient, although he hoped he wouldn't have to wait as long as Geoff had. Meanwhile, something else bothered him. "Look, is the wolf going to take over every damn time I'm around Zoey? I don't remember this happening to anyone else when they found a mate."

"That's because our numbers are small and most pairings are between Changeling and human. Our inner wolf only comes to the forefront when the mate is also a Changeling, and only because it needs to communicate with the other's wolf during the first mating."

"Zoey—"

"Zoey isn't a Changeling, I know," Jessie said. "But she may not be fully human. She has powerful gifts we haven't seen before. Frankly, I'm not sure *what* she is. And I don't think she knows either."

Connor remembered the split-second vision he'd had the night of the ice storm, when he'd first held Zoey Tyler. About the strange cavalcade of animals that flashed through his mind. But his *farsight* had shown him nothing more so he'd chalked up the incident to his own fatigue. Still did. As for gifts, many human beings had latent abilities—telepathy, telekinesis, precognition—but they went untapped and undiscovered. Zoey might have more talents than most, but she was still human. His wolfen instincts weren't telling him anything different. He shook his head and focused on his present dilemma. "So what the hell do I do?"

"You'll have to tell her what you are, and soon, before your wolf blows your cover. And, if I were you, I'd cement the relationship so your wolf will settle down."

Cement the relationship? "You mean—"

"Uh-huh. Getting married is nice too, but that's for your human side. Once it recognizes its true mate, the wolfen side declares its bond during sex. And as you know, it's for keeps."

He nodded. He knew that. No doubt a human male would be more than a little freaked out by the whole *mate-for-life* thing, especially on such short notice. Connor, however, was Changeling. He could easily picture spending the rest of his long lifetime memorizing every one of Zoey's freckles . . . and his body stirred to life at the thought. Still, he had a problem. "Jess, I'm not sure it's possible to cement anything with the wolf emerging at—uh—*critical moments*."

Jessie chuckled. "I imagine that's been mighty awkward for you. Don't worry, I have a gris-gris—a charmed amulet—that will keep the wolf at bay. It's impossible to Change while you're wearing it." Her expression sobered quickly. "Just don't forget to take it off when the bond is complete. The charm has residual effects, and you might not be able to Change for a couple of days or so. Meanwhile, you need to stay as close as possible to her, Connor. She needs your protection until we've dealt with Bernie. Lowen looked at her leg again tonight and it's not pretty."

"Well, sure, it's scary-looking with all that bruising but—"

"The wounds have opened up and started bleeding again like they were fresh."

Bleeding? "I know she was suddenly in a lot of pain and—" And he'd abandoned her to go after Bernie. He smacked his forehead with the palm of his hand. "I left her."

"She was in pain because her sire was here and *in wolfen form*. The presence of his powerful and discordant energies had a very grave effect on the original bite wound."

"The only thing powerful about Bernie is his breath. He's a damn nasty old drunk, but he doesn't have any power to speak of." As soon as the words left his mouth, he realized that the *nasty old drunk* had mysteriously overcome the effects of silver nitrate, and just outrun two younger, stronger wolves. How? He racked his brain, trying to think of some detail he might have missed during his visit to the Gervais farm, but came up blank. "I don't know what the hell to think, Jess."

"He's not the Bernie we know. Something's changed

and it isn't for the better. We'll figure it out tomorrow when the Pack gets together. Right now, you'd better look in on your lady."

Connor sighed. "Wish me luck, because I have no idea what I'm going to say to her. Where is she?"

"Out cold in the guest bedroom."

"*What?*"

"She's okay, just had a few drinks with Devlin. She'll probably have a helluva headache in the morning, but all in all, I figure it was a pretty good antidote to everything that's happened to her today. Probably good for you too," Jessie teased and called back over her shoulder as she walked away, "Buys you a little more time to think up something to say."

Connor shook his head and headed for the house. If he had years to think about it, he knew full well he'd still come up blank. Goddammit, he'd just been trying to make things right after walking out of Zoey's apartment earlier in the week. True, he'd had the chance to bring her luscious body to peak this time—and parts of him immediately stirred to rampant life—but he'd still gone charging off without a single word. He doubted that the orgasm he'd given her was going to gain him many points.

He stopped to examine Fletcher, who was stretched out beside a lawn chair. The yellow Lab was once again the epitome of placid friendliness.

Culley and Bill joined the tall vet as he knelt by the dog. Bill's reddish brows were knitted together in concern. "Is Fletcher all right then?"

"He's fine." Connor gave the dog a final pat and stood. "He was just being protective."

Bill spat. "Shouldn't have needed to be protective in his own backyard! That Bernie must be bloody mad."

"Crazy or not, Bernie shouldn't have been able to Change at all," said Culley. "We all know it's not possible with that much silver nitrate in his veins. But I've been thinking—what if there's something wrong with the silver?"

That just can't be . . . Connor felt in his jacket for the bottle. It was dangerous cargo for a Changeling, but it also had many uses for a healer, both metaphysical and medical. He always carried it with him, and had topped it up from the gallon glass jug in the clinic's pharmacy before he'd even met Zoey. Filled it again twice since then. The jug was silver nitrate without doubt—he'd spilled a tiny drop on his finger a couple months ago when the jug was new. The nitrate had burned like acid and rinsing the spot did no good. He'd finally had to ask Birkie for a charmed balm to douse the invisible fire. *Still. . . .* He pulled the little bottle out of his pocket. Silver nitrate was colorless and odorless. It looked exactly like water.

"Maybe the manufacturer labeled it wrong, maybe it doesn't have the potency it's supposed to," suggested Culley. "Does the stuff expire or something? We should get Devlin to do a test on it."

Connor stared at the bottle. *A test.* Without a word, he spun open the cap and splashed the contents over the palm of his hand.

Bill leapt backward off his chair to avoid the flying droplets. "Bloody hell, Connor! What are you trying to do?"

His friend needn't have worried. There was no pain. Nothing. *Not a damn thing!* Connor should have been writhing on the ground in agony. The fact that he wasn't didn't bring him any comfort. He would have felt much better if the stuff had burned a hole clear through his hand.

Cautiously, he sniffed the moisture in his cupped palm, touched a finger to it, then his tongue.

"Water." He looked at his friend and his brother with stricken eyes. "Dear God, it's just plain *water.*" Connor's mind reeled with the implications of his discovery. Small wonder Bernie could still *Change*, but that was far from the worst of it.

Culley said it aloud. His voice was low and calm but the words hammered at Connor nonetheless. "Zoey wasn't treated in time. Not treated at all. She's going to Change soon and she doesn't know a thing about it. And she's subject to that rotten bastard Bernie."

Connor closed his eyes as the full horror of the situation washed over him. Born a Changeling, he was subject to no one. But humans who became Changelings were in the power of the one who had bitten them, the sire. They could be found by their sire anywhere, anytime, summoned and even compelled to obey. Nature had intended it as a built-in safety feature. If you sired someone, you were responsible for them. You had to take care of them until they could control themselves—and once in a rare while you had to take control *for* them so they wouldn't hurt themselves or anybody else.

The potential for the misuse of such power wasn't a concern in most cases, since siring was usually done between mates. And the power of the sire wore off naturally with time, just as the need for it dissipated. His own mother had sired his father, and their loving relationship had now spanned centuries. Jessie had sired Bill just over a decade ago, and she wouldn't dream of so much as compelling him to take out the garbage. But Bernie was selfish at best, vicious and sadistic at worst. As a sire, he could force Zoey to do almost anything against her will. And he was no longer in control of himself. The fact that he had attacked a human being proved that.

Connor was sick at heart when he finally let himself into the guestroom, but even so, the sight of Zoey almost tugged the corners of his mouth into a smile. She was deeply asleep, her russet hair a riot of waves over the pillow. She was snoring loudly and her feet hung off the side of the bed. He set about rearranging her, easing her onto her side to quell the snoring. He kissed her forehead and gently pulled the bedding over her.

He'd like nothing more than to slip under the blankets too and hold her tightly. Instead, he settled into an armchair by the window and watched her. He'd never felt so helpless in his life.

A first Change always occurred on a full moon, although an experienced Changeling could shift at will. The light of the half moon glimmered faintly through the window and fell across the bed where Zoey lay. Connor had nineteen days at most to prepare her. *Nineteen days to win her trust, reveal my Changeling nature, break the news to her that she's going to turn into a wolf, and coach her on the upcoming experience. No problem.*

Christ.

Zoey awoke to a room ablaze with color. Vibrant sun poured in the window like a golden syrup, making every garish pink rose on the bright yellow quilt, the yellow wallpaper, and the yellow rug stand out with appalling clarity. She squinted at the spectacle, wishing she'd stopped at a couple or three or five drinks. This kind of decor could be fatal to anyone with a hangover, and she had a whopper.

She sat up on the edge of the bed with a groan, and stayed there for several moments until she was sure her brain wasn't going to burst from the change in altitude. *Eeyew.* Her tongue felt like a terrycloth towel left six weeks in a football player's locker. She needed water, aspirin, and especially a toothbrush. But in the end it was the need to pee that finally persuaded her to make a move. The en suite bathroom didn't look too far away. . . . Slowly she leaned forward to shift her weight to her legs and paused, hesitant to move further.

"Need a hand?" asked a deep male voice from the other side of the room.

Zoey jerked in surprise and swore as the jolt knifed through her brain. "What the hell are you doing in here?" she whispered fiercely. She didn't dare yell, although she certainly wanted to. She remained seated and turned— carefully—to peer at Connor through squinted eyes. "Can't a girl get a little privacy? I'm not—" She almost said she wasn't dressed but then realized she'd slept in her clothes. *Double eeyew.*

"Just watching over you while you slept. Thought that party-crashing wolf might have given you more night-mares."

"Thanks, but I've been able to sleep by myself since I was three." Aware that Connor's eyes were on her, she re-flexively tried to comb her hair with her fingers. A mis-take—even her scalp hurt! She gave up and glared at him as best she could while still keeping her eyelids shuttered against the blinding sunlit colors. Her body protested as she got to her feet only a little awkwardly, straightening her shirt as she swallowed a groan—then headed for the en suite bathroom with as much dignity as she could muster.

The bathroom turned out to be worth the trip, and not just because her bladder had been fit to burst. There was a welcome bottle of acetaminophen on the counter, a pitcher of ice water, a glass, and a brand-new toothbrush. Beside the fresh towels was a soft fleece jogging suit and a T-shirt with a note: *Thought these might fit you. Jessie.*

Zoey peeled her own clothes off gratefully, although every joint and muscle ached almost as much as her head. She didn't drink often, but she'd sure made up for it last night. Three drinks at least before Lowen showed up. She lost count of how many she'd had afterward with Devlin. She checked her injured leg and was relieved that the wounds hadn't bled through the bandages. Something to be grateful for. But Lowen had been unable to tell her why her leg had been bleeding in the first place, just suggested that maybe she hadn't been taking it easy enough. She supposed that could be true. After all, what had she done all afternoon? There'd been a fire, a big one, and she'd run around interviewing, photographing . . . She hadn't sat down for what, five hours? Six? Maybe she *did* need to take it easier. Elevate her leg, apply ice, and do everything that Connor had initially told her to do days ago and Lowen had reiterated last night.

Connor. She was still plenty annoyed that he'd ditched her the night before. Sure, Devlin said he'd gone after the wolf, but couldn't the man have said something? Was he going to act weird every time they became intimate? Maybe it was the hangover, but she felt even *more* annoyed that she wanted Connor naked and as soon as possible. It just wasn't fair to be so damn attracted to somebody you were trying to be mad at.

The shower did a lot to revive her. It was awkward trying to keep her leg out of the shower stall—or at least out of the stream of water—but she managed it. Mostly. She took her time drying her hair, aware that Connor was likely waiting for her, and she was determined to make him wait as long as possible. By the time she was ready to pull on the clothes Jessie had left, she was a lot less stiff—although she was grateful the clothes were soft and pliable. The heather gray of the knit pants and jacket was pleasantly neutral, while the red T-shirt loaned her complexion a little needed color. She surveyed her image in the mirror and decided that she no longer looked as bad as she felt, which was more than she'd hoped for.

She walked out and saw Connor looking out the window, and her eyes automatically took in his masculine backside. Appreciatively. Too appreciatively. Her insides clenched and she averted her gaze at once. She needed to clear the air between them, dammit, and buzzing hormones would only distract her.

"You took off on me," she said.

He turned around slowly. "Culley and I followed the wolf."

"Nuh-uh. You took off *before* it howled. You ditched me without a word and took off."

"I knew the animal was there long before it made a sound. I made certain you were all right and then my brother and I went after the wolf."

The words got through this time. Her eyes were wide open now, despite the way the light stabbed into them. "Wolves," she corrected. "There were two of them."

"Right, *wolves*," he amended. "I guess I was more focused on the one that attacked you, the one that was about to attack you again."

"The silver and black one was chasing it," she persisted. "Didn't you follow it too?"

"We followed the gray one."

That seemed more than a little strange to her. The new wolf had seemed intent on tearing apart the gray one. Why would it change its mind and leave once it was on the other side of the fence? She changed her line of questioning. "So you were what, trying to catch it?"

"We were trying to track it. We had the wolf in sight, followed it all the way out to the golf course. And then we lost it."

She could see more than frustration in his face. His eyes were storm-dark with fury. Anger again, she thought. His brother, Devlin, had been angry last night too. And Zoey hadn't needed her unpredictable psychic abilities to tell her that Jessie would like nothing better than to get her hands on someone or something. Yet all of them had been genuinely pleasant, even smiling. Nothing but concern was directed at her. The white-hot temper lurking beneath their friendly faces was all for the wolf. Why? It didn't fit, it just didn't seem like the right reaction to her. *Who gets mad at a wild animal?*

"So it's definitely the same wolf, the one that bit me?" she asked Connor.

He nodded curtly.

"And now there's another one. How many goddamn wolves are wandering the streets of Dunvegan?" *How long before someone else gets attacked?* The thought made her ill. "This is all my fault. I should have stuck with the truth and told readers about the wolf in the first place. I shouldn't have let the authorities pass it off. I should have yelled and screamed and beat on the police station desk until somebody listened to me." She closed her eyes for a moment and opened them when strong arms slipped around her.

"You've already warned people," said Connor, gently pulling her close.

"I didn't tell them it was a goddamn wolf!" Why had she been so careful?

"No, you didn't. Instead, you warned them in such a way that they'd be watchful without being panicked. Or skeptical." He tipped her chin up so she had to look at him. "Nothing would have happened differently if you'd called the animal a wolf instead of a dog in your article. Being more insistent with the cops or the game officials or the dogcatcher wouldn't have done any good either, just gotten you written off as crazy or hysterical.

"Besides, now the authorities know you were right. They know it's a wolf. Fitz was at the party last night."

"Sergeant Fitzpatrick?"

"He's out hunting for the wolf right now. So are Culley, Devlin, and several of our friends. Trust me, they'll find it."

She could read the truth in his face. And she did trust him, even though she wasn't even close to satisfied with his reason for leaving her so abruptly the night before. Zoey sighed and rested her face—albeit gingerly—against Connor's broad chest. "It's too damned early and I'm too hungover to be having this conversation. My brain hurts. I can't think straight. I can't even decide how pissed off I am at you for ditching me."

"I didn't ditch you. I was trying to protect you from the wolf."

"By leaving me? I ended up facing the wolf all by myself."

"The other wolf was there." His voice sounded odd. Strained. "You weren't alone."

"Right. Lucky for me that another wolf wanted dibs on eating me."

"It wasn't going to—" He broke off and sighed. "Look, I need to talk to you. It's important, Zoey. Meet me at the clinic later?"

"Maybe." She could barely picture walking outdoors

into the bright sunshine, never mind driving out to the clinic. "That's the best I can give you. I feel like crap."

"I know. I'd like to give you more time, but I've got to talk to you, tell you some things. Why don't you come out to my place around seven? I've got a great hammock under some shady trees, and you can just relax while I make you some dinner. Barring a five-alarm emergency, I'll be there." He paused and added, "Please."

"All right," she said at last. It still sounded ambitious, but at least there was a chance she'd feel more alive by then.

"I'll draw out directions and leave them with Jessie." He kissed the top of her head and left.

Chapter Fifteen

Zoey contemplated writing an article on the life-giving properties of a hot shower. Her head still hurt but she felt considerably revived as she wandered out of the room and found the kitchen. Fletcher padded over to greet her, his tail wagging steadily. "I'm glad to see you're feeling more like yourself today," she said as she buried her hand in the dog's thick yellow fur.

"Looks like you're feeling more like yourself, too, girl." Jessie came in the back door with an armful of herbs from her garden. "Bill said to go on over for breakfast if you had a mind to. He's doing the early shift at the diner this morning. Are you hungry?"

"Not yet, thanks, maybe later. I do want to thank you for letting me sleep over, though. Appreciate the clothes too."

"Thanks for not screaming when you woke up. Bill's mum used to live with us, and she had a thing for cabbage roses and bright colors."

"Especially yellow."

"Definitely yellow. That bedroom practically glows in the dark. Ada's been gone six years now, and I keep meaning to redecorate that room because it hurts my eyes, but Bill doesn't want me to. Now and then he sits in there for a while. I think he feels close to her amid all that, all that—"

"Splendor?"

"That's one word for it. How's your arm feel this morning?"

Zoey snorted. "I have an arm? Everything else hurts so much today, I can't tell. I intended to drink, but I don't usually drink so darn much."

"It was likely because you were with Devlin. I'm sure he showed off his bartending abilities to the max."

"I remember him putting some pretty exotic mixes in front of me." Zoey rubbed her head. "At least I remember *some* of them."

"He gets carried away demonstrating all his latest concoctions. I should have warned you." Jessie chuckled as she poured coffee for both of them. "Connor gave me an earful about it this morning, I can tell you."

"He has no right—"

"He cares about you and just like a man, he figures that gives him every right."

"I know he cares about me, but the way he disappeared last night was a pretty weird way of showing it." Zoey sipped her coffee and nearly whimpered with the welcome pleasure of it.

"He wanted the wolf stopped. We all do. It's dangerous if it's going to keep coming into town. You already know how dangerous it is."

"Connor *said* he left me so he could protect me. But—" But he had left her in the middle of some pretty passionate making out. Walked away without a word. What the hell was protective about that? "Look, Jessie, I'm having real trouble with this. He took off before the wolf howled, you know. Before Fletcher started barking, before anyone knew there was something wrong, yet he claims he already knew the wolf was there."

Jessie leaned back against the counter and looked at Zoey over folded arms. "Is that really so strange? You have gifts of your own."

"What?"

"G-I-F-T-S. *As in* abilities that are out of the ordinary, abilities that few others have. For instance, you know when things are going to happen, you see things that are hidden."

Zoey froze, unable to think of a thing to say. How on earth did Jessie know?

Her friend put her hands up. "Relax, girl. Your secret's perfectly safe with me. I have my own little talents. Like often recognizes like, don't you think?"

It was something that her mother had often said, but Zoey hadn't experienced it before. She wasn't sure she was experiencing it now—her so-called gift was offering no particular intuition at the moment. She sighed, both at the seeming flakiness of her ability and also because there was no point in denying the truth to Jessie. "Okay, I have a little bit of psychic ability. But it's totally unreliable."

"Well, Connor has some gifts too. And they're *very* reliable. That's how he sensed the wolf was there before anyone else did. He senses a lot of things. It makes him a damn fine vet for instance. You'll hear a lot of people tell you he has an uncanny way with animals. He knows what they're feeling, communicates with them."

Connor was psychic? Zoey could hardly believe her ears. "He never said anything about it."

"You haven't had much time together to share things like that. Have you told him about *your* little hobby yet?"

"Well, no, not yet. There hasn't—"

"There hasn't been an opportunity," finished Jessie. "And you probably don't share something like that with just anyone."

There was an understatement. She'd spent most of her life deliberately *not* sharing it with anybody. Trying to ignore her abilities. Trying to be normal. Trying to outrun the names she'd been called as a young teen. *The Weird Kid. Creepy Girl. Freakazoid.* All undeserved because she'd worked so hard not to stand out in any way. But it had been impossible—everyone in the frickin' free world seemed to have heard about her psychic family.

Zoey downed the rest of her coffee in silence and thought of the career she'd left behind in Vancouver. Thought of her present publisher, Ted. Sharing any mention of her ability with him would likely get her fired on the spot. She supposed she could keep that in mind if she ever really wanted out of her job in a hurry. She glanced up as Jessie leaned over and refilled her cup, then set a plate of toasted bagels on the table and sat down.

"Sorry to be so pushy. But I couldn't let you think badly of Connor. True, like a typical male, he thought he was being protective by leaving when you no doubt felt he ought to have stayed with you. But even *his* ability couldn't tell him what the wolf was going to do. All of us were surprised by what happened."

Zoey nodded but something still bothered her. "Hasn't anybody else noticed that the wolf population has doubled? I mean, do we have a whole damn pack roaming the streets when the sun goes down?"

Jessie stirred her coffee for some moments before replying. "Yes, there were two wolves, and believe me, I'm not happy that the pair of them ran right through the middle of my party. Because of the talents that I have, however, I know that the only wolf to worry about is the gray one. The other was there to protect you."

What? "You're kidding, right? I thought it was competing for drumstick rights."

"Trust me when I say that it was there for one reason only, and that was to defend you."

"Why on earth would a *wolf* want to protect me?"

"I'll leave it to Connor to explain that one." Jessie smiled, and pushed the plate of bagels toward her. "He knows a lot more about it."

"Because he's a vet?"

"Sort of. Ask him."

"You bet I will." Zoey added it to her mental list.

"You like him, don't you?"

"I like him a *lot*, but I don't know him very well yet." She hoped she wasn't blushing. She'd wanted to know every inch of him last night. Still did.

"Well then, as a friend, I should list all of Connor's virtues for you. He's compassionate and caring, honest as the day is long, and a heck of a lot of fun. And he's a big, strong, good-looking man, sure to get a gal's blood going. But you already know that," she added with a grin.

Zoey did blush then. "You saw, didn't you?"

"I may have noticed the pair of you waltzing off to a more private venue. But I was more than glad to see it. Connor's been alone for a long, long time. He needs something else in his life besides his work. Some*one*. And so do you, I think. Maybe that's why you're here."

She snorted. "It wasn't fate that brought me here, Jess. I had to get away from the city. I needed to get away from the violence, the crime, the politics. Everything."

"Makes sense to me. You only have man-eating wolves to deal with here."

"Right. Piece of cake compared to the city."

Jessie chuckled and stirred her tea. "That may well be. But I hear you left a successful career behind."

"I did," sighed Zoey. "That little gift we talked about? It's become more pronounced in recent years. I mean, it still comes and goes when it damn well pleases, which pisses me off. I wish it would either be useful or go away and just let me be normal. Still, when the gift decides to show me something, it's for real." *Usually.* Seeing a wolf in Connor's face had been just too weird for words.

"You distinguished yourself as a journalist. Surely psychic talent would come in handy in that line of work."

"I'll concede it was handy at first. But then I started arriving earlier and earlier to the scenes of accidents, murders, robberies. Never soon enough to stop anything, help anyone. Just always the first to break the story."

"I see. And that got to you after a while."

"God, *yes.* I wanted so much to prevent those things, but this stupid ability doesn't seem to work that way. I broke the story on some city scandals too, corruption by elected officials, stuff like that. My peers figured I had inside sources in the police department and in local government, feeding me information. Every reporter cultivates sources, but I guess they saw it as some sort of unfair advantage. They quit talking to me after a while."

"Sounds pretty lonely. And you couldn't explain, either."

"How could I tell them that I had seen a picture in my head? Or had a dream? And the information was seldom complete. Usually I just received clues—I'd see a building, a face, an item, a document. Or I'd know if someone I was interviewing was lying, or what they were really thinking and feeling. Most of the time, I still had to put the puzzle pieces together myself." Zoey shook her head. "My boss was furious that I wouldn't tell him who was giving me information, but he didn't dare fire me. He couldn't risk losing me to another publication."

"So there must have been a final straw, something to make you leave on your own."

"I just—" Without any warning, the memory burst into Zoey's mind, full-blown and raw. The wail of approaching sirens seared her consciousness as the sounds of traffic surged around her like the ocean. Screams and sobs emerged from the crowd that still hung back in shock and her own throat closed on a gasp. *Omigod, it's a child.*

A little boy of about eight years old lay crumpled on the pavement beside his bike. The pool of blood had trickled over the curb like a tiny cherry waterfall. His eyes were open, beautiful blue eyes with long lashes, doll's eyes. *Jerrod Matthew Copeland, the youngest victim of a gang-related shooting . . .*

"Zoey? Are you okay?"

She shook her head and came back to herself. "Sorry, Jess. Some things are still a little too fresh." She swiped the angry tears from her eyes with the back of her sleeve before they spilled over. "I just don't understand. What's the goddamn *point* of being psychic if you can't stop horrible things from happening?"

"Maybe there isn't a point, hon," said Jessie, handing her a napkin.

"What?"

"Think about it. Maybe there isn't supposed to be a point to being psychic anymore than there's a point to being freckled. It just *is*. It's just part of you."

"Well, it's a part I'd like surgically removed." Still, she'd never thought about her psychic ability in such simple terms. She'd always assumed it must—or should—have some greater purpose. Did it make it better or worse if it didn't? "Anyway, I decided to go somewhere where horrible things don't usually happen. Somewhere small where the crime rate is low, and my so-called gift can't show me things I'd rather not see. I thought maybe it would, I don't know, *go into remission* or something. I've never wanted to have it—I just wanted to leave it behind."

Jessie nodded. "What you have is not a comfortable gift. TV shows glamorize psychic ability, but it's not that much fun to live with. However"—she put her hand on Zoey's arm—"you're talking about it like it's a disease or a curse. To deny your gift is to deny your very self. It forces you to live out of harmony.

"Even in the middle of our peaceful little community, I doubt that you'll find much peace until you can discover a way to accept this part of yourself and who you really are."

"I don't know if I want to. Accept it, I mean."

"It's your choice, always. But strength comes out of wholeness. And when you truly need your strength, all of your strength, you'll need to draw on your whole self. Including those gifts you wish you didn't have."

Bernie's cabin was deserted. Connor had driven there with Culley right after leaving Zoey. The scent in the small gray building told them its owner hadn't been there for several days.

They searched the outbuildings and the barns but found no trace of their quarry. Finally, Connor spotted something in the trickling streambed a hundred yards from the house. A few prints in the mud. Lupine. Two toes missing on the left hind foot cinched the identification. Bernie had lost them to a trap a few years ago. The Changeling ability to heal declined with extreme age—hence the scars on his face—but even in a Changeling's prime, the regeneration of limbs was rare.

"About time we found something," said Culley as he glanced around quickly, instinctively making sure they were alone. A moment later, a pair of massive wolves trotted upstream, one black, the other silver with a blanket of black. Their noses to the ground, they followed the stream until it disappeared into the woods beyond.

Hours later, the brothers gave up and headed back to town. The trail was cold and they hadn't happened across anything fresher. Not a print, not a hair, nothing.

"He's obviously got a new hideout somewhere," said Culley. "I don't think he's coming back to his house again, not now that he's revealed he can still Change. Now that you know the silver was fake the first time, he knows you'll be coming after him with the real thing."

"We need to check on that."

At the North Star Animal Clinic, Culley and Connor inspected the pharmacy shelves. The brown glass jug of silver nitrate was in place, but the contents proved as disappointing as that of the little bottle in Connor's pocket. The tall vet realized that there was something else wrong.

"This is the very same jug with the very same silver nitrate that nearly burned a hole through my finger. See that spot of dye splashed on the label? I dropped a slide I was preparing and splattered everything on the counter with blue stain, including this container."

"So it wasn't any mistake at the factory then. Someone's deliberately filled the jug with water right here in your clinic," Culley pointed out. "One of your assistants? Most of them haven't been with you long."

Connor shook his head. "No, this has got to be Bernie's work—I threatened him with the silver nitrate after he ran amok and took down a dozen heifers from Ralph Wharton's herd. Maybe he was making a preemptive strike so he wouldn't get injected with silver, so he could still Change."

"I can see the logic, but not the method. There's no way Bernie could get in here without you catching his scent the next day. Hell, if he'd so much as set a toe on the property, Birkie would have known and turned him into a goldfish or some damn thing."

That was true enough. She wasn't a Changeling but her command of magic went far beyond even Jessie's. Even Connor's own father, Ronan, couldn't compete with Birkie Peterson. But Birkie was in Scotland, had been there since . . .

Connor went to Birkie's desk and searched through piles of papers. His young assistants had been taking turns handling the reception duties, but they hadn't kept up on the filing. Finally he found an invoice from AgriPharm. The veterinary pharmaceutical company came regularly to restock the clinic.

"They were here two weeks before the attack on Zoey. But Dave Anderson is the representative who makes the rounds, and this isn't his signature." He closed his eyes and brought the paper close to his face. He could scent the young woman who had held the paper—Joanne. But the other scent was male, and a mystery. "I don't recognize this guy."

"You weren't here?"

"No. I was on a farm call. One of the assistants signed off on it. She'd have no way of knowing that anything was wrong."

"So maybe Bernie paid someone to get rid of the silver nitrate? Who would he know? Nobody in town would do it for him, and I can't see him setting up something with an

AgriPharm rep on his own. I mean, that would take some real research and planning, wouldn't it? And probably a lot of money—you'd have to bribe somebody. Bernie might have the funds but not the connections."

"No, nobody in town would do it . . . so we're looking for somebody who *doesn't* live around here."

"And right now, the only stranger in town is that goddamn reporter who attacked Zoey."

"Helfren," spat Connor. "I don't know his scent, but it has to be him. Still, I don't understand why the guy would stick his neck out. Why go to all the trouble to get rid of some silver nitrate? And how would Bernie get him to do it—I mean, what kind of reason would he give him? Silver nitrate is pretty harmless stuff for humans."

"*Why* is easy enough—Helfren gets a story. He's already shown us he'll go to extremes when he put his hands on Zoey." Culley looked around. "Maybe he didn't get rid of the stuff at all. What if Bernie told him exactly what you were . . . wouldn't Helfren's next step be to try and prove it?"

A sudden chill went down Connor's spine as the realization dawned. *A waterlike substance could be hidden anywhere there was water.* The two men split up and moved slowly through the clinic, checking everything from the water cooler in the waiting room to the emergency eyewash station in the X-ray lab.

Culley found it first. A small water cooler stood empty in the corner of Connor's office. It was safe, but there was a tall refill bottle on the floor beside it. Carefully Culley opened the lid and touched the rim. Instantly his fingertip was on fire. "Dammit to hell! Right here waiting to poison you. You'd have been throwing up blood for weeks."

Connor suppressed a shudder. The effect of certain substances all depended on how you used them. Rubbing alcohol had been commonly used for decades to swab skin before a medical procedure. It didn't hurt. But the very same substance in the membranes of the eye or the nose was excruciating, even damaging.

Silver nitrate burned the skin of a Changeling, any skin that would produce fur during the Change. The substance produced no such sensation on the mouth or tongue, just as it produced no discernable sensation when injected into a vein. An injection of silver nitrate prevented the Change, with little other effect. But silver in the digestive system of a Changeling was a different story. . . .

Thank God he'd been far too busy in Birkie's absence to refill the damn cooler. He often came in hot and thirsty from surgery, from farm calls, from the clinic corrals. He likely would have filled up his water bottle and downed it before the taste registered. Agony would have followed rapidly. If he survived the internal bleeding, recovery would have taken many months. "Bernie would have gotten his revenge," he said grimly.

"And what would Helfren get?"

Connor frowned. What did any reporter want except a story and—

In an instant, Connor was on top of his desk ripping the grating from the heating duct. A moment later he tossed a handful of fine wire and a tiny silver box to his brother.

"There's what Helfren wants, Culley," he said, his voice hard and cold. "Live footage."

Chapter Sixteen

Shadows were long as the gravel road became dirt. Grass grew between the ruts. Zoey consulted the hand-drawn map on the seat beside her and hoped she was headed in the right direction. *Connor never mentioned anything about a damn goat path.* She'd attempted to nap twice, alternated drinking coffee and water all day long, and tried several headache remedies, but she still felt hungover. Her nerves were on edge as well—she'd been jumpy and distracted, and it had been an uphill climb to get even the simplest things done. Several times she'd come close to calling Connor to cancel, but although she couldn't imagine what he had to tell her, he had said it was *important.* Well, she sure wasn't going to dress up. At the last possible moment, she'd thrown on comfortable jeans and a soft cami, topped with a plaid flannel blouse, and forced herself to get in her truck.

Just as she was certain she must have taken the wrong road, she was relieved to see a mailbox with *Macleod* on the side, and turned in. A long tree-lined lane opened out to a pleasant farmyard, and she parked her old red Bronco behind Connor's clinic truck. "Will you look at this place? It's gorgeous!" She emerged from her vehicle slowly, trying to take in everything at once. The tall two-story house was freshly painted white with simple black trim. Overgrown gardens sporting tall irises and lilies fronted the shaded porch and flanked the steps.

Her publisher had warned her that his cousin's farm had been rundown when Connor bought it. To the south, she counted several weathered farm buildings. They were old and tired-looking, and a couple were definitely leaning. The red paint had flaked away from the weatherworn wood, and every roof was missing shingles. The fences weren't in much better shape, mismatched, propped up and no doubt held together by baling wire in spots. Yet everything was clean. There were no rusting equipment or abandoned cars, no stacks of junk and old tires. And the place didn't have that barren look typical of many farmyards. Thick stands of trees flanked the old buildings and dotted the corrals, offering inviting shade.

The quaint old place had character, she decided. She liked it.

Something strange was bothering her ears and suddenly she realized it was *quiet*. Perfect quiet. Only a soft susurrus came from the surrounding poplar trees as a faint breeze fondled the coin-shaped leaves. She sighed a little as peace wrapped itself around her. She breathed deeply, taking in the cool air and then held it—something huge and dark was moving between the buildings, gliding from tree stand to bush. The furtive movement reminded her all too much of the creature that had attacked her. Straining to see, Zoey could just make out some black fur and the waving plume of a black tail tipped with white as it disappeared around a building. With her heart in her throat, she hoped like crazy it was simply the giant dog that had been in Connor's office and not the massive wolf that had stood over her. . . . Suddenly strong arms wrapped around her from behind.

She nearly jumped out of her skin and the jolt made her head hurt. "Geez, Connor!"

He chuckled as she turned in his arms. Zoey shoved at him, but to no avail. He wasn't holding her tightly, but she was securely caged nonetheless. Since resistance was futile, she changed tactics, stepping into him and sliding her arms around his neck, tipping up her face just so. As she'd sensed, he didn't resist the invitation and bent his head to kiss her.

She bit his chin, hard.

"Ow!" He released her at once and held a hand to his face. "What the hell was that for?"

"Scaring me. And maybe for ditching me last night too, I'm not sure."

"Still hungover, are we?"

"Very."

Connor held out a hand. "I can make you feel a whole lot better. I've got a couple of great remedies."

She eyed him suspiciously, but sensed he was sincere. She gave in and took his hand, allowed him to lead her up the wide steps to the porch.

"I did try to make things easier for you, you know."

"How?" she asked.

"I told the welcoming committee to lie low. I figured they'd be a little overwhelming and probably much too loud. They get pretty excited around new people."

The welcoming committee . . . "You mean, dogs?" He looked at her and she grinned sheepishly. "What am I saying? Of course you have dogs. Every farm has dogs, and a vet with a farm probably has, oh, at least four. Maybe even five," she guessed, relieved and unable to stop blathering. He had dogs, lots of dogs. So there couldn't *possibly* be a wolf on the premises. "I just saw a dog in fact. I think it was that big black one from your office."

For a split second he looked surprised. "Right. Well, he's sort of new so I guess he didn't quite get the instructions. That's what comes of having so many dogs. There are fifteen or sixteen of them around here now."

Her eyes widened. She liked dogs but being greeted by an entire army of excited canines wasn't on her list of things to do. "Thanks for giving them something else to do. I guess I'm sorry I bit you," she added.

"That doesn't sound real convincing, but I'm definitely sorry I scared you." He tapped his chin thoughtfully. "You know, you could kiss it better."

"Maybe it'd be safer after the remedies you promised."

"Good point. Later then—but mind you, I *will* collect." Connor grinned and opened the door for her.

The interior of the sprawling old home had been renovated extensively, leaving it open and airy in design. It was more like an upscale lodge, with lots of wood and natural elements. The stone fireplace and large beams in the ceiling lent an earthiness that was relaxing and comfortable. Connor's house is just like him, Zoey realized. This was how she felt when she was around him. Grounded. Centered.

He motioned her to a plump armchair in front of the fireplace. "Relax for a minute and put your feet up. I'll get you something for that head."

She sank into immediate bliss and lay back with her eyes closed. The busy sounds from the kitchen barely registered and the next thing she knew, she was waking up to find that daylight had nearly become twilight.

"I have *got* to get one of these chairs," she murmured.

Connor appeared from the kitchen. "Great, aren't they?"

"How long was I out?"

"A little over an hour. You needed it. And I think you still need this." He handed her a glass of green liquid, and chuckled as she eyed it dubiously. "It's safe, I promise. It's one of Birkie's all-natural herbal elixirs and it's a terrific restorative."

Despite the unexpected nap, she had little doubt she could use some restoring. "I sure hope it regrows brain cells."

"If anything can, this'll do it."

Most hangover remedies tasted horrible, but this didn't smell bad. She sipped cautiously, played with it on her tongue, then drank it down. She could swear every cell in her body was suddenly reaching out for more. "Wow. Is there seconds of this stuff?"

"There can be. Let that settle, and I'll give you a short tour, get you some fresh air while dinner's in the oven."

The sun was skimming the horizon as they strolled hand in hand around the farmyard. Connor introduced Zoey to a variety of animals, both large and small, including the sixteen-dog welcoming committee he'd diverted earlier. They were calm and well-behaved but it was still a joy to watch her laugh and try to pet them all. Her interest in the other livestock was just as genuine, and she didn't hesitate to accept his invitation to scratch a three-hundred-pound pig behind the ears. She did hesitate at the next paddock, however, which contained a long-haired Highland bull with a great sweep of horns, but when Connor walked inside, she followed.

"This is Magnus, one of our herd sires." He rubbed the bull's brow, hidden beneath a heavy fringe of hair. Zoey reached out and touched the broad forehead tentatively.

"He looks like a leftover from the last Ice Age." The bull snorted. "No offense," she added hastily.

Connor chuckled. "Highland cattle are tough and hardy, perfect for our northern Canadian winters. Not only are they dressed for the weather, they're good at digging through the snow for forage—a lot of modern breeds have forgotten how to do that. Highlands will fight off predators too."

"Like wolves?"

"Like wolves." Ordinary ones at least.

No sooner had they left the bull's paddock than a wildly spotted horse came trotting over to them, putting his head under Connor's hands like a big dog asking to be petted.

Zoey laughed. "Looks like you've had a jailbreak."

"This is Charlie, and he's very good at opening gates. As you can see by his markings, he's an Appaloosa. He has a fancy pedigree that goes all the way back to the Nez Pierce tribe in the nineteenth century."

"You're pretty smart," Zoey murmured to the horse as she rubbed its speckled neck. "And really handsome too."

"He's certainly a looker. Charlie was born with a perfect coat, a beautiful head. Prettiest foal I ever delivered and could have been a champion in the show ring, except for a malformation of the front legs. They bow out quite badly, see?" Connor bent and ran his hands over the horse's legs, while the animal nuzzled the back of his head. He laughed and straightened up, rubbing his hand around the animal's ears. "As you've probably noticed, he's a glutton for attention."

"So you kept him?"

"The foal was breech and stuck in the birth canal when the owners called me in. It turned into a long night. The mare came through it fine, but the owners couldn't be bothered with the little guy after they saw his legs. They wanted him put down, so I traded them even. Tore up the bill in return for the foal."

"So now you have another horse. I've seen eleven so far. And twenty-some goats, a couple dozen mismatched sheep and some pigs, numberless cats, and sixteen dogs. You must rescue *everything*."

He smiled, a little sadly. "Not all—I'd be overrun in a week—but I do seem to bring home quite a few. Most I can find homes for, and those I can't find a place for just stay here."

Zoey shook her head. "That's a lot of extra work. You spend all those hours at the clinic and on call, then you have to come home and feed all these animals."

"I enjoy doing it when I can. It's kind of refreshing to hang out with healthy animals for a change. But lucky for these animals, Jim Neely looks after them, so they don't have to wait around for me to get home. And when Jim can't do it, one of my sibs does. Kenzie's been here lately, working on a book, so she spends quite a bit of time with the animals."

"That's your sister, right? The one who's in Scotland just now? I didn't know she's a writer."

"Actually she's an archaeologist, and she's away on digs more than she gets to be here. Although she says it's only because Jim's here that she dares leave at all. Most of my family have misgivings about a farm being in my black-thumbed hands."

"And Jim is your hired man?"

Connor laughed a little at that. *More like an* acquired *man.* Old Jim had been homeless, as much in need of a rescue as any of the animals. A small man with three missing fingers, he had spent most of his time drinking and getting into fights. But Connor had discovered by accident that Jim had a natural gift when it came to animals, and eventually persuaded him to move to the farm about four years ago. It had saved Jim, and in turn, Jim was a godsend to Connor. The old man blossomed, taking his responsibilities seriously and keeping the livestock end of the farm running smoothly.

"You could say that. I do pay him, but he's more of a friend than anything. He lives in a cabin on the other side of that far stable." He pointed. "Jim's at a cattle auction today, so I said I'd feed the troops."

"So can I help?"

"Next time. I already took care of that while you were snoring."

"I do *not* snore!"

He rolled his eyes. "That's what they all say." He laughed when she drilled his shoulder. "Keep that up and I won't give you Phase Two of your hangover treatment."

"Do I get another glass of that green stuff?"

"That was Phase One. Phase Two is PT, and I'll bet it'll be even more effective."

He could tell she was trying to resist asking, but finally she threw up her hands. "Okay, I give up, what's PT?"

"Puppy Therapy."

"Puppies? You've got even *more* dogs stashed somewhere? Oh!" She remembered the puppies. "Where is he? I want to see my puppy."

"Maybe we should eat first—" He turned as if heading for the house.

She grabbed Connor's hand with both of hers and dug in her heels. "My puppy. Now."

He laughed and threw an arm around her, gathering her to him so effortlessly that she might as well have been weightless. She squirmed but there was no escaping. He nibbled at the corners of her mouth. "Puppy," she murmured against his lips just before they took hers over. The kiss was long and deep, but still just a kiss—yet her nipples hardened almost to the point of pain, and her thong was suddenly soaked. The want, the desire for this man, pulsed raw and urgent within her.

She drew a long shaky breath and stepped back, and was both grateful and disappointed that he let her. He kept hold of her hand, however, and rubbed his thumb over it as he led her past several corrals and outbuildings toward an old barn that stood apart. Its hipped roof sported new metal cladding and the walls were neatly painted, yet the feeling of extreme age remained. Zoey figured the building was more than twice as old as she was. Maybe even three times . . .

"I have to announce our presence," warned Connor. He began to scuff his feet, then whistle, as they approached the barn. "Lila is a little protective for the first few minutes."

"You found a mother for the puppies?"

"Lila's one of the best surrogate moms around."

Zoey was about to ask questions when something enormous, dark, and shaggy appeared in the doorway. "A *bear*? Jesus, Connor, you gave the puppies to a *bear*?" Her grip on his hand tightened as she backed up several steps.

He burst out laughing. "I guess she does look like a bear, especially in the dark. Lila, come here and meet Zoey."

"But—" Zoey froze as the creature marched over. It was even bigger up close, and its broad head was level with her waist. It snorted loudly as it smelled her up and down with a wide black muzzle. Suddenly a huge tail emerged from the shaggy shape and began to wag. "Omigod, it *is* a dog!"

"Newfoundland. An old breed, specifically developed to

protect children and save people from drowning." Connor waggled his fingers and Lila went to him at once. "Here, pet her," he called to Zoey. "Lila's a great mom. She's fostered dozens of orphans over the years, even litters of kittens and a couple of piglets."

Zoey reached out tentatively and ran her fingers through the thick reddish-black fur in wonder. "It's so soft—and there's so much of it!"

"Don't be fooled, there's a lot of dog under it too. Lila's big, even for her breed. She weighs better than a couple hundred pounds, so don't let her lean on you."

Suddenly the high-pitched whine of puppies could be heard. The dog chuffed once and trotted into the barn.

"See?" said Connor, flipping on a light switch beside the door. "She's always on the job."

They followed the big dog and found her lying on her side as several puppies clambered their way to her teats. There were five big balls of fuzz—baby Newfs, Zoey assumed—and between them wriggled four small boxer pups, their white markings standing out in stark contrast to the ocean of black fur that surrounded them. Connor knelt beside the group and held out a hand for Zoey, pulling her down with him.

"They've grown!"

"The pups were small to start with but I think they've caught up nicely. Even yours isn't much of a runt anymore."

"He's not a runt!" she retorted. And he wasn't. Three of the pups were chestnut with white feet and white faces. Her puppy had those white markings too but the rest of his coat was dark and uniquely striped. *Brindle*, Connor had explained. She remembered the feel of the pup in her hands, so tiny as she tried to get him to breathe. . . . Now he was plump, almost roly-poly and every bit as big as his three boxer littermates. "He's gorgeous."

She couldn't help being glad, however, that he'd never grow as big as the Newf puppies would become. It would be too much like having a pony in her apartment.

"You got a gorgeous name for him yet?"

"No," she chuckled. "And it won't be a silly name either. I just haven't had time to think about it yet. When can I take him home?"

"Ideally, he needs about five more weeks, maybe six. We want him to get a good start. But he needs to be socialized, so I'd encourage you to visit a lot."

"I'd like to pick him up but he's busy eating."

"He's going to chow down a little longer and then he's going to fall asleep. Maybe we'll come back later, after we have our own dinner. It should be ready now."

"Okay." She trailed her fingers over his fuzzy little body. He was so warm, so soft. She jumped as Lila's wide black nose bumped her hand suddenly.

"She's just making sure you're being gentle enough," laughed Connor.

"I guess I don't have to worry about him with Lila on the job!"

"Not a bit."

Connor's arm was around her shoulders as they walked back to the house. When her heart began racing, she slid away and held his hand instead. The little extra distance didn't help much. She was finding it impossible to be close to this man and not want him. Any moment, she was in danger of drooling.

She almost did drool when he opened the front door but it was a reaction to the savory aroma that met them. Her stomach growled, and she was grateful for the distraction as she followed Connor to the kitchen, to the table set in a spacious breakfast nook. The bay window overlooked the back of the property, where the land sloped away to a river that ran silver beneath the twilight sky. The hills beyond had turned to dark blue and purple, while above them, the evening star seemed impossibly bright. "It's beautiful," she breathed.

"It is, isn't it? You can see why the dining room doesn't get used much." He lit a trio of votive candles on the table and switched off the overhead light. "You can see it better this way. I've got the same view upstairs too, from my bedroom balcony."

His bedroom . . . a tiny thrill shivered through her and her mouth went dry. She definitely wanted to see *that* room, and it was strangely irritating that she wanted it so much. The hangover made everything irritating, of course, but the nap and the elixir had taken the raw edge off that. Nope, it had to be plain old unfinished business—the business she and Connor had begun in the Watson side yard. Sure, she'd had the best orgasm of her life, but she couldn't help wanting more. Wanting it all . . . Flustered, she rubbed her hands over her face and through her hair, and tried to focus on the exquisite view, the pattern of the wood on the table, the color of the pottery dishes, anything but what she'd like to be doing with Connor Macleod.

Oven mitts in hand, Connor paused to look at Zoey, appreciating anew her thick russet hair. It wasn't tied back tonight, but fell free in soft waves that gleamed red in the candlelight. He wanted to gather it in his hands while he kissed every golden freckle on her body. She was staring out at the twilit scene, but he had the feeling she wasn't seeing it—and suddenly he caught the subtle scent of pheromones newly released. His groin tightened and the wolf within stirred restlessly, but remained at bay. He breathed a quick thanks to Jessie and the corded bracelet he now wore on his wrist. She'd made it look like simple braided hemp with scattered stone nuggets. Close inspection revealed tiny bits of fur and a wolf's tooth woven into it. A gris-gris, Jessie had called it. Whatever it was, he was damn grateful it was working. He was taking Zoey Tyler to bed tonight, come hell or high water, and his inner wolf wouldn't be able to get in the way.

He shook himself, struggling to get his mind back on food, and pulled a pair of steaming pies from the oven. Zoey jumped a little as he set them on the table, and he had the satisfaction of knowing exactly where *her* thoughts had been.

"Smells wonderful," she said.

So do you. "Before you get any notion that I can cook, this is strictly a Watson specialty," he said as he cut into one of the pies and set a slice on her plate. "Rosemary Chicken."

"Bill and Jessie do takeout?"

"Not exactly. They showed up at the clinic one day during winter calving season a few years ago and asked if I'd try the catering service they were starting. They offered to stock the fridge with meals at cost in return for getting feedback on the service. I was up to my armpits in cases and not paying enough attention, so I said *yeah, sure, fine.* As it turns out, the food was a godsend. Individual meals of every description, ready to nuke and serve."

"Perfect for a busy veterinarian."

"And his grateful assistants. Believe me, they were happy. Meanwhile, Bill and Jessie just kept stocking the fridge every week like clockwork. It was a month after calving season before I finally clued in that there was no catering service to be tested. Turns out that Birkie had given up trying to get me to eat properly, so she plotted with the Watsons to fix the problem. Worked like a charm, and the clinic fridge has been full ever since. This one too, when I'm not looking."

"Sounds like the Watsons have adopted you. Did you get to know them at the Diner?"

"Actually I met Bill when I was facedown in a muddy corral. Rob Garrick raises rodeo stock and I was getting ready to do a herd health inspection for him when his newest bull decided he didn't want me in the corral. Knocked me down without any warning." The bull, a 2,200-pound spotted monster with long curved horns, had been utterly unstable.

"My God, were you hurt?"

"He hit me pretty hard. For the first couple of moments I just lay there stunned," explained Connor. "Then this red-haired giant jumped the fence, hollering and swinging a shovel like an avenging angel with a sword. Hauled my sorry butt out of there. Probably saved my life."

In truth, if the massive animal had attacked him again, death wouldn't have been the worst outcome. Having his life in imminent danger would have triggered Connor's powerful survival instincts. He would have Changed to wolf form right there in broad daylight for anyone to see.

"Anyway, Bill drove me to the clinic, where Lowen told me I had a broken shoulder and five cracked ribs."

"Ouch. So you guys have been friends ever since?"

"Ever since we barbecued that miserable animal." And discovered they shared a passion for singing under a full moon. Connor had been aware of new wolves in the area for a few days. He had been delighted to discover his rescuer was one of them.

Zoey laughed. "You're kidding!"

"Really and truly. I told Rob plainly this bull would kill somebody if he took it on the circuit. He'd already had plenty of trouble with it so that was that. Both Bill and I had a freezer full of beef by the end of the week. I split mine with Lowen and Bev."

Zoey was quiet for a long moment. "Jessie tells me you can talk to animals," she said at last.

He looked at her steadily, and part of him couldn't help being captivated anew by Zoey's amber eyes. The flicker of candles brought out a golden light in them, reminding him once again of that long-ago falcon he'd treated. Fierce and beautiful. "Not in so many words. And not to that particular bull. I couldn't reach him at all. Didn't sense what he was about to do either. But usually, yes, I know what an animal feels, what it needs. Usually I can get across what I want them to do, too. Stand still, lift a paw, whatever. It comes in pretty handy in my practice. It also came in handy tonight—I told the welcoming committee to go hang out by the river until I called them."

"And they just went?"

"Sure they did. In their eyes, I'm their pack leader."

"I could certainly see that they adored you." She laid her silverware across her empty plate and sat back. "Look, I have to ask. Are you psychic? Jessie says that's how you knew the wolf was there last night before anyone heard it. Before *I* knew it was there."

"Yeah, that's right."

Her eyebrows shot up. "Just like that?"

"What do you mean?"

"You're so matter-of-fact about it. Your face, your expression—I don't know, it's like asking someone if the sky is blue. As if it were an everyday occurrence to know the future in advance."

"For some people, it is. Look at you, for instance. You know things too, see things. You saw a wolf in my face last night."

Zoey laughed at that. "That was hardly prophetic. That was just weirdness. I was bone-tired and had a drink on an empty stomach. Seeing things. That's all."

"Are you sure about that?"

"Yeah, I'm sure." She didn't sound certain at all. "Look, Jessie says your gift is really solid. But mine's flaky and seeing your face turn into a wolf just proves it. I'd been dreaming about that wolf, so it was already on my mind. Case closed."

"Uh huh. Is it my imagination or are you a teensy bit defensive about your gift?"

"I'm not—okay, I guess maybe I am. You and Jessie keep calling it a gift. My mom, her sisters, and my grandmother do too. Me, I'm not so sure." She told him what she had shared with Jessie, her fears and her frustrations. Especially the frustrations.

"So you want it to tell you things in advance, give you time to warn people, help people."

"Of course I do! What good is it if all I get to do is stand over bodies?"

"You write their stories. And you tell the truth. That's something."

"Not enough, not for me. I will *never* forget that child's face, the one killed by the drive-by—" She choked up then. And she obviously hadn't meant to say so much. Connor said nothing, just waited as she took a few breaths and cleared her throat. Her voice was much softer when she spoke again. "I don't want to just record tragedy. I don't think I can. I think it would break something in me after a while."

Connor reached across the table then and held her hand, stroking the back of it with his thumb. "Can't anyone in your family teach you how to focus your talent? I once heard psychic ability described as a radio receiver of sorts, and if that's so, perhaps you can learn to tune in to the signal."

She shook her head. "My mother, my aunts, my grandmother—none of them have a clue how to instruct in that area because they've all had their talent in spades pretty much since birth. And it's pretty hard to look for that kind of help in secret. I've always tried to keep it hidden from anyone outside of my immediate family."

"Why?"

"Are you kidding? Look, I don't know what kind of a world you grew up in, but you don't know what it was like. . . ." She rested her chin in her hand and sighed. "I'm sorry. I didn't realize how much the whole book thing still upsets me."

It was like pulling teeth, but Connor was prepared to ask questions all night if he had to. "What *book thing*?"

She took a deep breath. "My mother is Jayne Tallyson."

Connor whistled long and low. "I think I'm getting the picture now." Jayne Tallyson was a household name. The book was *Seeing with an Inner Eye*. He'd read it himself more than once, but decided he wouldn't get any points for saying so.

"It came out when I was in eighth grade and it became a bestseller."

"Did that make things hard for you?"

"People talk. Adults talk and their kids hear, and then their kids talk. My mom and Aunt Tildy were interviewed on TV. And somebody asked them if everyone in their family was psychic."

"They said *yes*," he guessed.

"They sure did. I don't think they realized what effect it would have on my life. I didn't share much of it with them for fear of hurting their feelings. But a lot of kids started pestering me to tell their fortunes—you know, tell them what they were getting for their birthday, who their boyfriend was going to be, that kind of stuff. I wouldn't do it—*couldn't* do it even if I wanted to—and they were mad. Some already disliked me because I got good grades, and they thought I cheated through my alleged psychic powers." Zoey pulled her hand away from Connor's and began toying with her napkin.

"So you caught a lot of grief over an ability you didn't even use. Sounds like high school was pretty rough."

She nodded. "Everyone talked about me—kids, teachers, neighbors, store clerks. I was kind of quiet and so they started referring to me as *The Weird Kid*. So I got even quieter. *Creepy Girl. Freakazoid.* The only time I was asked for a date in my hometown was when someone dared the guy to do it."

"Ouch. That had to hurt a lot."

"It sure does when you're a teenage girl. I applied to a college on the other side of the country, someplace where no one knew me. It was a breath of fresh air—for once, I was just like everyone else. I even made a few friends.

"Then my mother showed up on campus for a surprise visit and somebody recognized her." She shifted in her chair, stared out the window as if seeing the past before her. "My mother signed autographs for half an hour and accepted an invitation to speak at a sorority that night. I couldn't deal with it. I walked away and refused to be seen with her, but the damage was done."

"She blew your cover."

"Big time. She didn't even understand what was wrong, why I was upset. After she left, things were still okay with a couple of my friends, but others disappeared. You know, the paranormal is really trendy, but people aren't so excited about it when it turns up in their roommate or their girl-friend." She turned away from the window, and it hurt him to see so much sadness in her face. "That's when I decided to change my name. I had to. I changed my major and went to a different university."

"You didn't cut ties with them, did you?" He could understand that she might have been tempted. It had al-ways been difficult for the children of celebrities to have a life of their own, but in this century's media-frenzied cli-mate, it would be almost impossible.

"No, of course not. I phoned Mom every Sunday morn-ing like always. Still do. But I admit, the idea of not telling them where I lived crossed my mind." She laughed, but not with humor. "Only for about five minutes though. I mean, how do you hide from a family of psychics?"

"That'd be quite a challenge."

"No, the *real* challenge was making them all promise not to come see me, especially my mother. No more visits, sur-prise or otherwise. Ever. No mentioning my name in pub-lic, no showing family pictures to the media. They didn't understand then and they still don't get it. I love them but we still fight about it."

Zoey ran a hand through her hair, then put the heel of her hand to her forehead. "Good grief. I didn't mean to go on so much. It's just that it's a new experience for me to talk about this aspect of my life and not have someone think I'm strange or abnormal."

"You're not strange. Not even a teensy bit abnormal." He tried to make it sound light, but inside him sudden anger flashed like lightning toward whoever or whatever had made this vibrant woman doubt herself for an instant. "You're perfect just as you are."

Zoey took in a breath that was going to come out as a laugh—until she caught sight of Connor's face. His eyes had gone silvery, and the intensity in them had her swallowing that breath and feeling as if there suddenly wasn't enough air in the room. Maybe not in the entire atmosphere. . . .

Without warning, Connor was on his feet, and she was wrapped tight in his powerful arms. He had made love to her with his lips before, but these kisses were hard, hot and hungry, as if he desperately needed to express something he had no words for. As if he simply *needed*.

She had needs too. A bolt of pure electricity seemed to rocket through her core, ricochet crazily through her belly and zap her nipples to attention. In fact, every cell in her body was at attention and focused on this man. She needed. Now.

And this time, she was determined to *have*.

Chapter Seventeen

He was leaning into her yet Zoey didn't back up a single step. She matched his passion with her own, licked and nipped at his mouth, his tongue. Bit his chin again but lapped over it softly to ease the sting. There was no hesitation in her as her hands clawed lightly down his back, then slid around to flick open his jeans. Her fingertips circled upward, tugging apart his denim shirt. Buttons flew, but there was no pause, no uncertainty as she brushed her lips across his bare chest and gently seized a nipple in her teeth.

He froze, sucking in his breath. Her tongue played with the captive nipple, then she nuzzled her way to its mate before resuming her original mission—to get this man naked. Her hands outlined the hard muscles of his upper body, rubbed up and over his broad shoulders, then eased the shirt down his powerful arms, over the strong hands. She held the warm garment close to her face as she stepped back for a moment, instinctively drinking in the scent of him as she took in the sight. He stood perfectly still, allowing her to look.

Fully clothed, the man was sigh-worthy. Shirtless, his jeans unbuttoned and riding low on his hips, he was simply heart-stopping. The candles' glow revealed a powerful body that combined strength with an easy grace, yet she sensed that the difference between *Day Connor* and *Night Connor* went deeper than appearance. There was something dangerous here, a force barely leashed. It radiated from him, unseen yet palpable. She hesitated. . . .

And he winked.

Just that quickly he was back to the Connor she knew, his pale gray eyes amused. She laughed a little, more at herself than anything, but didn't move closer, not yet. Instead her fingertips moved to the buttons of her blouse. The amusement vanished from his face. It was his turn to watch, to look. To want.

Peeling away the plaid material, she dropped it to the floor and ran her hands over her lace-trimmed cami. There was no bra beneath it and her nipples stood out plainly. His eyes followed her fingertips as she slid first one thin strap off her shoulder, then the other—

She never saw him move. In one heartbeat, she was standing, in the next, she was tangled on the floor with Connor. He peeled away the camisole as he mouthed her throat, running his tongue and teeth over her pulse. He devoured her breasts as he shucked her jeans. She nearly came as he clutched her ass hard, his big, work-roughened hands rasping deliciously against her skin. Connor was all raw need, hungry and wild, and Zoey urged him on, the wildness thrumming in her own veins as well. All conscious thought had fallen away and what was left was basic, primal—and urgent.

She wrapped her long legs around him, pulling him into her, chanting *now* with every breath. The unyielding floor should have been uncomfortable. Instead she reveled in the way it gave her leverage, allowed her to angle her hips upward in a way that buffered nothing and accepted everything. And everything was exactly what she wanted. *Now* turned to *Yes* as he thrust hard and drove deep, shocking the breath from her as her core exulted.

Yes. The rhythm pounded in her body, in her veins, in her mind.

Yes. Tension throbbed and built, roiled and grew rapidly to impossible heights. As burgeoning clouds before a thunderstorm yearn for the lightning, her body craved the explosive release even as she feared its intensity.

Yes. Yes. YES. She imploded on a stuttered gasp, just as Connor poured himself into her. For the longest of moments she was suspended in pure sensation, unseeing save for strange sparkles of blue light behind her eyes. And for one brief second she thought she heard the howl of a wolf.

Connor's senses returned slowly. First was smell. The air was satisfyingly ripe with sex. Better still was a scent he had already memorized in every cell of his body. He pulled that scent deep into his lungs like a drowning man draws air, then released it with a soft growl. Woman scent. *His* woman. Zoey.

The candles had guttered out and twilight had given way to darkness, yet nothing was hidden from his Changeling vision. He could easily see the unique color of Zoey's hair and the golden freckles that blanketed her skin, and he couldn't be more pleased that, yes indeed, those freckles covered her shapely ass too. He'd have to make a point of counting—and kissing—every last one of them.

As his awareness expanded, there was warmth and softness along the length of his body where her skin pressed against his. Her head was pillowed on his shoulder. Closing his eyes again, he found it hard to tell where she left off and he began, as if they had melted into each other. Even their hearts beat together.

His heart was hers, permanently, and he knew it. It had been tipping and teetering since he met Zoey, but tonight his heart had just plain fallen off a cliff and might never reach bottom. That was all right with him. He could feel, too, the immense satisfaction of his inner wolf, content and peaceful now that it had found and claimed its mate at last.

Mate. He had a mate. He'd half given up hope of ever finding one. Wolves mated for life and so did Changelings. Changelings, however, lived longer than wolves, much longer than humans too. Because of that, relationships with humans were not formed lightly. There might be sex now and then with a willing partner, but the drive was infrequent. But all that changed when the inner wolf recognized its mate.

Connor nuzzled Zoey's soft hair and sighed. He hadn't intended to lose control. He'd been a more considerate lover behind the damn garden shed at the Watsons' than he'd been tonight. Still, she'd surprised him by accepting the wildness he couldn't contain, taking it in and giving back. *And then some.* He'd thought her passionate the night of the party. Now, he realized that term didn't come close to describing her.

Still, passionate or not, Zoey probably wouldn't be comfortable waking up on the kitchen floor in the dark. Connor gathered her closer to him and maneuvered until he could roll to his knees. She was a tall woman, curvy and solid. To his Changeling strength, however, she might as well have been a child, and he stood effortlessly without waking her. Instead of taking her to bed right away, however, he paused for a moment to wonder at the marvel in his arms. Two weeks ago he'd been alone and half expected to remain that way. Now he was skin to skin with this exciting woman, and she was his *mate*. It should feel strange at best, scary at worst, but instead it felt good, natural, even normal—as if she'd always been with him.

Connor crossed his fingers that Zoey felt the same as he carried her upstairs. *I've got a helluva lot to tell her.*

Connor banged his elbow twice as he tried to maneuver them both through the bedroom door, and Zoey couldn't help giggling.

"You're not asleep," he chided.

"I confess. I just wanted to be carried," she laughed. "It was pretty nice, too."

"You didn't seem to like it much when I carried you up to your apartment that first night."

"That was completely different."

She squealed as he tossed her into the middle of an enormous bed and pounced on her with mock growls and gentle bites. She tried to fend him off with both hands, squirming out from under him and finally making a break for the floor. He let her go—she knew darn well she had little hope of breaking free unless he permitted it—and she bounced over to the middle of the room.

And *what* a room. It was enormous, almost the whole of the second story. Zoey spotted a switch on the wall and flipped it, sucking in her breath at what the myriad of recessed lights revealed. Great ivory beams converged to a peak along the center of the high ceiling. A stone fireplace with a tall slender window on each side graced the east end of the room, but it was the west end that was particularly inspired. The entire wall, floor to ceiling, was made of windows.

She exhaled slowly as she let her gaze travel appreciatively over the decor. There was little in the way of furniture, but it was well chosen and natural colors prevailed. The enormous bed was near the center of the room, facing the wall of windows. It was simply framed in dark wood and dressed in rich earth-toned sheets and comforters. A glance around the broad headboard revealed a sitting area backed against it, opposite the fireplace. A sumptuous leather couch was made even more inviting by the dozen or so richly textured pillows scattered over its cushions and stacked on the thick furry rug in front of it. A half dozen books were comfortably piled on an end table. Zoey could easily picture herself relaxing in front of the fire on a cool evening with the latest paperback. Although, with a hot naked man in the house—like the one currently sprawled across the bed—she doubted she would get any reading done.

"This is really beautiful," she breathed. "There's a harmony here. No distractions. Nothing jars the eye. Everything is very functional, yet it's warm and inviting at the same time. And there's all this glorious space."

"You like it."

"Very much. Did you design this yourself? What am I saying, of course you did, just like you did the downstairs. What a wonderful sanctuary."

"That's the right word," he said. "Everyone needs a refuge at the end of the day. I like open space, and I like comfort, plus I love to look at the sky. This is the next best thing to sleeping under the stars."

"Better. There are no wolves."

He made an odd choking sound and had to clear his throat. "Well, not every night."

She laughed at that and switched off the lights, standing still until her eyes adjusted. "It's even beautiful in the dark."

It was. The pale beams were silvery and the rising moon cast the faintest of light into the eastern windows. It pooled on the dark floor like water.

"Come see the outside." Connor rose from the bed and extended a hand, leading her to a door in the glassed wall and out onto a wide deck. Treetops framed it on each side but nothing obscured the view of the hills in the distance or the glistening river. "The stars are just coming out."

Zoey looked up at the night sky in wonder. Connor was right. New stars seemed to appear even as she watched. A cool breeze reminded her that she was stark naked and yet it felt like the most natural thing in the world to be standing outside beneath the stars. With Connor. She nestled back against him comfortably, grateful for his intense body heat, for his powerful arms wrapped around her. *Safe and warm.* Maybe not so safe. . . . She grinned as she felt his erection nudging at her hip. She stroked it softly with her fingertips, felt it rise and bump her hand as if asking for more. She slid her hand along the fiery length of it and gripped it hard. Connor was a large and powerful man— but it satisfied her tremendously to feel the tremor that passed through him from her touch. To her surprise he removed himself from her grasp, turned her to face him and held her at arm's to length.

"God, baby, don't do that just yet or I'll lose my mind again." He grasped one of her hands and held it to his lips, kissed each fingertip gently. "I was too rough with you before. I didn't mean to be."

"Maybe I liked it."

"Only maybe?"

She made a grab for him but he eluded her easily. "No

fair! Your arms are longer." Before she could blink, she was wrapped up tight against him.

"Can you reach me now?" he grinned.

"Much better," she laughed and wriggled, rubbing her breasts against his hard chest, rocking her pelvis against his powerful thigh. She was gratified to hear the hiss of breath drawn in through his teeth. Without warning, he scooped her up. She didn't have time to protest before they were through the door—and no elbows were banged this time—with Connor striding across the room. To her surprise he bypassed the bed and set her feet on the deliciously soft rug in front of the couch.

"Sit down," he whispered.

She sat a little gingerly, expecting the leather to be cold. Instead its buttery soft surface warmed immediately to her skin and she relaxed back. Connor knelt and lightly stroked his strong hands over her, ankle to thigh, fingertips to shoulders. His great strength was leashed, his touch tender as he traced tiny circles and swirls over almost every square inch of her. And the *almost* was driving her crazy. Calves and belly, collarbone and ribs. Places that seldom received much attention were extravagantly fondled, traced, and teased. Zoey squirmed, craving Connor's touch and yet it left such heightened sensitivity in its wake that her skin felt electrified. Her breasts were aching, her nipples straining, begging to be kissed. Yet Connor ignored their call, simply continuing to stroke the unsung parts of her body with his fingertips. Zoey could feel the moisture pooling between her legs and yet he didn't touch her there either. She was buzzing with sensation, her body taut and yearning.

"Turn around," he whispered and her core clenched hard. It was all she could do to move as he guided her into position, knees on the seat of the couch, her arms resting on its back. *Oh God, oh God.* She jumped as he ran his hands gently over her hips, the roughness of his palms rasping lightly over her back, her shoulders. Soothing and igniting at the same time, delicious torture. She trembled as he stroked the back of her thighs, still drawing endless patterns upon her. She was wet for him, so wet that a droplet of moisture trickled down her inner thigh with the same painstaking slowness as Connor's caresses. She wanted him to take her, needed him, she was so damn ready for him. . . .

All of her senses were startled as he kissed her ankle. A single hot, openmouthed kiss, followed by a light swirl of tongue. She shivered as he breathed over the spot and planted another kiss on the other ankle, then eased her legs apart. She trembled as he kissed his way slowly up her left leg, taking his time until she was sure she would scream. She did cry out as he kissed her right leg, above and below the bandages, but it certainly wasn't from pain. Eventually he lapped up the little droplet of moisture on her inner thigh, and the ones that had followed it. Closer, closer. . . . His hot mouth kissed its way over her cheeks, adding soft gentle bites. She was shaking, she couldn't help it, and she was on the verge of begging when his big hands suddenly parted her and his hot wet tongue slicked over her in one long stroke from clit to tailbone.

The orgasm slammed into her with all the force of a tsunami, and she might have been knocked from the couch by the intense wave, except that Connor held her securely, his big hands cupped around her hips. As her body throbbed and pulsed, he breathed over her folds and began lapping at them again, penetrating them with his tongue, licking around her swollen pearl until she came a second time.

The pleasure was nothing short of devastating. Finally he

stood behind her, using the head of his cock like a giant's finger to stroke the length of her crease. Breathless, Zoey managed to call Connor's name. It was both a plea and a summons, and he answered it, sliding smoothly into her until he had filled her completely. To her surprise, he stopped, holding himself there in perfect stillness. For an instant she savored his size, the incredible heat that radiated from him inside her. So big. So hot. And then some primal instinct erupted and she thrust her hips wildly, impaling herself gladly and still unable to get enough. She nearly wept with relief when he pulled her from the couch and flipped her over on the plush rug, plunged into her deep and hard. Faster and faster. She dug her fingernails into the muscles of his butt, needing to pull him into her even further, needing to be in one skin.

They imploded together, and it was as if they had leapt from the balcony. Zoey felt airborne, ethereal—and inextricably blended with Connor like twining breezes among the stars. She drew a great shuddering breath and the physical world returned. Connor was half-draped over her, sheltering her, warming her, the weight of him a secure blanket. She planted a kiss on his chest where his heart pounded in rhythm with hers, and received a warm kiss on her forehead in return. Sighing, she closed her eyes and allowed sleep to take her.

Instead, a dream took her over.

In it, Zoey wandered to the balcony. The bright stars seemed to direct her to the stairs and she followed them down to the yard. But it was not Connor's farmyard. There were few trees here, and the buildings were painted dark, perhaps red. It was hard to tell when the light of the waning half-moon washed away all color. Clumps of brush and wild grass dotted the yard and surrounded a small house with a swayback roof. The open windows emitted the sound of a television cranked up as loud as it would go. The owner must be deaf or nearly so—

Zoey spun as frantic bawling erupted from a nearby corral. Cattle stamped and ran, their flanks heaving. Several bashed into the wooden rails of the fence, knocking it down. A dozen cows poured through the break, stampeding wildly into the night. And close on their heels was her own worst nightmare, the grizzled gray wolf. Soundlessly it followed the cattle, slashing at their flanks with gleaming teeth. Finally, it singled one out and leapt for its throat, bringing the big animal down as easily as a lamb. Terrified, Zoey pressed herself behind the wall of a shed, watching in horror as the enormous wolf gave chase and pulled down each of the cows in turn until all lay dead or twitching on the ground.

The sound of the television stopped abruptly, leaving an eerie stillness in its wake. A porch light came on and a man emerged from the house, silhouetted in the doorway long enough for Zoey to see that he had a gun. Slowly, cautiously, he stepped down into the yard, looking this way and that. As the moonlight illuminated his face, Zoey was certain that she had seen him before, but she didn't know his name.

Suddenly he spotted the broken fence of the corral and ran to it, yelling. He swore at the dead cattle inside, then looked wildly around for the rest of his animals. "Dammit!" he yelled again as he spotted dark heaps scattered around the farmyard. "Goddammit to fucking hell!" He fired his gun into the air, the shot a punctuation mark to his frustration and anger. He kicked at a dead cow and turned away—

Almost right in front of him, the enormous wolf rose

from a clump of tall grass like a lion on a savannah. Its tongue lolled from wide grinning jaws.

Frightened, the man backpedaled and stumbled. He struggled with his gun, trying to bring it to bear as the wolf walked stiff-legged around him. He fired off a shot but missed. The wolf leapt and snapped at his leg, the empty ring of its jaws sending a shiver down Zoey's spine. The gun fell to the ground as the man crab-walked backward, then turned and ran for his life.

No, thought Zoey. *No, no, no!* She raced from her hiding place, heedless that she was naked, and tried to grab the gun. She couldn't. Like a ghost, she wasn't truly there, was only a helpless observer. She swore, and ran toward the man's screams.

He was silenced before she got there.

Zoey watched with angry tears streaming down her face, her fists clenching and unclenching. The wolf shook its lifeless victim by the throat like a rag doll. She could plainly see the terror and surprise still stamped on the man's face, the same expression she had seen on those people killed by the drive-by shooting, and that she had witnessed in the eyes of the child who lay dead on the sidewalk. . . .

Horrified, she cursed the gift that didn't enable her to intervene, only to see too late. Then she saw something else—the wolf was greedily drinking from its victim's torn throat. As it drank, the creature was making a strange chuckling sound as if it were laughing. Zoey's stomach heaved and her lungs were suddenly not getting any air, yet she was unable to look away. And as she stared, the wolf lifted its dripping muzzle and looked directly at her, its eyes glowing with unholy light.

You.

The word was in her head. In. Her. Head. The wolf had put it there. The murderous creature before her had put a word in her *mind*.

You're going to Change for me, sweetheart. I own you and I'll have you.

The words weren't loud and yet they shook her. She felt violated, dirty. She tore at her hair as if she could pull the words out of her head. And then she saw the wolf lope toward her, its bloodied jaws gaping wide as it leapt. . . .

Chapter Eighteen

"I've got you! I've got you, baby. Wake up!" Connor was frantic. Zoey was screaming, yanking at her hair and clawing at her head, and he couldn't seem to reach her. Finally he pinned her to the rug, grasping her wrists before she hurt herself. "Zoey!" he shouted, adding a psychic punch to his words. At last he saw her jerk her eyes open. They were uncomprehending at first, wide and terrified. And then she saw him, truly saw him.

"He's dead," she blurted. "He's dead, and I couldn't do anything. Nothing!" She shattered into sobs that shook her whole body.

"Shhh. Who's dead, honey?" Connor gathered her into his lap and cradled her, rocking back and forth as if soothing a child. He kissed the top of her head, nuzzled her hair.

"The-that man. A farmer." Tears ran down her face and trickled onto Connor's chest. It was several moments before she could speak again. "I don't know him. He has cows and the wolf killed them, killed all of them. And then, and then—oh God, he was so scared." The racking sobs overtook her again.

"The same wolf that attacked you." He made it a statement, knowing the answer.

Zoey nodded through the tears, the sobs starting to catch in her throat.

Jesus, she's frozen. She was cold all over and shaking. Connor picked her up and carried her to the bed, climbed in with her and pulled the blankets over them both. He held her tightly as his thoughts whirled.

It hadn't been Zoey's screams that woke him. It was the sudden burst of energy from her that intruded on his mind, radiating from her like a star gone nova. He'd been fully awake and staring at her, trying to comprehend what was happening, when the screaming began.

It was no nightmare that brought her to such a state, he was certain of that. This could only be the result of the extrasensory talent that she'd inherited, and he could easily see why she didn't consider it a gift. *Poor little falcon.* Taking the edge of the sheet, he used it to gently dab at her face. She was almost cried out, the sobs transmuting to shuddering hiccups. He kissed her head tenderly, tucked her closer to his heart and wished he could protect her from the terrible truth they would surely hear within hours.

Bernie had finally killed someone.

Connor awoke first. Daylight came early this far north. It was probably only five A.M. but the busy sounds of nature poured in the open window, a cacophony of birdsong and insect buzz, as if it were midday. As if a man wasn't lying dead in a field somewhere, his life cut short by a rogue Changeling.

I've got to tell the Pack. Connor looked down at the woman in his arms. Zoey was sleeping peacefully at last. He eased away from her and tucked the comforter close around her. Then went downstairs to make a phone call he wished he didn't have to.

Jessie's voice was quiet and soft, as it was when she was truly angry. "It's one thing for Bernie to dare to invade my territory, flip the finger at the Pack in a situation where we were surrounded by humans and couldn't Change. There's no Pack law against being an asshole. But this . . . this is my mistake. He'd already crossed the line when he attacked Zoey and I foolishly thought that binding his wolf would be enough. Harming a human is forbidden, and there's only one penalty for killing one. Bernie's life is forfeit."

Connor knew it. Changeling law was strict. Bernie would not be allowed to live. He had no love for the vicious old drunk, but still he felt responsible. "I should have stopped him."

"It's not your fault for not being omniscient. You don't control what your gift shows you—or what it doesn't."

Hadn't he just tried to say the same thing to Zoey the night before? Small wonder she hadn't found it comforting. Didn't do a damn thing for him either.

"Will you call the Pack?" he asked, knowing that Bernie's sentence would be carried out quickly.

"Yes, but not you."

"What?"

"Your job is to keep your mate close. Bernie still wants her and until he's dead, she's in danger."

"I—"

"I'm sure you want a piece of him, Connor, but even if you didn't have Zoey to protect, I would forbid you to be involved. This is too personal for you."

Shit. Jessie was right. He wanted to kill Bernie with his bare hands for *very* personal reasons. And because of that, he needed to step back. But it would be damn hard.

He returned to the bedroom to find Zoey out on the balcony, clad in only a bath towel. Her freckles were pure gold in the morning sun and his body shot to attention at once. Her russet hair was freshly washed, and the moisture in it made it curl and wave even more than usual. He couldn't help wondering what it would feel like to have that long lovely hair gliss slowly over his cock. . . . She turned and smiled at him, and concern replaced arousal. Her smile was much too brave, he thought. Her eyes were deeply shadowed, more from stress and tears than lack of sleep.

"I borrowed your shower," she said.

"Sorry I missed it." He slid an arm around her and kissed her thoroughly, tenderly. "Need some breakfast?"

"No. Not ready for that. The dream . . ." She let it hang, knowing he understood.

"You still need to eat something. How about some coffee and one little slice of toast? Just to make *me* feel better," Connor coaxed.

"Maybe in a while." She slid her arms around him and they stood for a while, drinking in the fresh morning air. "You're so warm. Don't you ever get cold?"

"High metabolism." He was just contemplating removing that towel from her and warming her up too, when she stopped him with a question.

"So, yesterday you said you had something important to tell me?"

Every sense Connor possessed shot to high alert. The moment of truth had arrived, the conversation that every Changeling dreaded. He had to tell her, and there wasn't a damn thing he could do to make it easier. And considering the horrifying vision she'd had in the night, it was the worst possible time to be having this talk. Normally he'd put it off, tell her tomorrow or next week or next month. But the pale half moon hung in the bright morning sky, like a ghostly hourglass ticking away time. Eighteen days. Christ, only *seventeen* now.

Connor grasped her hand and took a deep breath—or tried to, since it didn't feel like he was getting much air. "It *is* important. And it's difficult to explain, so I might have to take a couple of runs at it. You have a psychic gift, so you know there's more to the world than most people are aware of."

"Some gift," she said bitterly. "Why didn't it tell me what was going to happen in advance? Maybe I could have warned the guy. Maybe you and I could have gone there and shot that damn wolf before it got a chance to do anything. Instead, that poor man is dead and it's my fault."

"It sure as hell *isn't* your fault!"

"See it from my side, will you? This is exactly what's been happening to me more and more over the past few years. I'm not a journalist, I just record the mess after it's happened."

He couldn't think of a thing to say to that, so he simply guided her indoors before she caught a chill. They sat on the bed together, his arm around her shoulders.

"I guess your gift is different from mine," she said at last.

"Not that much. It didn't tell me what was going to happen to that farmer either, and it bothers me too. I don't get to control what my precognition tells me and that sucks. It's not like my other gifts."

"Your other—oh, you mean communicating with animals. So you have control of that?"

"I do, most of the time," he nodded. "But don't forget that crazy bull still caught me with my pants down. So you see, it doesn't always work the way I'd like it to. Neither do my *other gifts*." He emphasized the last part deliberately, waited for her to pick it up.

"You can do more?"

"A whole lot more."

"Like what? Hey!" Zoey eyed him suspiciously. "You can't read my mind, can you?"

"No, nothing like that. Your thoughts are your own." He conjured up a ghost of a smile as she looked relieved. He loved her expressive face. He loved her. And he had to get this out before he couldn't. "Zoey, not only can I communicate with animals, I can become one."

"Excuse me?"

"I'm a Changeling. Part of me is man and part of me is wolf."

She mouthed the word *wolf* and then laughed. "You had me going there for a moment. Yeah, I'm really going to believe you're a big bad—"

"Werewolf."

She smiled up at him and then the smile disappeared as she realized he wasn't kidding. "Connor, quit it."

"Zoey, there are legends of men who shapeshift in every culture in the world. Every single one. The Navaho have the Skinwalker, the French have the Loup-Garou, the Chinese have the—"

"I don't give a damn what the Chinese have. Stop it, will you? This isn't funny in the least. I just had the worst dream of my life, saw a wolf *kill* someone for God's sake, so this is a damn poor joke."

"Honey, I wish I *was* kidding." He meant it. At this moment in time he would have traded every one of his extraordinary abilities to be an ordinary human male. To not have to see the mix of hurt and confusion on Zoey's face. "But I'm not."

She scrambled off the mattress and began yanking on her clothes.

"Zoey, you have to hear this."

"I don't have to hear your lame-ass excuses. I thought we had something good between us, something real, but if I was wrong, have the guts to say so. Don't dick around with my head with bizarre stories—"

He was in front of her in a heartbeat, startling her into backing up. He followed, deliberately stalking her until she was against the wall, holding her shirt in front of her like a shield and glaring fiercely. "I love you, Zoey. I want more than a relationship with you, I want a life with you. I want children with you, I want all of it, everything. With. You."

"Then why the hell are you—"

"*Because* I love you, I have to be up front with you and tell you everything about me. Including something you don't want to hear. I'm not fully human. And you're not either."

She blinked at him. "How *dare* you! How dare you say something like that? Last night you called my ability a *gift* and this morning I'm back to being a goddamn *freak*?"

"Hell, no!" He had to find a way to stop putting both feet in his mouth. "I wasn't talking about your psychic ability. I meant you're going to Change."

"Change how?"

"It wasn't a wolf that attacked you. It was another Changeling."

"A werewolf? You're saying I was attacked by a *werewolf*? You're as crazy as that asshole reporter, Helfren."

"I agree he's an asshole and a dangerous one, but he does have a few facts straight."

She stared at him wordlessly for a long time. Moisture welled up in her amber eyes but he knew she was willing the tears not to fall. His own heart bled on their behalf.

"I'm going home now," she said at last, sliding out from

between him and the wall and walking over to the center
of the room to finish dressing.

"You love me." He felt like the ground was being pulled
from under him.

"It sure felt like it. But that was when I thought I knew
you. I don't know the guy who's standing in front of me
spouting all this B-movie crap."

"You *do* know me. Nothing's changed."

She shook her head. "This is probably my own fault.
This is what I get for making excuses for you."

"What the hell do you mean by that?"

"Come on, Connor, you go along for a while being Mr.
Wonderful and just as I think you're Mr. Right, you do
something bizarre. Like that time we got all hot and heavy
in my apartment and you took off like the couch was on
fire. And at the party? We all but had sex standing up and
bang, you disappeared without a word." She jammed her
feet into her shoes. "And now? I just had the best night of
my life and now you're telling me the wildest, most ridiculous story I've ever heard. I don't know what the hell is the
matter is with you, but you've got *serious* issues with inti-
macy, mister!"

He stepped in front of the door just before she reached
it.

"Get out of my way," she said through gritted teeth.

"No. Not until you hear me out. I left your apartment in
a hurry that morning because my inner wolf was not under
control. It was reacting to you, and I couldn't risk Changing in front of you."

She all but rolled her eyes at that and it pissed him off,
even though he could hardly blame her. She tried to move
past him, but he blocked her and tried a different tack.
"You've already seen my wolf side, Zoey."

"I'm seeing your lunatic side right now!"

"I didn't ditch you that night at the party. I was standing over you, protecting you. You've been dreaming about a wolf with unusual markings, a silver and black wolf. And you saw that wolf in *my face* in Jessie's kitchen. You saw it because you have a gift, and it tells you things that are normally hidden, things that most people don't see, *can't* see. If you'll just listen to your gift, you'll know that what I'm saying is true."

She hesitated and he knew he'd struck a chord. But damned if he had any idea how to follow it up. He wished he had something brilliant to say but all he had was the truth, a truth that was completely impossible in the human world she lived in.

"Are you going to stop me from leaving?"

His heart sank and he stepped back to let her pass, then yanked on his jeans and followed her down the stairs. She beelined out the front door. "Zoey, wait!"

She paused at the bottom of the porch steps and turned back. The morning sun haloed her hair as she stood by the riot of flowers and his heart stuttered at the sheer glory of her. Why the hell did he have to tell her these things? Why couldn't they simply be two people in love?

God help him, he almost gave in. Almost told her what she wanted to hear, almost said, hey, just kidding, everything's fine . . . and then he saw it. The faint shell of the moon in the bright morning sky.

Connor walked down the porch steps like a condemned man. Only he wasn't the one condemned. He stopped in front of Zoey, gently caressed her shoulders with his hands, remembering the glorious freckles that adorned them like flakes of gold. She looked at him with hope in her eyes, waiting. Waiting for him to take it all back, to make it all better between them again.

"Zoey, I love you with everything I've got in me and then some. But I will not lie to you, not even to make things easier to hear. I'm a Changeling, but that's not the problem."

"It's a pretty damn big prob—"

"You're going to become one too."

She slugged him then. He saw it coming and allowed her to hit him, permitted her fist to connect with his jaw. Part of him was impressed with the power of her human punch, although it barely moved him. The rest of him understood how far she'd been pushed, how much she *needed* to strike back at the terrible words, words that seemed like horrible lies to human ears. She drew back her fist for another punch and he seized her wrist in a movement too fast for her to follow. Held it. "One is all you get," he said simply. "Now we talk."

"*Talk?* There's no use in talking if you're just going to spout more of this werewolf bullshit."

He ignored her and continued. "Bernard Gervais is a Changeling. He bit you and you're going to become a Changeling in a little over two weeks. I tried to stop it and I couldn't." He told her about the silver nitrate, in spite of the fury in her eyes and the disbelief. "Changelings can call out the wolf at any time, become one whenever they want to. But that first time, the first Change, always happens on the first full moon after a bite."

Zoey yanked her wrist and he released it. She backed up a couple of steps and folded her arms. "Prove it then. Do it now. Show me you can do this."

"Fine." Frustrated, he called the Change—and was shocked when nothing happened. Nothing at all. There was only a faint whine in the back of his mind as if his inner wolf was complaining. *What the hell?* Then he remembered. The goddamn *gris-gris*. He ripped the hemp bracelet from his arm and hurled it across the yard, startling several chickens into brief flight.

Connor tried again to call his wolf. Again, the Change wouldn't come, and this time he recalled Jessie's warning. There were residual effects to wearing such a powerful amulet. It might be a day or two, maybe more, before he could run as a wolf.

Which didn't do him one damn bit of good as Zoey watched him with folded arms and raised eyebrows.

"I'm waiting," she said, as if he didn't already feel like a complete idiot.

"I was wearing a charm. I didn't want to Change by accident around you," he said.

"A charm. Is that as in *magic*?"

This day couldn't get any worse. "Yes," he admitted.

"I see." It was obvious she didn't. Zoey turned to leave and Connor grabbed her arm.

"Whether or not you believe it, you're going to Change on the full moon. And whether you like it or not, you need my help."

"I need you to let go of me. I need you to stay away from me. I need you to get some help for yourself. You're out of your fucking mind, Connor Macleod."

She yanked her arm and he released it, watched helplessly as she stalked to her truck and drove away. Connor stood with his hands jammed into his pockets as Zoey's vehicle disappeared from sight. He continued to glare out at the gravel road until the dust had settled and there was no sign she had ever been there. The wolf within him clawed wildly for release, to no avail. His heart slammed painfully against his ribs and his insides felt as if they were being pulled in different directions, but the Change would not come, thanks to the damn amulet that lay somewhere in the yard where he'd thrown it.

"Stop it *now!*" he ordered his alter ego in a voice that allowed no argument. For once, his inner wolf appeared to listen and settled uneasily, waiting. Connor stalked into the house and grabbed the rest of his clothes. Called the North Star Animal Hospital, told them he wasn't coming in and instructed them to send emergencies to the clinic over in Spirit River.

Lastly, he went to the gun case in the spare room. He might be stuck in human form, but not having fangs and claws didn't stop humans from being the deadliest creatures on the planet. He passed over the lighter rifles that would take down ordinary game and instead selected a .375 and loaded it, stuffing spare shells into his jacket pocket. The H&H magnum rifle had enough shocking power to stop a charging grizzly—or a very powerful Changeling. Connor stowed the weapon behind the seat of his pickup and drove to town.

Zoey might not want him within a hundred yards of her but whether she liked it or not, she was getting a bodyguard.

Chapter Nineteen

Doug Peters and Greg Simmons had been at Al Menzie's farm since six A.M. The Fish and Wildlife officers had scoured the dry ground for prints, and the bloody carcasses of twenty cows for tooth marks, evidence of bite pressure, the whole nine yards. Tipped off by the police scanner in his van, Tad Helfren made sure he showed up just after eight with doughnuts and coffee.

The three of them leaned against the government truck, coffee in hand, waiting for Horizon Dead Livestock Removal to show up and haul away the ravaged remains.

"God, what a mess," said Helfren, pretending to be a little squeamish. In truth, he found the carnage exciting. It was evidence that he was getting closer to his own quarry. *The thrill of the hunt, boys and girls.* "I don't know why you guys aren't sick. Anyone find the owner yet?"

Peters shook his head. "Jeff Maguire, the hired man, came home from the bar last night and found the cattle like this. Nobody home at Al's. Maguire figures his boss went early to a farm auction. There are three of them out by Spirit River today and tomorrow, and they tend to go dawn to dusk."

"Al's sure gonna be pissed when he finds out these heifers are dead," added Simmons. "They were purebred

Murray Grays. He just got them a month ago at a dispersal sale, bred to an expensive bull to boot. It's a huge loss."

"Surely there's insurance on something like this, right?" Helfren already knew the answer yet played the men along. He knew there was no glamour attached to their job, and it was likely that no one bothered to ask their opinion about much of anything. It was a safe bet that they'd be glad to share everything they knew with an appreciative audience. And he knew how to be appreciative.

"Most farmers don't carry insurance on livestock," explained Simmons, biting into a chocolate cream doughnut. "Costs way too much."

"But isn't it a crime for a neighbor's dogs to kill your cows? I mean, there must be some sort of victim's compensation or something," Helfren persisted.

Peters and Simmons exchanged glances. "No dogs did this," said Simmons. "Had to be a big animal, maybe a bear attacked these cattle."

"I say it was wolves," declared Peters.

Yes! Inside, Helfren did a touchdown dance. On the outside, however, he kept up the act. "Really? But wolves don't actually attack things, do they? I heard that was a myth."

Simmons shrugged. "They go after livestock once in a while, but they'd focus on one and then eat it, leave the rest alone. Wolves don't go on a killing spree. And none of these animals has been eaten. I say it was a grizzly."

"Grizzlies don't kill everything in sight either," retorted Peters.

"Maybe this one did. We didn't find all the cows. Twenty dollars says a griz dragged one off and cached it, buried it under leaves and dirt for later."

The officers argued. More coffee was consumed. Over

the next hour, the officers showed Helfren every piece of evidence they'd found. Tooth marks on bone, stray hairs—everything that fairly shouted to the practiced eye of the paranormal investigator that this wasn't the work of wild dogs. Or bears. Or anything else belonging to the natural world. Too bad, though, that the ground was so frustratingly dry—there wasn't a print anywhere. Still, Helfren took careful notes and shot photos, even getting the men to pose in front of their truck.

Finally the livestock removal truck lumbered into sight and the officers went to talk to the driver. Helfren strolled around the farmyard alone, looking for anything he might have missed. Dead cattle were scattered like discarded toys. He was standing by one that had been killed near an outbuilding, when he spotted the telltale buzz and swirl of flies over tall grass down by a creek. One more cow, but he ought to check it for clues just the same.

It was no cow.

For a long moment, Helfren stared at the dead man, taking in the position of the body, the open staring eyes, the terror permanently etched in the lines of the face, the throat below it almost completely missing. Shouldn't there be more blood? He'd seen bodies before, but the sight chilled him nonetheless. Gunshot victims were one thing. But this. . . . Slowly he moved forward, circling the body carefully, scanning the ground. And hit pay dirt. Three bloody footprints, faint but distinct. Unmistakably wolf yet larger than any wolf had a right to be.

Grinning, he lifted his camera. It would be a great lead-in to the best story of his life. Capped with a few shots of that long-legged editor changing into a beast from hell, his reputation—and better yet, his fortune—would be assured. He shot several dozen frames from all angles, double-checked the digital screen to make sure he had what he needed, then carefully backed away from the sordid scene. A glance at the officers on the other side of the yard showed them busily directing the livestock removal. They hadn't noticed where he'd been or what he'd been doing. *Good.* It was best if no one knew he possessed photos of the victim. How many great stories had been spoiled by a court ban on publication, or worse, by confiscation of camera equipment in the name of evidence? Never *his* stories of course—he was much too careful.

Helfren ambled casually back to where the trucks were parked. He helped himself to a jelly doughnut with powdered sugar and took his time savoring it, then checked his watch. He imagined it would be thirty or forty minutes before either the livestock removal crew or the Fish and Wildlife officers worked their way over to that last cow near the stream—and stumbled over the farmer's body.

He called out a good-bye to the men, got an answering wave and headed to his van, humming a little as he tossed around captions in his head. This was going to be the best damned edition of the *OtherWorld News* in its thirty-three-year history. And with plenty left over for his book.

He still had to get his hands on Little Miss Editor of course. But not yet. No point in rushing things. She wasn't going to be useful until much, much closer to the full moon.

And then she'd be gold.

Bernie was exultant. Giggling laughter bubbled up in him as he sat atop the tallest standing stone in the circle at Elk Point. The formation was said to be the meeting place of the gods and revered for centuries as a hallowed spot by various native peoples. Now it was mostly forgotten, hidden by tall trees and unknown except to the occasional hiker or hunter . . . and Changelings. They could feel the energy of the place and the Pack held it to be sacred.

Sacred, my ass. Bernie swung his feet, his entire body abuzz with sensation. There were lines of invisible energy flowing deep within the earth and this spot was an intersection of sorts. He'd never been able to tap into it before, but now it energized him almost as much as Al Menzie's blood had hours earlier. Normally a Changeling could assume wolfen form only once or twice a day at most because it required massive amounts of energy. Three times was dangerous and nearly unheard of. Four times would be fatal. Bernie had Changed not once but several times in the night, simply because he could. And he wasn't tired in the least. *Menzie, you really recharged my batteries. Who'd have thought a dried up little runt like you would have so much juice?*

But Menzie couldn't hold a candle to that red-haired newcomer. Bernie had gotten only a single bite, yet that one taste of the woman's blood had revealed she was fairly bursting with power, a strange and pure power that eclipsed that of any human he'd killed to date. The energy had shot through his system like the most potent drug, surprising and distracting him. Then the woman had surprised him further, daring to defy him, to fight back. *Cut my face.*

He'd have killed the stupid bitch, of course, killed and drunk every last drop of her blood as she lay in the street. He'd finally have had the power he craved, the means to get everything he'd ever wanted—except Connor Macleod had showed up and interrupted everything. Bernie leapt to the ground effortlessly, crouched as if in wolfen form. Fury blinded him, nearly choked him. *I found her! She was mine, her blood was mine!* He howled long and loud in frustration, the sound all the more chilling as it erupted from his human form.

Damn the Macleods! They were always ruining things for him. They'd done it again when he'd livened up that party in the Watson's backyard. He'd meant only to stir the pot, provide a little footage for Helfren, a sample of things to come. Bernie hadn't known the red-haired woman would be at Watson's like an inviting snack just begging to be nibbled. But his hopes for another energizing bite were dashed by Connor Macleod. Who'd have thought the bastard would risk Changing in the middle of all those humans?

Bernie automatically bared his stained teeth in a snarl. Those interfering Macleods wouldn't be so high and mighty once Helfren revealed them to the world. Instead, they'd be freaks. *Freaks!* The entire clan would be hauled off to some secret government lab and studied for the rest of their unnatural lives. Or hunted down and shot dead. Either way worked for him.

In the meantime, the Pack was onto him, watching for him, even hunting him. They'd never be able to trail him of course. His new power had provided some unexpected benefits. *This old dog has learned new tricks.* Thanks to the network of waterways that connected the entire region, he had an innovative way of getting around that other Changelings would never even think of, never mind detect.

But it was the principle of the thing—the Pack would pay for *daring* to hunt him, starting with the Watson bitch who led them. He'd be the one doing the hunting soon—but first he had to get to that red-haired woman and her incredible blood. He had no idea why it possessed such potency, and he didn't care. The problem was how to reach her with the Pack's eyes everywhere. . . . A member of the Pack was even in charge of the fucking cops. Bernie refused to risk having the Macleods or anyone else interfere in his plans again.

His rage disappeared abruptly as an idea popped to the surface of his chaotic brain. He didn't need to waste time stalking the woman. He was her sire, wasn't he? Hadn't he given her the wolf? Wouldn't she Change at his command? Normally it couldn't work at such a distance—after all, he couldn't see the stupid bitch from here and she couldn't hear him—but he was so much stronger now. Much more powerful. She *would* Change. And she would come to *him*.

It was damn fucking perfect.

Bernie rubbed his crotch, indulging the unexpected erection there. He felt virile, young, and oh-so-potent. Maybe he could have a little fun with that red-haired woman before he killed her. After all, he could tell her to do whatever he wanted and she'd have to do it. Have to. He'd tell her to peel her clothes off for starters. He'd like a good, long look at her rack. She'd turn those strange gold eyes on him, those hawklike eyes, and they'd be full of hate, but she wouldn't be able to do a fucking thing about it. Not a thing.

And then he'd tell her to give him head. *Oh yeah.* He got even harder just thinking about it. A new Changeling had no choice but to obey the one who sired them, and he could make her do anything he wanted for as long as he wanted. As long as he enjoyed her. And when he got tired of her, he would simply drain her dry, lap up every last drop of her luscious blood until he was damn well invincible.

Hell, he was already strong enough to take on the whole stinking Pack. He knew it, could feel it. He growled low, drawing his lips back from teeth that had suddenly gone long and sharp, crowded grotesquely in a mouth that wasn't designed for them. *I'll show you. All of you. Every damn one of you.*

Suddenly Bernie giggled and shook himself. The teeth retracted, became human again. *First things first.* He had a little call to make.

A routine investigation by Fish and Wildlife into the deaths of twenty-two purebred heifers took an ugly turn Sunday morning when the body of Allan Ralph Menzie, 76, was discovered on his farm.

The dead livestock had been reported earlier that morning amid speculation that a large grizzly bear or possibly a cougar was responsible. Acting coroner, Dr. Lowen Miller, has not yet confirmed the cause of Mr. Menzie's death. . . .

Zoey leaned back from the keyboard and sighed. Nothing like being right back where she'd started. She'd left the city, thinking she could leave the violence, the death, and more importantly, her own psychic visions, far behind. *Ha.* Maybe that's what they—whoever *they* were—meant when they said *you can run but you can't hide.*

She had no hope of hiding from the ghastly images in her head, those remnants of the horrible dream that had proved all too true. A man was dead. Officials weren't saying the word *wolf.* At least not yet. But in her heart she knew without doubt that it wasn't a bear that killed Al Menzie and his cattle. The creature that had attacked her, whose bite she still bore on her leg, was still at large and very, very dangerous.

Yet until the police could confirm the animal's identity,

she couldn't tell anyone. Oh, she could, she supposed. But who would believe her? Zoey knotted both hands in her hair in frustration. Her family claimed that her psychic ability was a precious gift. Connor seemed to consider it a gift too. All her life she'd wished she could give the useless talent back, but never more than right now. Of course, reporting the news was a mere formality in a small community. News traveled faster on the grapevine than by any other means, and, by Monday morning, it was unlikely that there was anybody left in town who hadn't heard about the death of Al Menzie. The *Dunvegan Herald Weekly* had been a zoo all day. Reporters from surrounding communities hung out in the coffee room, making it impossible for staff to get a break from the constant questioning. The phone seemed to ring without stopping. Local residents stopped by too. Some people were merely curious, wanting to know if the newspaper staff "had heard anything yet." Others had theories to offer, some sound, some bizarre. Ted Biegel had bodily removed the seventh or eighth person who had the temerity to bring up the word *werewolf*.

Zoey had decided against going to the Menzie farm herself. The RCMP had it cordoned off anyway. Instead, she assigned the sports reporter to drive out and take a basic shot of the farm site from the road. That was all that a tasteful small town newspaper had any business publishing anyway. There was no hope for an interview with officials either, not yet. The RCMP was being closemouthed until they concluded their initial investigation into "an unattended death." Fish and Game might think it was an animal attack, but the last word would come from Lowen Miller. She wondered what it would be like for the gruff doctor to step into a coroner's role again. Would he feel as frustrated as she did? Had he and Bev also been trying to leave the big city violence behind them? Or would it simply be like putting on a familiar pair of shoes?

Maybe she could visit the Millers, ask them about it sometime. And while she was at it, maybe she could ask them about *lycanthropy*. That was the word she'd come up with after researching half the day on the Internet in between poring over financial papers in preparation for the Village Council's budget meeting that night. Although she'd be surprised if the councilors got around to discussing the budget at all. At the request of the mayor, the RCMP had promised to stop by and report what they could on the Menzie issue.

Lycanthropy. The belief that one can become a wolf. Zoey had heard the word but hadn't known it was a medically-recognized condition, treatable with antipsychotic drugs. And it certainly seemed to fit Connor's wild story to a tee. Except that he had no other apparent symptoms, appearing to be a perfectly normal specimen of the human male in every other way. And an exceptional specimen in many ways. . . . For the hundredth time, Zoey's mind wandered happily to that subject until she yanked it back in angry frustration.

Damn you, Connor Macleod. Things had been fine between them, great in fact. Hell, they were flat-out wonderful. So why did he have to get so weird on her? What was it that compelled him to tell her such crazy stories? Was he a compulsive liar? No instinct she possessed sent up any alarm bells at his words. To her way of thinking, that could only mean he believed his own story. It sure as hell wasn't a joke—one look at his face proved that—so what was his motivation?

She had no answers, just more pain than she'd ever

known. This wasn't heartache, this was being sawn in two with a dull knife. How could she have come to love someone so much in such a short time? And Connor certainly seemed to feel the same way. Not only had he said he loved her, he'd declared his desire to marry her and even said the C word (although she wasn't terribly certain that she wanted children).

I love you but I turn into a wolf. He was trying to be honest, he said. Honest about his mental condition? Did Connor realize he had a problem? If so, did he know what it was? Zoey had scoured the web for information on every mental disorder she could come up with. She even researched the phenomenon of multiple personalities (although she wasn't sure that applied if the other personality was an animal). *Lycanthropy* was the only thing that seemed to fit—and yet it didn't. Medically, lycanthropy was considered an offshoot of a larger problem such as schizophrenia, bipolar disorder, even clinical depression. Zoey wasn't a doctor, but surely she would have seen some sign of such things. Wouldn't she? Maybe she just hadn't known Connor long enough. Hell, she barely knew him at all.

Zoey held her head with both hands as a headache began to wale on the back of her head with the force of a two-by-four. A pair of tears slid down one cheek in quick succession, annoying her. There was no way she was going to cry. No way. *At least not here and not now.* Another tear defied her and she might have broken down completely except for a tiny detail that slid into her awareness like a note slipped under a door.

Jessie. Her friend had been convinced the saddleback wolf that stood over Zoey at the party had been protecting her. And didn't Jessie say to ask Connor about that? When Zoey had asked why, Jessie had simply said he knew a lot

more about it than she did. The more Zoey thought about
it, the more it seemed a very strange thing to say.

Exactly how much did Jessie know?

Slowly Zoey sat up. It was definitely time to visit the
Finer Diner. She shut down her computer and was about
to get up when the phone rang. *Crap.* It was after six
o'clock, the office was officially closed, and she had a raging migraine, but pure reporter's reflex had her picking up
the receiver anyway. The voice on the other end was low
and gravelly.

"I know where to find the animals that killed Menzie."

Great. Another wannabee tipster. "Who is this?"

"A musher has been crossing big malamutes with wolves
and he can't control them. Very vicious."

"Are you sure about this? Why haven't you gone to the
police?"

"The police won't take me seriously, lady, because I
drink a little too much. But this guy is keeping these animals near my farm and I'm afraid they'll get my horses.
Meet me and I can tell you more."

"You're going to have to tell me who you are."

"Bernard."

Bernard Gervais? Had to be. "Aren't you one of the guys
that claimed to have seen a werewolf?"

His voice sounded almost contrite. "I was drinking that
night, lady. I'm not drunk now. Come and talk to me. I can
give you the whole story. I'm really scared for my horses."

Zoey considered the fact that she didn't really know the
man, had only seen him once. And he'd been drunk and
raving about werewolves at the time.

"I'm sorry, I'm really busy. If you have something to say,
you'll have to say it now."

"I want you to Change when the moon clears the horizon."

"Pardon me?"

"*Change.* When the moon is up. And then come find me."

He laughed, a thick chortling sound that sent unexpected shivers down her spine. Zoey slammed the receiver. "Stupid drunk." But she was shaking as she closed down her office and gathered up her things to leave.

Chapter Twenty

Connor held a newspaper in his hands, but his eyes weren't scanning the print. Instead they looked out over the page, as they had most of the day, studying everything within a block in either direction of the *Dunvegan Herald Weekly*, watching for the slightest sign that anything was amiss. Seeing nothing. Still, there was a gnawing in his gut that said something was wrong.

Hell, wasn't everything wrong? A rogue Changeling had started killing people and the Pack couldn't seem to find the bastard. His long-awaited mate was right there inside the newspaper building yet he was out here with his pickup truck doubling as a proverbial doghouse. It hadn't been boring, however. That damn reporter, Helfren, had made several appearances throughout the day. Mailing a letter. Drinking coffee. Window shopping. And every time, he was watching the office of the *Dunvegan Herald Weekly* just as intently as Connor was. A fact that made it difficult for Connor to resist cleaning the guy's clock. Especially when the vet had more than mere human impulses to resist. Deep within him, his inner wolf was growling long and low.

Luckily, Culley had been on the job. Connor had spotted him shadowing the reporter so cleverly that Helfren never noticed he was being tailed. Of course, Culley added his own flourishes to the task. Connor couldn't help enjoying it when a monstrous black dog knocked the reporter over by running between his legs. The huge animal had vanished before Helfren could regain his feet—but Lucinda Perkins and several members of the Dunvegan Neighborhood Patrol had rushed to help him. And stayed to grill him.

With Helfren under such close surveillance, Connor was free to watch the street, the alley, and the back and front entrances to the newspaper office. The *Herald* would be closing soon. Bernie could be anywhere, and he was just crazy enough to make a move on Zoey in broad daylight.

Connor turned a page of his newspaper as he glanced at his side view mirror. Culley and Bill were approaching the truck.

"I'm not in the mood for company," warned Connor as his brother slid smoothly into the passenger seat beside him. Bill, too, ignored Connor's comment. The red-haired giant simply passed a steaming cup of coffee forward as he crammed himself into the rear seat of the pickup. Connor took the cup without looking, keeping his eyes on the newspaper building. The staff had started filing out at last. But the woman he most wanted to see hadn't yet emerged.

"So you and Zoey had a falling out?" asked Culley.

"How the hell would you know that?"

"Only that I found the North Star Animal Hospital shut down on a weekday with a cheery sign on the door for folks to take their emergencies elsewhere."

"Maybe I'm busy."

"Maybe you're miserable. I could feel the vibes from four blocks away. So since nothing else was likely to pull you two apart, I'm guessing you must have told her about your secret identity."

There was no point in denying it. Culley was a prankster and often impulsive, but he was also smart and perceptive. And Bill, who was sitting silent in the backseat, was the best friend a guy could hope to have. Connor sighed. "Yeah, I told her what I was, and then I told her what she's going to become."

Culley whistled long and low. "Christ, you gave it to her with both barrels?"

"Do you think I wanted to dump it on her like that? There are only sixteen days before the full moon. Just sixteen, Culley. I didn't have the luxury of breaking it to her gently."

"Maybe not, but how the hell are you going to prepare her to be a Changeling if she's not speaking to you?"

Connor glared at his brother. "Why aren't you watching Helfren?"

"He got a sudden call from his buddies at Fish and Wildlife. Seems they found wolf prints all around their truck while it was parked outside their office."

"You didn't—"

"Hey, it was time to create a distraction. Because we've got news, bro."

"What news?" Connor watched Ted Biegel leave the office and stop to talk to someone on the street. Still no sign of Zoey.

Bill leaned his beefy arms on the back of the seat between the brothers. "Fitz called Jessie an hour ago—he looked at the body and it's plain that Bernie drank from the kill."

"What?" The newspaper slid from Connor's fingers as the words sank in. Pack law forbade the harming of humans. Bad enough that Bernie had killed, but drinking human blood complicated everything. It was said to bring incredible power to the renegade who indulged in it—and complete madness. *Goddammit!* He pounded on the steering wheel. "Goddammit to hell!"

"Now we know why Bernie was able to outrun us the night of the barbecue," said Culley. "It finally makes sense. And the bastard's stronger and faster than ever now, maybe stronger than any of us."

"The night of—but Menzie hadn't been killed yet! Bernie pulled away from us like he was on wheels." Puzzle pieces fell rapidly into place in Connor's mind.

Bill said it first. "We figure Menzie couldn't have been Bernie's first victim. He's killed before. He must have been a lot more careful; maybe he hadn't gone starkers yet and that's why no one found the bodies, but he's killed before."

"Good Christ, I should have stopped him," said Connor. "I could have stopped Bernie long ago, if only I'd—"

"If only you'd had a crystal ball? Don't even go there." said Culley firmly, reading his brother's face. "You've got the gift of *farsight* but it doesn't tell you everything. You had no way of knowing what the old bastard was going to do."

"I knew he'd killed livestock. I knew he was getting out of control."

"As far as anyone knew, Zoey was the first human to be attacked. And you took action on it pronto."

"Some action. I injected the bastard with fucking *water*."

"Fine," said Culley. "If you want to beat yourself up, go ahead. But at least save your energy and wait until we've dealt with Bernie."

Connor's eyes hardened, the pale gray going storm dark. He'd deal with Bernie all right. *Personally.*

"It's up to the Pack to deal with him," Bill said, picking up Connor's vibes immediately. "Not any one Changeling.

And knowing the rotter's been supercharged, no one should make the mistake of approaching him alone. It's a right good thing that Fitz warned us or one of us might have gotten killed as well."

Connor could hear the sense in his friend's words, but it didn't change the way he felt. Or what he would do if he caught Bernie's trail. But he could agree about Fitzpatrick. Every member of the Pack felt lucky to have a Changeling heading the police detachment. It added another layer of security to their secret lives, but even Fitz wouldn't be able to help them if Bernie wasn't stopped soon. "Any clues?"

"Nope," said Culley. "We searched the area all day for a trail, couldn't get even a hint of one. Jessie and Devlin are still out there, but they won't be for long."

"Oh?"

Bill put his hand on Connor's shoulder. "Jessie's put the word out not to Change unless you have to, mate. There's been a swack of cops and volunteers beating the bushes with guns since noon, looking for something to shoot. There were wolf prints by the body. Big ones."

Connor swore. "People are scared then."

"Terrified is more like it. Fish and Wildlife called in a helicopter to search the area." The big man's voice was quiet, subdued. "They didn't take tranquilizer guns, mate. Devlin was at the airstrip, tinkering on his plane when he saw them loading the rifles."

"If we don't Change, it's going to make it a lot harder to hunt down Bernie, and until we do, the killing's not going to stop."

"The bastard's right off the deep end, that's sure. I see you're prepared though."

Connor caught Bill's eye in the rearview mirror, saw his

friend look down at the floor where the .375 lay amid empty bottles of cattle vaccine. "Absolutely."

Culley glanced into the backseat. His eyebrows went up but he didn't mention the rifle. "So, about Zoey. Is she okay?"

"As fine as can be expected. She's been at work most of the day." Connor snorted. "Now ask me how *I* am. I just got a goddamn text message from her suggesting the name of a psychiatrist who specializes in lycanthropy."

"They have shrinks for werewolves?" asked Culley.

"No, they have shrinks for people who *think* they're werewolves."

"Oh. Well, shit."

Bill shook his head. "Let me guess. She thought you were lying, trying to play mind games with her. Then she figured out you were sincere and concluded you were just plain loopy."

Connor picked up the coffee and gulped it quickly without checking its temperature. He didn't care if he scalded his throat or not. The pain helped offset the ache in his heart. "That about sums it up." He looked back at Bill suddenly. "How did you know?"

"Come on, mate, I was new to this game once too. When Jessie told me what she was, I just laughed— thought it was a big joke. Then she wouldn't let it go. I told her it warnt funny no more and when she kept it up, I got plenty mad. Figured she was making up some elaborate story so she could dump me." The big man shook his head, remembering. "Then I felt sorry for her, her being so deluded and all."

"So how did you get past it? How did Jessie convince you?"

"She Changed. Right there in my motel room." Bill

grinned at his friend. "Of course, I went more than a little crazy at first, mind you. Fainted dead away—and don't you ever tell no one that, mate! You either, Culley, or I'll have to kill you. Anyway, when I came to, Jessie was still a wolf, just lying there waiting for me to wake up. And then she played with me."

"She what?"

"Played. You know, like a big dog, all puppy-like and cute until I wasn't afraid no more. And then she Changed back. I can't say as I was able to take it all in at once, but she kept Changing every time she was with me until I got used to it."

Like a big dog. Connor turned it over in his mind, remembering Culley's goofy dog act in the clinic office. The idea had possibilities—if Zoey was ever willing to let him within a mile of her. Suddenly he saw her shapely figure slip out the back door of the *Dunvegan Herald Weekly*. The sweep of her russet hair caught the fading light of the sun and his heart flared painfully within him, a burning ache that crept into his throat.

Mercifully, Culley and Bill were silent as they got out of the truck and disappeared into a nearby store. Connor watched as Zoey tossed her camera bag and an armload of papers into her old Bronco and drove off. Putting his own vehicle into gear, he followed.

Attending a municipal budget meeting wasn't on Zoey Tyler's list of *Ten Favorite Things to Do on a Monday Night.* Or any other night for that matter. As editor, she could have assigned one of the other reporters to cover the event, to write up the article explaining the rationale for the tax increases scheduled to be announced tonight. With the growing migraine sending sharp knives of pain in through her right eye and out through the back of her head, she *should* have assigned someone else. But her publisher had other ideas.

"The RCMP announced they're going to share what they know about Menzie with the mayor and her council tonight. I want a professional on this story, Tyler, and that means you. I need someone I can trust to keep a lid on the speculation. This newspaper reports facts, not fantasy."

She hadn't needed to ask what he meant. Ted Biegel had made it his mission in life to protect the town from three things—the installation of parking meters, Sunday shopping, and most of all, rumors of werewolves. Notwithstanding the fact that those rumors were already flying thick and fast.

Despite the undercurrent of anticipation regarding what the police might say when they arrived, the meeting started like any other. The village secretary, Floyd Melnick, read off the minutes of the last meeting. Mayor Jenny Galloway called for approval of the agenda. The evening droned on. Zoey rubbed her head and tried to remember exactly when she could take another dose of painkillers. It was hard to focus her attention on the meeting. Heck, it was hard to focus her *eyeballs*. Nausea was starting to roil in her stomach from the migraine and she gritted her teeth, determined to hold on.

The council was debating the cost of snow removal and whether global warming would preclude purchasing a new plow before next winter when Sergeant Fitzpatrick finally entered the room. Dr. Lowen Miller was with him. Zoey was thankful when the mayor immediately cut off the discussion and invited the men to take the floor.

"We won't take up much of your time," said Fitzpatrick,

a sheaf of papers in his hand. "You've asked for a report on the incident at the Menzie farm. You know the basics already. Twenty-three cattle killed, and the owner, Allan Ralph Menzie, found dead at the scene. You all know Lowen here. He's the acting coroner, and I'll let him give you the details." He stepped back to give the doctor the podium.

Lowen barely glanced at the audience, electing to simply cut to the chase. "The man's death was not due to natural causes. He didn't die of old age or a heart attack. He didn't shoot himself accidentally or on purpose. He was killed by a large animal, and I believe it's the same animal that killed his cows." The doctor folded his arms as if bracing for questions. They weren't long in coming.

"What kind of animal?" asked the mayor. "Somebody said it was a grizzly."

"No one's seen a griz around here in years. We have mostly black bears," argued Elva Peters.

Lowen shook his head. "I don't believe it was a bear. I've seen the results of bear attacks and there are no claw marks on the body. The predator went straight for the throat with its teeth. That's not bear behavior either. We've ruled out a cougar as well. Again, no claw marks. Plus, a big cat typically attacks from above or behind, ambush-style. Allan Menzie was facing his attacker."

"What the hell does that leave?" demanded Melnick, forgetting completely that he wasn't a councilor and technically was not permitted to speak.

Fitzpatrick exchanged a glance with Lowen and took the podium again, his face grim. "We've got samples of hair, tooth marks on bone plus photos of tracks that were found near the body, all pointing to a single animal. It's been suggested that the killer might be an extremely large and vicious dog, and all the evidence indicates that we're dealing with a wolf or a wolf-dog hybrid."

Zoey gripped the edge of the table as the council chamber erupted with loud protests, arguments, and questions. The noise was excruciating, almost as if her brain were trying to escape from her head. Perspiration beaded on her forehead, ran down her back. She hadn't noticed the heat when she came in, yet it was sauna-like now. Then a shiver ran through her and she was instantly chilled. Her gut cramped hard. *Am I coming down with something? Please God, not the flu. Anything but that.* Her notes swam in front of her and the air seemed thick and hard to breathe. She had to get out, had to go home, but her legs wouldn't obey the order to stand.

From his truck parked directly behind Zoey's old red Bronco, Connor had staked out the village office building for the past hour, until the sense of *something wrong* that had dogged him all day suddenly began screaming at him. His inner wolf clawed at his insides, wanting out, wanting to get to Zoey, but the effects of the charm hadn't worn off yet. Instead, Connor leapt from the truck on two legs, racing into the building and up the stairs to the council chamber.

He didn't need Changeling senses to hear the muffled commotion on the other side of the heavy double doors. Cautiously, he pulled one door open. The wall of noise hit him first. Everyone in the place seemed to be on their feet, arguing. Except Zoey. He finally spotted her sitting alone in the far corner at a desk reserved for members of the media. Her head was in her hands and she didn't look up, but every other eye in the place was fastened on him. *So much for trying to sneak in.*

"Dr. Macleod, I'm relieved to see you! Maybe *you* can help us make sense of this situation," said the mayor. She waved a dismissive hand at Lowen and Fitz, who were standing their ground grimly in the midst of the melee. "These men are claiming there's a killer wolf out there." Her angry tone said it all. She didn't believe it. She didn't *want* to believe it.

The president of the Chamber of Commerce piped up. "I will not have this nonsense starting up again. Local retailers are having a hard enough time without somebody crying wolf. It's bad for business."

"For heaven's sake, Brady, those werewolf stories a few years ago brought a ton of people to town," declared another man, the utilities manager. "They all had to eat, buy gas, and rent a motel. Maybe it's exactly what we need to boost the economy around here."

Connor exchanged glances with Lowen and Fitz, glad he wasn't in their shoes and not keen to try them on. Something was terribly wrong in this room and he couldn't see it. He scanned the furious faces, but no one was even looking at Zoey. All of the anger and outrage was being directed at Lowen and Fitz. But all the attention was squarely on him.

He took a deep breath. "I didn't come here to take part in this discussion, but I will say that these men are experienced professionals and Dunvegan is damn lucky to have them. Fitzpatrick worked homicide for twenty-two years in three cities, and I shouldn't need to remind you that Miller is one of the most respected doctors in the country in the field of forensics. So if they say there's a *wolf* out there killing people, I'd start figuring out what to do to protect people instead of complaining because it's not what I wanted to hear. That's all I'm saying."

There was shocked silence for a moment, then an eruption of indignant comments, which Connor ignored as he made his way around the room to the news desk. "Zoey," he whispered fiercely. "Zoey, are you all right?"

There was no response. She continued to look down at her notepad, holding her head in her hands. Connor searched for words. "Look, I know you're pissed off at me and maybe you don't feel like talking to me, but I just need to know—" He felt it then. Electricity hovered in the air around her, invisible but building fast.

Quickly Connor sat on the edge of the table, shielding Zoey from view as he yanked her hands from her face. Powerful static looped and crackled around his fingers. She blinked up at him in surprise. Her eyes sparked with green fire.

God in heaven. "Honey, we need to get you out of here, okay?" he whispered, his heart in his throat. In case anyone was watching—although everyone seemed to have returned to arguing among themselves—he felt her forehead and her cheeks. She was burning up and cold at the same time, but it was no fever. Connor was about to ask if she could walk, but quickly decided appearances just didn't matter at the moment. He scooped her up in his arms and walked out with her. "Flu," he said as loudly as he could to Lowen as he passed. He lowered his voice however—and no one but a Changeling would hear him above the raised voices in the room—and said to Fitz, "*Lupine* flu. I'll be at the clinic. Bring the doc."

He was confident that Fitz and Lowen would cover his exit. They'd extricate themselves and come to the clinic as quickly as they could, although he doubted either could do much to help in this situation.

Connor didn't know what he was going to do either.

The clinic was the only safe place he could think of to go in a hurry. It was close by, yet isolated at the edge of the village industrial park, surrounded by corrals and sheds. Zoey's apartment was not an option. If Zoey Changed, there would be pain. A lot of it. He winced as he remembered the screams of that frightened teenager in the woods. . . .

Zoey was curled in a shuddering ball on the seat of the truck beside him. Pale beyond pale. Static energy lifted wisps of her russet hair, made it dance and float. Her eyes were glassy, unseeing. Connor drove with one hand while he gripped hers in the other. "Stay with me, honey. Hang tough for just a few minutes, okay?" *Dammit, wake up,* wake up*, you can't do this!* He hit the remote on the dashboard and drove inside the back bay of the North Star Animal Hospital.

There was no time for gentleness. He carried her straight to the shower in the back of his office and shoved her inside. Turned the cold water on full blast. He held her there for a moment, then gritted his teeth and stood under it too, holding her to him. Holding her up. "Come back to me, Zoey. Can you hear me?" *Look at me. Listen to me, just to me. The wolf is calling you but listen to me instead. Listen to your mate. Come back now.* There was no response except for a soft moan. "Don't do this, honey, you're not ready for this yet. For God's sake, wake up!" Her eyes were closed but he didn't need to see the green glimmer in their depths to know that the Change had not retreated. The wolf in him could feel it.

Connor had never known such fear. There was no way for Zoey to successfully Change, not now, not so soon. The Change required vast amounts of energy, both from the body and from the elements. Connor was practiced enough to draw it from the air if need be. With some coaching, a new Changeling was able to draw from the ground where the energy was most easily available. But Zoey hadn't had any instruction at all. Nor could he hope to teach her now. She was long past even being able to hear him, never mind understand what he was telling her.

Christ. She didn't even know what was happening to her. If he didn't find a way to stop this, she would never even know what killed her. Because Changing unprepared was almost always a death sentence. There was no being "stuck" partway between human and wolf like in a bad movie. Just death—pure, simple, and final.

Zoey's body was limp beneath the icy shower spray, her skin nearly transparent. Connor shook her fiercely, calling to her both aloud and in her mind, aware that time was rapidly running out. Again and again he reached out with all the psychic power he could bring to bear. Finally, he slapped her. For a flicker of an instant he felt her try to respond, then her awareness slid away again. "I won't let you go! Zoey!" He slapped her face again, much harder this time, *willing* her with everything he had to come back to him. He waited in agony.

Suddenly she gasped for air like a drowning swimmer. Her eyes opened wide and she held up a hand to fend off the spray of freezing water. "Goddammit, Connor! What the hell are you doing!" She sputtered and choked and cursed him, but it was music to his ears. The hellish green light had disappeared from her amber eyes, replaced by pure feminine fury.

Outrageous relief flooded his senses and jellied his knees. Connor gave up trying to stand. Instead, he opted to simply slide to the shower floor with Zoey clutched tightly in his lap. With one hand he reached up to turn on the hot faucet and let the water warm their shivering bodies.

Chapter Twenty-one

"A *flu*? This was all because of a flu bug?" Zoey was incredulous. "The last thing I remember is sitting in the council meeting and the next thing I know, I'm being drowned in a cold shower." She'd elbowed her way out of that shower in a fury, ran straight into Lowen as he came in the front door of the clinic and all but demanded that he take her home. Immediately. He'd compromised by taking her to his clinic first, where his wife had made her a soothing tea and found her some dry clothes.

Lowen nodded as he leaned over Zoey. He pumped up the blood pressure cuff and applied his stethoscope to the inside of her elbow. "No problem here," he announced as he ripped off the cuff. He turned his attention to her eyes, fingering the lids open wide and shining a penlight into the pupils. She winced.

"Light still smarts?"

"Oh yeah."

He put the light away. "You told me you came down with *the migraine from hell* to start with. Your pupils match. No broken vessels in the retinas either, but the surface of your right eye is mightily bloodshot, which can be symptomatic of a real thumper. You took medication?"

"Twice, but it didn't help."

"Hmpf. Headaches sparked by a virus seldom respond to conventional treatments. I'll have George at the drugstore send over something else. Head still hurt?"

"Yeah. At least it's down to a dull roar. Now the rest of me feels like crap."

"I'll bet it does. Get some solid rest." He pointed his finger at her. "*Real* rest, hear me? Lots of fluids. I'll write you a note for work. Bev will drive you home and I want you to stay there."

"Okay, but the shower thing—"

"Still ticked over that, are you? It was damn fine first aid in my book. Connor says you were dangerously feverish. Christ, your temperature was still 102 when you got here, and it's not normal yet. Combined with a migraine, I'm not a bit surprised you passed out. You're lucky you weren't alone when it happened."

"Okay, okay," She could accept that. And she could almost accept that Connor had taken her to an *animal* clinic. Habit, she supposed. And probably the closest available shower stall. "You seem to have a lot of respect for Connor's medical skills."

"More than I have for most human doctors, frankly. But if it's credentials you need, I suggest you check the wall in his waiting room sometime. He's got more than veterinary science diplomas up there."

She would be certain to do just that, but right now she wasn't concerned about Connor's qualifications. "Actually, I'd like to ask you about his mental health."

Lowen stopped writing on the prescription pad and stared at her. "*Connor's* mental health?"

"I don't think that's such a strange question. I have reason to wonder if he's prone to delusions, hallucinations—

anything like that. He's told me some pretty disturbing stories."

"Stories," repeated the doctor. "So I take it you don't believe whatever he's telling you?"

"Well, of course not!"

"Have you ever known Connor to lie?"

"Look, I'm sure he believes what he's saying and that's why I need a professional opinion—"

"You care about him?"

Why was he giving *her* the third degree? "Look, Connor says he can become a *wolf* for God's sake. All the caring in the world doesn't make that normal!"

"Normal," Lowen snorted, ripping off the prescription sheet and handing it to her. "Young lady, the older you get, the more you realize that *normal* is just a word somebody made up. But since you asked for my professional opinion, here it is—there isn't a damn thing wrong with Connor Macleod."

Zoey sat there, openmouthed, as the doctor left the room. She didn't even notice Bev behind her until she spoke.

"I'm sorry, dear, but Lowen tends to be rather direct."

"Yeah, I get that. Well, at least I don't have to waste time wondering what he's thinking."

Bev chuckled. "No one does. I've warmed up the jeep if you'd like to go home now."

"Thanks, I'd really appreciate the ride," said Zoey and stood up. She still felt a bit shaky, but better than when she'd come in. No wiser, however.

There isn't a damn thing wrong with Connor Macleod. She wondered about Lowen's words all the way home.

* * *

It was 6:45 A.M. and her head swam with great pounding waves of pain. *Damn migraine. Damn stupid stinking migraine.* This one had been building for two days, ever since she'd been home. It might even be the same migraine from the night of the village council meeting. It wouldn't be the first time a skull-splitter had fooled her into thinking it had left, only to ambush her again later. The change in weather might have triggered the migraine too. The overcast sky was iron gray, and there were reports of thunderstorms in the foothills with unusually heavy rains. A far distant dam on the Peace River had been forced to discharge water, and Zoey had called the sports reporter to investigate reports of flooding upstream.

As for herself, she wasn't going anywhere. Her stomach roiled with nausea and moving was out of the question. Zoey laid her head gingerly on the little bistro table in her kitchen and closed her eyes, grateful that she wasn't at the office. Wishing she had the energy to put herself to bed now that she'd finally finished the front-page story.

Officials hadn't released enough details for a thorough report in last Monday's paper. Now she had something to work with, and work she had. Zoey had put in hours on the Al Menzie article, and several others related to it, less to please her publisher and more as a matter of professionalism. Menzie had lived alone and had no relatives in the area, but he had farmed that same spot for 53 years. Long enough to have accumulated a lot of friends, neighbors, and acquaintances, most of whom would be reading the newspaper. She had wanted every detail to be both accurate and sensitive, and had written and rewritten everything into finely polished pieces.

The fact that the task had kept her mind off Connor for whole minutes at a time was a bonus.

Maybe I could nap or something right here at the table. Maybe I'll wake up in a couple of hours and my headache will be gone. Maybe I'll sprout wings and fly. She knew that the pain in her head would stand between her and sleep, just as it had much of the night even though she was exhausted right down to the bone. What little sleep she'd snatched hadn't been rewarding. Whenever she had nodded off, she'd dreamed again of a great grizzled wolf attacking poor Al Menzie—and then stalking *her.*

Damn wolves. Thinking about them naturally led to thinking about Connor. If she was honest with herself, she missed him. A lot. So much so that sometimes she almost didn't care if he thought he was a wolf. And when Zoey caught herself thinking things like that, fear and anger grabbed her by the throat. Fear that her heart was no longer her own, and anger that she had let it happen, that somehow she had lost control. *You'd think I'd be mad at Connor, but instead I'm just mad at me. Why is that? I should be furious with* him, *the way he's insinuated himself into my life, the way he's pulled all these emotions out of me. I probably wouldn't even have this damn headache if it weren't for him.*

"It's all your fault, Connor Macleod," she muttered into the place mat.

"Probably."

Zoey nearly fell off her chair in her scramble to sit up, the pain in her head screaming at her for moving so fast. She put one hand to her stomach to hold it in place, the other hand to her pulsing temple, and blinked to try to focus through the rush of agony. Connor was leaning in the glass doors to the balcony.

"Sorry to startle you, honey. I thought you were asleep until you spoke. Are you all right?"

"Actually I was having a near-death experience, but it wasn't as pleasant as I'd been led to believe it would be."

He didn't laugh. "Another migraine," he guessed. "A bad one too. I can see it from here. Will you let me help you?"

"I already took something for it. I'll be fine, thanks. Now what the hell are you doing here?" The pain prevented her from achieving much of a glare, and it was hard to feel assertive from a sitting position, but she worked at it. "Since when do you just walk into my place? And did you *climb* or something?"

"Since you haven't answered your e-mail, your text messages, your phone, or your door, I was concerned."

"I'm sure your pal Doc Miller told you I'm supposed to be resting."

"Ha. Nice job of that. I ran into Ted Biegel today. He told me all about your articles, so I know you haven't been taking it one bit easier than usual."

"Hey, I stayed home, didn't I? So now you've seen me, you know I'm alive, you can leave." She meant to say it casually, flippantly, but it didn't come out that way. In fact, the words almost didn't come out at all. In spite of the pain in her head that was almost blinding her, the pain in her heart was much worse.

He sighed. "I don't know what you took for that head, but it's not working. I can see you haven't been sleeping much either. And *don't*"—he pointed at her, and his voice took on a warning note—"say you're *fine* one more time or it's really going to piss me off."

Abruptly he was standing by her chair. She hadn't even seen him move. "Don't touch me," she ordered, but it came out as a whisper.

"I need to help you with this, honey. Do you think I'd hurt you? Are you that afraid of me?"

It was the right button to push. "I'm not afraid of you. I just don't need—" Zoey hissed as Connor's large, powerful hands gently cupped her pounding head. Long, strong fingers rested lightly over pulse points. She shivered as her vision swam, as the pain reared up in a searing wave. For a fleeting moment she thought she would faint.

"Steady, baby. Just breathe." Connor's voice was both a balm and an anchor. "Breathe with me, okay? Nice and slow. One, two. . . ."

She gasped in a shuddering breath, then let it out. Did it again. There was an odd warmth spreading from Connor's fingers. It seeped into her skull, smoothed the jagged throbbing edges of the migraine. Miraculously, the pressure eased, the roaring waves of pain began to recede. His fingers were gentle as they combed through her long russet hair, uncovered the back of her neck.

"Hell of a knot here, little falcon." He circled it lightly until the tension slipped away, then ran his hands along her shoulders, and planted a kiss on the top of her head.

Zoey opened her eyes slowly. The light didn't stab at her. She turned her head from side to side, cautious, testing. And blew out a breath. "God, that's better. That's a *lot* better. I feel almost human." She eyed him warily. "How did you do that?"

"You sound like I used black magic. It's just a skill. The lady at the health food store over on Third can do the same thing. It's a matter of shifting energy, balancing it."

She'd heard of it, although she hadn't experienced it before. "Thanks. Whatever it was, it did the trick. I appreciate it." Something twigged at her memory. "What was that you called me?"

"When?"

"A few minutes ago when you were working on my head."

"Oh. *Little falcon*."

"I see. I've been demoted from *honey* to a predatory bird?"

"It's not—well—" He looked almost sheepish. "I've been calling you *little falcon*, at least to myself, from Day One. It's the first thing I thought of when I saw you on the roof of your truck. You were soaked and frozen and scared but still ready to take me on if I so much as breathed the wrong way. That ferocious look in those amber eyes of yours reminded me of a falcon that was brought into the clinic once."

"Still doesn't sound like much of an endearment."

"Trust me, it's a compliment. I was very impressed with the courage and tenacity of that angry little bird." He held out his left hand and turned it just so. "See? I still have a scar on my thumb."

"How sweet. And this reminds you of me?"

"You're brave and strong and beautiful, just like the falcon."

There was nothing but sincerity in his voice. She studied his face, his eyes, and was startled to see them drawn and exhausted. Apparently she hadn't been the only one missing sleep. A stray lock of dark hair hung over one of his eyes and she found herself wanting to smooth it back. She'd been ready to tell him to leave, plead her need to sleep and send him away. But she couldn't make herself do such a thing now.

Perhaps he sensed the change because he pressed his advantage. "We need to talk, Zoey. We need to set things right between us."

"I know it," she said quietly, realizing there was no sense putting off the discussion any longer. She rose carefully, relieved that she was no longer dizzy or nauseous, and followed Connor to the living room. What he could say to make things better, she couldn't imagine, but she was praying fervently he would come up with *something* she could accept. Because she'd tried to imagine a future without him in it, and it was a bleak and aching void. She wrapped her arms around herself as much for comfort as to defend against such a prospect.

"Come sit down, honey. I have a lot to say and you need to be comfortable."

"What I *need* is a damn good explanation, Connor."

"I have one. Come and sit."

He patted the cushion next to him, but she chose the far end of the couch instead. She didn't trust herself to be too close—it would be far too easy to melt into his arms, to start kissing him and not stop. She needed to hear what he had to say first. She resisted the silly impulse to clutch a throw pillow in front of her like a shield.

"I'm sorry I didn't handle things well the other day," he said.

Relief flooded through her. He was apologizing. Things were going to be okay—

"I've been thinking a lot about what I might have done differently, but there just wasn't enough time."

"I guess I left too soon." She could meet him halfway. "I was really upset."

"I know you were, and I'm sorry it had to be that way. There's even less time now."

"We've got lots of time. We can take all the time we want to work this out."

He shook his head. "There are only two weeks before the full moon."

Full moon? She jumped to her feet. "No way, not this crap again. Don't you dare—"

He was off the couch and had hold of her upper arm in a flash. "No, don't *you* dare. This time, you're going to listen." His eyes had gone dark with barely repressed fury. "Just because you don't understand something, it doesn't make it any less true. Do you think I'm getting off on this? Do you think I've made all this up so I can get my jollies by torturing you with it? I wish like hell I had buckets of time to ease you into this gradually, but I don't. Or more accurately, *you* don't. Whether you like it or not, whether you believe me or not, *your life is on the line.* You've got to trust me and let me help you."

Zoey studied the man looming over her. His anger made him seem even larger than usual. There was no possibility of getting her arm back—he wasn't hurting it, but until he relaxed his steel grip, she knew she wasn't going anywhere. Still, she wasn't afraid of *him*, not yet, anyway. It was his delusions that were terrifying her. "Why are you doing this to me? Why are you telling me these things? I don't understand, Connor."

"I'm telling you the truth. Feel it, read it in my mind. You have enough of a psychic gift to at least sense it if you'll let yourself." He let go of her arm and began to pace the apartment. Told her the story all over again. *He was able to become a wolf. She was going to become one too.*

It didn't sound any more plausible to Zoey the second time around. Or the third. Or the fourth. She tried hard to wrap her head around what he was saying, tried to look at it symbolically, metaphorically, in fact, every way she could think of. Except literally, of course, although Connor kept insisting she should take it that way. Finally she buried her face in her hands. Her head was pounding again, she was tired beyond belief, and her heart felt as if it had been ripped out by the roots. She loved Connor Macleod more than she'd thought possible to love anyone—and some terrible mental illness was standing between them like an iron fence. A movement caught her eye and she pushed her hair out of her face with her hands and slumped to sit on the floor with her back against the couch. She watched bleakly, too miserable to even be curious, as Connor abruptly shoved the coffee table to one side. For a moment he just stood there in the open space, holding her gaze with those pale gray eyes that moved her so. And then a flash of green fire appeared in their depths.

Zoey had been on a golf course once when a lightning bolt struck just yards away, an explosion of light and sound and raw power that had shaken the ground beneath her. She could feel something like it now, right here in her living room. A sudden sensation of static electricity, the lifting of the hair on her neck, the ozone whiff in the air, a thrum of power that vibrated bone-deep. . . . She was about to warn Connor, when suddenly he wasn't there anymore. In his place stood an immense wolf, bright sparks of static crackling in its fur.

Chapter Twenty-two

Had she snapped? Had Connor managed to pull her into his fantasy world? Zoey swallowed hard and took a slow, shaky breath to steady herself. Now was not the time to figure out how a wolf came to be in her apartment. *Options. There have to be options.* Maybe she could lock herself in the bathroom or barricade herself in the bedroom. *Too far.* The wolf would be on her before she could make it. The hallway—if she could make it to the hallway of the apartment building, she could close the beast in, call for help. But the wolf was between her and the door. A weapon? Maybe she could hit it with something, stun it, distract it just long enough. . . .

So far, the wolf hadn't moved. It merely sat and regarded her, its head tilted to one side, its great jaws gaping into a huge sharp-toothed grin. Could she catch it off guard? The door to the hallway was to her right. She made a feint to the left and gasped as the massive wolf leapt to its feet—but it didn't attack her. Instead, it jumped into her recliner with enough force to open it up. She was about to make her break for the door, when the wolf caught her attention. It was lying on its back across the chair, feet paddling the air, head hanging over the end of the footrest, mouth open, tongue lolling.

My God, is it crazy? Maybe it's rabid. It was far too big for the chair. The powerful creature looked absolutely ridiculous. *I must be nuts too. Stop looking at the wolf and get out of here!*

But she couldn't take her eyes off the wolf. It rolled onto the floor and crouched there, bouncing on its front paws like an oversized puppy, filling the air with little excited barks. Then it seized the remote off the coffee table with careful teeth and tossed it at her.

Zoey caught the remote more out of instinct than intent. The enormous wolf was looking at her expectantly and yipped again. She found herself wanting to respond, wanting to join in the insanity and toss the remote. Quickly she shoved the impulse away. There was something else pressing on her conscious mind, something familiar that she should know but couldn't quite grasp.

The wolf wouldn't give up, however. It came creeping toward her on its belly, whining softly, wagging its tail. She was so mesmerized by its silly performance that she failed to realize it was within reach of her foot. Before she could yank it away, a broad pink tongue flicked out and licked her bare toes.

"Don't do that!" Zoey yanked her foot away. *Great, now I'm talking to it!* She felt behind her for the couch, wondered if she could jump up and over it successfully before the beast got any closer. Would that give her a second or two to make it to another room? Suddenly the huge animal was right next to her. It rolled onto its back, still making soft little whining sounds, nudging her leg with its nose.

His nose. The animal was definitely male. The wolf wriggled itself up close to her, begging for her attention like an oversized dog. Hesitantly, knowing it was insane but still unable to resist, Zoey reached out and touched the silvery fur on the animal's chest, then found herself looking directly into its strange pale eyes. Pale *gray* eyes. . . .

Several things rocketed through her brain at once. Silver pelt marked with a black saddle. The wolf that had protected her. In her dreams. In reality.

"Connor?"

The wolf yipped and rolled upright. She reached out to touch him again, an expression of wonder on her face. Ran her hands through the thick soft fur around his muscled neck, inhaled the primal scent of him. The wolf from her dream. The man she loved. "You're the same. Omigod, you're the same. All this time. I didn't know, I didn't understand."

The great wolf leaned in to nuzzle her russet hair, licked her face softly, washing away the tears that ran freely.

You had no way of knowing, little falcon.

Zoey jumped backward as if the animal had snapped at her. The words had resounded clearly in her head. "You didn't . . . you couldn't . . . you just—"

Talked to you. Yes I did.

"I can hear you! Omigod, I can hear you! Connor!" She automatically touched her ears with her hands, although she hadn't heard the words physically.

Of course, you can hear me. You're psychic, remember? Most of the Pack can talk to each other just like this.

"Of course I can . . ." She laughed a little desperately, and shook her head. "Good grief, look at me. I'm sitting in my living room with a telepathic wolf."

Changeling.

"Changeling. Wolf and human together. Is it—are they

equal parts of you? Are you really half and half or is one side in charge of things?"

His snort of laughter tickled the inside of her head. *Some days I wonder. But both sides love you with everything they have.* He licked her face once more then backed away a few steps, holding her gaze with his.

Electricity suddenly crackled through Zoey's hair and prickled her skin. Something unknown called her, pulled at her, brought forth a strange yearning from deep within her . . . In an instant it was gone and she saw Connor's face appear through a whirl of blue sparks. Without thinking, she leaned forward to brush the hair back from his eyes.

"Ow!" A powerful static charge snapped from his face to her fingers as she accidentally grounded the electricity. He had the nerve to laugh, even as he took her hand and kissed it better. "I'm afraid you have to watch out for that, honey. It's like shuffling your feet across the carpet and touching a doorknob, but a helluva lot stronger." He sat down beside her at the foot of the couch and gathered her under his arm, kissed the top of her head. "Devlin developed a theory about how much power is collected, so after a few beers one night, he set a lightbulb on the floor beside him and Changed while we all watched to see what would happen. The bulb lit up all right, then it exploded. Culley and Kenzie picked a lot of glass slivers out of his hide that night."

Zoey turned to study his face. "I'm not dreaming. Unless I've fallen down Alice's rabbit hole, it's all really true, isn't it? I'm going to wake up in the morning and this will have really happened."

"Yup, 'fraid so."

"And your brothers are like you?" Her thoughts tumbled like stones in a polishing drum, becoming brighter and clearer with every turn. A lot of things were beginning to make sense.

"My whole family actually. You've already met Culley in his furry form."

"I have?"

"The clinic. My office."

"The big black—but that was a dog!" Suddenly she wasn't sure.

"No, it was a big black *wolf* doing a terrific impression of a big black dog. What can I say? The boy's got a helluva knack."

Werewolves doing impressions . . . She filed that surreal thought away for the moment. "How about your friends?"

He nodded. "The Watsons are Changelings. A few others as well."

"Aha!" She pointed her finger at him. "Lowen Miller, right?"

"Nope."

"No? But he didn't seem very surprised when . . ." she trailed off.

"No doubt you told him I thought I was a wolf. And Lowen didn't react because he's known about Changelings for years."

"You're kidding. There are ordinary humans that know about you and it hasn't been on CNN or National Geographic? How can that be?"

"Maybe Changelings choose their friends well."

"And maybe nobody believes anybody that talks."

"That helps a lot."

"But Helfren believes. And I'll bet a lot of his readers believe too."

"His belief didn't give him any credibility in your office."

"No. No, it sure didn't."

She leaned over and laid her head on his shoulder, shaken to the core by the wonder and the enormity of what he'd revealed to her. The world as she knew it had abruptly changed forever. "I guess I'll have to apologize for not believing you."

"No need. It's too much to ask anyone to believe all at once," he said, stroking her hair and leaning down to brush it with his lips. "You were pretty damn brave, you know. Bill fainted when Jessie Changed in front of him the first time. And don't ever tell him I told you."

"You gotta be kidding. Bill? But he's a wolf too, right? I mean, he can be a wolf when he wants to be?"

"Yes. Jessie gave him the gift. She's Pack leader, by the way. We usually run together."

Sure you do. It still sounded bizarre to Zoey. Maybe it wouldn't in time, but today? Definitely the stuff that role-playing video games were made of. Still, Bill and Jessie seemed normal, appeared to be perfectly happy. They ran a business, held barbecues for their friends . . . Why wasn't she surprised that Jessie was a pack leader? *You think size matters?* Zoey found herself chuckling at this new spin on her friend's words.

Connor squeezed her shoulders. "What's so funny?"

"Well, it all makes the Hollywood stereotype seem so silly—you know, *tormented human turns into werewolf and eats everyone in sight.* Bill and Jessie are so friendly and sweet, it's—" Suddenly her own words sank in. "Omigod," she whispered, covering her mouth with her hands as if to stifle the words. *Menzie.* Images of the farmer's terrified face, his torn body, flashed through her mind. Was there something Connor wasn't telling her? Was there a dark side to his dual nature? What about his family and friends? They all seemed like normal human beings by day—but what were they, really, by night?

And dear God, what was she about to become?

"You're not going to turn into a vicious killer." Connor followed Zoey throughout the house as she paced. She was frantic and frightened, but he had to give her credit for holding herself together.

"He bit me. You told me he's my sire. If I can get this goddamn werewolf virus from him, why not the homicidal tendencies?"

"Bernie's crazy for a reason, and it has nothing to do with a virus or genes or anything else." Connor searched for a way to address her fears. "He can't pass that on to you."

"And no one else has whatever he has? Because I need to know that he's the only one, Connor. Tell me that the rest of you don't go out in the middle of the night and gobble up hitchhikers and homeless people."

He didn't know whether to laugh or be pissed off at that. "You've been watching way too many bad movies, honey."

"Don't take that tone with me. I don't have any reference points for all of this. I had no idea that werewolves—"

"Changelings."

"—*werewolves* existed until today. On top of that, you're telling me I'm going to become one. If that's true, how do I know you didn't plan it this way? Maybe you didn't want a human lover, maybe what you really wanted was for me to be just like you. Well, *I* don't want this, Connor Macleod. I don't want any of it, do you hear me?"

"I didn't do this to you," he growled. With a quicksilver motion, he reached out a powerful arm and gathered her back against him, nearly taking her off her feet. Wrapped his other arm around her as well and held her. She struggled a little, then made a disgusted noise and settled for glaring up at him with furious eyes. His own anger began to dissipate. Zoey might be putting up a brave front, but he could sense the fear, scent it on her. She wasn't afraid of him—but she was terrified of the unknown. "I didn't do this to you," he repeated, gently this time. "I would never put you through this unless you asked me, and even then, not until you'd had more time in our world and understood what you were asking for."

"You wouldn't have turned me into a wolf?"

"Never. Not unless you truly wanted it. And if you didn't want it, then we would continue just as we are. And I happen to think we're pretty damn good together." He waggled his brows at her. "You sure didn't need to be a wolf to drive me crazy the other night."

She seemed to relax a little at that. He kept his arms tight around her just the same, but took a chance and planted a gentle kiss on her head, nuzzled her thick russet hair. "We have to deal with what is, Zoey. It's not fair that you've been bitten, not fair that you have no choice. It's against all Changeling law. But it's done. We have to go from here and make the best of it."

"Easy for you to say. I don't know what to do. I don't see an instruction manual anywhere. What if I can't Change, what if I don't do it right? What if I change into a Labrador Retriever or something instead of a wolf? I read about shapeshifters who can become anything. I could end up being a groundhog or a goddamn chicken!"

He was certain that if he gave in to the laughter that was threatening to burst out, she'd get even more upset. "Okay, sure, there are legends of people who can become any animal they want. But I've never met any. Or heard of anyone who has. You'll be a wolf, I promise. You won't even have to think about it."

Zoey looked unconvinced. "Does it hurt?"

He wished he could say *no*. Instead, he nodded. "The first time, yes it does. Not so much for those who are born Changelings, but there's a great deal of pain for those who are human to start with, I'm afraid. Most of the pain is in the bones, like a severe case of arthritis. It's because they have to shift proportions so dramatically, much more so than any other part of the body. The most important thing is not to fight it. It's painful but you have to keep your fear under control. If you panic and start resisting, the pain gets worse."

"I can hardly wait," she said ruefully, then searched his face. "Does it hurt you to Change?"

"No, not at all. Like I said, it only hurts the first time. The next time and every time after that, you don't feel a thing. It's like your body knows the way, has created a pattern to follow. And it comes faster. After you've Changed a few times, it becomes pretty much instantaneous."

"Do you have any idea how surreal this is? Or how scary? You've grown up with the concept of people turning into animals. I haven't known about this for twenty-four hours yet."

He leaned down and touched his forehead to hers, rested his broad hands on her shoulders. "I'll be with you every step of the way, I swear it. I'll help you. We'll get through it together." Now he was the one putting on a brave front. The whole idea of Zoey going through the first Change scared him to death. He certainly understood now why Geoff Lassiter had waited so long—almost three years—before allowing his human wife, Melly, to join him. There was always a certain amount of risk involved, just as there was with childbirth. If a problem developed, however, no human hospital could help.

Connor wished that Kenzie and Birkie were here. He could call them, he knew, and they would come home immediately. But good Christ, he didn't want either of them within a thousand miles of Dunvegan until Bernie was dead. No, better to leave things as they were, with the women safely in Scotland. If Zoey wasn't so close to the Change, he'd send her there too.

"You're frowning," she said.

"I just remembered that there's no one looking after the farm but me today. I need to drive out and feed some animals, check on things. Maybe that's a good thing. You look like you could use some fresh air."

"I don't know, Connor. I think I'd rather stay here and lie down."

He shook his head. "You can lie down at the farm if you like, but we're not splitting up again for any reason. That damn reporter was parked outside your building when I came in." He waved a hand at the window.

"I'm not surprised. He phones a dozen times a day," she sighed. "But I'm perfectly safe in my own apartment. There's a deadbolt on the door and I'm on the third floor, for heaven's sake."

"If you were on the *twentieth* floor, I'd still be worried about Bernie. The crazy old bastard's still at large and he's targeted you. And believe me, he could climb to your balcony just as easily as I just did."

"He's an old man!"

"No, he's not. He's old as dirt, all right, but he's a Changeling. You saw the gray wolf at the party—did he look old and decrepit to you? Or the night he bit your leg—I'm betting he didn't look too geriatric then either."

Zoey shivered. "Okay, okay. I get the point."

Connor slipped his arms around her. "Besides that, we're a team now." He nuzzled her ear, brushed his lips over her temple, her brow. "I don't ever want to be without you again. These last few days were hard enough. So I'm thinking you should marry me, and the sooner the better."

"Don't you want to wait and see what I look like as a wolf first? I might be ugly and then you'd be stuck. The other Changelings would make fun of you."

He laughed then. He couldn't help it. "I'll take my chances. Is that a yes?"

"No, it's a *let me take something for the headache I'm getting, and I'll get ready to go.*"

His hand found the back of her neck, rubbed it gently. "Another migraine already?"

"Yeah. I usually only get a couple in a month, but lately it's been one after another." She laid her head on his chest and sighed as he massaged her shoulders, her neck, the back of her head.

"I'll bet it's because the first Change is coming on. Your hormones are probably all over the map as your body adjusts to accommodate it."

"Hormones?" She gripped his arms. "Please, *please* tell me I don't get PMS with this."

"I sure hope not," he chuckled. "But anything's possible. The good news is, after you've gone through the Change once, the migraines will stop. In fact, you'll probably never have another one. Never have a cold either. Changelings are remarkably healthy."

"No migraines? Ever? You should have told me that first—I might have volunteered to be a werewolf!" She smiled then, the first real smile he'd seen in days, and it was like the sun coming out from behind the clouds. Still smiling, she stepped into him, fisted her hands in his hair and pulled his face down to hers.

"I need you, Connor," she whispered. Her amber eyes were lit with tenderness, with love, with desire. With a hundred emotions that were all for him. "Now; I need you right now and right here."

He meant to say *I need you, too*. Before he could get the words out, however, something primal slipped its leash. What possessed him went far beyond a human need and he wanted, hungered and *craved* with a soul-deep yearning that shook him. Before, he had always been careful, even gentle, not wanting to overwhelm her with his strength. Now, without any warning, he was a creature maddened by thirst, balanced on the brink of deep mountain lake.

In the blink of an eye, he yanked her hard against him. Took her lips in a bruising kiss and thrust his tongue deep, clutching her ass in viselike hands. What small part of him was still sane expected her to protest such tactics and shove him away, yet he couldn't make himself pull back. Instead, a faint growl escaped him. Then her tongue flicked lightly at the corners of his mouth, slid teasingly between his lips. One slender hand knotted itself in his hair as her pelvis rocked into his. The surprise of it held him still for a fraction of an instant, long enough for her to unhook his straining jeans and slide her hand inside.

As her cool fingers caged his rampant cock, he sucked in an empty breath—the air had long since left the room. Slowly, slowly, her hand began to slide up and down and the beast that had wanted so badly to ravage and take was suddenly at her command. He opened his eyes to find her amber ones fixed on him—and in them was the same primordial need that had overtaken him.

In a heartbeat they were on the floor. A wild desperation to be in one skin drove them to tear at each other's clothes. She was wet as he pressed against her, wet and hot and hungry for him as he stroked into her. She urged him on, wrapping her legs around him, pulling him in harder, deeper as her pleasure gathered and spiked. Wrapped her arms around him as his body throbbed out his own bliss.

When sense finally returned, they were gasping and laughing in a comfortable tangle of arms and legs. The tangle of clothing was less comfortable. Connor kicked away his jeans from one ankle. Zoey's bra was looped crazily around an elbow and her shirt was attached by only a cuff.

"I sure hope the neighbors are at work," she giggled as she tried to free herself from her sleeve. "I don't want the cops at my door asking what all the noise was about."

"Don't worry, I'm sure they'll only write you a ticket."

"Write *me* a ticket? What about you? You all but howled at the end!"

"Fitz is a buddy of mine. I'm pretty sure I can get off with a warning." Connor helped her turn the tangled cuff and undid the button. "Maybe I'll put in a good word for you too. After all," he grinned. "I love you, Zoey Tyler."

She stripped off the offending shirt with a sigh of relief. "I love you too. I didn't stop, you know. Not even when I thought you were, well—"

"Crazy? That's good to know. So you'll stand by me if I develop any mental problems in the future?"

"Absolutely."

"Even if I do something crazy like this?" He nuzzled her face, sought her mouth and kissed her long and deep.

Roved his hands over her pliant body, skimming his fingers lightly over her soft skin until she shivered. Palmed the moist heat between her legs until she moaned aloud.

"Okay, yes, *especially* if you do something crazy like this." She gasped as he slipped a finger into her, trembled as he swirled it slowly around. "Omigod, I don't think we can do this again already."

"Bet we can." He grinned. "We'll just take it long and slow. Very, very slow."

The colorful shades were drawn and the *Closed* sign swung in the window of the Finer Diner, but Culley walked in the front door just the same. Most of the Pack was already there, including the RCMP sergeant, all watching a disheveled Devlin as he taped district maps to the candy display. A bundle of colored markers rattled in his shirt pocket and Culley chuckled to himself. *My brother the geek.*

Culley raised a hand at Lassiters and McIntyres, nodded to Holt LaLonde and Fitzpatrick, winked at René Ghost-keeper, then took a seat in a booth across from Bill and Jessie. Jessie looked exhausted and grim, leaning back against her husband as he rocked her gently. Culley knew that she, as well as most of the people in the room, had been hunting for the rogue Changeling almost around the clock since the night of the barbecue. Still, the Pack leader managed a faint grin for him.

"What are we looking at, Dev?" Culley called out.

His twin ran a hand through his hair, unaware that the gesture only made parts of it stand up straight. "I thought if we looked at where Bernie's been, we could spot some sort of pattern."

"What, like in Scooby Doo?" Holt snorted. "That stuff only happens in the movies."

"Yeah, well so do *monsters*," said Culley. "But we seem to have one anyways."

Jessie rose to her feet. Despite her obvious weariness, her voice was clear and firm. "Ideas, people. We need ideas and we need them now. Bernard Gervais has eluded our best trackers and we don't know how he's doing it. I don't even *care* how, as long as we figure out where he is so we can stop him. So all ideas need to be on the table no matter how silly or farfetched you might think they are."

"Motive," said Fitz. "If we know what he wants, we could figure out where he's going."

Geoff Lassiter rolled his eyes. "Bernie's crazy. Who knows what the hell he wants?"

"Crazy, and grouchy as an old bear. Have you ever met anyone so rude?" asked his wife, Melly. Her makeup didn't hide the circles under her eyes.

"More than rude. He *hates* us—does that count as a motive?" Culley ventured. "Of course, I don't know if he hates the Pack as a whole or each of us individually."

"Both, and some more than others," said Devlin.

Bill shook his head. "Bernie's a right miserable cuss, but it's not members of the Pack he's attacked. He's picked on humans, and one for sure that he didn't even know."

"Zoey," said Culley. "But maybe Bernie doesn't attack Changelings because he knows he can't win. Like an angry bully who only picks on kids smaller than him."

"Well, if he's attacking humans at random, I don't know how we can predict what he'll do next," said Melly. "For all we know, he's picking on humans just to make life hard for *us*."

Fitz looked thoughtful. "You know, Mel, that makes a lot of sense. Bernie doesn't have to fight any Changelings in order to make life miserable for every one of us. He just has to scare the general population. It's going to be tough to be a wolf in these parts soon. Some people are already out hunting."

"You're talking like that old coot has a plan," said Holt. "I think Geoff had it right. What if Bernie's just batshit crazy? That means there's no motive, no pattern, no nothing."

Culley sat back as the meeting got "lively," as Jessie often termed it. As a species, Changelings were strong-willed and intelligent, and that usually translated into strong opinions too. This type of an assembly tended to resemble a gathering of relatives at Thanksgiving when the subject of politics came up. It was going to be noisy for a while. . . .

Devlin was busy circling things on the maps and Culley strained to see what his twin was doing. Finally, he got up to take a closer look. "Are these all the places Bernie's been spotted?"

"Well, not quite all." Devlin made a couple more circles with a marker. "Holt caught sight of him *here* and chased him for a short ways until he vanished without a trace. And here's where the McIntyres saw Bernie, up on the ridge. By the time they got there, he'd disappeared and there was no trail to follow."

Culley's gaze flicked from one circle to the other. "I can see roads intersecting these locations. But even if Bernie was driving or taking the damn bus, there'd still be a trail of scent in the air." He closed his eyes, tried to picture each location, conjuring not just the image but the smell. If a Changeling had been somewhere in lupine form, then his brain automatically had the location mapped out in im-

mense detail by scent. Culley knew all of these places inti-
mately, right down to the smallest clump of earth and the
types of plants that grew there. Slowly, he drew in a long
breath of air as he savored each scent stored in his mind,
noting the odors common to all the locations—

His eyes flew open. "Devlin, we need a more detailed
map."

Half an hour later, it was Culley standing in front of the
Pack. Emotions were still running high but the Changelings had settled into relative quiet. For the moment. At the
new map, hastily scanned and enlarged at a local geological
survey office, Devlin traced something in blue highlighter.
At first, the thick colored line resembled a tree, branching
out in all directions. Little Burnt Creek wound its way
along the edge of town, a tiny stream as it passed under the
Gamble Street Bridge. But by the time the creek made its
way to the Peace River, it wasn't tiny anymore. Instead,
countless streams had trickled through the rolling land-
scape to join it, swelling it to a respectable size before it
merged with the mighty river.

"This is the old Gervais place." Devlin made a square
with green marker, then drew two more. "This is Menzie's
farm. And *this*, over here, is the local golf course outside of
town."

"They're all linked," announced Culley. "Everywhere
Bernie's made an appearance, he's been able to get there by
water. Water is the key."

"What, he's swimming?" Holt didn't clue in at first.

Jessie did, immediately. She sat up and pounded her small
fist on the table hard enough to rattle the salt and pepper
shakers. "Goddammit. He's using an old fox's trick."

There were nods around the room. It was one of the

most basic of strategies, employed by many animals. A fox pursued by a dog would enter a creek and walk downstream for a time before returning to dry land. The pursuer would have a difficult time finding the scent where the quarry had left the water.

"Yes and no," replied Culley. "I think he's taken the old trick to a whole new level. I think Bernie's using the water system in this area as his own personal highway. In fact, I'll bet he seldom leaves the waterways except to commit some new atrocity."

Geoff wasn't convinced. "Come on, Culley. We're good hunters, all of us, and Changelings have keener senses than even real wolves do. Holt and I followed the stream by Menzie's for nearly four miles in each direction without ever catching a hint of that bastard's scent. It just plain wasn't there. Water can hide tracks and trail, sure, but we'd be able pick the scent out of the air itself if we had to."

"True, but I'll bet more than the water is hiding him from us," said Jessie. "By now, Bernard's accumulated a great deal of power from the blood he's spilled. Enough power to almost seem like magic. If he's walking along a creek bed, he might very well be able to wrap the energy of the water around himself like a blanket."

"Is that even possible?" asked Holt. "Sounds like science fiction."

"I have seen it done," she replied. "And I think it's more than possible in this case."

Frowning, Melly leaned forward. "I'm confused. Are you saying this energy, this power, acts like some kind of camouflage?"

Jessie nodded. "Not only would we be unable to scent him, we might not even be able to *see* him when he's traveling along the water."

"Bollocks." Bill sat back. "That means the rotter can come and go as he bloody well pleases."

"So what do we do? Bernie's running around like a mad dog and people are dying," said Geoff. "There must be some damn way of using this information."

Fitzpatrick nodded. "Maybe there is. We could try to anticipate who might be targeted next. If he's using the water system like Devlin says, then what other farms are along it? Where is Bernie most likely or most able to strike again?"

Devlin squinted at the map, pulled a red marker from the bundle in his pocket and made four new squares. "Tom Yasinski has a big bison ranch north of town. This creek right here passes through it. Quinn Madden has a farm south of Dunvegan, and I think this is Anna Webber's sheep operation to the southeast. Both of them are linked by a sizeable stream."

"I want two members of the Pack on each of those places. I want them watched around the clock," said Jessie. "Make sure one of you has strong mindspeech abilities so you can get a message to me if you spot Bernard. If necessary, get out your damn cell phone and call me, so I can mobilize the Pack. But don't engage him on your own."

Culley glanced back at his brother. Devlin was standing silently, staring at the map with his finger on the fourth red square. "What it is, bro?"

"Connor's place. This one is Connor's."

Chapter Twenty-three

"Quite a spread." Tad Helfren left his van and stood for a few moments with his hands on his hips, surveying the scenery. The farm was the last one on a dead-end road, but it was easily the largest. According to the district map, everything Helfren looked at in every direction belonged to Connor Macleod. Between the stands of trees, he could see far across the lush fields to where the land dropped away steeply into the river valley. Even with the sky dark and overcast, the scenery was impressive.

He'd heard that the place had been a fixer-upper. The sprawling house was certainly old, but there was a new roof and fresh paint. It looked decent on the outside at least. He couldn't say as much for the rest of the farm. Obviously Macleod hadn't gotten around to fixing up the many barns and outbuildings, or perhaps he just didn't give a damn about them. The only thing different between this and a hundred other tired old farms in the area was the number of trees. Most farmyards were bare. This one had tall stands of poplar between the buildings and in the corrals. Was it a case of a werewolf preferring to have ample cover handy, or was it simply nature reclaiming the neglected place? A thick forest of poplars and spruce flanked the south side of the yard. Beyond that, he knew from the map, the woods gave way to more fields. Just wild grass, according to some other farmers, no crops planted in years.

Of course, what use would a werewolf have for wheat or soybeans? Behind the fences were a considerable number of cows, horses, pigs and what-have-you. Maybe it was a private buffet. *Dinner on the goddamn hoof whenever he wants it.*

Helfren glanced to his right and spotted a swatch of black and white beneath a thick patch of blueberry bushes at the side of the house. Ever curious, he wandered over, his camera at the ready. *Looks like fur . . .*

Pushing a branch aside, he could see that the fur belonged to a dog, a Border Collie. Its throat was torn out and its blood was soaking into the grass. Helfren was puzzled as he studied it for clues. Why would Connor Macleod kill a dog? For fun? Sport? Maybe werewolves just plain didn't like dogs. Practice? That must be it, Helfren decided. The red-haired editor was new to being a werewolf, so it stood to reason that Macleod would make her practice her skills. Apparently she hadn't killed anything at Menzie's farm. The police report had stated it was probably the work of a single animal. So maybe she'd just watched. And learned.

Helfren raised the digital camera and snapped a couple of frames. Lowered it and considered the dog. The kill was very recent. Too recent. He'd bet the dog had been dead an hour, maybe two at the most. Yet he'd been keeping close tabs on the editor, and checked her apartment building once more before he left town. Her truck had been parked in front all day, and he'd seen Connor Macleod pull up and head into the building—alone.

As he straightened up, he spotted another lump of fur amid the leaves. *What the hell?* Parting the branches, he saw several more dogs, all shapes and sizes and colors. All freshly dead. All deliberately piled in the midst of the bushes, like broken toys. And in the flower bed beyond that—he strained to see, unable to move closer because his feet seemed rooted to the ground.

There was a body. A human body.

Helfren's mouth dried and he backed out of the brush quickly, his gaze darting everywhere at once. Was there another werewolf? The vet had brothers and a sister who lived in the area. Shitfire, what if the entire frickin' family could shapeshift?

The man's heart raced and he was having trouble pulling in enough air. If he was dealing with a whole nest of werewolves instead of just one or two, then he needed to regroup and reconsider. Refine his strategy. And from a safe distance, which meant getting the hell away from here now. *Right now.* Helfren made his way back to the driveway as quickly as his shaky legs would take him. But as he rounded the van to the driver's side, he saw an old man half sitting, half lying, on the porch steps leading up to the house.

"Gervais? What the hell are you doing here?" His voice sounded strained even to himself as he gripped the door handle of the van.

"Just waiting for Macleod and his bitch to come home," the man giggled, and slid down one stair. A large empty vodka bottle rolled to the ground. "I've got a lil' surprise for 'em."

Every one of Helfren's survival instincts was screaming at him to open the damn door and get in the van. Instead, his reporter's instincts considered Bernard Gervais. The guy was drunk as a skunk—but maybe he hadn't been in this condition an hour or so ago. In fact, it was highly likely that Gervais was the one who had killed the dogs. He was mean enough to do it, and certainly pissed off at Macleod.

But was he crazy enough to kill the man in the flower bed too? And what the hell had he used for a weapon? A hatchet?

You sick old bastard. Yet the bastard seemed to be in a good mood and maybe the vodka had made him talkative. There didn't seem to be any weapon other than the empty bottle, and it had rolled out of reach. Helfren took a deep breath, then another. Reminded himself that he was no mere reporter—he was a paranormal investigator, a professional. And a professional would damn well investigate. He forced away his fear and slid his hands into his pockets to control their shaking. A moment later he was the picture of casual friendliness. "Hey, nice job with the dogs." He considered himself a good actor, but still he had to force out every word. "That oughta burn Macleod's ass. Perfect way to get even with a veterinarian in my books."

"Hell, yeah."

"And that guy back there, he musta tried to stop you. Guess you fixed his wagon."

Gervais grinned. "Not done yet either." He made a sweeping gesture at the paddocks and corrals.

Helfren struggled to hide his revulsion. He wasn't much for law enforcement as a rule, but he'd call in an anonymous tip to the cops the minute he was on the road and headed for town. "I've really been depending on your expertise, Mr. Gervais. Thanks to you, I've got great footage of some wolves running through the golf course and some wolf prints near Menzie's body. My readers are going to like that, but I need more. I didn't get a damn thing from the vet clinic. No footage of anyone turning into a werewolf yet. I'm hoping you might know a little more than you've been telling."

" 'Course I do."

"Is it a question of more money? 'Cause I thought I was paying you pretty well."

"Don't need your damn money."

"What do you want then? I'm willing to negotiate but I need to know about the Macleod family. Are they all were-wolves?"

"Every goddamn one of 'em. Think they're safe here, think they're protected. Wouldn't feel so fuckin' secure if there wasn't a cop on their side."

"A cop? One of the RCMP? What about him?" Helfren had drawn his pocket recorder and clicked it on, without even being aware he had done so. "Does he know about the werewolves?" Hell, maybe the guy was on the take. Maybe he was being paid to ignore evidence or something. According to his sources in town, the Macleods were far from poor.

"The sergeant's one of *them*." The old man spread his arms wide. He burped loudly, then followed it up with a long, drawn-out fart. "Too damn fuckin' many of 'em now. Hate 'em all."

"There are *more* werewolves?" Helfren didn't have to fake his amazement.

"Shit, yeah." Gervais spread his hand, counted awkwardly on his fingers. Wrapped his mouth around the names even more awkwardly. "LaLonde. McIntyre. Beauchamp. Lassiter. Rousseau. You see those names around here, there's bound to be Changelings nearby. Then there's Ghost-keeper—"

"What?"

"That's a Métis name, city boy. Look it up in a fuckin' history book." Gervais's expression hardened, his eyes narrowed. "And don't forget those goddamn Watsons, too.

That little bitch thinks she should lead the Pack, but she's wrong."

Helfren's mind was whirling, and the dead dogs, even the dead man, faded in importance. This was beyond anything he'd ever dreamed of. He was in goddamn Werewolf Central. He could almost taste the books, the interviews. Hell, just think of the *documentaries* . . . He swallowed hard and found his voice at last. "So, these werewolves—are they working together?"

"Not all of 'em."

Maybe there were different factions. Perhaps each family was a separate pack or clan or something. Helfren's head was swimming as he continued questioning the old man. "But the wolf that did the killing over at Menzie's. That was Macleod, right?"

"Ha. Not him. He doesn't have the stomach for it."

Helfren frowned. "But I thought you said—" he began and then corrected himself. No point in antagonizing his source. At least until he got all the information he could from the guy. He tried another tactic. "I guess I was mistaken, Mr. Gervais. I thought you knew who the killer werewolf was."

"Haven't figured it out, have you?" sniggered the old man.

The reporter drew on his patience, found the reservoir a little low. But he could *act* patient, by God. And humble. It always paid to act humble in an interview. You always learned more by appealing to someone's sense of importance. "Mr. Gervais, you're the only one who can help me. You're the only one who knows the truth, who knows what's really going on around here."

"Damn right. Damn fuckin' right I do." The drunk giggled hysterically and slid down to the last step. Closed his eyes.

Helfren took a deep breath. "Please tell me who the killer is, sir. Where is he?"

Gervais said nothing, only chuckled deep in his throat. Helfren waited in the maddening silence, but the drunk was either playing him or he didn't know as much as he'd said he did. Or maybe the vodka had finally knocked him out. Hell, if he'd consumed the entire bottle in one sitting, it was amazing he wasn't dead. Disgusted, the reporter turned to leave.

And found himself *face to face* with the old man.

"How—how the hell did you do that?" Unnerved, the reporter backed up a step. Then a few more. Gervais followed, his gait steady, his eyes clear and focused. On Helfren.

"You really don't know much of anything, do you Mr. Bigshot Reporter?"

The man's voice had changed, dropped a couple of octaves and was suddenly free of its drunken slur. But it was the gleam of insanity in his eyes that made all the hair on Helfren's body stand up. He continued backing away from Gervais, who was now between him and the van. The old man's hands held no weapons, but Helfren was far from reassured. He struggled to find his voice, regain control of the situation. "Come now, Mr. Gervais, we had a business arrangement. You called me, remember? You called me to come up here and write a story. You wanted somebody to tell the truth about the werewolves."

The old man seemed to consider that for a moment. "Of course," he agreed. "That's what this is all about. You want to know where the killer is, don't you?"

Helfren nodded because he was expected to, not because he wanted the answer.

Slowly, Gervais's lips drew back in a crazed and distorted grin. His teeth were long and pointed. "He's right here."

Hide. Gotta hide. Tad Helfren didn't think for an instant that there was any place on Earth he could go where the monster couldn't sniff him out. But there was a slim chance he could get off the creature's radar if he wasn't in plain sight. After all, what had once been Bernard Gervais was now preoccupied with chasing down and slaughtering every single animal on the Macleod farm, and, lucky for Helfren, Connor Macleod had kept a lot of livestock.

He couldn't drag himself very far. He'd awakened in the flower bed by the front porch amid a tangle of crushed irises and lilies. The big purple and white flowers looked funereal to him and that had been enough to jolt the cloud from his brain and get him moving. Slowly, anyway. The taste of copper was in his mouth, and he was bleeding badly from dozens of bites and slices. For some insane reason he thought of an old phrase—*Nature, red in tooth and claw.* Insane because nature had nothing to do with the thing Gervais had become.

Helfren nearly blacked out a couple of times as he pulled himself by inches toward the porch. If he could just get underneath it . . . Blood ran into his eyes, half-blinding him. He could hear bone-chilling howls from elsewhere on the farm and animal screams that made him want to scream himself. His head spun as he finally got a hand on the lattice work, almost wept when a loose panel gave him access.

Once beneath the porch, he pressed the corner of the

panel back into place and crawled farther into the sun-dappled dark. The earth felt cool and refreshing at first, then seemed to draw all the heat from his body. As he shivered, he drew the cell phone from his pocket. Sheer reporter's instinct—or fucking insanity—had possessed him to snap a photo of his attacker, somewhere between having his leg broken and his scalp nearly sheared off. *Sick but slick.* It was that gutsy quality that made him the best damn investigator in the entire paranormal business.

He fumbled with the phone, squinted to see and swore at the signal bars. Only one out of three. Nevertheless, the web came up on command and he readied an e-mail to *OtherWorld News*. It would be the best damn front-page photo in the paper's thirty-three year history.

And his last. He knew he was dying, but at least he'd finally be fucking famous. This once-in-a-lifetime photo might even get him nominated for a Pulitzer—posthumously of course. He grinned as he clumsily tapped out his message on the keypad with fingers he could no longer feel.

The cell phone went dark just as he was about to press *send*.

"No, no baby, don't do this to me." Helfren scrabbled at the keypad but the screen remained dark. "No, no, *nooo*," he moaned. As he clutched the phone to his chest, frustrated tears joined the blood on his face. He was well and truly fucked. Visions of his name living on faded even as his breathing slowed but his mind continued to race. There would be no legacy, no final discovery to rock the scientific world and immortalize him. Sure, someone might find the damn phone when they found his body, but who would bother to charge it up, look at what was on it? It wasn't like there'd be cops looking for clues—he'd be all too obviously dead of an animal attack. Case closed. *Shit.* Helfren couldn't feel his body, couldn't feel the cold anymore. Couldn't see much of anything either. He was going to die alone under a dark porch like a damn rat.

I brought it on myself. The thought came out of nowhere, but it rang true and a few more tears leaked out. He might have been a great reporter but he hadn't exactly been a stellar human being. It hadn't always been that way, but somewhere along the line his ethics had disappeared. The story became everything. And he'd *done* just about everything to get his stories. Assumed identities, stolen artifacts and evidence, paid off authorities. Befriended others in his field only to rip off their leads and their contacts. Hell, he wasn't James fucking Bond, he was just a jerk and an asshole.

What a crappy legacy. I wish . . .

His world went dark and still.

"Okay, you have to tell me what happens to your clothes. Every werewolf movie I've ever seen has the guy's clothing in shreds, but I *saw* you. Your clothes were not only still on, but in perfect condition when you turned from wolf to human. So what's the secret?" Zoey nestled her back against Connor, basking in his heat. She felt totally relaxed, thoroughly adored. And certain that the satisfied grin on her face was never going to come off.

Connor brought her hand to his mouth and kissed her fingertips one by one. "That's a good question. I'm not sure how well I can explain it—Devlin's the quantum physics expert in the family. He says the clothes go into some little pocket or compartment in another dimension."

"What, like a parallel universe or something?"

He laughed. "This isn't science fiction, honey."

"Spoken like someone who is just *way* too used to being a werewolf!" She rubbed her forehead, thinking. "I know that according to Einstein, there are actually four dimensions, not three. Some scientists are now saying there are more, maybe even ten. I suppose there'd be room in one of those for an interdimensional clothes closet for werewolves."

"You're going to get along great with my brother. And it's *Changeling*, not werewolf."

"Semantics. So you send your stuff off to this other dimension, and then what?"

"You don't send them. The clothes automatically go there when you become the wolf. But they don't come back on their own. That's where the skill comes in—you have to *learn* to bring your clothes back with you when you Change."

"Bet you could lose a lot of clothes practicing. So is it difficult to learn?"

"No." He ran a gentle hand along the side of her face, trailed fingers down her throat. "It's not a step-by-step procedure like programming the TiVo—which I still rely on Culley to do, by the way. It's more a case of getting the right *feeling*, of pulling your clothes to you with your mind. You get pretty good at it after a while, enough that all the things in your pockets come along too, whatever you had with you, whatever was touching you or your clothing. Books, tools, ID, and so forth." Connor laughed suddenly.

"What's funny?"

"Devlin took that to new heights once. Our mother wanted her piano moved upstairs, so Devlin figured if he was holding on to it while he Changed, then he could just run upstairs as a wolf and then Change back. Voilà, the piano would be moved."

Zoey rolled her eyes. "Oh come on, Connor, there's no way that would work. It's not fair for you to try to put stuff like that over on me just because I'm new to all this."

"Actually, it worked just fine. He Changed and the piano reappeared. But he hadn't anticipated how much energy it would draw from him. He was so exhausted, he was bedridden for more than a week. According to my folks, Devlin would have been far better off to have stayed in human form and single-handedly carried the piano upstairs."

She just shook her head, her mind boggling. "I still think you're pulling my leg. It all sounds like magic."

"Maybe that's what magic really is. Using natural principles, even ones we don't understand, to accomplish things."

"Now it sounds dangerous," she snorted.

"Not really. People do it all the time. Do you understand how your truck works? Yet you're not afraid to drive it. And then there are computers. Most of us haven't a clue how they work either, but we use them. Or we try to," he said with a laugh. "The bottom line is, I don't know how my clothes disappear and reappear, I only know that they do. And lucky thing too, because I'd hate to turn up bare-assed naked in the middle of the woods some night."

"What if you were holding someone's hand? Or accidentally brushed against someone when you Changed?"

"First of all, no one ever Changes close enough to a human to hurt or endanger them. It's a cardinal rule. It's drilled into all of us as children."

"But what if another werewolf touched you? Would it hurt them?"

"Remember when you touched me right after I Changed? Multiply that to the power of a hundred or so if you'd touched me *while* I Changed." Connor chuckled and lay back with his hands behind his head. "My oldest brother James and I got into a helluva fight when we were kids. We—"

"Wait a minute. James? There's more of you?"

"I guess I forgot to tell you. There's six altogether. You've already met Culley and Devlin, and you'll meet Kenzie when she gets back. Carly lives in Wyoming right now."

She waited a beat, then two, but Connor offered nothing more. The laughter in his eyes had been replaced with a faraway look, however. "Is James still living?" she asked carefully.

"Yes." He blew out a breath. "And no. James lost his wife some years ago. Grief makes people do things, whatever they have to do I suppose, in order to survive the pain. He turned into a wolf and as far as I know, has never Changed back."

"As far as you know. You mean, you don't know where he is?"

Connor shook his head. "Nobody does. He's been spotted once in a while near here, like he's checking up on us or something, and then he's gone again."

"I'm sorry. That must be pretty rough on you, on the whole family."

"Yeah. I miss him all the time."

Zoey slipped her hand into Connor's. "Finish the story you started. About when you and James were kids."

"It's not a very long story. We were fighting again, something we did a lot because he was a year older and figured he should get to tell me what to do. We were pretty much the same size, but I was losing as usual. Finally, when he was holding me down and punching me, I Changed. James got a shock much bigger than you did, enough to throw him clear across the room and stun him. He wasn't injured but he had a headache for a week."

"So Changelings fight dirty, do they?"

He laughed a little then. "I've heard it said that if something's important enough to fight about, then there's nothing unfair about using whatever you have to in order to win."

"I'll just remember that."

Connor leaned over and lightly swatted her butt. "Lucky for you, I have a code of honor. Let's get going. I've got animals to feed, and I'd like to get it done before it rains. Then maybe we can find something to eat for ourselves. I'm starving."

She pulled her clothes on and headed into the bathroom to adjust her makeup, brush her hair. When she emerged, Connor was sitting motionless on the edge of the bed, staring at the cell phone in his hand.

"Is it the clinic? Do you have a call to go to?"

He turned to her and she was shocked to see his eyes filled with fury and grief. "No. It was Jessie, calling from the farm. Seems Bernie's been there ahead of us." He took a deep breath as if it were difficult to push out the words. "Jim Neely's dead."

The laneway was jammed with vehicles. Three police cruisers, an ambulance, a fire truck, the coroner's van, the pickups of several curious neighbors and a Fish and Wildlife jeep. Connor parked his truck along the road. When he got out, however, he leaned back against the vehicle for support, blinking as if trying to clear his vision.

"Are you all right? What is it?" asked Zoey, taking his hand.

"Death. Good Christ, it's everywhere. I can feel it, smell

it, taste it." He made a sweeping motion with his hand. "They're all dead, Jim and all the animals too. Everything. Every damn living thing that was here." He shook himself and straightened, but it was as if he was lifting an incredible weight on his shoulders. His eyes hardened until he looked at her. "I shouldn't have brought you here. I don't want you to have to see this. Or feel it either. Your psychic senses are already showing you this shit, aren't they?"

There was no denying that she'd felt the discordant energies coming from the farm long before the truck stopped. Now she was picking up flashes of images in her mind of what had happened here, things that turned her insides to water. But she wasn't about to give in. Not this time. "I can see it, yes. But I'm staying."

"The Pack is here. Let me call Culley or Devlin to take you home. They'll stay with you, watch over you until I can get back."

She shook her head, resolute. "You said we're a team, remember? Wherever you're going, I'm going too, so get used to it, Connor Macleod."

He was quiet for a moment, then nodded and took her hand. Together, they walked up the long, long drive beneath the somber sky.

Sergeant Fitzpatrick met them near the house. Other officers were keeping the little knot of neighbors back. "I'm sorry, Connor."

"Not as sorry as I am." Jessie appeared at the vet's elbow, with Bill behind her. "Devlin figured out there was a danger, and I brought the Pack on the double." Her face looked stricken. "We weren't in time."

"Bernie's going to pay, Jess." Connor's voice was steel. Zoey shivered at the force of the emotions radiating from him. The hot fury had returned to balance the icy current of grief deep within. Even more intense was the guilt that ripped at him—guilt for having drawn such danger to the old man. Jessie had said that even a Changeling would have had little chance against what Bernard Gervais had become. A human would have no chance at all. And Neely had been very much human. Of course Connor would blame himself for his death. But she couldn't tell him it wasn't his fault, not yet. His heart wouldn't be able to hear it.

"Bernie's going to die," said Jess. "And it still won't be enough to balance this."

Fitz put his hands up. "Stop right there. Do *not* say things like that," he ordered. "Not now, not here, do you understand?"

"You're addressing the Pack leader," reminded Bill, and although his voice was quiet, Zoey could see the tensing of his muscles. Jessie herself looked irritated.

The sergeant glanced around, then lowered his voice to a fierce whisper. "Look, Lowen's here and he says Jim Neely died from an animal attack, just like Al Menzie. But I've got officers all over the place here, *human* officers. You can't walk around mentioning Bernie's name in connection with Neely's death unless you want even more werewolf rumors flying around this town.

"I've got guys asking questions already because we've found dead animals piled in the bushes, stacked in the barn. Deliberately thrown in the pond. What wolf does that? On top of that, there's almost no blood left in or around the human body." He yanked off his hat and ran a hand through his hair, then jammed the hat back on. "And you sure as hell *cannot* be talking about someone having to *pay*. This is a small town and, believe me, someone will hear it and that someone will remember you said it. And in the human world, a court will treat those words as an uttered threat if Bernie winds up dead or missing. So I've got plenty of reasons for telling you—even you, Jessie—to keep a lid on it."

No one spoke for a long tense moment. Then Jessie put a hand on his arm. "Of course, Sergeant. Emotions are running high right now. Thank you for reminding us that we cannot let our guard down," she said graciously. "We rely on you to keep the peace between our two worlds, and our trust is well-founded."

Two worlds. Human and Changeling. Until very recently, Zoey had known of only one. Funny how fast things could change. . . .

"I've got the Pack divided into groups, searching for Bernie," Jessie said to Connor. "Right now we're going to join them, but we'll be back later to help you bury your animals. Take care of Zoey."

"Thanks, Jess. I will."

Bill put a huge tattooed arm around Connor's shoulders. "Jim Neely was a good man, but no one knew it till you came along. You made his last years some of the best, mate."

Connor couldn't say anything to that, only nodded.

Zoey watched Bill and Jessie walk away. "How many Pack members are out there?" She squeezed Connor's hand, seeking to distract him from his sadness.

He blinked like a man waking up. "Twenty now. Jessie and Bill will make twenty out there."

"They'll have to work fast," said Fitzpatrick. "I can't keep the Fish and Game guys busy forever. Luckily their helicopter is over in the next district doing a moose count today, but they booked it for daybreak tomorrow if the rain holds off. I figure we have till then to find Bernie, before

it's too dangerous for us to be in wolfen form out there."
He nodded toward the open land. "They'll be shooting
every wolf they spot, just to be sure."

"Can't we stop them?" asked Zoey.

Connor shook his head. "They have no choice, not with
two men dead. It's a matter of public safety now. Not only
will it be hell on the wolf population, but it's going to
make it difficult to be a Changeling in this region for a
long time to come. Maybe years."

"Right now, we've got other things to take care of. Did
Neely have any family?" asked Fitzpatrick.

"No, there was no one. He's—he was—a widower, no
children. No siblings living," said Connor. "We were his
family, these last few years. Do you need me to identify
him?"

"No, that's not necessary. He'd been in enough scrapes
back in his drinking days that we can officially identify him
with fingerprints."

"I'd like to see him just the same."

The sergeant nodded. "You'll get a chance to do that
after he's been taken to the morgue."

"I'm his friend. I'll do it now," said Connor.

"Procedure—" Fitz began, then stopped. "Hang procedure. Over here." He led the way around the side of the
house.

The group passed the blueberry bushes. RCMP officers
with latex gloves were pulling the limp bodies of dead dogs
from the patch and laying them out on the grass, where
two Fish and Wildlife officers were examining them.

Connor looked over at Zoey. "You okay?"

She nodded and ran a nervous hand through her hair,

wondering if any of them would ever be all right again. "I've already seen this." And she had. But despite the ugly previews her psychic abilities gave her, the real thing was always worse.

A pair of officers was standing with Dr. Lowen Miller beside a bed of purple monkshood. Through her research of werewolves, Zoey had learned that these flowers were also known as wolfsbane because they were supposed to repel shapeshifters. It certainly hadn't worked here. Most of the flowers had been crushed and in the center of the plants was a glaring yellow tarp. It seemed far too bright for the tragedy it covered.

To her surprise, the gruff doctor walked to Connor at once and put a hand on his shoulder, patting him like a child. Lowen guided him over to the flower bed and dismissed the officers.

"But sir—" began one.

The doctor glared. "Take a hike, son."

The officers left.

Lowen knelt at one end of the tarp, holding a corner, watching for Connor's nod that he was ready. The tarp was peeled back. Zoey didn't look at what lay beneath it. What she did see was Connor's face, stricken suddenly as if by a physical blow. Then his eyes closed in pain and grief.

"Goddammit, Jim," he said quietly to the dead man. "This shouldn't have happened to you."

Lowen straightened the tarp and stood up. "I have some tests to do, but I think he had a heart attack. He may have been gone before the first blow landed, Connor."

Zoey stared at the tarp and nodded. She could see it in her head, just as the doctor described. "He saw the wolf, and he died. He didn't even have time to be scared. The wolf was surprised and—and disappointed." Suddenly she was aware of both Connor and Lowen staring at her. Unbidden, she heard words from her past, the names that had both labeled and dismissed her. *The Weird Kid. Creepy Girl. Freakazoid.* Felt the sting of them again, even as she shoved them back into whatever mental closet they'd fallen out of.

She turned and walked off, heading for the front of the house, wanting to get away from the death and destruction. But there was no escape. Many of the vehicles had gone, most of the people associated with them as well, giving her a clear view of the entire farmyard. Hapless creatures large and small lay scattered as far as the eye could see. From here, she could identify the largest shapes by their color—the great shaggy heap that was certainly the Highland bull, the dappled gray hide of one of the horses, a pair of big pink sows. Her heart bled at the immense sadness of the scene, but she knew it must be worse for Connor.

"Thanks for that." His voice behind her made her jump. Before she could recover, his powerful arms simply slid around her and gathered her back against him.

"Thanks for what?"

"It helps, knowing that Jim didn't feel what that bastard did to him, that he was already gone. Bernie's still responsible but at least Jim didn't suffer."

Connor took a great shuddering breath and Zoey squirmed, wanting to hold him but his grip was so tight that she couldn't turn around. She had to settle for nuzzling and kissing the arm closest to her, placing her hands over his.

"I wish I'd been able to do more, see more," she said, her voice tight with tears. "I wish I'd seen this in advance so we could have stopped it."

He turned her around then, cupped her face in his huge hands. "Don't do that to yourself. It's bad enough that I feel that way, don't you go there too."

"I'm already there, dammit!" She burst into hot, angry tears then. "I've been there for years now. Always too late, too damn late to do any good at all. You and Jessie keep saying this ability is a gift, but I don't see it that way. It's a horrible thing to have, and I wish it didn't exist. All it does is leave me standing over the dead. Helpless."

Chapter Twenty-four

The coroner's van pulled away with its sad burden, followed by the RCMP cruisers. Connor watched them go without seeing them, without seeing anything. He felt like he was underwater. Everything was distorted through a watery lens and he was moving in slow motion, pushing against the current along the bottom of a cold river.

Every living thing on the farm had been chased down and slaughtered, from the herd of cattle in the pasture to the smaller animals that ranged free around the yard. Blood seemed to be everywhere, soaking into the hard clay, splattering the fence rails and feeders, even splashed against the walls of the white barn like garish paint. Still, he'd made a thorough check of every animal, from the biggest draft horse to the smallest cat. He'd known they were dead before he touched them. But he'd needed to touch them. And each one reinforced both his anger and his decision. White hot fury hardened his resolve to diamond.

Bernard Gervais had run rampant long enough. He had to be stopped, permanently. For Jim Neely and for Al Menzie, for every victim known and unknown. For those intended to become victims, like Zoey. And for all the helpless and innocent creatures.

Connor stood and scanned the surrounding land. The

forest, the fields, the coulees dropping away to the river valley. He surveyed them until gradually a silvery thread appeared before his eyes. *Farsight* had come to his aid at last.

He had Bernie's trail.

Zoey paced the house, rubbing her arms as if she was cold. In truth, she didn't know what she was. She couldn't seem to feel much, except anxiety for Connor. He'd asked for some time alone in the farmyard, and she could certainly understand that. She was tired and knew she should be hungry, but although she warmed up some soup, she couldn't bring herself to eat it. Nor could she sit down and rest. Her mind and heart were with the man she loved. And so she kept returning to the living room to watch Connor through the windows. She'd seen him kneel by every last animal, saw him touch each and every one. Was he saying good-bye? Praying for them? What did Changelings do? Whatever their custom, she thought of her own loss when Fester died, and thought how much worse this must be for the gifted veterinarian. His heart was already sore from the loss of his human friend. But the animals had been his friends too. She remembered the night she first walked through the farmyard with Connor, remembered how he had introduced her to each animal that lived there. They were all individuals to him. And they obviously adored him, couldn't get close enough to him.

Oh Jesus—she suddenly remembered Lila and the puppies. *Her* puppy. She dashed out the front door, but paused at the top of the steps when she spotted movement on the far side of Connor's truck. Connor himself emerged from the backseat, pulling something with him. Then in a blurred motion almost too fast to follow, he spun away.

He Changed. He must have. Because in the next instant

all she could see was a massive black and silver blur moving between the trees.

And then it was gone.

"Wait," she mouthed although Connor was no longer in sight. Something was niggling at the corners of her awareness, something huge and dark. Suddenly her physical sight was overwhelmed by her inner sight.

She was flying high overhead, eagle-like, following a wide river. The water was turbulent, swollen with rain and debris. Trees were gouged from the banks and carried along in the torrent. As she watched, she noticed several places where the hillsides had given way and slid into the river. One spot in particular drew her attention, about four miles downstream from the first. Where the toe of raw earth met the river, an enormous tree lay on its side, its roots half-buried in the slide and half in the air, its broken crown nearly submerged in the river, spanning a third of the way across the wild, churning water.

The tree was important. She *had* to get there. It was important, as necessary as breathing.

She dove toward it—

—and found herself on the ground at the foot of the stairs, staring at an empty vodka bottle that was wedged under the bottom step.

Zoey eased herself to her feet, brushing off her clothes. She'd have bruises, no doubt, but that wasn't bad considering she'd tumbled down six or seven stairs. It was the vision that bothered her. What the hell did it mean?

She paced and swore repeatedly in pure frustration at the strange gift that had set her apart, made her different, disrupted her career and her life. Why the hell couldn't it work the way it did in television shows? Often she received nothing, no hint at all of what was to come. Other times, she'd been led to scenes after the event had already taken place. Sometimes she just received incomprehensible clues, like these. A landslide, a flooded river, a fallen tree . . . She sank to the bottom step and willed her brain to work through the puzzle. The river in her vision had been very wide and the coulees that flanked it were a signature of the Peace River, the same river she could see in the far distance as a glimmering thread. But it gained its name from its serene surface. Sure, the calmness was deceiving—the Peace actually boasted a strong, swift current—but it was hardly the raging floodwaters she'd seen in the psychic vision.

Or was it?

She glanced at the lowering sky. It hadn't rained here yet, but she knew that it was still raining heavily in the mountains and foothills. The dam had been forced to release more water. How long did it take for all that extra water to travel a couple hundred miles or so along the winding river? Zoey held her head in both hands in an effort to focus, to discern the meaning of the images she'd seen. Why was it so important? What was it she needed to do? Did any of it have to do with Bernie or was it just a distraction?

Connor had headed into the forest that flanked the farmyard on the south. The river was west. If there was a connection, she couldn't feel it. She got to her feet again and as she turned to begin pacing, her foot brushed the vodka bottle. A sudden tingle went through her as if she'd touched a tiny electric current. Puzzled, she knelt and reached for the bottle—and as her hand closed around it, thoughts and images burst into her brain. Not so much an epiphany as an *explosion* in her head.

Zoey lost her balance and fell backward onto the grass, overwhelmed. She knew without a doubt that Bernard

Gervais had touched the glass, had wrapped his fingers around it. And she suddenly knew something more, something new. Because he had touched this object, she could *use it* to enhance and direct her gift! In the past, in the city, her growing psychic ability had led her to places and events by thought alone. Never had she intentionally or inadvertently touched anything associated with a crime scene. And so she'd never known, never even thought or imagined, where her talent truly lay.

Please, please, please. Zoey held the bottle in both hands, clutched it close to her, tried to open herself up to her gift. *Show me. Tell me.*

It did.

With horrifying clarity, she could see exactly what her vision had meant. Bernie was near the river, lying in wait. Connor was going after Bernie.

And neither would survive.

The faint silvery thread of *farsight* led into the woods and straight into the shallow stream. Connor found himself racing along the streambed, driving the cold water into plumes around him. Miles later, his psychic guideline had not altered. Bernie had clearly used the little creek as a personal pathway. How long, how far, Connor couldn't begin to guess, but it didn't matter. The water didn't slow him in the least. An adult wolf was a perfect running machine, able to cover fifty to sixty miles in a day. A Changeling, twice that distance. An angry Changeling, maybe more.

The psychic trail led Connor to where the land dropped away into the river valley in runneled cliffs and coulees of sandstone and clay. The saddleback wolf trotted along the tops of the cliffs on silent feet, keeping to the cover of trees and brush. His *farsight* had subsided, but he didn't need its help anymore. Bernie had left the water's camouflage and Connor could sift the rogue's scent easily from the air. Knew he was close by.

Without warning, an enormous grizzled shape crashed through the bushes and broadsided the saddleback wolf. Connor simply rolled beneath the force and regained his feet, launching himself straight at his attacker's throat.

The creature twisted and leapt aside, Connor's jaws closing just shy of the vulnerable throat. Instead he got a mouthful of the gray ruff. He used his momentum to pivot, scoring a long ragged gash along Bernie's ribs.

At least he thought it was Bernie. Changelings were naturally larger and more powerful than ordinary wolves, and Connor was one of the largest in the Pack. Yet this incarnation of Bernie outweighed him easily. Only the color of the creature's hide and the madness in its eyes identified it as once having been Bernard Gervais.

Connor dodged and wheeled as the monstrous rogue charged him again and again with snapping jaws and deep-throated snarls. He delivered quick slashes of his own, then leapt barely out of reach as the beast whirled on him. The battle became a blur of savage growls and lunging forms. Droplets of spittle and blood flew from gnashing teeth. The rogue wolf was pure killer instinct, all fang and claw, muscle and teeth. His madness had lent him unnatural strength and speed. Connor left off trying to get to the throat and instead sliced at the rogue's legs at every opening. If he was lucky, he might be able to slow Bernie down, disable him. But each time, Bernie managed to shake him off—often twisting away from Connor's jaws like quicksilver—and delivered vicious bites of his own.

Despite Connor's best efforts, the rogue gained ground, backing the saddleback wolf onto a narrow promontory of land that fell away steeply on three sides to the river valley below. Connor was bleeding from many deep wounds while Bernie's injuries seemed few and shallow by comparison. Determined, Connor made another try for Bernie's throat and found himself abruptly slammed away by a paw that felt more like a fence post. He landed hard near the edge of the cliff, raked with deep parallel gashes over two, maybe three, cracked ribs.

Apparently satisfied that he had his enemy both cornered and subdued, Bernie backed away and sat down at the root of the outcropping, effectively blocking any hope of exit. The rogue was barely breathing hard although his opponent's sides were heaving. Still, Connor got to his feet quickly, braced for another attack. And recoiled in pure shock as he got his first clear look at his enemy.

The only wolflike features Bernie had left were his ears, which looked out of place perched on top of his widened skull. His lips drew away from powerful jaws with multiple rows of long needle-like teeth. His skeleton had shifted, broadened, to support muscle that would have been outsized on a Kodiak bear. In fact, he looked like a grizzly on steroids, complete with a massive hump of muscle over the shoulders. His front feet, braced in front of him, revealed additional toes with wickedly hooked claws. As Connor watched, the rogue's hide seemed to move, almost as if live things snaked and bunched beneath the skin. As if his body were still in flux, still changing.

Like the upgrades, Macleod? As you can see, I've evolved.

Bernie's words popped into Connor's head. They felt dark, almost oily. The old Changeling had been verbally belligerent most of his life. But this was different. Not because of the physical alterations, but because of what Connor could sense within Bernie. Pure evil. Instinctively he

masked his own thought processes, locked them away deep
where the monster couldn't read them. Wished he could
keep the monster's voice out as well.

*You're looking at the future, Macleod. And after I've killed all
of you, I'll start a race of new and improved Changelings. Together, we'll hunt the weakling humans instead of being hunted by
them.*

*Sounds like a bad movie to me, Bernie. Are you going to pro-
claim yourself Emperor too?*

The rogue snapped his foam-flecked jaws together,
opened them with a deafening roar. *You should be on your
knees to me! All of you! Every damn one of you! And you will be
before I kill you!*

Connor noted with amazement that Bernie had just sev-
ered the end of his tongue—yet he seemed unaware of it.
The rogue continued his mindspeech rant as if nothing had
happened, although blood ran freely from his jaws.

Pretending to quake in fear, Connor hunched down as if
submissive. It wasn't hard to fake defeat. Wounded and
bleeding, he was trapped between Bernie and the cliff. He
had to buy time, had to keep this insane monster busy
gloating as long as he could. It was plain now that Bernie
couldn't be taken down by ordinary means. Pack law was
clear on the rules of fair combat between enemies, and also
clear on the fate of rogues—only tooth and claw were
honorable to use between Changelings. But the horrific
creature in front of him was no longer a Changeling at all.
It was an abomination.

*Maybe I should call your woman, have her watch while I tear
you apart.*

It was all Connor could do to keep a leash on his temper. He had to wait, had to watch for the right moment,

the right opportunity. Still, a long, low growl escaped him. *Keep her out of this, Bernie. It's between you and me.*

The creature laughed horribly, a high-pitched gurgle. *I'm going to have fun killing you, Macleod. But it's really all about her. She's got the bloodline, you know, the power.*

What the hell are you talking about?

Bernie fell back on his haunches and hooted, hyena-like. *You gotta be kidding me, Macleod. You don't know? Then let me be the one to tell you what I'm taking away from you. Your red-haired bitch is* theriona.

Theriona. Connor hadn't heard the word since he was a child, when his father told him stories of the ancient race. While Bernard Gervais was a well-known liar, he was also far older than any Changeling Connor knew of. Was there a chance he could be right? Jessie herself had said that Zoey wasn't exactly human, that she had powerful gifts. But Jessie, for all her wisdom, hadn't known what Zoey *was.* No one did, not even Zoey. *C'mon Bernie, there aren't any of those left.*

You know nothing, you stupid pup. But I do. And once I open up her throat, all that power is going to be mine at last.

I think you're full of shit, Bernie. And you'll never touch her again.

The beast roared, spittle and blood flying from the dreadful teeth as its powerful forefeet clawed the ground. *You've forgotten I'm her sire—think about all the things I can tell her to do. I can even make her like it. Maybe I should keep your woman alive for a while, Macleod. Use her for breeding. Maybe I should use* her *to create my new race.*

Maybe you should ask her what she thinks about that. Connor deliberately flicked his gaze over Bernie's shoulder. The rogue fell for the ruse and turned with a savage snarl, giving Connor the split-second opening he needed. Calling on all the energy he could draw from the earth and the air, he Changed to his human form. The .375 was cocked and loaded in his bleeding hands.

It happened fast. With a deafening roar, the demon that was Bernie spun and leapt at Connor. Just as his feet left the ground, the blast of the rifle echoed off the valley walls. Momentum carried the creature forward, but the rogue was dead before his massive bulk slammed to the ground, missing one eye and most of the back of his skull.

"Evolve from this, you murdering bastard." Connor emptied the rest of the shells into the carcass, obliterating the head. Changelings could recover from wounds that would be fatal to a normal wolf, and he was taking no chances in case the rogue's healing ability had been as enhanced as his muscles and teeth.

The ringing echoes had barely subsided when Connor became aware of a strange crackling in the air around him. The hair on his head lifted, floating as if he was underwater and he realized with a jolt that the death of what once was Bernie had released energy.

A ton of it.

There was a sudden wrenching groan from deep in the earth. Connor jumped back as the ground trembled, shifted, but there was nowhere to go. The very hillside itself gave way beneath him and slid several hundred feet to the river below.

Chapter Twenty-five

The jeep bumped and lurched over the increasingly rocky terrain, as Zoey drove as fast as she dared, and then faster. The gravel road had given way to twin ruts running between fields. But the ruts had proved easier going than the potholed goat path she was currently on. Still her senses pushed her forward, leading her—she hoped—to the place in her vision. Praying she would be in time.

Without warning, the voice in her head shrieked at her to stop. She jammed on the brakes, rammed the shift into *park* and ran from the truck, not even bothering to close the door. The field was rimmed with trees and brush and she could just see the valley beyond it, so she knew she was near the edge of—

The grassy field vibrated beneath her feet, resonating through her entire body until she could feel it in her bones, her teeth. Then it stopped.

Zoey backed away on jellied legs. Where trees had stood moments ago, there was only a great sprawling spill of earth. For an instant it was like looking straight down a long ski slope. Then the scene resolved into churned soil and tumbled rock, broken trees and buried brush. It was sheer luck that the slide had started just beyond her and hadn't taken out the spot where she stood.

Heart pounding, she drew a shaky breath as her senses returned. Her psychic senses returned too, leading her eye down the length of the slide to the river below. The Peace River was no longer peaceful, no longer the calm blue ribbon that looped through the valley. Even from the top of the coulee, she could see the water was wild, swirling with mud and debris from this and several other slides.

Suddenly she spotted the tree from her vision.

The massive root ball protruded above the fallen debris in a sweeping half circle. The rest of the tree was in the wild water. With most of its branches stripped away, the broad trunk of the old forest king looked like an incomplete bridge. The psychic message persisted—somehow she *had* to get to that tree. And she had to do it fast. She had no idea what she would do when she got there but the vision she'd received had been plain. Connor would be somewhere in the midst of the angry river, battling to keep his head above the deadly water. Getting to the fallen tree was her only hope of saving the man she loved.

Zoey forced herself to take a step forward. The entire slide area looked unstable. Here and there clumps of dirt and rocks tumbled down its face. She looked for a way to climb around it but the swath of destruction was wide, fanning out even farther as it approached the riverbank. She took another step and another, and watched in horror as her feet sank and her movements set loose a shower of unstable soil. How could she hope to get to the tree in any kind of a hurry? Connor was going to die before she could make it partway down the goddamn hill.

"Help me, I don't know what to do!" She reached out to

embrace every nuance of her psychic gift, opening herself up to it completely as she had never dared before.

Something inside her answered. Something she'd never heard before yet was strangely familiar. Something decidedly not human. Still, she knew without doubt that it could help her, that it was the answer she sought.

There was no time to ponder the insanity of it all, to consider pros and cons or even to feel the fear that was turning her insides to water. No time to consider that she had no idea what she was doing. Connor was in danger, and so she had to try. Jessie had said that strength came out of wholeness. *When you truly need your strength, all of your strength, you'll need to draw on your whole self.* Calling on every bit of courage she could claim, Zoey gave herself up to the energy, the entity within.

Immediately she was hot, so hot. Sweat soaked her clothing, ran down her face. Her breath hitched and she was suddenly *more*. What was within her was moving to the surface rapidly, almost frantically—but it wasn't alien in the least. With a burst of insight, she realized that this inner self was as much a part of her as her freckles. *Yes.* She spread her arms wide and closed her eyes, embracing the sudden duality of awareness. For an instant she was in harmony with everything within her and around her. The sun, the sky, the grass, the earth—all one with her, all feeding her their strength. Tiny sounds like paper crumpling signaled the buildup of electricity in the air.

And then it began.

Zoey fell awkwardly to her knees, buried her hands in the dry grass, knotted her fingers in it, clung for support as she began to shiver uncontrollably.

Bones lengthened, others shortened. Muscles heaved and

joints popped. She gritted her teeth, cursing, moaning, clinging to the image of Connor in her mind with all her strength. The moans turned into a sharp prolonged cry as her face contorted and lengthened, as her tailbone uncurled and extended. Fingers shortened, toughened and became paws. Fair skin darkened, blushed gold as soft fur erupted everywhere at once. Blue sparks flew from the tawny pelt.

The cry became a scream. It echoed over the valley and bounced back to her as a long, drawn-out howl.

Then silence.

Zoey drew a deep breath, then another. She could hear the beat of her own heart, the surge of blood in her veins, the rush of air into her lungs. Her awareness fanned outward. The air made delicate sounds as it moved through the blades of grass. Insects thrummed. A tiny rodent wandered nearby and she could hear its footsteps, hear its teeth as it sampled a plant stem. She drew the air through her nostrils and tasted the scents that came with it, sorted out the one that was *mouse*. She shook herself all over, felt the slide of skin and the toss of fur over her entire body. Did it again because it felt so good. Glanced down at her hands. *Omigod, I have paws.* She picked them up one at a time. Her limbs were altered, different. For one surreal moment, she panicked at the strangeness of it all. Then ordered herself to *get a grip*, shook herself again and stepped forward tentatively, testing her balance. To her surprise, it was unexpectedly natural to walk with four legs instead of two.

She raised her head. Her eyesight was keen, the focus sharp and bright. She swept her gaze over the slide, down to the river. Saw the wild water and the fallen tree. *Connor. Connor would be there.*

Without hesitation, Zoey threw herself over the edge of

the coulee, hitting the loose ground running. And took the fastest, most direct route to the river—straight down the very back of the barely-settled slide, racing flat out, uncaring if she brought the whole cliffside down.

Connor was fighting for his life. The slide had thundered down beneath him, forcing him to scramble and fight to stay on top of the tumbling earth. It was like riding the back of an avalanche. He had nearly made it, too, almost escaped when a poplar tree had been flipped end over end by the slide. The uppermost branches had caught him and swept him into the flooded river.

He was pulled under immediately and had to battle to regain the surface. But it wasn't much safer up there. Huge chunks of debris pushed at him, crashed into him, threatened to shove him under again. The wild current was far too strong for him to be able to fight his way to shore. Fingers of colder water pulled at him from beneath, an undertow that could drag him down. The roar of the water was deafening.

Changeling instincts brought out the inner wolf when threatened and Connor had to fight to persuade his body to stay human. His wolfen form would be disadvantaged here. His only hope was to be able to grab something and hang on, and for that, he needed human hands.

He clung to a heavy tree limb, grateful to ride along for a moment and conserve his strength. He had little left, and he was having trouble drawing much from the water. The roiling energy it contained was too chaotic to control. He was chilled to the bone, wounded, exhausted, and his body was being hammered and scraped by the debris in the water. A human would have drowned already. But even a

Changeling wouldn't last forever against the force of the turbulent river. If he didn't think of something fast, he'd die here.

Finally Connor caught sight of what might be his best chance. Far ahead, a sliver of earth jutted into the river, the result of another slide. A giant of a tree lolled on its side, reaching nearly a third of the way across the river. The branched crown had been battered away by the brunt of the current and the debris—but half of the tree's massive root ball was still buried, anchored now by the very slide that had torn it from the hillside far above.

Connor also saw that the powerful current would take him past the tree, swing him just out of reach unless he started angling his way over to it now. Reaching deep for everything he had, he let go of the limb and swam for his life.

He snagged the tree with the tips of his fingers, caught and clung to the end of a broken branch. Muscles screamed and cracked ribs shrieked as he fought to hang on against the force of the current. The tree was a thick and ancient poplar, with a profusion of small branches down the entire length of the trunk. Handholds galore, an abundance of hope. With them he might just make it to the roots at the toe of the landslide—and safety.

The greedy undertow sucked at Connor's body, dragged at him, as he struggled to pull himself along. He wound his hands, his arms into the blessed branches and allowed himself to rest a moment. His lungs burned and ached, it hurt to breathe, but he could no longer feel the rest of his body. He was cold and tired, so very tired . . . then a sudden movement of the massive poplar jolted him into full alert. He turned his head in time to see the root ball that anchored the tree roll ever so slightly. A couple of inches maybe.

Shit. The toe of the slide was probably unstable, the current gouging away the dirt beneath. He had to move, had to get to shore before the tree washed away. It was only thirty, maybe thirty-five feet away from him but it looked like a mile.

It was a battle to persuade his numb body, his rubbery arms, to cooperate. He managed a few feet, stopping frequently to rest and seek his next handhold. It was brutally hard going, but he was going to make it—

Without warning, a terrible impact slammed the breath from his lungs, stunned him. Above the roar of the water he thought he heard his own ribs breaking. Then he knew nothing at all.

Grateful for the speed of her new form, Zoey raced down the ruined hillside, leaping broken trees, clambering over rocks and debris. Finally she rounded the exposed roots of the forest king and leapt onto its broad trunk.

Connor! He was unconscious, his face barely out of the water. His arms and hands were wound in the tangle of broken boughs, but lax and sliding. Only his shirt, snagged on a jutting branch, kept him from being swept under by the brutal current. And the shirt wouldn't hold him for long.

Zoey tried to walk out to him but the bark was smooth and wet, the trunk shuddering and vibrating with the force of the wild river. Worse, the tree rolled slightly. Her wolfen feet slipped again and again, claws scrabbling wildly, finding little purchase. She would never get to Connor in time. Even in human form she wouldn't have the surefootedness to reach him or the strength to pull him to safety. On top of that, the tree was being tugged loose from the spill of earth that held it. Eventually it would give and pitch them both into the raging waters to their death.

That cold realization cleared her mind. And allowed her to hear something inside, calling out to her, offering what she needed.

It was outrageous. It was desperate. And it was necessary. She had no reason to hope it would work, but she had nothing else left to try. Trembling, she closed her eyes for a split second and focused. She needed balance, balance and muscle, and claws for when balance and muscle failed. She needed something she had seen enough to be able to build a detailed picture in her head. Then she knew. A photo assignment had once entailed several visits to a wildlife rehab center. And had gotten her up close and personal with a creature being prepared for release.

She Changed, instantly and easily. And ran to Connor on sure feet.

A puma's body was amazingly strong, all muscle. A big cat could easily break the neck of an elk, an animal far bigger and heavier than itself, then grab the carcass in its jaws and drag it wherever it pleased. But, Zoey thought as she gently seized the back of Connor's shirt in her teeth, the puma wouldn't have to be careful of its prey, wouldn't be restricted to moving scant inches at a time. She could tell that Connor was terribly injured, and prayed that she wouldn't make his wounds worse. His heavy denim shirt tore a little and she was forced to pause and shift her grip.

The trunk beneath them shuddered violently, swung a little, and Zoey used her long curving claws to dig in and steady herself. It would take forever to reach the foot of the tree at this rate.

Suddenly she heard Jessie's familiar voice shouting over the rushing water. "You can do it, girl! We're right here. We'll take him from you when you get here."

Out of the corner of her eye Zoey spotted Jessie and Bill, standing knee-deep in the wild river at the foot of the tree, hanging onto its branches as the water gouged at the slide beneath it. As she watched, two wolves ran up behind them and resolved into Culley and Devlin. More wolves were racing along the riverbanks. She could see Geoff Lassiter and Holt LaLonde. Even little Jeannie Rousseau appeared. The cavalry had arrived if she could just get to them. She *would* get to them. She had to.

The tree abruptly rolled a few inches and swung farther out into the current. Zoey was forced to scramble for balance, raking the thin smooth bark into ribbons with her claws. When things settled again, she fixed her eyes forward on the roots, half in the air and half in the unstable ground and prayed they would hold just a little longer.

A dozen feet. Ten. Time slowed to a brutal crawl. Eight. Mountain lions were strong but Connor's tall and muscular build translated to pure dead weight. The water dragged at his body, and every branch along the tree's trunk impeded Zoey's progress. Six feet. Five. Her shoulders felt broken, her jaws ached, and her claws threatened to pull out of her toes. Three feet. Two. Home free. Gratefully she surrendered her precious burden to the outstretched hands of her friends. Culley, Devlin, Bill, and Holt carefully supported Connor's battered and bleeding body between them and carried him to safety. Zoey leapt down from the tree and staggered up the bank after them, to collapse in a heap in the mud.

*   *   *

Culley couldn't stay in the house a minute longer. He'd been up all night but was forced to concede that he couldn't do a thing for his injured brother except worry. Time to see what he could do outside. Horizon Dead Livestock Removal had finished their grim task and gone, but they dealt only with large animals. The smaller victims of Bernie's bloodlust, such as the dozens of dogs and cats, still needed to be buried.

It was heartbreaking work. He chose a spot between the oldest barn and the crabapple orchard, and opened up a long deep trench with a backhoe. That was the easy part. The hard part was gathering up all the creatures that Connor had adopted over the years, and laying them carefully, one by one, in the earth. He'd managed only a handful before Bill found him and joined in the sad task.

The sun was long gone before they finished. They walked back through the silent farmyard, by the empty corrals and paddocks. Culley sighed. "It still doesn't feel clean. Maybe we could call Eddie Melnick to bring his water truck out in the morning, see if the blood can be hosed off the walls of the buildings. Or maybe someone's got a pressure washer."

Bill nodded. "It'll help. But the only thing that'll heal this place is new life."

Connor would no doubt fill the place with rescued pets from his practice again, thought Culley as they walked up the steps to the porch. If he recovered. *When. When he recovered.* He sighed and stuck his hands in his pockets. He was filthy, tired, and hungry, but he wished more than anything for something else to do, something to occupy his mind and keep it from worrying about Connor.

As if in answer, his attention was caught by the enormous flower bed below, the broken irises and crushed daylilies, and the odd pattern they made, as if something had been dragged through them. "Bill," he said. "Isn't that blood on those flowers there?"

"There's blood over half this farm today, mate."

"Yeah, but—" Culley didn't finish. Instead he leapt down into the midst of the garden. And discovered a great deal of blood among the green leaves. Normally he could scent it, even in human form, but today his senses had been overwhelmed. He'd been smelling blood and death all day. Probably one of the poor dogs had been killed in this spot. Yet something about the scene niggled at his instincts. *Ah, hell.* He called the Change, instantly becoming a great black wolf.

And just as instantly he discerned that the blood was not canine. It was human and he knew the scent.

Helfren.

In a split second, Culley had nosed out the scene and realized that the trail of blood led under the porch. He pressed a paw against the latticework panel. It moved.

"Are you finding anything, mate?" called Bill from the porch.

Culley didn't answer, but shouldered the loose panel out of the way and slipped beneath the decking and into the darkness. The scent led in a wobbly line through the loose clay soil, and Changeling sight revealed what looked like a pile of rags far back against the foundation of the house. He approached on silent feet, nosed at the body to determine if there was life. He could have spared himself the trouble. Tad Helfren's eyes flew open and he began screaming.

Shit! He couldn't calm the man as a wolf, so Culley immediately resumed his human form without thinking. He cursed as he cracked his head against the decking above him. "Helfren, it's okay. Settle down, man. Help is here."

"Get away from me! I know what you are!"

Something whizzed through the air and Culley instinctively caught it before it hit him. He couldn't see much in his human form, but the feel of it in his palm was enough. A cell phone. He slipped it into his pocket to check out later. "How bad are you hurt?"

There was no reply. Culley felt for a pulse, was relieved to find one. It was faint and thready but Helfren was still alive. He must have passed out.

"What have we got, mate?" Bill had taken off the lattice panel and was leaning in.

"Big trouble, and he's going to die if we don't hurry."

Faint sunlight flickered over Connor's face, teasing at his awareness until he opened his eyes a little and blinked. Slowly his bedroom came into focus. Try as he might, he couldn't imagine how he had come to be there. An icy thread of unease ran through him.

Where was Zoey?

Connor tried to find his voice to call her, but managed only a faint croak. He gave up and searched for Zoey with his mind. He felt unspeakable relief when he found her immediately. She was close, very close. Beside him, in fact, sound asleep. Connor moved his left hand a little, was surprised that his entire chest erupted with pain from the small effort. Was even more surprised when his fingers encountered not warm, soft skin but thick, plush fur. *Fur?*

"Zoey," he whispered haltingly. "Zoey, wake up." Connor had to fight to find the strength just to turn his head. He managed it just as an enormous mountain lion yawned hugely in his face. Shock was far too tame a word for what went through him as tremendous fangs gleamed scant inches away. The jolt was complete when the powerful jaws closed and he could see the creature's eyes. Brilliant shining amber like a falcon's eyes. His little falcon.

"Honey, what big teeth you have!" He mustered a weak grin even as he struggled to keep unconsciousness from claiming him again.

"The better to save your ass with." Culley's voice came from somewhere to his right, but Connor didn't take his eyes from the puma.

"Is she okay? What the hell happened?"

"Everything happened, it seems, just before we got there. The whole Pack turned out to trail you when we realized you'd gone off on your own. The valley was a frickin' mess, slides everywhere—"

"Zoey. Tell me about Zoey."

"Right, well she hasn't quite got the hang of mindspeech yet, so only Jessie's been able to communicate with her. All I know is that we thought you'd been caught in one of the landslides and so the Pack was searching the slopes and the riverbanks. Suddenly I spot the biggest mountain lion I've ever seen in my life, and it's got you by the scruff of your shirt, carrying you like a damn antelope. And then Jessie says it's not a lion, it's *Zoey*. She must have plucked you out of the water, but I don't know how. That damn tree you were on was rolling like a ship on high seas. She got you to shore just before the river took it away."

"Why the hell is she a lion? How the hell did she Change in the first place? Who helped her?"

Culley shook his head. "Nobody, bro. She didn't have anybody with her, she did it all on her own. Gives me the willies to think of her Changing without any help. She could have—well, you know what might have happened. But I guess she was trying to save you, and she's one determined woman."

Connor felt the blood in his veins turn to ice water. "Jesus."

"It probably helped that she had some natural ability to help her, some instincts to guide her."

"What instincts could she possibly have to draw on?" Connor didn't think Zoey's psychic abilities would be much help in such a situation. "She wasn't born a Changeling."

"Well, that's where the lion thing comes in, bro. Jessie says she's *theriona*, that she can probably become anything she wants."

Theriona . . . "Christ, Bernie was right."

"Bernie? He had this figured out?"

"Not until he first ran into her, but yes. It's why he targeted her."

"Makes a weird kind of sense—I mean, he was practically prehistoric himself. No one's run across one of the *theriona* for centuries. But Jessie's been on the phone for three days with your folks over in Scotland, and they've been researching Zoey's family tree. Seems like some of the right names are on it, going all the way back to Celtic times in Wales and beyond. Apparently Tallyson is just an Anglicized version of Taliesin."

Taliesin. *Holy-o-shit.* Connor's mind boggled as the pieces fell into place. The Welsh bard had been a known shapeshifter, and rumored to be a descendant of Merlin himself.

"Jessie figures Zoey had a recessive gene and the Changeling bite just activated it, the way it activates dormant genes in humans."

Suddenly Connor remembered the night he'd found

Zoey and the strange, brief vision he'd had, the silvery images of animals, many animals, that had burst through his mind and vanished. He'd dismissed the experience, thinking that his *farsight* had been affected by his fatigue. He should have known better. . . .

"You know what this means, don't you?" asked Culley.

That I'm a complete idiot. "Not a clue, but I'm sure you're going to tell me."

"It means that the silver wouldn't have helped, bro. If Helfren hadn't messed with your silver nitrate and you'd given it to Zoey just like you planned, it still wouldn't have helped. Jessie says nothing would have changed the outcome once the *theriona* gene had been activated."

Well, hell. Connor took a long breath. Then another. He hadn't realized how heavy that particular bundle of guilt had been. He'd been so certain he'd failed Zoey. He'd still failed her in some ways—he hadn't been there when she Changed, and he'd promised her she wouldn't be alone. He sighed. At least he'd dealt with Bernie. At least he'd done that much for her. She was free of her sire and out of danger. Mostly. "Why is she still a lion? Is she stuck?"

"Jessie told her not to Change back yet."

Alarm seized his heart. "She's not hurt, is she?"

"No. Not hurt at all, just tired out." Culley squirmed a little. Actually squirmed. Connor narrowed his eyes at his brother until he capitulated. "Okay, okay. Don't tell Jessie I told you. Zoey was pretty drained when we brought her here. She's okay but she needs to rest up for a while and recharge her batteries before she resumes her human form. She Changed twice out there, trying to get to you."

"Twice!" Connor struggled to rise up on his elbows, but instantly a massive golden shape pinned his shoulders to the bed with paws the size of his face. The mountain lion pressed its broad nose to his and he could see Zoey's amber eyes glaring at him.

"Is she *growling* at me?" Connor was incredulous.

"She's definitely not purring, bro. You're under very strict orders not to move."

The big cat withdrew and curled up beside Connor, all in one fluid motion that barely sent a vibration through the bed. The fierce, bright eyes remained open, watching him. Warning him.

"You're worried about Zoey, but she just needs rest. You're the one that was injured. You were in pretty rough shape when we dragged your butt in here, you know." Culley ticked things off on his fingers. "Punctured lung, five broken ribs, punctured liver, dislocated shoulder. Not to mention you were bleeding bad from a variety of war wounds. Lowen stayed here for the first three days, nursing you around the clock. Changelings heal fast, but he was plenty worried. We all were."

"Just how long have I been here?"

"Five days, nine hours, forty-three minutes and"—Culley checked his watch—"Twenty-nine seconds. Not like I'm counting or anything."

Connor closed his eyes. "Sorry."

"You probably will be. Jessie's pretty pissed that you took on Bernie by yourself. She's just waiting for you to heal up so she can put your ass in a sling. I'm thinking I might help her, although I have to say you did a damn fine job."

"Apparently I wasn't by myself," said Connor, and he patted one of the enormous paws beside him. "I've got terrific backup." To his surprise, the lion leapt gracefully from the bed and padded away on silent feet, flicking the end of its tail as it left the room.

Culley whistled softly. "Looks like me and Jessie will have to get in line. Zoey's been worried sick about you. You know, she might have been able to Change by now but she hasn't been resting like she's supposed to because she watches over you constantly. Jessie says her energy levels won't be high enough until tomorrow or the next day at least."

Connor sighed. "I guess I have a helluva lot of making up to do. Do me a favor, bro?"

"Do I have to?" he teased. "I mean, you're not on your deathbed now, so technically—"

"*Culley.*"

"Fine. What do you need?"

"Great grandmother's ring. Our folks have it." He had the satisfaction of seeing his brother's eyes goggle, then Culley gave him a broad grin and two thumbs up.

"Now that's *making up* in style. I'll call Mom right away." He headed for the door, then caught himself and came back. "There are a few other things you should know. We cleaned up the farm for you, buried the animals."

Connor closed his eyes, saw again the slaughtered creatures scattered as far as the eye could see. He didn't even know how many animals there had been—he'd lost track long ago. But he had known them all. "I don't know how to thank you for that. It had to have been a tough job. And Jim?"

"When you're up and around, we'll have a service for him. I, ah, I took the liberty of getting a permit to bury him in our family cemetery on the farm."

"We don't have a family cemetery. They don't even allow such things anymore."

"They don't allow *new* ones. They have to allow pre-existing ones."

Connor's eyebrows went up. "I'm scared to ask what you did."

"Suffice it to say that Devlin and I took care of it. All it took was a little finesse with the computer to create a few old records."

There was an understatement, Connor thought. Culley was to computers what Da Vinci was to canvas. There was very little he couldn't do.

"After that, we fenced off an area out in the northeast corner under the crabapple trees, mowed it and spiffed it up a little. It's pretty there. And it's close to where we buried the animals. They were sort of his family, so I thought Jim would like it."

"I think he would too. I like it. Thanks."

"There's a little bit of good news as well. We found a few of the animals still alive. That Appaloosa of yours that opens gates—"

"Charlie? Charlie's alive?"

"Alive and kicking. He had three other horses with him when he showed up in the driveway yesterday. They must have high-tailed it out of here when Bernie showed up. Five goats were eating the flowers on the porch this morning when I got up. And then this ginormous shaggy dog nearly took Devlin's head off when he went up into the loft for some hay. She's got a bunch of puppies hidden up there, all safe and sound."

Connor couldn't speak for a long moment. There was a lump the size of a tennis ball in his throat. *Zoey's going to have her puppy after all.*

"Which brings me to the bad news. Something else turned up alive that's not nearly so cute." Culley sat on the bed then, shaking his head. "We found Helfren under the porch. He'd been bleeding bad, but the clay earth must have helped to stop it."

No. He couldn't even make his mouth form the word, but his face must have said it because Culley nodded.

"Bernie had chewed on him pretty good. Don't know why he didn't kill him, but we've got problems now. More than a day had passed between the time he was attacked and the time we found him."

It wasn't hard to do the math. Connor knew that no amount of silver nitrate would do Tad Helfren any good if it wasn't administered within twelve hours of being bitten. "The full moon?"

"Eight days."

Chapter Twenty-six

Twilight had just given way to full dark when the moon cleared the horizon. Only two days shy of being full, it glowed like a frozen pearl just above the coulees, reflected in the wide glittering river in the valley below Elk Point. A cool wind stirred the needles of the tall spruce that surrounded the rocky plateau, swirled bits of dry grass between the flat-topped boulders that formed a natural ring there.

Zoey leaned back against Connor, glad to be sitting on one of those rocks now. The heat of the day had been captured in it, and it radiated warmth almost as pleasantly as Connor did. She wondered if she would develop a higher body temperature now that she too was a Changeling. *Not tonight, apparently.* A sudden gust of wind had her pulling her jacket around her tightly and crowding even closer to Connor.

Connor was as quiet as the rock he sat on, contemplative, as was most of the Pack. Even Culley's face was uncharacteristically sober. The issue at hand was serious, and the boulders of the sacred circle were covered with Changelings from the entire region. Some were wolves, most were in their human form. She recognized many of them. And knew that all of them were deeply concerned.

Wolves, real wolves, were not a protected species outside of national parks. Bernie had not only terrorized the people who lived here, he had resurrected the old stories from Dunvegan's distant past. From the post office to the coffee shop to the hardware store, *werewolves* surfaced in every conversation sooner or later. Often with a laugh. Sometimes, with a quick glance over the shoulder.

"It's going to be a long time, years maybe, before things settle down again," said Jessie. She sat cross-legged on the ground by the fire in the center of the circle. But there was an unmistakable aura of power about her and the flames turned her mahogany skin to gold. "We have no way of setting fears to rest, no way to explain the deaths of Jim Neely and Al Menzie, and no way of letting people know that the killer is gone."

"I heard that you found the location of Bernie's body. Why don't we dig it up and turn it over to the cops?" said Geoff Lassiter. "There are so damn many hunters out there right now that it's not safe for my family to Change on our own land."

"Devlin? Will you address that?" Jessie asked.

Culley's twin nodded and explained. "Usually, the testing of DNA won't reveal anything out of the ordinary. Over the past couple of years, Connor and I have taken samples of hair from different members of the Pack in their wolfen form, and sent it out to different labs. So far it's always come back as pure wolf and nothing else. But that may not last. For one, the testing is getting better all the time. And two—Bernie was different, something wasn't right about him. Every instinct I have says this is a bad, bad idea."

Lassiter persisted. "The bastard's still going to have two toes missing on one foot, still likely to have bits of Jim

Neely's shirt in his claws or even in his stomach. There's some positive ID without ever having to look at DNA."

"Once we give over the carcass, we have no control over what tests will be done. Samples of the body are likely to be sent to many different governmental departments as well as top researchers at universities," said Devlin. "Why? For one thing, the wolf is unusual because of its size alone—biologists will be interested in learning if it's a new subspecies or just a big hybrid. But mostly, it's because wolf attacks are so rare that everyone will be wondering what was *wrong* with this animal, why it acted in such a way. They'll be looking for disease, for injury, for aberrations of any kind, including genetic anomalies. And they might find something we didn't expect."

"They sure as hell will," declared Connor. "He didn't even resemble a wolf at the end. He'd mutated into a monster, thanks to all the energy and power he absorbed from killing human beings. We don't dare hand the authorities something like that. Because in addition to the woods being full of hunters, they'll be full of biologists searching for a brand-new species of predator. Not to mention it'll attract every cryptozoologist on the planet."

"Yeah, but you're the only one that saw him," said Jeannie Rousseau. "Maybe you were already punch drunk from the fight. Kudos to you for killing the old bastard but you took a hell of a beating, Macleod. Maybe your memory's not accurate?"

Culley stood up then. He walked over to Jessie and flipped open a cell phone, called up an image and showed her.

The Pack leader was rarely surprised but Jessie's eyes widened as she took the phone and studied the photo. "Are you saying this is Bernard Gervais?"

"It is. This was taken by a human survivor of the attack at Connor's place."

"Helfren?"

He nodded.

Jessie glanced over to where Tad Helfren was sitting propped against a rock between two wolves. "You're very cool under pressure, mister. My hat's off to you." The man simply shrugged and looked away.

She handed the cell phone back to Culley. "Has that photo gotten out?"

Culley shook his head. "The guy tried to send it to his newspaper, but the battery was too low. I powered it up, retrieved the e-mail he'd composed and trashed it." There was a faint moan and a muttered curse from Helfren's direction. "I canceled the phone's service too and did a little tweaking. The phone's just a handy way to display photos now—it can't do anything else, not even download to a computer."

"Well done. Show this to Lassiter first. Then pass it around. I want every member of the Pack to see it. After that, destroy it."

"Happily."

Jessie sat for several minutes in silence as the photo was shown. Finally it was Zoey's turn to see it. She reached for the phone but Connor intercepted it.

"Let me hold it for you. God knows what you'll see if you touch it."

He was right. Now that she'd finally figured out that she was a touch-telepath, she had to be careful what objects she picked up. Laying a finger on the phone might plunge her into a vision of the entire *Gervais versus Helfren* scene. Of course, her errant talent might decide to award her the vision anyway, but there was little she could do about that—or wanted to. Jessie had been right. Zoey felt whole now that she had finally accepted her abilities. "Thanks for the intervention," she said and leaned in to look at the photo. For a few moments she couldn't say anything, only stare at the horrific image. Finally she found her voice. "Connor, it doesn't even look like a wolf. It doesn't look like anything on this planet. You fought this thing by yourself?"

"If I say yes, are you going to yell at me again?"

"Probably. Only because it scares me so much that I might have lost you."

He cuddled her close and kissed the top of her head. "Then I think we're even because it scared the hell out of me that you Changed by yourself. So maybe we should just let it go. Agreed?"

"Deal." She grinned at him and Connor passed the cell back to Culley, who was rolling his eyes. He went to the center of the circle and bashed the cell phone with a rock until all that was left were tiny fragments of plastic.

Jessie spoke again. "As you already know, it's going to be dangerous to Change, dangerous to run as a wolf for a very long time. Many real wolves have already been shot. Some of you have brought us news of traps being set."

René Ghostkeeper voiced a question that many were thinking. "Will the Pack be disbanded then?"

There was a flurry of murmurs as Jessie shook her head. "I know that some of you are already making preparations to disperse, and it's your choice. However, I won't disband the Pack just yet. Bill and I will stay on here for a few years more until everyone has found new territory."

It came as no surprise to Zoey. Culley had been talking about moving to Alaska eventually. Others were planning to leave right away. Fitzpatrick had applied for a transfer.

The LaLonde and McIntyre families had already put their homes and businesses up for sale.

"It seems so unfair that everyone is being forced to start over, all because of the actions of one," she whispered to Connor.

He pulled her closer. "None of us can stay here forever, little falcon. Twenty years, maybe thirty at most and then it's time for any Changeling to make plans to move on."

"Because you live so long?" She was still trying to wrap her head around that little tidbit. At first she hadn't believed how old Connor said he was. It didn't seem possible. But then, considering she was sitting around a campfire with enough werewolves to make up a couple of pro football teams, who was she to say what was possible?

"And that we don't age at the same rate as humans. I've already been practicing here in Dunvegan for about fifteen years or so. A few more and someone may start to notice that I don't look any different from when I first started."

Zoey shook her head. "I don't think that's a legitimate issue anymore. These days, more and more guys are dyeing their hair, getting plastic surgery and so forth. I saw it a lot in the city, especially in the corporate types." She grinned. "The townsfolk will just think you're incredibly vain."

"If that's all they think, I'll be happy. Maybe the current youth trend means I have a little more time before people get suspicious. But someday, we'll still have to leave Dunvegan, at least for a few decades."

"We? You mean I'll look too young to keep my cushy editor's chair?" Zoey had decided to stay on at the newspaper. It was hard to believe she'd once worried that her publisher might find out about her psychic abilities and fire her. Ted would likely have a heart attack if he knew what she could do now!

Connor nuzzled her hair. "You look too young for that already. I always thought editors were crusty middle-aged types with glasses and a comb-over."

"You've been reading way too many comic books." She sighed inwardly and hoped they wouldn't be forced to leave Dunvegan too soon. She had been starting to feel at home. But then, what was home, really, but being with the people you loved? She was with Connor, and she would be at home wherever he was. Still, the idea of the Pack dispersing seemed terribly wrong and she rose to her feet. Waited until Jessie spotted her and nodded permission to speak.

"I think we need to stand our ground," Zoey began. She was unsure of what she was going to say, but it felt right, even though she could hear the murmuring among some of the assembly. She knew what they were thinking, that she was new to the Change, new to the Pack, and she couldn't possibly know what she was talking about. Many would want to dismiss her idea, dismiss *her*—and she wasn't going to allow it. She reached out with her senses, seeking the words to explain. "I'm new at being a Changeling but I'm not new to some other things. I know that in the distant past, many of you have been forced from your homes, forced to start over. I've had to start over too. And I've learned that you lose something when you let fear push you into leaving what you've built, when you give up ground.

"All of us are afraid right now, but it's important to realize that we are *not* helpless. Maybe it wasn't possible to turn the tide of public opinion a century ago, but things are very different now. Maybe wolves aren't a protected species in this country at present, but there's a worldwide movement that would rally to that cause if we wanted it. This is our home. I say we don't give up without a fight. Today's weapons aren't tooth and claw, they're words and net-working, and they're powerful. We can change the tide of public opinion. It'll be hard after what Bernie did, after the loss of life here. But we aren't guilty of anything and it just doesn't seem right to skulk away as if we are." She looked around at all the faces. Some were nodding, some were frowning. "That's all I have to say." Zoey sat down as voices erupted around the circle.

Jessie allowed the din to continue for some time before calling the Pack to order. "Each wolf will have to choose for himself, of course, but Zoey's words are worth consid-ering. Sometimes new blood brings new wisdom." She winked at Zoey before continuing.

"We have one final issue to discuss," Jessie said. "Bernard hoped to betray us by revealing our secrets and our identi-ties to a human being who had not proven himself to be a friend to the Pack. He's here, and we need to decide what to do with him."

That sounded like a cue. Slowly, painfully, Tad Helfren used a crutch to get to his feet and shuffled to the middle of the circle where the small dark woman was holding court. *Yea, though I walk through the Valley of the Werewolves . . .* He felt no fear, just resignation. They were going to kill him, and maybe it would be doing him a favor. He had no idea why he wasn't dead already. He'd chased monsters his whole life, looking for physical proof of their existence. Now he'd finally met one face to face and had proof in spades . . . and wished he didn't.

He cleared his throat, tried to straighten up. There were rows of stitches on his forearms and on the backs of his hands. Stitches across his belly held closed deep gashes, and a cast on one leg ran from ankle to thigh. There were even two jagged trails of stitches across the top of his head, knitting together his scalp. Try as he might, he couldn't remember getting a single one of those sutures. Hell, he couldn't remember being rescued, never mind being treated for his wounds.

He remembered every detail of how he had gotten them, however, and that was where the real damage lay. In his head. Every time he closed his eyes he saw Bernard Gervais turn into a creature from hell. The nightmare stalked him 24/7 and he no longer knew what it was like to sleep without screaming.

Jessie motioned for him to sit, which he did gratefully. Both his body and mind were exhausted. He glanced around and recognized many of the faces in the assembly, knew most of them by name now. Funny, he'd expected them to look at him with hate or loathing or disgust. Instead, he could swear he saw something like pity, perhaps even concern. He chalked it up to imagination.

"This is Tad Helfren, a reporter—"

"Investigator," he corrected. He didn't want anybody writing *reporter* in his obituary. He was a professional.

The Pack leader cocked an eyebrow at him and continued. "An *investigator* for *OtherWorld News*. He came here to write a story on werewolves. However, he now has a vested interest in keeping our secrets rather than publishing them," she said to the group. "He's been bitten and the full moon is only two days away. He could not be treated with silver in time."

There was a collective gasp. Oh yeah, there's another good reason for not hanging around, Helfren thought. *Going to turn into a monster in two days? Just let me check out now.* "Can I ask how you plan to kill me?" he said. "I've already been torn up once, so I'd like to choose something quick if that's allowed."

There was silence for a long moment. Great, he'd pissed them off. So much for the quick death.

"You believe we want to kill you." Watson made it a statement.

"Why not? You're werewolves."

"Changelings," somebody corrected.

"You think we're all killers like that rotter, Bernie." Watson's husband, Bill, folded his tattooed arms indignantly. "We're just bloody animals to you."

Helfren simply shrugged. *If the shoe fits . . .* "Can we just get it over with?"

Jessie Watson shook her head. "We're not going to kill you, Tad. We can't undo what has been done to you, but we can help you get through it, teach you how to live with it. You can be one of us."

He stared at her, incredulous. "This is a joke, right?" He looked around, but no one seemed to be laughing.

"You've been Changed without consent," she continued. "Your sire is dead, and you are the Pack's responsibility now. We take that very seriously."

No. No way in hell was he buying *this*. "Seriously enough that I could join up and become the Pack flunky, you mean." Just how dumb did they think he was? "I guess somebody has to order the pizza, be the designated driver, and bury the bodies, but you're going to have to get somebody else."

There were surprised murmurs around the circle. Some faces were amused, some angry. Bill Watson was definitely on the angry list and looked as if he was going to come over and do something about it until a new voice broke in.

"For Christ's sake, Helfren, this isn't *Dracula*. We don't turn people into our personal minions." Helfren turned and saw that it was one of the Macleod twins. "I do my own laundry, just like everybody else."

"Culley, you're always talking our sister into doing your laundry," said Connor.

"Hey, well, she's not here right now, is she? So I'm doing my own laundry like I said."

For a split second it sounded normal. *They* sounded normal. Just regular people with regular families. Helfren sighed. He was afraid of being taken in by this charade— but a tiny part of him wanted, *needed*, hope. "Do you really expect me to believe that there are no strings? That I could just learn to be like you and that's it?"

"You're really waiting for the other shoe to drop, aren't you?" Jessie shook her head. "There are no strings here, Helfren. That's not the way we work. You'll have a lot to learn, some adjustments to make. But your life is your own."

He took a breath and allowed himself, just for a moment, to believe they weren't going to kill him. That he wasn't going to die. But the life before him looked terrifying and fear overwhelmed him. "I can't do this," he said quietly and wondered if he could cowboy up enough to shoot himself.

"You have to do this and you will. But not alone." Jessie spoke to the assembly. "Bernard Gervais is dead. Someone must take on the responsibilities of teaching this man in the sire's stead."

"I think I'll take that bet." It was Culley Macleod. He rose and walked over to Jessie. "He's a jerk and an asshole, but I think he's got potential. Besides, I like a long shot."

A *Macleod*? A Macleod was going to be his guide to

werewolf life? Helfren blinked, glad he was sitting down. This couldn't be good. Out of everyone present, the Macleods had the most reason to kill him. He'd spied on them, harassed them. Worst of all, he'd gotten carried away, so damn intent on breaking this story to the world, wanting that fame and fortune so bad that he'd put hands on Zoey Tyler, threatened her. Hell, he'd almost hit her. Yeah, the Macleods had plenty of reason to take him out and he couldn't blame them a bit.

"Culley, this is a commitment, not a prank," said Jessie. "You're sure about this?"

"Yeah. I'll do it."

The Pack leader folded her arms and surveyed them both. "I'm not sure who's getting the worst of this bargain, but I'll accept it." She rose and walked a few steps away. "It's a terrific life, Tad. I think you'll find happiness in it." In the blink of an eye, she was gone and in her place stood a wolf. Tiny blue sparks winked out in its rich fur. It wasn't the horrific monster that Bernie had been but Helfren's heart skipped several beats just the same. With a wave of her tail she loped away. Several others Changed and followed after her, as he stared.

"You look like you're having a panic attack," interjected Culley. "Better take a breath there, bud."

Helfren shook himself and sucked in air until he felt as normal as he was going to get. He put his hands up. "Look, why the hell do you care, anyway? What is it you want?"

"Maybe I just want to see if there's a human being under that obnoxious reporter shell of yours. And maybe I got a glimpse of it that gives me hope." Culley lowered his voice. "I saw you in the grocery store parking lot one day helping Enid Malkinson. That old cat of hers, Poodle, jumped out of the car and ran off. You helped her chase it down."

Helfren scowled. "Big deal. All I did was get a damn cat for a little old lady."

"Uh-huh. And you had to crawl under a grain truck to do it." Culley grinned. "Don't give me that look, Helfren. I know you've got a heart. It's rusty and shriveled with disuse, but we can work with it, maybe do a little remedial charm school once we get the Changeling stuff down. Who knows? Maybe one day you'll even apologize to Zoey and Connor. They'll probably just eat you, of course, but you'll go out with a clear conscience."

He felt the color draining from his face.

Culley simply chuckled and shook his head. "You're *way* too easy, bud. Nobody's going to lay a finger on you, I promise. So what do you say?" He held out a hand.

Tad Helfren sighed then and gave up. Just gave up and gave in. He was going to be a werewolf—*Changeling*, he corrected himself. And apparently he was going to have a wise ass for a mentor.

He took the hand.

Epilogue

The wind whipped a flurry of golden poplar leaves down the dark, deserted street, mixed them with a few wet snowflakes. The Village Council's monthly meeting had gone overtime again. That was almost a tradition. The new publisher of the *Dunvegan Herald Weekly* was the last one out of the building. That was well on the way to becoming a tradition too.

I've got to start finishing my story notes at home. Or hire another reporter. It's got to be after 11 o'clock. Camera bag in hand, Zoey headed toward the only vehicle left on the street: her old red Bronco. Suddenly her peripheral vision detected a large dark shadow moving stealthily along the bushes toward her. She stopped dead, heart pounding.

The shadow resolved itself into an immense wolf.

"Connor Macleod! That's *so* not funny!"

The silver and black wolf bounded into the amber glow of a streetlight, jaws grinning, tongue lolling. A moment later, a tall man leaned on the hood of her truck and smiled innocently at Zoey as blue sparks spiraled to the ground around him. "Come on, you weren't really scared, were you? I told you I'd be waiting for you."

"More like lying in wait! Good thing there's nobody around to see you at this time of night!" She dodged his embrace and put the camera bag on the front seat. Sighed as he moved in close behind her. Sighed more deeply as he brushed aside her long hair and began warmly kissing the sensitive spot on the back of her neck. She felt herself melting and slipped easily into mindspeech. *Mmmm. You get around me every time.*

Not every time. You bopped me when I surprised you in your office last week.

Yeah, but I only hit you once. And I generously forgave you for sneaking up on me like that, since you were kissing me so nicely.

"I did a helluva lot more than kiss you," he murmured. The two of them had ended up making love amid the stacks of newspapers in the darkened print room. Later, it had taken quite a while to shower the stubborn ink off their skin—but that just provided an opportunity to enjoy each other all over again. *Come to think of it, I'd like to do a lot more than kiss you right now, little falcon.*

"Really?" She grinned and leaned back against him, enjoying the warmth that radiated from him. "Now why would that be?"

"Because my life's goal is to finally count all of my wife's freckles. For some reason I keep getting distracted and having to start over." He slid a hand over her hip and cupped her bottom. "I think I left off about *here* last time."

She laughed and glanced down at the antique ring on her hand, a Macleod family heirloom. Two silvery wolves entwined around a large moon-white pearl. Connor had gently slid the band onto her finger only a few months ago, during an intimate ceremony with family and friends at the Macleod farm. At the first touch of the ring, her psychic gift had shown her a beautiful dark-haired woman, smiling at Zoey as if she heartily approved.

It had been one of the nicest visions Zoey had ever had,

almost like a wedding present from her extra-sensory side. And maybe it had been a sign as well. Accepting her abilities had caused them to grow and flourish. Embracing a relationship with Connor had done the same. It had seemed the most natural thing in the world to say yes when he asked her to marry him. The fact that she'd been a mountain lion at the time notwithstanding . . .

"I have an idea," she murmured.

He nuzzled her hair until he could brush his lips over her ear. *And what's that?*

"Let's forget the truck and run home."

His mouth traveled down her sensitive neck in long soft kisses and gentle bites. He slid his big hands under her jacket, her shirt, seeking skin. "And then what?"

"Oh, I don't know." The frosty night air and the heat from his strong fingers was a delicious combination. She shivered, but not from the cold. "Have wild and crazy sex all night?"

"Mmmm . . . Just how wild and crazy are we talking?"

She whispered in his ear.

Connor stepped back immediately and Changed. The saddleback wolf loped to the middle of the street, where he paused and looked back, waiting. In a moment, a sleek golden wolf joined him. Together they ran through fallen leaves and skiffs of snow, dodging in and out of shadows until they reached the edge of town.

Suddenly the golden wolf vanished and a tawny falcon took to the dark sky.

No fair! Connor's voice protested loudly in her head.

She only chuckled and soared higher. Zoey watched her mate admiringly as he raced over the moonlit fields, then, with a flip of her wingtips, overtook him. *Last one home makes dinner!* Out of the corner of her falcon's eye, she could see the great saddleback wolf redouble his pace. He was close, but no way was he going to catch up to her.

He knew it too. *I always end up making dinner because you* cheat. *I could really lose my motivation here!*

Not if you make dinner naked *tonight. And I'll provide dessert . . .*

Fine, but I want dessert first!

Zoey laughed and flew like an arrow for home.

Don't miss BODYGUARDS IN BED,
the anthology from Lucy Monroe, Jamie Denton, and
Elizabeth Naughton, out now!

Turn the page for a preview of Lucy's story . . .

Danusia wiggled the key in the lock on her brother's apartment door. Darn thing always stuck, but he wouldn't make her another one. Said she didn't come to stay often enough for it to matter.

Yeah, and he wasn't particularly keen for that to change either, obviously. He'd probably gotten the wonky key on purpose. Just like the rest of her older siblings, Roman Chernichenko kept Danusia at a distance.

She knew why he did it at least, though she was pretty sure the others didn't.

Knowing didn't make her feel any better. Even in her family of brainiacs, she was definitely the odd one out. They loved her, just like she loved them, but they were separated by more than the gap in their ages. She was seven years younger than her next youngest sibling. An unexpected baby, though never unwanted—at least according to her mom.

Still, her sister and brothers might love her, but they didn't get her and didn't particularly want her to get them.

Which was why she was coming to stay in Roman's empty apartment rather than go visit one of the others, or Heaven forbid, her parents. She did not need another round of lectures on her single status by her *baba* and mom.

The lock finally gave and Danusia pressed the door open, dragging her rolling suitcase full of books and papers behind her. The fact the alarm wasn't armed registered at the same time as a cold cylinder pressed to her temple.

"Roman, I swear on Opa's grave that if you don't get that gun away from me, I'm going to drop it in a vat of sulfuric acid and then pour the whole mess all over the new sofa Mom insisted you get the last time she visited. If it's loaded, I'm going to do it anyway."

The gun moved away from her temple and she spun around, ready to lecture her brother into an early grave, and help him along the way. "*It is so not okay to pull a gun on your sister. . . .*" Her tirade petered off to a choked breath. "*You!*"

The man standing in front of her was a whole lot sexier than her brother and scarier, which was saying something. Not that she was afraid of him, but *she* wouldn't want him for an enemy.

The rest of the family believed that Roman was a scientist for the military. She knew better. She was a nosy baby sister after all, but this man? Definitely worked with Roman and carried an aura of barely leashed violence. Maxwell Baker was a true warrior.

She shouldn't, absolutely *should not*, find that arousing, but she did.

"You're not my brother," she said stupidly.

Which was not her usual mode, but the six-foot-five black man, who would make Jesse Jackson Jr. look like the ugly stepbrother if they were related, turned Danusia's brain to serious mush.

His brows rose in mocking acknowledgment of her obvious words.

"Um . . ."

"What are you doing here, Danusia?" Warm as really good aged whiskey, his voice made her panties wet.

How embarrassing was that? "You know my name?"

Put another mark on the chalkboard for idiocy.

"The wedding wasn't so long ago that I would have forgotten already." He almost cracked a smile.

She almost swooned.

Max and several of Roman's *associates* had done the security at her sister, Elle's, wedding, which might have been overkill. Or not. Danusia suspected stuff had been going on that neither she nor her parents had known about.

It hadn't helped that she'd been focused on her final project for her master's and that Elle's wedding had been planned faster than Danusia could solve a quadratic equation. She'd figured out that something was going on, but that was about it. This time her siblings had managed to keep their baby sister almost completely in the dark.

A place she really hated being.

Not that her irritation had stopped her from noticing the most freaking gorgeous man she'd ever met. Maxwell Baker. A tall, dark dish of absolute yum.

Once she had seen Max with his strong jaw, defined cheekbones, big and muscular body, not much else at the wedding had even registered. Which might help explain why she hadn't figured out why all the security.

"It's nice to see you again." There, that sounded somewhat adult. Full points for polite conversation, right?

"What are you doing here?" he asked again, apparently not caring if he got any points for being polite.

She shrugged, shifting her backpack. "My super is doing some repairs on the apartment."

"What kind of repairs?"

"Man, you're as bad as my brother." They hadn't even

made it out of the entry and she was getting the third-degree.

Really as bad as her brother and maybe taking it up a notch. Roman might have let her get her stuff put out of the way before he started asking the probing questions. Then again, maybe not.

"I'll take that as a compliment." Then Max just paused, like he had all the time in the world to wait for her answer.

Like it never even occurred to him she might refuse to respond.

Knowing there was no use in attempted prevarication, she sighed. "They're replacing the front door."

"Why?"

"Does it matter?" Sheesh.

He leaned back against the wall, crossing his arms, muscles bulging everywhere. "I won't know until you tell me."

"Someone broke it." She was proud of herself for getting the words out, considering how difficult she was finding the simple process of breathing right now.

This man? Was lethal.

"Who?" he demanded, frown firmly in place.

Oh, crud, even his not-so-happy face was sexy, yummy, heart-palpitatingly delicious. "I don't know."

Try THE DARKEST SIN by Caroline Richards,
out this month from Brava!

R owena Woolcott was cold, so very cold.

    She dreamed that she was on her horse, flying through the countryside at Montfort, a heavy rain drenching them both to the skin, hooves and mud sailing through the sodden air. Then a sudden stop, Dragon rearing in fright, before a darkness so complete that Rowena knew she had died.

When she awakened, it was to the sound of an anvil echoing in her head and the feeling of bitter fluid sliding down her throat. She kept her eyes closed, shutting out the daggered words in the background.

"Faron will not rest—"

"The Woolcott women—"

"One of his many peculiar fixations . . . they are to suffer . . . and then they are to die."

"Meredith Woolcott believed she could hide forever."

Phrases, lightly accented in French, drifted in and out of Rowena's head, at one moment near and the next far away. Time merged and coalesced, a series of bright lights followed by darkness, then the sharp retort of a pistol shot. And her sister's voice, calling out to her.

The cold permeated her limbs, pulling down her heavy skirts into watery depths. She tried to swim but her arms and legs would not obey, despite the fact that she had learned as a child in the frigid lake at Montfort. She did not sink like a stone, weighted by her corset and shift and riding boots, because it seemed as though strong hands found her and held her aloft, easing her head above the current tried to force water down her throat and into her lungs.

She dreamed of those hands, sliding her into dry, crisp sheets, enveloping her in a seductive combination of softness and strength. She tossed and turned, a fever chafing her blood, her thoughts a jumble of puzzle pieces vying for attention.

Drifting into the fog, she imagined that she heard steps, the door to a room opening, then the warmth of a body shifting beneath the sheets. She felt the heat, *his heat*, like a cauldron, a furnace toward which she turned her cold flesh. Her womb was heavy and her breasts ached as he slid into her slowly, infinitely slowly, the hugeness of him filling the void that was her center.

Was it one night or a lifetime of nights? Or an exquisite, erotic dream. Spooned with her back against his body, Rowena felt him hard and deep within her. She slid her hip against a muscular thigh, aware of him beginning to move within her once again. She savored the wicked mouth against the skin of her neck, pleasured by the slow slide of his lips. Losing herself in his deliberate caress, she reveled in his hands cupping and stroking, his fingers slipping into the shadows and downward to lightly tease her swollen, sensitized flesh.

"Stay here . . . with me," he whispered, breath hot in her ear.

And she did. For one night or a lifetime of nights, she would never know.

Good girls should NEVER CRY WOLF.
But who wants to be good?
Be sure to pick up Cynthia Eden's latest novel,
out next month!

Lucas didn't take the woman back to his house on Bry-ton Road. The place was probably still crawling with cops and reporters, and he didn't feel like dealing with all that crap.

He called his first in command, Piers Stratus, to let him know that he was out of jail and to tell him that there two unwanted coyotes in town.

The woman—Sarah—didn't speak while he drove. He could feel the waves of tension rolling off her, shaking her body.

She was scared. She'd done a fair job of hiding her fear back at the police station and then at the park, at first any-way. But as the darkness had fallen, he'd seen the fear. Smelled it.

Sarah had known she was being hunted.

He pushed a button on his remote. The wrought-iron gates before him opened and revealed the curving drive that led to his second LA home. In the hills, it gave him a great view of the city below, and that view let know him when company was coming, long before any unexpected guests arrived.

When the gate shut behind him, he saw Sarah sag slightly,

settling back into her seat. The scent of her fear finally eased.

Like most of his kind, he usually enjoyed the smell of fear. But he didn't . . . like the scent on her.

He much preferred the softer scent, like vanilla cream, that he could all but taste as it clung to her skin. Perhaps he would get a taste, later.

With a flick of his wrist, he killed the ignition. The house was right in front of them. Two stories, Long, tall windows.

And, hopefully, no more dead bodies.

He eased out of the car, stretching slowly. Then he walked around and opened the door for Sarah. As any man would, Lucas admired the pale flash of thigh when her skirt crept up. And he wondered just what secrets the lovely lady was keeping from him.

"We're going to talk." An order. He wanted to know everything, starting with why the dead human had been at his place.

She gave a quick nod. "Okay, I—"

A wolf bounded out of the house. A flash of black fur. Golden eyes. Teeth.

Shit. It wasn't safe for the kid. Not until he found out what was going on—

The wolf ran to him. Tossed back his head and howled.

Sarah laughed softly.

Laughed.

His stare shot to her just in time to catch the smile on her lips. His hand lifted, and, almost helplessly, he traced that smile with his fingertips.

Her breath caught.

Lucas ignored the tightening in his gut. "Shouldn't you be afraid?" After the coyotes, he'd expected her to flinch away from any other shifters. And Jordan was one big wolf, with claws and teeth that could easily rip a woman like Sarah apart.

She looked back at the wolf who watched them. "He's so young, little more than a kid. One whose glad you're—"

No.

Understanding dawned, fast and brutal in his mind. *I'm more than human.* She'd told him that, he just hadn't understood exactly *what* she was. Until now.

His hands locked around her arms and Lucas pulled her up against him. Nose to nose, close enough so that he could see the dark gold glimmering in the depths of her eyes. "Jordan, get the hell out of here." He gave the order to his brother without ever looking away from her.

The wolf growled.

"Go!"

The young wolf pushed against his leg—*letting me know he's pissed, cause Jordan hates when I boss his ass*—and then the wolf backed away.

"Now for you, sweetheart." His fingers tightened. "Why don't we just go back to that part about you not being human?"

Her lips parted. She had nice lips—sexy and plump. He shouldn't be noticing them, not then, but he couldn't help himself. He noticed everything about her. The gold hoops in her dainty ears. The streaks of gold buried deep in her dark hair. The lotion she rubbed on her body—that vanilla scent was driving him wild.

He was turned on, achingly hard, for a woman he barely knew. Not normally a big deal. He had a more than a healthy sex drive. Most shifters did. The animal inside liked to play.

But Sarah . . . he didn't trust her, not for a minute, and

he didn't usually have sex with women he didn't trust. A man could be vulnerable to attack when he was fucking.

"You know what I am, Lucas," she said and shrugged, the move both careless and fake because he knew that she cared, too much.

"Tell me." Her mouth was so close. He could still taste her. That kiss earlier had just been a tease.